Educated at Hampton Grammar School and the University of Nottingham, Graeme Roe had a marketing career working for major international companies.

He then founded and built an extremely successful advertising agency. At the age of forty he decided to take up riding and under David Nicholson's guidance gained an amateur National Hunt licence. His biggest success was winning the Ayr Yeomanry Cup on Dom Perignon.

He then took out a Jockey Club permit quickly followed by a full licence. Amongst his many winners were All Bright, Dom Perignon, Kitty Wren, We're In The Money, Le Grand Maitre, Fairly Sharp and Bad Bertrich.

Graeme now runs a corporate communications company. He has written two books on business. *Too Close To Call* follows *A Touch of Vengeance*, *Odds on Death* and *Dangerous Outsider* (in that order).

'Roe is becoming the Jeffrey Archer of the racing thriller. His increasingly familiar cast of sleekly menacing business sharks, fresh faced young jockeys, dodgy bookmakers and quick-witted East End fixers are all linked through the authentically presented County View stables, where you can almost smell the straw and hear the creak of the stirrup leathers.'

Robin Oakley, *Spectator*

TOO CLOSE
TO CALL

GRAEME ROE

ROBINSON
London

Constable & Robinson Ltd
55-56 Russell Square,
London WC1B 4HP
www.constablerobinson.com

This edition published by Robinson,
an imprint of Constable & Robinson, 2008

A copy of the British Library Cataloguing in
Publication Data is available from the British Library

ISBN: 978-1-84529-577-6

Printed and bound in the EU

3 5 7 9 10 8 6 4 2

Acknowledgements

I have already paid tribute to so many different people for the help they've given me during the planning and eventual writing of my first three novels in this series. Many have been equally helpful whilst I've been working on *Too Close to Call* – so many that it's almost impossible to single out some without fear of offending those I have not been able to mention in this list. To those of you who undoubtedly deserve my thanks, please accept them even though you are not mentioned.

It would be quite wrong not to include Mark Kershaw, Edward Gillespie, Simon Lee, Becky Green and Fergus Cameron, who have all been enormously helpful at the racecourses where they operate. Once more, John Killingbeck has given me valuable information in relation to veterinary equine activities, and so many journalists have been more than kind in what they have said about my books. With some difficulty I single out Chris Smith of the *Racing Post*, Robin Oakley of the *Spectator*, and Tom Richmond of the *Yorkshire Post*.

Last, but by no means least, I must thank my daughter, Jessica, for her guidance on what really happens in Las Vegas, and Katie Jarvis for running a critical, but always constructive, eye over the manuscript.

To all my readers who have made my books a success, my sincere thanks, and particularly to those who have gone out of their way to say kind words in letters, phone calls, and at the many race meetings where I've met them.

I hope you all enjoy *Too Close to Call*.

Author's Notes

A number of non-racing people who have read my books have commented on how often champagne seems to be drunk by both the heroes and villains. Interestingly enough, this is one of the areas of the book which is not total fiction. It's true that champagne is drunk in quantities at Wimbledon, in corporate hospitality boxes at rugby and soccer, and indeed, at the bars of many other sports. Yet in my experience there's no sport where a bottle of bubbly or a glass of fizz seems to be so deeply entrenched in the traditions as it is in racing.

Why this should be I have no idea. Yet, it is reported that 170,000 bottles of champagne were drunk during Royal Ascot and over 10,000 at the Cheltenham National Hunt Festival. One major brand of champagne informs me that about 10 per cent of their annual sales are at race meetings and this is a brand that does little in the way of racing sponsorship.

Once more, I must insist that it is a work of fiction, and if names of real people or real horses, other than those that are obviously quoted, are used, it is in ignorance and I apologise. Likewise, I hope there will be a little indulgence if some of the events seem not to fit exactly into the sporting calendar, and if every racecourse is not, in reality, exactly as described.

Alterations to the positions of jumps and where races start occur so frequently it's almost impossible to be totally accurate when a manuscript is completed some months before the book appears in bookshops.

As I've said before, racing is an amazing sport, and in spite of the criticisms and a few less than savoury episodes, it continues to excite, fascinate and thrill me and millions of others. Our debt of gratitude to the magnificent animals which provide such wonderful and exciting spectacles is huge.

Prologue

It was mid-afternoon, and the dimly lit bar was almost deserted. In an alcove well away from the bar itself a young couple sat opposite each other. He was tall, handsome and powerfully built; she was blonde, extremely attractive, with a Midwestern American accent.

'What's the drama?' he asked.

'I had a phone call from Eddie downstairs on my way back from the airport,' she replied. 'My flat's been raided by the police.'

'Christ. What did you have there?'

'The last shipment. The one I brought in from Amsterdam two days ago.'

'What have you got with you?'

She opened her airline holdall and passed him a fake Louis Vuitton beauty case. 'I picked this up in Brussels this morning.'

He took it and quickly hid it under the table.

'What the hell shall I do?' she asked.

He thought for a moment. 'How are you off for cash?'

'I've got plenty in the bank, but none with me.'

'When was the raid?'

'Two hours ago.'

'Right.' He was decisive. He walked across to the bar, paid the bill for their two unfinished glasses of white wine, and led her out. Hailing a cab, he directed it to the Lower Regent Street branch of Lloyds TSB and told the cab to wait. He accompanied her in to the bank where she produced her passport and withdrew £2,000 from her account. He held her hand reassuringly while the transaction went through and then took her round the corner to the ATM. She withdrew another £500. Jumping back into the cab, he instructed the driver to take them on to his flat. He let himself in and they went up to his apartment on the second floor.

He poured her a large brandy. 'Sit down by the window,' he said, and left the room.

A moment later he returned with a camera. He took two or three photographs of her head and shoulders. 'Stay here,' he said, 'and find the next few planes from Heathrow to the States, but not on a line where you're likely to meet anyone you know. I'll be back in two or three hours.'

She made the calls and noted four flights leaving between eight o'clock that night and seven thirty the next morning. Less than three hours later he was back. He reached into his pocket and drew out two envelopes and passed them to her. She opened the thin one. Inside was a UK passport with a name which was certainly not hers and a copy of one of the photographs he had taken that afternoon.

'You are English but went to school and university in the States,' he told her, 'hence your accent. The passport is a real one. It was bought from a girl with a real cash problem.'

She opened the other. In it were two hundred $100 notes. She looked at him gratefully. He smiled. 'You're worth it, to quote the ad. Now let's look at the flights that are available.'

She showed him. He quickly made a call to the airline with a flight taking off three hours later. He booked her a first-class ticket in the name of the passport he had given her, and paid for it with a credit card which was valid and his own, but which did not bear the name he generally used.

'Come on,' he said, and walked into his bedroom. He took out a suitcase and found a few T-shirts, two pairs of jeans, a cashmere sweater and some trainers. He put them in, along with a couple of novels. She looked enquiringly at him.

'You can't travel first-class with no luggage,' he explained, and tossed in the Vuitton beauty case, now emptied of the plastic bags it had contained.

'Let's go,' he said. They left his apartment and took a lift to the basement. He ushered her into one of the cars there, opened the automatic garage door and drove rapidly but carefully out of central London and down the M4 to Heathrow. Pulling up in front of the terminal, he looked at her.

'Thanks for everything, darling. Good luck and I'll be in touch.'

There were tears in her eyes as she leant across and kissed Kerry Nixon tenderly. She got out and, without looking back, walked into the airport. An hour and forty minutes later, this time feeling relieved, Honey gazed down as the aircraft crossed the Welsh coastline on its way to New York.

Chapter One

The short, wiry man in his early thirties limped out of the betting shop. He had the dejected look of someone who had lost, which in his case was more than true. Lenny Brown had been a top jump jockey. Although never champion, he had always ended the season in the top five or six of the winning riders' list. The yard he rode for was one of the most successful and he had good horses in the top races. Among his successes were no fewer than eleven wins at the National Hunt Festival. It was there at Cheltenham that his life took a terrible turn downhill. A crashing fall at the open ditch down the back straight left him with a left leg broken in four places, and not even the most skilled surgery could repair the extensive damage. He was left with a pronounced limp and his race-riding career was over.

He could hack horses and canter and could also drive the horsebox, but his high-income days were finished. Unhappily he could not get used to his new lifestyle. He had always lived rather high off the hog: his father had often told him, 'Lenny, you've got champagne tastes and beer pockets. You've just got to take it easy and save some money.' The advice went unheeded and Lenny rapidly got through his meagre savings. He took to drinking and gambling and soon lost his driving licence.

His employer was sympathetic and kept him on at the yard as little more than a groom, but at least he had a roof over his head and a regular though restricted income.

He was now worried not so much about the small amount of money he'd just lost in the betting shop, but about the very substantial debts he'd run up with one of the bigger bookmaking firms. The Kent brothers were well known for frequently offering slightly better odds than their competitors. This had tempted a number of celebrities to bet with them, including several well-known footballers. Along with this went a reputation for coming down hard on people who owed them money. Lenny was now very much in this situation and was becoming increasingly concerned as demands for payment became more insistent and indeed more threatening.

Turning off the main street of the small town, he became aware of footsteps behind him. Turning, he saw two men following him. He hurried as fast as his limp would allow in the direction of the stables. Rounding the corner, he was confronted by two more men. Without a word they grabbed him and shoved him into the back of a people carrier which was parked round the corner. They all drove off without a word and stopped once they were outside the town. One of the men sitting in the front turned round.

'The boss is not very happy with you, Lenny,' he announced. 'When's he going to get his money?'

'As s-soon as I can,' Lenny stuttered. 'I thought I'd have some of it today but the bloody horse fell at the last fence when in the lead.'

'We're not interested in that,' came the reply. 'Time is running out.'

Lenny thought frantically for something to say. 'I've got a bit of information which might help.'

'Oh, yes.' The tone was deeply sarcastic.

'Coming Good is due to run in the big race at Worcester on Thursday. He's not at the top of his form and the guv'nor doesn't want to run him, but the owner has sponsored the race and is insistent. He'll start a hot favourite and I'll eat my boots if he wins. I look after him and he's just not himself.'

The man in the front seat paused for a moment. 'I'll talk to the guv'nor about it. But, Lenny, if you know what's healthy for you this information had better be good, and you'd better find some way of raising the money, or at least half of it, and pretty damn quick or it won't just be your left leg giving you problems.'

With no further ado they bundled Lenny out on to the road and drove off.

The man in the front seat dialled a number and briefly relayed the conversation to Garry Kent, who grunted, 'We'll see how good this information is. If it turns out to be worthwhile I might just let him off the hook for the time being. If it's not, God help him.'

Three days' later Garry Kent was sitting in the back of his Bentley. He was driven by a grizzled but neatly dressed man in his late forties. 'Boxer' Stead had been a rather unsuccessful middleweight fighter, and when his brief career in the ring had ended he'd resorted to petty crime with a number of his East End friends. He'd been caught, and after one spell in jail had vowed never to go back. So far he had achieved that objective.

For several years now he had worked as driver and gofer for the brothers, and particularly for Garry. On the whole he avoided the sometimes dubious debt collection and other borderline activities in which the brothers indulged, but his still close contacts with the underworld normally meant that he could find the right person for any specific job. The Kent brothers' reputation ensured that such assignments were always completed with the utmost discretion. It was Boxer who had sent the four heavies to confront Lenny.

Garry had the day's *Racing Post* and a number of form books on the seat beside him, but his mind was busily engaged upon a long-term plan which had been given impetus by the events of the last few days.

Coincidentally, one of Garry's mates had been in a pub called the Shepherd's Rest located near County View, the training establishment of Jay Jessop, the champion National Hunt trainer. Supping his drink, he had overheard two men at the next table saying that an unraced horse called Red Squirrel was extremely highly thought of and was having her first public appearance in the same race as Coming Good. Their opinion was that she would be a lively contender, and even though the experience of some of the other horses would probably tell, these men were confident that the County View horse would figure in the first three. Garry had by now virtually finalized an idea which had been simmering in his mind for some time. This afternoon he was going to have a trial run to see if his plan would be as profitable as he'd hoped.

As Garry arrived, Worcester racecourse was bathed in glorious September sun which made the grass look almost emerald green. It wasn't one of the biggest racecourses in Britain, but its location almost always ensured a good crowd and competitive fields.

16

The fourth race that afternoon was a novice hurdle, not particularly valuable for a sponsored race but still worth winning. This had attracted two previous winners – Coming Good which had won at Huntington and Director's Perk which had won at Sandown. It also had two other horses which had been placed in better class races at Ascot and Newbury. These four led the betting at prices varying from 2 to 1 on Coming Good to 5 to 1 on Director's Perk.

The race was approximately two miles, which meant that the field would pass the winning post twice. Going down the back straight the second time, these four well-backed horses had drawn away from the other eleven runners and the TV cameras were trained on the leaders. Garry, a well-built man in a rather loud check jacket and smart grey trousers, was watching the race intently through his powerful binoculars. Interestingly, he was not watching the first four horses which had drawn several lengths ahead of the main pack. His glasses were trained on the following group which, with the exception of two stragglers, were still closely bunched. As this group jumped the last hurdle down the back straight, he noticed with some satisfaction that one horse was moving smoothly through the pack and was making ground on the four leaders. Although Red Squirrel had not run before, she had started at 10 to 1 largely because she came from County View and was trained by Jay Jessop. By the time the four leaders were approaching the third last hurdle in the home straight, Red Squirrel had attached herself to the back of this group. Between this hurdle and the penultimate one Coming Good, the favourite, and Director's Perk, the Sandown winner, had drawn clear of the other two members of the quarter. It was clear that

17

Coming Good was now struggling to keep up the pace. The County View horse moved past the third and fourth horses and was soon within a length of the two leaders. Director's Perk gradually drew ahead of the favourite who seemed to have downed tools, his jockey accepting defeat.

David Sparrow, Red Squirrel's young jockey, sat quietly and let her natural ability move them up to within half a length of Director's Perk. As they approached the last hurdle, the two of them jumped it fluently, and with a shake of the reins and a slap on the neck the County View horse moved smoothly away to win by a comfortable length and a half.

Garry Kent hung his binoculars round his neck and smiled contentedly to himself. This had not only been a successful race for him financially, but it confirmed the idea he had been mulling over for some time.

Garry and his brother Tony were two East Enders. They had built up an extremely successful on-course bookmaking business which was supported by a big credit betting operation and three very profitable betting shops, one in the East End and the other two in Essex. They were also in the final stages of buying a small but growing and profitable internet gambling operation. Garry had been at Worcester that afternoon as a result of the conversation overheard at the Shepherd's Rest – which had been made even more interesting by Lenny Brown's information.

Having got to the racecourse, he had waited until he had had a look at the horse in the pre-parade ring and then phoned his brother. Quick telephone calls resulted in the odds on the four best-fancied horses being lengthened and those on the County View runner being shortened. This attracted a considerable volume of bets on these four horses which far outweighed the small amount of money which had been placed on Red Squirrel to win.

Having spoken to Tony and found out how successful the afternoon had been, Garry walked into the bar and bought himself a large scotch. He noticed that Jay Jessop was sitting chatting to a smartly dressed woman in her fifties. He surmised that she was the winning horse's owner. He was right. Laura Pearce had been completely surprised when, on the death of her cousin, she had inherited two young horses. Like Eva, Jay Jessop's wife, she was South African, and the two had met socially quite frequently and had become good friends. Red Squirrel and her other horse, Golden Moment, were soon ensconced at County View. She was obviously thrilled that her first runner had been a winner and insisted on buying a bottle of champagne. Jay had already arranged for David Sparrow to drive him home as the jockey had travelled with the horse to Worcester in order to have plenty of time to walk the course before racing, and also to relax before his afternoon became really busy.

Garry had another whisky, phoned Tony to say he was on his way, and walked across to the car park in the middle of the racecourse where Boxer was already sitting in his Bentley. Because they left before the last race they weren't held up, and in just over three hours he was sitting in his office near the Elephant and Castle discussing the day's activities with Tony. They also discussed their weekend shooting plans. Both were excellent shots and travelled all over England and Scotland to indulge their passion.

Back at Worcester, Jay and Laura found themselves joined by another big man. Frank Malone was also a bookmaker but on a much bigger scale than the Kent brothers. He and Jay had become friends some time ago and Frank had been very helpful to Jay when a number of strange events had taken place involving County View and some of its horses.

Frank had several very good horses with Jay but still enjoyed racing even if he didn't have a runner. He sat down and congratulated Laura warmly. They knew each other from previous meetings on Jay's gallops. After discussing her horse's triumphs and enquiring after one or two of his own favourites, he changed the subject.

'There's been some pretty strange betting on your race,' he informed Jay. 'The Kent brothers must have made a small fortune this afternoon. They lengthened the odds on the four short-priced horses and shortened them on yours quite dramatically. It was almost as if they knew your horse was going to win.'

Jay laughed. 'That's more than I did. I knew she would run very well but she was up against some stiff opposition, and you know I'm always cautious in my assessment of our horses' chances of winning.'

'Well, in that case the two brothers must have been inspired. I wish I'd done the same as them.'

Chatting for a little longer, he said he wanted to be ready to leave as soon as the last race was over. He gave Laura a friendly peck on the cheek and was on his way as David Sparrow walked in to join the owner and his trainer. Frank was extremely fond of young David, who had joined County View a few years earlier and had moved from being a very promising novice to winning the Conditional Jockeys' championship. He was now among the most successful jockeys in the country. Jay and Frank quietly believed it wouldn't be long before he was champion. Apart from riding the pick of County

View's horses, he was starting to be booked by outside trainers for good horses in major races.

Frank congratulated him on Red Squirrel's win and reminded him he would be riding two of his horses the next day. 'So don't drink too much of the fizz,' he warned the young man, and cheerfully made his way out to his car.

On his way home Frank phoned his son Lance, who was not only in Frank's business but had become his right-hand man. Frank, as always, was being driven by Peter Enfield who had worked for him for over twenty years as his secretary and Man Friday. He always referred to him as 'my boy', although Peter was now in his early fifties.

'Would you be free for dinner tonight?' he asked his son.

'Absolutely, Dad,' was the answer. 'I'll phone Mother and let her know.'

Lance lived with his mother. Frank had divorced her some years ago; he now lived alone and was looked after by an elderly but super-efficient housekeeper who came in seven days a week. He phoned Winnie and told her his plans with Lance.

'Don't worry, Mr Malone,' she said. 'You know I always keep a few things I've cooked in the freezer. I'll get out one of my chicken casseroles and I'll put some potatoes in the oven if you call me when you are nearing home. You can finish it off with that lovely Stilton which somebody gave you a few weeks ago.'

'That sounds wonderful,' agreed Frank, and settled down to have a quiet kip in the back of his car as Peter drove him home.

Meanwhile, Jay was on his way back to County View driven by young David. He phoned his home to let Eva know he would be there in about an hour

21

and she immediately wanted to know how things had gone.

'Pretty well,' he told her, 'but I'll give you all the news when I get back.' He didn't want to discuss the rather odd betting in front of the Sparrow.

An hour and a half later he was sitting down with a Scotch and water in his hand and relating the afternoon's events. He explained how Frank had seen Garry Kent at the races and that there had been a very strange betting pattern on Red Squirrel's race.

'I don't think it's anything to worry about,' he assured his wife, 'but it is odd that Garry Kent should be there when he or his brother had adjusted the odds on our horse and the favourite so dramatically. Apart from anything else, Frank assures me it is unusual for either of them to go to racecourses that far away from London.'

Eva shrugged her shoulders. 'Well, I'm sure none of us are involved so there's no reason to lose any sleep over it,' she reassured her husband. 'Come on now, let's have some supper. I imagine you're starving.'

With their young son Max, they were soon tucking into a lamb casserole while Max described his day at school and told them how much he was looking forward to the next round of the county badminton championship in which he was progressing rapidly.

Chapter Two

Back at the Elephant and Castle the two Kent brothers were calculating how much they'd won on that particular race, and were more than satisfied. Altogether they'd had a pretty good day, with a number of favourites losing both there and at the other tracks where racing had taken place. Red Squirrel was a bonus.

'I've had an idea,' Garry announced. 'If we could get twenty to thirty races like the one at Worcester this afternoon we could do really well.'

'Sure,' agreed Tony, 'but how often are we going to get lucky and have one of our mates overhear a conversation like that?'

'We don't get lucky, we make it happen.'

'How the hell have you worked that out? Have someone sitting in every pub near every racing yard in Britain?'

'No,' replied his older brother. 'We find half a dozen or so informants in the big yards. We pay them well for their information and we make sure that it can't be traced back to us. We mustn't be too greedy, and if we keep our nerve we could do really well.'

'Carry on,' prompted Tony.

'My idea is that we go around the top six to ten

yards and do some real homework on the stable staff who have been at the yards for a while. Even head men are not paid well, and if we offer say five hundred quid a month with an extra five hundred if their information turns out to be accurate, this could make a huge difference to their financial situation. It would also allow us to adjust our books and make a few killings like this afternoon.'

'The horseracing authorities would come down on us like a ton of bricks if they found out. We'd get warned off and so would they.'

'I know,' agreed the older Kent, 'but this is my plan. We get a couple of our reliable East End friends to go round the yards and discover where the guys meet socially. They find out who really knows about the horses, then get friendly with them, check out how reliable they seem to be and gradually put the idea in front of them. They would explain that the money would be paid into a Swiss bank account but they wouldn't be able to touch it for five years. However, they would know the money was gradually accumulating for them and there would be a nice nest egg at the end of five years. If the information turned out to be good and reliable, we could then offer them another five years.'

'How are we going to get the information from them?' asked Tony.

'Remember Oscar Fry, the banker who nearly got caught embezzling money. If you recall, we bailed him out and he took early retirement and is now in Spain. I happen to know that he could do with a bit more money. They could phone him in Spain and he would then forward the information to us. He would have two phones with separate numbers. That ought to keep us in the clear.'

Tony gave it some thought. 'It sounds good to me. How do we get the guys who are going to contact the stable staff?'

'I think we can leave that to Boxer,' replied Garry. 'He knows a hell of a lot of people and I don't think anyone he chose would be unreliable as far as we are concerned. They know it wouldn't be safe to talk about us or what we're doing.'

'I think you're right. Let's go for it. Now, how about a drink?'

At seven thirty that evening Lance Malone drove up to the iron gates at his father's house. He had a remote control to open them himself. Frank heard the car coming up the drive and Hun, his German shepherd, barked a couple of times then rushed to the front door. Frank opened it to greet his son, and Hun bounded down the steps and across the yard to give Lance the most enthusiastic of welcomes. Hun was Frank's pride and joy. He was an extremely good guard dog but gentle and affectionate with Frank, Lance and their immediate circle.

Giving his son a hug, Frank led the way into the dining room where a log fire was burning cheerfully. They sat down on big easy chairs in front of the fire. Frank poured himself a Scotch and water and a vodka and tonic for Lance. They'd already agreed that Lance would stay the night so there was no problem about him driving home. Lance brought his father up to date, and explained that they'd had a fairly good day as a large number of favourites had been beaten.

'Not as good as the Kents had,' his father chuckled. 'They must have had second sight or something,' and he recounted what had happened at Worcester.

'That's interesting,' remarked Lance. 'One or two of our regulars sometimes bet with the Kents, and several of them didn't bet with us today. In fact we took very little money on that race, far less than we would normally.'

'Well, that would figure if the pros looked at the odds carefully,' replied Frank, 'and I'll wager a few other bookmakers laid off some of their books on that race with the Kent brothers.'

'Almost certainly,' agreed his son.

'Let's eat,' suggested Frank. The two of them fetched the casserole and the baked potatoes from the Aga, and put the Stilton and some fresh bread on the table. Frank opened a bottle of claret and they chatted about racing in general.

'How's your mother?' enquired Frank, out of politeness rather than genuine interest.

'Just the same. Goes to the gym every day, has a huge lunch with one of her girlfriends and complains she's putting on weight. Then in the evening she tucks into another large meal.'

'Sounds like your mother to me,' chuckled Frank. 'Does she still moan all the time?'

'I guess so,' replied Lance, 'but she's not too bad to me.'

'I know,' said Frank. 'You mean the world to her and that's why I never made any effort to encourage you to leave her and come and live with me. I suspect she'd really take to the bottle if you did that.'

'I think she probably would too,' agreed his son.

After dinner they sat back in the two fireside chairs with a glass of brandy each. Frank enjoyed a cigar but his son didn't smoke at all. After a little more idle chatter, Frank looked at his watch.

'I've got an early start tomorrow,' he said. 'I want to be at Ascot fairly early. Let's turn in.'

Lance stood up, gave his father a hug and went upstairs. Frank went to the front door, opened it and let Hun have his freedom. The dog loped round the grounds just inside the high stone wall surrounding the property, which in turn was topped with razor wire. Cameras were placed at strategic points, and infrared beams illuminated the area if anyone walked through them once Frank had closed the front door and turned the system on. He never kept large sums of money at home but was always aware that criminals might not know that and assume a major bookmaker would always have a pile of cash around. Hun soon returned, panting and wagging his tail. Frank went through the procedure of locking the doors and turning on the security system. He then made his way upstairs accompanied by Hun. He cleaned his teeth, washed his face and climbed into bed. Within moments Hun had climbed on to the foot of his bed, curled up and was snoring very gently. Frank smiled to himself. The snoring never worried him, and like his dog Frank was soon fast asleep.

Chapter Three

Tolchester racecourse was one of the stiffest in Britain and was situated in the northern part of the Midlands. It was owned by Tolchester Holdings, a publicly quoted company on the AIM stock exchange, and was one of a total of six racecourses owned by the company. These were spread around the UK, all of them in good geographical positions from the point of view of easy access to large catchment areas. Most of them were close to motorways, all were close to good road systems, and three of them had railway stations attached to the actual courses.

Each of the courses had originally been family owned, but as racing became more competitive and commercial it became clear that there was a strong case for courses to join forces. A number of established tracks had already come under central ownership and management.

The chairman of the holding group was Adam Forsyth, the only son of wealthy parents. At fifty-two, he was a well-respected and highly successful businessman with interests in many different areas. He had been clever at school without being outstanding, and had achieved an upper second in Economics at Cambridge. It was there that Adam had met Jay Jessop and Percy Cartwright, through their mutual interest in racing even then. Jay and Percy had been close friends ever since. Adam was on good terms with them but had never been very close, although his racing interests meant he saw Jay more often than Percy. He was a little older than both of them, having spent a few years in his father's US business and then another year in South America before going up to Cambridge.

Percy was the owner of a highly successful international insurance business and had a number of first-rate horses trained by Jay at County View, his now famous training establishment.

Adam Forsyth owned 20 per cent of the equity in the holding group, and the other four original company directors each had 10 per cent. This was because Adam had owned Tolchester and Avon Park racecourses and the other directors just one each. They were Jon Gormley, Rupert Jonson, Norman Parry and Monty Raymond, who had all inherited their racecourses from their families. Thirty per cent of the shares were owned by the public, most of them by a private bank and a venture capital company named New Opportunities. Percy and Jay had 5 per cent each.

When Adam had first discussed the idea of combining a number of similar-sized racecourses he realized that it would be a great advantage to have at least two non-executive directors on the board. This was agreed by the board, so once the deal had been done he approached Percy and Jay. Although they were both extremely busy in their main occupations, they thought this would be an interesting additional activity and would also provide an opportunity to put something back into National Hunt racing which they both loved so much. They had such excellent reputations that Adam had no difficulty in persuading his board colleagues to extend the invitations.

Jay and Percy had arrived at the racecourse three hours before racing was due to start in order to attend a board meeting of Tolchester Holdings.

The main item on the agenda had been tabled by Adam Forsyth who thought the company should be more aggressive in its attempts to expand some of its other services, and even to take over other racecourses. He pointed out that there was no racecourse in the Birmingham area nor in Manchester, both of which had supported major racecourses in the past. Aintree and Haydock were close to Manchester, but he still felt there was the possibility to have a further racecourse on the other side of the city. Birmingham had a number of racecourses nearby, including Uttoxeter, Worcester and Stratford-on-Avon, all of which were excellent, but none were really major courses. It soon became obvious that the other directors were rather more conservative than Adam in their attitudes. They were comfortable with what they were getting from their shareholdings and did not really welcome change. This was really frustrating for Adam Forsyth, a view shared by Jay and Percy.

Percy had also suggested that the racecourses which they already owned could be developed to offer a wider and better range of services. They could work hard on building up conference facilities, and at least two courses had enough spare ground available to accommodate a reasonably sized hotel. This had already proved successful at other courses including Wolverhampton.

He also felt that real attention should be given to the catering services, and that top-class retired chefs should be employed to work with younger chefs to offer exceptional food, not only on race days but on Friday evenings, Saturdays and perhaps even Sunday lunchtimes. As well as race days, they could cater for weddings and perhaps even concerts. This would obviously require significant investment.

The other directors were still dubious about this, but two of them looked more amenable when Percy pointed out that first of all they'd have to get planning permission for the hotels, and also that it would not be difficult to set up a pilot activity at one of the racecourses to see if the catering experiment worked. Again no conclusion was reached, but there wasn't the really positive reaction to these proposals which Adam, Percy and Jay had hoped for.

The two friends left the dining room, which had been used for the board meeting, and went down to the owners' and trainers' bar where Eva was waiting for them. She could tell from their expressions that they were not particularly happy.

'Whatever's the problem?' she asked Jay.

'I'll tell you about it later, darling. It's not a good moment, and Percy and I would both love a cup of coffee.'

She looked at them with a smile. 'Percy, have you got your driver here?'

'Yes. Francis never misses a trip to the races.'

'Well, I'll drive you home, Jay. I think perhaps a bottle of champagne would be a little more appropriate at the moment. We'll leave it at that.'

Soon Eva returned with a beaming smile, bearing a tray loaded with an ice bucket, a bottle of champagne and three glasses. She poured each of the two men a full glass and herself a modest half measure.

She looked at Jay. 'Have you spoken to Percy about your ideas concerning Jed, Danny and Vicky?'

It was clear from Percy's expression that whatever was under discussion was news to him.

'I'm sorry, Percy, but a couple of days ago Cathy came to see me and was concerned that Jed was beginning to find the pressure of work too much.'

Cathy was Jed's wife and had been very much part of County View ever since her husband had joined Jay as assistant trainer. Although much older, Jed was a longstanding friend who had been a well-respected trainer. Jay had ridden for him when he was an amateur jockey. His main owner, Howard Barrack, had joined the board of County View right at the outset and was now one of their most enthusiastic owners. Cathy wanted her husband to withdraw as far as possible from the strains of his job as he did not enjoy the best of health. Jay understood, but pointed out that Jed was such an important person he did not want him to retire completely. It would probably not be good for Jed either.

While County View was developing, a young city financier called Roddy Clinton-Bowes had joined the board and had been building up a separate stud business which was now very successful. It had operations in France, Australia, New Zealand, South Africa, and more recently Ireland. It had occurred to Jay that although Jed was not an expert in stud management he had a wonderful eye for a good horse and would be an ideal right-hand man for Roddy, not only helping him to choose brood mares but also to select those young horses which were most suitable for augmenting the County View string, or those which would be more sensibly entered into the sales. Although there would be a fair amount of travel, if Cathy went with him Jay was certain that Jed would not overdo it. Jed had given

32

County View such good service he deserved to be well looked after.

Percy nodded his agreement to this idea.

'That leaves a hole in my staff,' Jay continued. 'I've talked to Danny in the past and he's always made it quite clear he loves being head man. There's no way he'd agree to being assistant trainer. He feels he doesn't have the social graces to handle the job. He's much more a hands-on man, doesn't have the diplomatic skills you need to be a trainer or an assistant. I've chatted to Eva about this and I have a rather unusual idea. You know Vicky Benson, the ex-amateur jockey who's done very well with her small string in the north of England? We always got on well together, I think she's under-capitalized and has probably gone just about as far as she can. I haven't spoken to her yet but I think she might well jump at the idea of becoming my assistant. She's showing real ability as a trainer with limited resources. She's also got a great deal of style and I'm sure she would charm the owners.'

Eva gave him a hard look. 'I'm not too sure that it's only her professional qualifications that appeal to Jay.' She smiled at Percy. 'She's a remarkably attractive woman.'

Percy decided that discretion was the better part of valour and said nothing.

Eva continued, 'I'm only joking. I really think that if we could persuade her to join us it would be a huge help. I also think, by the way, that Jay is now being overstretched. He's running the biggest National Hunt yard in Britain, he's very involved in the National Trainers Federation, and this Tolchester business seems to be taking up more and more time for both of you. We also have an eight-year-old son who adores his father and is rightly very demanding in terms of Jay going to school activities. In short we've got a hell of a lot of responsibilities, not only to the other shareholders in County View but also to our owners and staff.'

Percy nodded. 'I think it's an excellent idea. I've met Vicky a few times at the races and I'm sure that she would live up to your hopes for her. Let's toast the future.'

They all raised their glasses and sat back to relax for ten minutes. Jay looked at his watch. He got up. 'Come on. We've got work to do with our two runners.'

The first of the runners was Eva's horse. Jay had bought Sharp Focus for Eva on the advice of Freddy Kelly, a retired champion jockey who had also ridden many winners for Jay. He now had his own blood-stock business in Ireland. The horse had won a point-to-point there and Freddy was very enthusiastic. At first Jay had been disappointed but suddenly Sharp Focus had developed in leaps and bounds, and in just a few weeks he was beginning to look as if he would turn into a really useful animal. Danny, who rode the horse most days, was even more enthusiastic.

Soon the horse had been saddled and was walking around the parade ring like an old professional, led by Patsy, his doting groom. Tolchester racecourse was definitely the stiffest of those in the group. After a long tough uphill finish, the track dropped rapidly away from the stands towards the back straight where there was a sharp incline followed by another long downhill slope, which continued halfway round the final bend, before the long climb to the finishing post in front of the stands. Sharp Focus looked wonderful and had gone to the start with that long lazy stride which had been one of the key factors in Jay's decision to buy him.

Although he had run over three miles in Ireland in point-to-points, Jay decided to settle for two and a half miles in his first chase under rules in England. Furthermore, he felt the stiff uphill finish would help to bring the horse's obvious stamina into play. The two-and-a-half-mile start was at the beginning of the back straight which meant the horses had nearly two complete circuits to travel.

David Sparrow had been told to stay in touch with the main pack for the first mile and a half at least, and then to ensure he was in the first four or five as they turned for home on the final circuit. There were fifteen runners in this novice chase with two previous winners, No Slouch and Silver Earl. Of the other runners, Gentle Jenny, Night Alarm and Happy Hours had all been placed earlier in the season. No Slouch was a firm favourite at 3 to 1.

To Jay's surprise Sharp Focus was only 7 to 1, largely because of his point-to-point win in Ireland coupled with County View's reputation. The fifteen runners were soon on their way without any problems at the start. All had racecourse experience in either bumpers or hurdles, or both. The exception was Sharp Focus who had clearly benefited from his point-to-point experience.

The pace was good but not too ambitious, with two and a half tough miles in front of them. Silver Earl, the second favourite, led. He was a confirmed front-runner and ensured that there was a good gallop. There had been no incidents as they turned for home and faced the open ditch followed by two plain fences before passing the winning post for the first time. Taking the bend and before the course took the downhill slope there was a water jump, which all cleared well with the exception of Gentle Jenny, who dropped her hind legs in the water and lost several lengths in so doing. Sharp Focus was in the ideal position from Jay's point of view, about seven lengths behind the leader in fifth position.

The pace increased going down the hill. It was clear that with his long stride Sharp Focus wasn't totally comfortable and he lost two places but only a couple of lengths. David Sparrow sat quietly, letting the horse negotiate the downhill slope in his own way. As soon as they met level ground, he quickly made up the two places he had lost and resumed fifth position. Going round the bend and beginning to meet the uphill ground, Sharp Focus jumped the plain fence and moved smoothly to fourth and then third place. No Slouch had now taken the lead. He was distinctly increasing the pace and showing no sign of fatigue, and was beginning to draw clear of a tiring Happy Hours in second place. The Sparrow gently urged Sharp Focus to pass this horse and to go in pursuit of the still strongly galloping favourite. Approaching the open ditch, Sharp Focus was closing steadily on the leader. Both of them jumped it smoothly and Sharp Focus reduced the gap between him and No Slouch to two and a half lengths. There was no change in the situation as they reached the second last, which both cleared fluently, but Sharp Focus had reduced the deficit to barely a length. Approaching the last, Eva's horse had cut the lead to half a length but the favourite was still galloping strongly as he and Sharp Focus headed for the finishing post. Eva, Jay and Percy were now really excited as her horse slowly but surely reduced the gap, but No Slouch was game and was showing no sign of weakening as they approached the winning post. With fifty yards to go Sharp Focus had reduced the deficit to a mere neck. It was a slow but steady wearing away of the leader's advantage, but as Jay had suspected there was no kick at the end. Passing the winning post, Sharp Focus was beaten by a head. Although everybody was pleased, there was a slight disappointment that he hadn't quite made it.

Giving his wife a hug and a kiss, Jay said, 'Well, we always knew he would need a longer distance and his jumping was immaculate. Next time out we'll go for three miles.'

Percy looked at them with a grin. 'I know it's a long way from a novice chase to Aintree, but I think you might have a real Grand National horse in the future.'

Eva pulled a face. 'Well, fortunately it's a while before we have to make up our minds about that, but I'm not sure that my nerves would stand it.'

They hurried across to the winners' enclosure in time to greet and congratulate the Sparrow. His elation was obvious.

'He jumped super, madam!' he cried. 'Another half furlong and we would have won.'

Percy gave him a pat on the back. 'Another fifty yards and you'd have won.'

'That's great,' said Jay. 'Now go and weigh in. We don't want to lose the second prize money, do we?'

With a cheerful grin and a touch of his cap, the Sparrow left for the weighing room.

At that moment Howard Barrack, as always smartly but slightly flashily dressed, came up to them. He was not only a founding director of County View but a close friend. Giving Eva a big kiss on the cheek, he shook hands almost violently with both Percy and Jay.

'I got here in time to watch it. Didn't he run a cracker? I thought he was going to win.' The words tumbled out in his enthusiasm. 'Come on, I'll buy you all a drink.' Without waiting for them to answer, he turned round and bustled his way to the owners' and trainers' bar. Another bottle of champagne appeared and again Eva insisted on just half a glass.

'I'm driving the guv home,' she said with a grin. 'And what about you?'

'Don't worry, my love,' he said. 'I've got one of Benny's lads driving me.'

Benny was an East End character who, along with his brothers, had performed a number of services for Howard over the years and some really important ones for Jay and County View. Sometimes his methods sailed close to the wind, but he'd never actually been nailed for anything illegal. He also had a surprisingly good relationship with a number of policemen, including a senior officer, Harvey Jackson, who had been involved in two extremely worrying situations concerning County View.

By the time they'd finished talking about the race and trying to cool Howard's expectations of his horse down to some sort of reality, it was time to saddle his mare.

Pewter Pearl was the first foal of a wonderful grey mare that Howard owned named Pewter Queen. She had won a number of top-class hurdle races including one at the Cheltenham Festival, and was her owner's pride and joy. In her early days Jay had ridden her, including to success in her first ever race at Sandown. Her daughter was almost a carbon copy of her dam in her youth. A steely grey, she looked and moved like a real aristocrat. With age her mother had got whiter and, as Howard said, looking adoringly at

38

the filly as she walked round the parade ring, 'God, she's the spitting image of her mum. I hope she turns out to be half as good.'

'Well, we'll get a clue today,' said Jay, 'and I don't think you'll be too disappointed.'

Pewter Pearl was running in the last race of the afternoon, a two-mile National Hunt flat race. This was how her mother had started her career at Sandown, with Jay riding her and beating his rival and great friend, Freddy Kelly, in the tightest of finishes. As this was her first visit to a racecourse, the filly was very much on her toes and looking around in an alert and interested manner. She wasn't pulling her young groom, Tina, around the ring, but she was still striding out and needed a little restraint to keep her a sensible distance behind the horse in front. A kick in the parade ring was the last thing she needed before her first race, or indeed any race for that matter.

The Pearl was being ridden by Vijay Hassan, a young Asian conditional jockey. To everyone he was known by his nickname, Ali, after his hero Mohammed Ali. Young Ali was an extremely accomplished boxer and had won the stable lads' championship for the previous two years. He had worked like a Trojan when he joined Jay's yard, had eventually been given a licence and had now chalked up nineteen rides. He had been placed seven times out of his nineteen rides, but hadn't yet notched up a winner. Jay had talked long and hard to Howard before making the decision, and Howard had been his usual supportive and enthusiastic self.

'I've seen the lad ride a few times,' he said, 'and I know you wouldn't put him on the Pearl if you didn't think he could do her justice. And, after all, he does get a few pounds off her back.'

'That's true, but he looks after the Pearl when Tina's not there and rides her in all her serious work. The two know each other well,' Jay added.

Ali walked into the ring, touched his cap to all four of them, and took the opportunity to congratulate Eva on Sharp Focus's run. He turned to Jay.

'I'm not going to tell you what to do but remember, if she's anything like her mother she'll have a good finish even though it's a stiff uphill climb. Because there are so many young and first-time horses, there are bound to be one or two who are a bit over-keen, so don't get galloped off your feet in the first mile or so.'

'Right, guv,' said Ali and, turning, he had a quick look around the ring where he saw his parents who had driven all the way from Bradford. He gave them a little wave just before the bell rang, and Jay walked across and legged him up on to Howard's lovely horse. Tina led her out on to the track. Going past the grandstand, the Pearl ducked away from the crowd but the movement wasn't too sudden or dramatic and her young jockey stayed firmly in his saddle.

At the start, one or two of the inexperienced horses were playing up and the starter was not satisfied with their first approach to the tape as one of the runners turned around completely and a couple of the others were side on. The jockeys were instructed to take a turn before lining up and coming in for a second time. This time he released the tape and the field were off.

As Jay suspected, three of the horses dashed to the front and it was clear that the pace they were setting would be unsustainable over the stiff two-mile course. By the time they had gone between the wings of the first hurdle which had been removed, the field

40

was already strung out, with Pewter Pearl sitting in about ninth position of the twenty-one runners. It was a little like the charge of the Light Brigade as the field streamed past the winning post for the first time.

As always, Howard was on tenterhooks as his horse went past, and his eyes were glued to his binoculars as they swept down the hill towards the far side of the track. By this time the three horses that had gone off at a breakneck speed were already beginning to tire. Halfway down the back straight they were engulfed by the pursuing pack. Turning for home, Pewter Pearl crept up to seventh place and was making steady progress as they turned to confront the stiff climb to the finish. She was now in fifth position, but her young jockey sat still on her, letting her make ground in her own time. With a furlong to go, she had moved into third place and was only half a length behind the second and a further length behind the leader.

At this stage Ali gave her a slap on the shoulder and she showed that surprising acceleration which had been a feature of her mother's racing. She rapidly moved into second place, and with fifty yards to go she was soon neck and neck with the leader. Her superior finishing speed told quickly and she flashed past the winning post with a length and a half to spare.

Howard was ecstatic. The rest of the party were equally pleased though not quite so vocally demonstrative as her owner. They followed him as he rushed across the lawn to the winners' enclosure where he grinned from ear to ear as his horse was led in by a glowing Tina and an equally cheerful Ali. When the jockey jumped off, Howard gave him a huge hug. He kissed Tina, before enthusiastically patting his winner.

41

Jay quickly congratulated Ali on his first win, adding that he'd ridden the horse with great maturity and his timing had been perfect. The young man was positively beaming as he looked past Jay to see his delighted parents waving enthusiastically to him. The racecourse photographers engulfed them and pictures were taken of all concerned, with the steaming grey looking every inch a star.

'Come on, you and I will go and weigh in,' Jay said, 'then you can go and have a chat with your parents. Eva, be a darling – pop over and explain to them what's happening.'

With that, he led the young man into the weighing room where the formalities were completed. Though Ali didn't drink, Jay suggested he might like to meet his parents in the owners' and trainers' bar.

Howard was still ebullient as he and Percy made their way to the bar where Jay knew yet another bottle of champagne would be opened. He crossed over to Ali's parents, who were still chatting to Eva, and explained that they would be very welcome to join them and there would be a Coke ready for their son. His parents were also teetotal, but said they would love to join the rest of the party for a cup of coffee. They were clearly over the moon at their son's success, and Jay and Eva made them even happier by praising the way in which Ali had ridden the horse.

A few moments later he joined them and got a huge kiss and hug from his mother which clearly embarrassed him, while his father shook hands, giving Jay a big wink over his son's shoulders.

The celebrations continued for twenty minutes, when Ali's parents announced they must be on their way as they had to drive back to Bradford.

'I think we should all be on our way now,'

suggested Jay. Shaking hands with Howard and Percy, he promised to be in touch with them in the next few days. 'In fact,' he said to Howard, 'I'll call you tomorrow to reassure you that the Pearl is none the worse for her race.'

'I'm sure she won't be.'

With more warm handshakes all round, and kisses for Eva from both of the men, they separated and made their way towards their cars.

Jay's spirits, damped after the board meeting, had lifted again with the two successes and a significant amount of champagne. He sat contentedly beside Eva as she negotiated her way out of the car park and on to the main road. As soon as they were well on their way, she gave her husband a quick glance. 'Well, tell me about today.'

Jay explained that Adam had put forward the idea of possibly acquiring other courses and had suggested further significant developments for Tolchester Holdings, including at least three of the courses that were already in the group. Reaction had varied between negative and lukewarm. The proposition about developing conference and entertainment facilities, with high-class catering, had been met with much the same attitude by two of the directors, but a slightly more positive reaction from the other two.

'Tell me how each one reacted.'

'Well, Monty Raymond, who owns Arden Park, was completely negative, and so was Norman Parry, who owns Essex Park. Rupert Jonson, who owns Stockton Park, was negative about the major expansion, but a little more interested in Percy's proposals about expanding our services, and Jon Gormley, who owns Mussfield, was at the best lukewarm about the major developments but seemed far more interested in the second of our proposals.

'Adam is extremely disappointed. You know how enthusiastic he is. His whole business life has been focused on expansion and he's used to getting his own way. He's particularly disappointed with Jon Gormley as they both sit on the board of some other company and Adam thought he could count on his support. I can see friction developing between now and the next board meeting.'

'Ah well,' sighed Eva, 'let's enjoy the success we've had today, and get home and have a cheerful evening with Max.'

Jay gave her hand on the steering wheel an affectionate squeeze, and they both sat back and listened to one of Jay's CDs which featured a number of country and western songs, which were among his particular favourites and were tolerated by Eva.

They'd been travelling for a little over an hour when Jay's phone rang.

'It's Adam here,' announced the familiar voice. 'Jay, are you racing tomorrow?'

'No,' replied Jay. 'We've got a runner at Plumpton but Jed is going down with Cathy because they always see a lot of their old friends there. You probably remember that he trained in Sussex before coming to join me?'

'That's right,' said Adam. 'He was pretty good but never top-class, I seem to remember.'

'He was very good but he never had any really top-class horses. Pewter Queen and the Conker were only just beginning to race and show their real ability when he and they joined with me at County View.'

'How did that come about?' asked Adam. 'I've often wondered.'

44

'Well, he had a bit of a heart scare. The doctor told him that he should cut out smoking, and that he was overdoing things and should do something which was a little less stressful. Coming to be my number two suited him, Cathy and me wonderfully. He is incredibly knowledgeable, has a very cool head, and is a wonderful man in a crisis. He's been an invaluable part of the growth of County View.'

'Well, that's not what I phoned you about, Jay. I'd like to come and talk to you tomorrow if that's possible, both about today's board meeting and also about my son.'

'Tomorrow would be fine as I'm not racing,' Jay replied. 'If you want to come and watch the gallops, you'd need to be here at seven-thirty for first lot and nine for second. Alternatively you can come down in time for lunch.'

'I'd love to watch the horses,' replied Adam, 'but I've got a breakfast meeting tomorrow which could take a couple of hours, although that would still give me plenty of time to get down to you between half past twelve and one. Would that suit?'

Jay was slightly surprised at the comment regarding his son, but assured Adam that he would be most welcome.

Putting down the phone, Jay looked over at Eva and outlined his conversation with Adam.

'I didn't think he'd waste much time before getting down to business after his rejection today. I wonder what he wants to discuss about his son, though? I've seen him ride a few times and he's not without ability. I think he finished about sixth in last year's amateur championship, but a long way behind Robin Haslett who has won it for three years in a row.'

Eva had an idea. 'Seeing as Adam's visit is likely to

cover some very confidential matters, I suggest we have lunch at County View. Do you want to talk to him alone?'

'Not at all,' replied Jay. 'You're a director of County View so I'd appreciate your views about anything he has to say, as well as your company,' he added with a grin.

'What do you really think about him?'

Jay thought for a moment. 'Hard one. He's a very tough man who has a reputation for being pretty ruthless in his business deals. On the other hand, he seems to keep the key people who work for him for long periods. He's always been polite and charming to me without going over the top, but there's something about him that concerns me. Sometimes I think he could be almost dangerous in his pursuit of excellence and success. I suppose I could be reading too much into his reputation rather than the man himself.'

Eva smiled. 'Well, it'll be interesting to be alone with him. I'll give you my views after the meeting.'

With that they sat listening to the music and were soon back at County View where they were met by an enthusiastic Max who was wild with delight because he'd won a big badminton match that afternoon. Quite where this enthusiasm for badminton came from was a mystery to both his parents, but he was turning out to be much more than just adept at it and was already in the county junior side.

While Eva prepared supper Jay phoned Vicky and outlined his plan. She was clearly taken back. 'That's an amazing offer, Jay, but I'll need to give it some thought.'

'Of course. There's no desperate hurry, although I'd like it settled reasonably soon. There's no one else in the running at the moment so don't feel pressured.'

'Thanks, Jay. I'm really flattered and I won't waste your time.'

'I'm sure you won't. Keep those horses of yours running well. Talk soon. Goodnight.'

Jay left his office and related his brief conversation to Eva.

'Well, it's going to be a bit of a learning curve for all of us,' his wife replied enigmatically, and went back to her cooking.

For once they had a relaxed evening with only two telephone calls from owners enquiring about the well-being of their horses and when they would run next. There was also a call from the *Racing Post* who wanted a comment on Jay's two runners that day, and another from the local press wanting the same.

Max went off to bed and both parents went up to say goodnight to him a little later. They then sat and enjoyed an hour of relaxation while Jay smoked a Montecristo No. 3 and Eva put on the recordings of their two races that afternoon. It was wonderful reliving the excitement and satisfaction of their runners' performances. Having done that, they made their customary early way to bed as Jay was always up before six, and Eva no more than forty-five minutes later.

Chapter Four

The following morning Jay was out early on the gallops sitting in the Land Rover with Jed beside him. He'd had a look at the previous day's runners and they had come out of their races in excellent order, having eaten up all their evening meals and cleared their mangers at breakfast.

Jed had watched the previous afternoon's races from Tolchester on *At the Races* and was enthusing about both their runners' performances. Jay took the opportunity to mention his approach to Vicky and to discuss Jed's impending transfer to the bloodstock side. He knew it was the right thing for his longstanding friend, but was anxious that Jed did not think he was being passed over.

'What do you think about the idea of working with Roddy now that you've had a chance to consider it?' he asked the older man.

'The more I think about it, the more sensible I believe it is. You know Cathy has been worried about my health, and to be honest, Jay, it would be really nice to see something of the world at a more leisurely pace. I know Cathy would love it. Of course I'll miss County View, but I'll keep in touch and I'm sure I'll be welcome here and at the races.'

Jay grasped his colleague's arm. 'You know damn well you will be,' he said with feeling, 'and I hope you'll come racing whenever you feel like it.'

'You bet,' the older man replied. 'By the way, we are going to move back to Sussex. We've got so many old friends there and it will be convenient for both Gatwick and Heathrow when I travel for Roddy, and easy for me to meet him in London. It will also mean Vicky has a place on the spot if she agrees to join you.'

'Hang on. You don't have to go. That's your place as long as you want it,' Jay insisted.

'I know, but we really do want to go back to Sussex, and I'm sure it would be best for me and Vicky if I just visit rather than sit here and breathe down her neck.'

Jay thought. 'OK, but don't make up your mind too soon.'

Jed nodded.

At that moment their attention was switched to the string coming up the gallops towards them. Both of them were particularly interested in two young horses which had won their bumper races and were now ready to run over novice hurdles. Tobago King was really quick and was destined for a career as a two-miler – at least in his early races. Terrific Terrier was owned by a relative newcomer to the yard called Luke Quinlan. This horse was not as quick as Tobago King, but had demonstrated amazing stamina at home. He would start his campaign over two and a half miles and was expected to graduate to three miles very quickly.

'Have you made up your mind where you're going to run them?' asked Jed.

'Yes,' Jay replied. 'I'm going to run Tobago King at Kempton. The flat track should suit his speed, and

49

I'm taking Terrific Terrier to Sandown. I believe they're both very decent horses, and although the races will be probably be fairly high class, it doesn't worry me. The alternative is I might take the Terrier to Wincanton. A lot will depend on the going as neither of them would like it too heavy.'

The two horses in question were side by side in the string, behind two of the yard's high-class chasers with a number of top-class race wins between them. The younger horses showed no difficulty at all in matching the older horses' speed, and Jay drove the Land Rover to the end of the gallop to discuss how Danny and young Ali felt, having ridden the two that they were particularly interested in that morning. Both of them enthused about their horses' performance and confirmed that no race would come too soon for either of them.

Returning to the yard, Jay left Jed to supervise the second lot, including selecting six horses which would be schooled over hurdles. These would include Tobago King and Terrific Terrier who had gone straight to the schooling area from their gallops. Jay settled down to a mountain of office work, including entries, knowing that the schooling session would be in good hands under the watchful eyes of Danny, who would be riding, and Jed, who would be supervising.

After half an hour or so on administration, he picked up the phone and made a call to Vicky Benson.

'Have you had a chance to think about the proposition I put to you?' asked Jay. 'I know it's only last night we talked but both Eva and Jed are all for it so I thought I'd let you know.'

'Yes,' Vicky replied. 'I am interested but obviously we need to talk about it in rather more detail than the brief conversation we had on the phone.'

'Of course,' replied Jay. 'Are you likely to have runners in the Midlands or further south?'

'Well, I'm going to be at Chepstow in a couple of weeks, if that's any use to you.'

'Absolutely,' replied Jay. 'I'm planning to run Vital Clue and Sweet Caroline there. Vital Clue, you may recall, is owned by Jemima Philips, Sweet Caroline is a County View horse. Caroline is running in a novice chase and Vital Clue in the handicap hurdle. What's your plan?'

'I'm running Happy Horoscope in the handicap hurdle too. It will be interesting to see which of us comes out on top.'

'It looks as if it will be a pretty hot race. I'd be happy if I'm in the frame. How about you?'

'I would too, but I think he might run very well indeed. I've never had him working better at home.'

'Right,' said Jay. 'Would you like to come and have dinner with us afterwards and stay the night? It will give us an opportunity to have a leisurely chat in privacy.'

'That would be great,' replied Vicky. 'It would be nice to have a proper look at County View again, and also get to know Eva a bit better. Why don't we meet for lunch before racing?'

'Deal done,' replied Jay. 'See you then.'

Shortly after noon Adam's chauffeur-driven Lexus pulled up. A uniformed driver leapt out and opened the rear door. Adam, in his usual beautifully cut dark grey worsted suit, stepped out. He had a document case in his hand, and his sparkling white shirt showed off his claret Hermès tie and the ruby-studded gold links which glowed from the two inches of shirt cuffs. On one wrist was a thin copper bangle, and on the other a discreet Cartier tank watch with a crocodile strap.

Immaculate as always, Jay thought, as he greeted his guest on the front doorstep. Entering the rather small but light dining room at County View, Adam was really surprised. The rest of the house had walls covered in pictures of a few very special horses which had figured in Jay's riding and training careers. Almost all of the rest of the wall space was covered in photographs of moments of triumph.

This room was totally different, with just three beautiful originals painted by Dufy, Spencer and Flint. They stood out like beacons of beauty. Adam stopped and took them in. 'I didn't realize art was such a passion of yours, Jay.'

'It's not. It's mine,' interjected Eva. 'These are wonderful but I wish I could afford the real Impressionists. I find them truly inspirational.'

Adam looked at her in a slightly different way. 'So do I, my dear, but at least we can still look at them in some of the great art galleries and enjoy the amazingly good reproductions which so many books now give us. Still,' he added jokingly, 'if Jay keeps going like he is and we have the confidence to put thousands on his runners, perhaps one day we will be able to.'

Turning to Jay, he said, 'I'm sure you're as busy as I am. Let's talk business.'

The two men were soon sitting down with a glass of champagne, and almost immediately Eva joined them. They talked generally about the previous day's racing, then Eva got up and returned with plates of finely sliced avocado pear accompanied by almost transparent Parma ham.

The general conversation continued through this course, and Eva quickly cleared it before returning with a fish pie which was one of her specialities. Adam was quick to compliment her on the excellent food which he was enjoying enormously. Finishing his plate and taking a sip from his refilled glass of champagne, he looked at Jay and Eva and said, 'Can we start talking business without boring Eva?'

It was Eva who responded. 'Business never bores me, Adam. I was brought up with it. In South Africa I worked in my father's business until he died, and I've been deeply involved as a director of County View ever since we started. It fascinates me, and as long as you feel comfortable about talking in front of me, I'm more than happy to listen, and learn,' she added with a twinkle.

Adam returned the smile.

'Right,' he said, looking at Jay. 'I thought the board meeting was extremely disappointing. We can't just stand still. In my view Percy's recommendations about improving the facilities and services on our existing racecourses are fundamental to maintaining their profitability and indeed our standing not only with the racing public but also with the authorities. We need to keep up those standards to ensure we continue to have good racing fixtures. We are fortunate in that we have at least one really important race a season at each of our courses. It is equally important to make sure that we have good handicaps with good prize money. A part of this, we both know, will only come through attracting good sponsors, but the facilities that we were discussing yesterday are a significant factor in that. We need good hospitality facilities for them if they are going to put thousands of pounds into a race.'

Before Jay could make a reply, Eva chipped in. 'Percy has told me about his plans and I think they're first rate. Though racecourse food is improving, it started at a pretty low level at most courses. The sort of sophisticated upmarket food that Percy has in mind would be a huge attraction to non-racing as well as racing customers. It is a tragedy that these facilities are only used a few times a year, and a number of racecourses have already shown how successful this type of development can be.'

Jay supported his wife. 'You know that I'm completely behind you and Percy in this view, but we've got to get at least two of the other directors on board.'

'I know,' agreed Adam. 'I think our best chances are with Jon Gormley and Rupert Jonson, and I was hoping that you might talk to them. I suspect that in some ways they rather resent me, and see me as a bulldozer. They like Percy, but I think they find him slightly aggressive. I know it's only his enthusiasm, but he does sometimes come across a little too strongly.'

Jay couldn't help smiling. 'I know exactly what you mean. It's his enthusiasm. He's not a bully in any way.'

'Well, that's where you come in,' continued Adam. 'They have a huge respect for you and they don't really associate you as closely with hard business life as they do Percy and myself. I know in many ways they're wrong, because building up County View as you have, and also your previous success with your publishing company, shows that you are no slouch when it comes to finance and planning the development of a business. The fact remains they see you as perhaps rather more accommodating than either of us. What I was hoping was that you could arrange to meet them individually and persuade them to back our view.'

'I'll do my best,' said Jay. 'I'll think about the most appropriate way to approach them. Perhaps they'd like to come racing with me one day, or alternatively meet me for lunch in the Turf Club. Anyway, I'll get in touch and follow up.'

'Much appreciated,' was Adam's reply. 'Now, the next matter I want to talk to you about is going to be more difficult, but what is your view about us acquiring other courses or else building a new racecourse in either the Manchester or the Birmingham area?'

Jay thought for a moment. 'Well, to be honest I think it's a really good idea, but the big problem is whether we would get the fixtures which we would need from the British Horseracing Board. It's no good having a really big and rather grand racecourse if we don't have the fixtures to go with it, so we'd have to sound them out first.'

'Which of the two sites do you think would be more appropriate to start with?'

'Well, I guess it's Birmingham really,' was Jay's reply. 'Although Manchester doesn't have a course of its own, it is well served by both Aintree and Haydock, and there are a number of good courses like Doncaster and York not that far away. I'm not saying it wouldn't work but I think the Birmingham one would probably be my preference.'

'I agree. What do you think we should do first?'

'Well, there's no point approaching the racing authorities if we can't find the appropriate venue, so I think it's really important to find a site and see if we can get planning permission, and at that stage we could approach the BHB. We'd need to have a very good business plan to put to them. There's a school of thought that there are probably too many racecourses rather than not enough, but a really good one is likely to be more acceptable than a medium run-of-the-mill course.'

'All right. I'll get on to that. Now what about acquiring other small courses?'

'Well, I think that idea has considerable merit as long as we don't have to pay too much. They would need to fit into the plan that we're talking about with the existing ones. In other words it would be important that there was enough land for us to develop them and to build a hotel. It would also be important that whichever racecourse we approached already had a number of good races because, as I said earlier, the fixture list is key to making these courses work.'

'I understand that, and I think perhaps I may have found a couple, but I want to do a little more research then I'll come back to see what you think about the location and the potential.'

'Fine,' said Jay, and thought that would be the end of the meeting.

He was wrong. Adam looked at both of them and said, 'I've got a favour to ask you. You probably know that my son Leo is a very enthusiastic amateur jockey. He's hell-bent on being champion, and I know that means a lot of hard work for him. He'll also need a number of good horses which he can ride. I'm wondering if you would be prepared to help him.'

Jay had forgotten Adam's remark the previous day and gave some thought before he replied. 'You do realize that Robin Haslett, the current champion, is very strongly in control of the title? The last two years he's won by a significant margin. Not only does he have several good horses himself, but his sister has some which he rides as well from time to time. What's more, a lot of the top trainers use him in amateur races, and on really busy days he'll be used in professional races when the top jockeys are not available.'

'I know, but I'm still anxious to give him an opportunity. What would you say if I bought five horses and put them with you, and took the four he's got with a couple of other trainers? That would give him nine of his own to ride.'

'Well,' replied Jay, 'I wouldn't want to take the horses from the existing trainers. They're both good friends of mine and are not particularly big yards. I imagine you sent Leo's horses to them because you knew they'd get special attention.'

'That's true,' agreed Adam, 'but I think we've now got to a stage beyond that. Leo would work really hard, and I don't think he's without ability. I've brought a tape of four or five of his recent rides which I thought you might like to look at before you decide. If you agree, I would leave the buying of the horses up to you.'

Jay nodded. 'Right, let me look at the tapes along with Jed and Danny and I'll come back to you. I'll be perfectly frank with you. If I don't think it's a realistic opportunity I'll tell you.'

'That's all I'm asking for,' said Adam. Turning to Eva, he continued, 'Thank you so much for a delicious lunch, and I hope that I'll see more of you in the future.'

With that he got up, gave her a quick peck on the cheek, and shook hands with Jay who accompanied him out of the front door. James, his chauffeur, leapt out of the car and opened the rear door. With his document case firmly clutched in his hand, he levered himself into the back of the car. Jay gave him a wave, and couldn't help wondering what was in the document case which he hadn't used at all during their meeting but seemed to be extremely attached to.

Going back into the kitchen where Eva was clearing up the lunch plates and cutlery, he gave her a questioning look.

'What do you think?'

'I rather liked him,' said Eva. 'I do see what you mean about there being a pretty hard streak there, but I thought he was frank in what he had to say. I was particularly impressed with his realistic view of his son's chances.'

'I'm not quite so sure,' replied Jay, 'but we'll see.'

At the end of the afternoon Jed and Danny came in. Jay put on the tapes. They all watched the five races in silence, before Jay turned to them.

'What do you think?'

It was Danny who spoke first. 'Well, he doesn't look too bad but he doesn't know how to ride a finish and he waves his whip all over the place.'

'I agree,' said Jay. 'I also think that he rides a little too short. It's a common fault with amateurs if they think they've got ability. They often feel it makes them look more professional. You know Freddy's old saying, "Ride long and live long."'

Jed smiled to himself. He remembered in Jay's early amateur days saying exactly that to the young man who was soon to be the most celebrated amateur jockey in the country and was now the champion trainer.

'Are you two willing to give it a go?'

'Absolutely,' replied Jed, 'but we've got to be realistic. Robin Haslett, the champion amateur, is only thirty-three years old and rides like a real professional. He's very popular with his fellow amateur jockeys, and indeed with a lot of the top trainers. If he hadn't been born into a rich family, he could almost certainly have made a very good living out of being a professional jockey. He is one of those young men blessed with confidence which stops well short of arrogance. He's well accepted in the weighing room among his peers. Even if he beats one of the top jockeys there's never any acrimony afterwards. They know he always gives his horse a good ride and has worked hard to achieve his results. He is extremely fit and strong, has a dry sense of humour, and is one of the real characters of National Hunt racing.'

Jed looked at Danny and grinned. 'Does that description remind you of anyone sitting in this room?'

Danny roared with laughter and Jay looked slightly embarrassed. Ignoring their banter, Jay went on to explain that Leo's mother had died when he was born and that Adam tried to do everything he could for the young man without putting too much pressure on him. He felt that Jay's team could be tough on him without causing any resentment. He also felt that Adam wanted Leo to succeed in his own right rather than thinking it all came from his father.

Jed nodded. 'If we're going to buy five horses, we'll have to buy five which are a credit to our yard as well as to this young man, but they'll also have to be horses which teach him a lot. There's no point in buying five armchair rides for him. He's got four of those already. I've seen that done before, and it's not going to get this man past the current champion. It'll also be interesting to see how hard he's prepared to work. He'll certainly need to ride out here at least five days a week if he is to make it. Just think how hard Hansie worked and he had a big job in the City.'

Hansie was a young South African who had spent

two years in England, and with County View guidance had become very competent.

Jay looked thoughtful 'Before we buy a single horse, I'd like to put him on Control Freak at Towcester,' he said. 'The fences there are big and challenging and it's an extremely hard course. I'm sure that Percy would go along with this because he's also a director of the Tolchester company and he knows that it would take a really bad jockey to put his horse on the floor. Young Leo is certainly not that, so let's see what the young man's made of.'

Control Freak was a nine-year-old handicap steeple-chaser who had won four and been placed nine times. Not top-class, though still very good.

Jed half nodded, before turning to Danny. Danny was completely in agreement with Jed. 'He's not a bad horseman,' he said. 'I've seen him ride a few times. Whether he's got the guts and the dedication to be the champion amateur jockey is another matter, but there's not much doubt that Freak would sort him out, and so would Towcester.'

Jed phoned Percy and explained the situation. Percy readily agreed. 'I'll be there to see what happens,' he promised.

Jay then called Adam and suggested that before he invested the considerable amount of money which would be involved in buying five horses, he should see how well his son performed on a reliable horse in a tough race on a very tough course. He added that Percy had already agreed Leo could ride his horse. The older man was thrilled and all was set up.

Two weeks later the big day had arrived. In all fairness Leo had come out and ridden two lots every day. He was clearly fit and very enthusiastic. It was Danny who had made an interesting comment.

'I almost wonder if he's too enthusiastic,' he said. 'There's something slightly manic about his dedication. I have a feeling he's not doing this for himself or the horse, so much as to prove himself to his father.' Jed and Jay looked at each other and there was a nod of agreement between them.

'Well, let's see how things go on the day.'

Unusually Jay only had Control Freak running at Towcester. This gave the whole team the chance to watch Leo in some detail. Percy's horse was led out looking gleaming and perfect as always. Maria, the young groom who looked after him, won the best-turned-out prize, and the proud father was in the ring as Jay legged his son up.

'Remember this is a very stiff course,' he said. 'Some of your competitors will go far too fast early on. These races are won from the bottom of the hill the last time. Don't get too far out of touch, but don't worry if some horses get a long way ahead of you, they normally come back to you coming up the hill.' Leo nodded.

The race started at the bottom of the hill and then had two full circuits to complete. As they arrived at the second fence, there was complete mayhem. The leading horse, which was being ridden by a particularly young amateur rider, took the top of the fence out completely, crashed to the ground and brought three other horses down. To Jay's relief, Leo's horse avoided the mêlée, but lost some lengths by passing the fallen animals. Control Freak now found himself in seventh place of the nine remaining runners. Climbing the hill past the grandstand, they turned and took the downhill fence, and on this occasion no incidents took place. There were no more problems as they made their way along the back straight and turned for home with the hill still before them for the second of the three times. By now the unrealistic pace of some of the young amateurs was beginning to show and the horses were becoming strung out. Control Freak had moved into fifth place and went past the winning post for the second time in good order. There were now only five horses in contention and Percy's horse was still lying in fifth place behind the closely bunched quartet. It was not until the last fence down the back straight that another incident occurred. This time the leading horse, which was clearly still more in control of what was happening than the jockey, took off too soon, hit the top of the fence, and sent his young rider into orbit. Fortunately none of the other four horses were impeded and Percy's horse was now fourth.

Standing next to the young man's father, Jay mentioned that he was riding rather well. Jed was just behind them, also watching intently.

'He should be getting up closer,' Adam said.

'I don't agree,' replied Jay rather tartly. 'It's a long way to the top of this hill.'

As they turned up the hill with four fences still to jump, Percy's horse moved from fourth to third and from third to second. Jumping the last, the father was furious.

'He should be in the lead now. He should be in the lead. He could have won this race.'

Jay said nothing but, looking at Percy, raised an eyebrow. Within the next hundred yards Percy's horse swept past the previous leader and won by a length and a half. Everybody apart from Leo's father seemed delighted. They hurried to the winners' enclosure where Jay and Percy congratulated the young man. His father was less enthusiastic. 'You almost left it too late. What were you playing at, you fool?'

'No, I didn't,' replied his son. 'I could tell the other horse was labouring and mine was still running on very strongly. I wanted to make sure we jumped the last fence correctly. Did I do the right thing, Mr Jessop?' he asked, turning to Jay.

'You certainly did. You rode the horse extremely well. In fact I don't think you could have ridden it better.'

His father changed his tune and now, glowing with pride, patted his son on the shoulder and said, 'Sorry, son. Let's all go and have a drink.'

'I think we'll make sure he weighs in properly first,' said Jay, 'and then we'll meet you in the owners' and trainers' bar.'

This was duly accomplished and they all met in the bar. By now the father was ecstatic and was talking about the number of horses that he would buy for his son.

'I think we need to take this carefully,' said Jay. 'Your son rides extremely well but he's still got a lot to learn.'

To Jay's delight, Leo didn't look put out by this, and said, 'I realize that, Mr Jessop.'

'I think what we need to do is find two or three useful but experienced horses that can give Leo a couple of months of real practice in hunter chases and amateur racing, then we can look for a couple of better horses which might give him a chance to go for the championship.'

Adam thought about this for a moment. 'But why don't we find all five so you can get them ready and Leo can become used to them?'

Jay paused before replying. 'If you insist, but I'm all for taking this a little more carefully. If we don't win the championship this year, we still have next season and Leo will be far more experienced by then.'

This clearly did not sit well with Adam. 'I hate procrastination, but it's your call.'

Jay could see Leo was in a quandary. He did not want to upset either his father or Jay and looked hopefully at his new trainer and mentor.

'OK,' laughed Jay. 'I'll do it your father's way. I can remember how impatient I was at your age.'

Adam was clearly delighted at the outcome. Jay was not too sure if this was for his son's sake or if it was because he felt he had got his own way.

'Here's to the next amateur champion jockey,' Adam toasted.

It was Jed who slightly surprised Jay by saying, 'Well, let's see how that goes. I'm sure he can do it eventually, but let's not run before we can walk.'

The older man was obviously not too pleased by that remark but took it quietly. They all downed their champagne, shook Leo's hand, and made their way out of the bar.

'Is there anything else you're thinking of doing?' Jed asked Leo.

'I'd like to go and make sure the horse is all right,'

'Quite right,' said Jed. 'I expect you to do that any time you ride one of our horses, whether you own it or not. Shall we see you tomorrow?'

'Of course,' was the reply. 'And thank you all – especially you, Mr Cartwright, for letting me ride Control Freak.'

'My pleasure,' grinned Percy. 'Let's hope it's the first of many.'

Jay, Percy and Jed set off towards the car park.

64

'Adam might be a bit of a problem,' Percy suggested. 'He's more controlling with his son than he seemed at first.'

'I agree. We'll have to watch that and make sure he doesn't start telling us what to do as well as his son.'

'So you'll be your normal diplomatic self,' was Jed's rather sarcastic comment. 'I can't wait to see it.'

Percy roared with laughter. 'Me too,' he hooted, and shaking hands with both of them he made his way to his car.

Chapter Five

As things turned out, Jay had just one runner for Chepstow. This was Vital Clue in the valuable three-mile handicap hurdle in which Vicky's horse, Happy Horoscope, was also taking part. Sweet Caroline had bruised her foot the previous day and, although it was nothing serious, she was not fit to run.

He was slightly surprised earlier that morning when Leo approached him and asked whether he might go with Jay. He explained that his Mini was being serviced and he fancied an afternoon at the races. Jay readily agreed. The young man was working hard and making progress. Jay welcomed the opportunity to spend some time chatting to him.

Although there were no complaints from the yard, Leo was rather reserved and nobody really seemed to know what made him tick or what he did when he wasn't at the yard or riding races. It was clear that he didn't always spend the night in his cottage on the outskirts of Newbury. Although he was never late, he sometimes looked very tired in the morning.

Fifteen minutes before Jay had said he was leaving, Leo arrived. Somewhat to Jay's surprise he had his racing kit with him. 'I didn't realize you had a ride this afternoon,' Jay commented.

'I don't,' smiled Leo, 'but I always take it with me just in case a spare ride comes up.'

Jay nodded appreciatively. He'd done the same thing in the early days of his amateur career before he'd become so well known that he was nearly always booked up two or three days in advance. He recalled it was a very unlikely spare ride that led him to winning the Gold Cup some years earlier on a fantastic horse called Splendid Warrior. This was thanks to Freddy Kelly who had been injured in an earlier race that afternoon and had assured the owner and trainer that Jay was the right man for the job.

They were soon crossing the Severn on the famous suspension bridge, and fifteen minutes later pulled into the car park opposite the racecourse. They walked through the owners' and trainers' entrance, and Leo, thanking Jay for the ride, said he would pop his head into the weighing room just in case anything happened.

'See you after the fourth race,' he said to Jay. 'Good luck.'

The fourth race was the handicap hurdle in which Jay's and Vicky's horses were running. Unusually for Jay, he'd booked a table in the Silks Restaurant at the top of the grandstand and had barely sat down when Vicky Benson joined him. They chatted about racing in general and their opponents in the hurdle race that afternoon. They had a tacit agreement not to discuss her potential move to County View until they were in the privacy of Jay's home.

Jay was looking at Vicky across the lunch table as she chatted. Almost subconsciously he was comparing her to Eva. His wife was tall and blonde with a willowy grace, almost Scandinavian in her looks. Her striking face was just a little short of being

67

classically beautiful, but if this was a defect it was more than made up for by the warmth of her manner and the charm which had endeared her to so many people from vastly different backgrounds.

Vicky on the other hand was considerably shorter and almost wiry. She had a good figure which, in Jay's view, had improved with the extra pounds she had acquired since giving up the rigours of competitive riding and the constant riding out and schooling which were an integral part of being a top steeplechase jockey, whether amateur or professional. At the same time her diet was far less restrained than had been the case in her competitive days. Although she was still lithe, her rounded bosom was much more to Jay's liking than her previous boyish figure. Her short dark curly hair, Mediterranean complexion and huge brown eyes added up to an extremely sensuous appearance. There was almost a conscious sexuality in the way she walked, although Jay was quite certain she would be mortified if she knew that many men thought she deliberately flaunted it.

At the same time Vicky was having similar musings about Jay. Sitting opposite him, she observed that age had been very kind to him. In the decade she'd known him he also had gained a certain amount of weight which took away the almost gaunt look which he'd had at the height of his riding career. His hair was beginning to show a touch of grey at the temples, and he had a smile which was both warm and slightly roguish. She found him physically enormously attractive and had often wondered how he would compare with the significant number of lovers who'd shared her bed since her late teens.

Although tempted, she had always resisted the urge to give him any encouragement in that direction, partly from a fear of rejection but also from a concern that any such liaison would make their working relationship difficult if not impossible in the long run. Her thoughts were interrupted by Jay.

Let's go,' he said, looking at his watch and putting his coffee cup down, 'I suppose we'd better start working.'

'I guess so. I really enjoyed that, Jay. Thank you very much.'

Side by side they walked to the weighing room, collected their saddles and made their way to the saddling boxes. On the way there, an announcement came over the public address system.

'Will Leo Forsyth please report to the weighing room immediately.'

I wonder what that's about? thought Jay, but gave it no more consideration as he started getting Vital Clue ready for his exertions.

A few minutes later Vicky was standing at one end of the parade ring with Happy Horoscope's owners, while Jay was standing with Jemima Philips. She'd been an owner with Jay for some time and had been lucky enough always to have good horses. Her runner in this race had already won two good handicaps and was therefore carrying the second highest weight. Vicky's horse had also been successful but in rather lower grade races, and was receiving eight pounds from Vital Clue. Within a few moments they were joined by David Sparrow; he had always got on particularly well with Jemima who had a very soft spot for him.

After a brief conversation about the race, it was time for David to be partnered with his horse. Within minutes they were walking round the parade ring before going down the chute on to the racecourse. Jay had already explained to Jemima that her horse would be held up in the middle of the pack and that David would save as much energy as possible for the very steep climb and the four flights of hurdles which faced them on their way to the finishing post.

The race started at the beginning of the back straight, and within a few moments the fifteen-runner field was under way. As they had three miles in front of them, the jockeys were travelling at a sensible but still competitive speed. David had his horse settled in about sixth position, and Jay noticed that Vicky's horse was several lengths in front lying fourth.

The first circuit and a half passed without event and the field was still closely packed as they continued away from stands, round the uphill bend to the start of the back straight. Suddenly, there was a significant injection of pace by the leading horse which was carrying bottom but one weight. It was clear that the jockey was hoping he could use his weight advantage to test the stamina of the runners behind him, and to a degree he was successful. Several of them started to struggle but Vicky's horse moved smoothly into second place. David was still biding his time but now moved up to fourth. Jumping the last hurdle down the back straight, they were still in the same positions. The leading jockey asked his horse for yet another additional effort, which Jay thought was distinctly on the early side with four hurdles and a sharp incline ahead of them. Nevertheless, turning to face the first of these four hurdles the leader had now increased the distance between him and Happy Horoscope to six or seven lengths.

Vicky's jockey sat patiently where he was and jumped the third last hurdle in the same position.

Moving between that and the penultimate hurdle he came within three lengths of the leader and David, responding to this move, encouraged Vital Clue to move to only a length behind Vicky's horse. They jumped the penultimate hurdle in the same order, and approaching the last Vicky's horse started to make steady inroads into the front runner's lead. Jumping the hurdle he was level and started to move away on the long run-in. As soon as he had cleared the final obstacle, David went in pursuit of Vicky's horse and was making significant headway. Suddenly something happened and Jay saw David pull the horse across to the middle of the track out of the way of the rest of the runners. He quickly jumped off.

It was obvious to Jay that Vital Clue was very lame. Turning to Jemima, he said, 'That looks pretty serious. I think he's broken down.'

David stood by the horse as the rest of the field went by, and shortly afterwards the horse ambulance arrived on the scene. The horse was gently coaxed into the back of it and David was picked up in a Land Rover and driven back to the stands. Jay and Jemima met a very disconsolate-looking jockey.

'I'm sorry, Mrs Philips,' he said, 'but I think he's broken down quite badly.'

'You go and wait for me in the owners' and trainers' bar,' Jay said to the tearful owner. 'I'll go down to the vet's box and see what the situation is.'

Minutes later he was talking to the vet. 'It's not good, Jay,' he said. 'I'll strap him up so you can get him home, but I think you're looking at a minimum of a year off. Whether or not he'll race again you'll have a better idea when he's been scanned, but I wouldn't be too hopeful.'

'Well, at least he won't have to be put down,' said Jay. 'His owner's got a farm and I know that she'll retire him there if his racing days are over.'

'That's good news,' said the vet. 'Well, there's another horse that needs my attention so I'll go and have a look at him if you don't mind, Jay.'

'Of course not, and thanks for seeing to him so quickly.'

'That's what I'm here for,' grinned the vet.

Jay returned to the stand and found Jemima. He explained the situation 'Well, at least he's going to survive,' she said. 'I was terrified it might be fatal.'

'I knew you were,' said Jay. 'Now let me buy you a stiff drink.'

'I think I'll take you up on that,' she said. 'I've got a driver to take me home, so if you don't mind I'll have a large brandy.'

'Seems very reasonable under the circumstances,' agreed Jay, but as he was driving he settled for a spicy tomato juice.

While all this had been going on the subsequent race had taken place without Jay being able to give it any attention but, glancing at the TV monitor, he was somewhat surprised to see Leo being led into the winners' enclosure, grinning from ear to ear.

Well, luck was on his side today, thought Jay.

Twenty minutes later a beaming Leo joined him and Jemima.

'How did that happen?' asked Jay. 'Well done, anyway.'

'Well, it seems that Harry Fowler, who was due to ride the horse, phoned to say he wasn't feeling very well. He thought he'd be all right but he was sick during the night and continued to be ill right up until the time he was due to come here.'

'Bad luck on him, good luck on you.'

'Yes,' replied Leo, 'but he seemed fine last night. I had dinner with him in Newbury. Fortunately we had different food, and perhaps it was the prawns he ate that upset him.'

'Well, whatever the reason it's another winner for you,' smiled Jay. 'I'll see you at the car in fifteen minutes.'

'Right,' said Leo, and turned to Jemima. 'I'm really sorry about your horse, Mrs Philips.'

'Thank you, Leo, but at least he's going to survive.'

At that moment a jubilant Vicky arrived with her owners, Colin and Sue Vickery. She left them for a moment and walked across to Jemima. 'I'm so sorry about Vital Clue. I'm sure he would have given us a real fight.'

'That's very kind of you, my dear. I'm sure he would. Now you go off and have fun with your owners, and very well done.'

'See you later,' Vicky said to Jay. 'It's OK if you want to go. I can remember the way,' and smiling to all of them she returned to an already opened bottle of Lansen Black Label and a full glass.

'What a nice girl,' commented Jemima. 'Is she having supper with you?'

'Yes. She and Eva are great pals and she's going to stay the night.' He was slightly exaggerating the closeness of this relationship.

'Well, she'll be in a good mood,' commented Jemima. 'I'll be on my way.'

'I'll call you in the morning as soon as the vet has seen him,' promised Jay.

'I know you will. Well done, Leo,' and she hurried away.

Fifteen minutes later Jay and Leo were on their way

back to County View, Leo talking enthusiastically about his win and how strange it was that Harry Fowler had been taken so ill.

'Ah well, these things happen,' said Jay. 'Are you doing anything exciting tonight?'

'I'm not sure,' he said. 'I'll probably give a couple of my friends a call and see if anything is going on.'

'I expect you'll hear from your father,' Jay suggested.

'Only if he was watching the racing on television,' pointed out Leo. 'He didn't know I was going to ride.'

Getting back to County View, Leo thanked Jay again for the lift. 'Do you mind if I don't come in until second lot tomorrow?' he asked.

'Not at all,' said Jay. 'You deserve an extra hour in bed.'

As he left Leo, Jay couldn't help thinking it was strange that he was clearly planning on a late night even though he'd said he didn't have any particular plans.

Leo found Danny, who had promised to take him to the garage where his Mini had been serviced that day. Dropping the young man off, Danny again congratulated him on his win and went back to County View. Leo got into his Mini, feeling extremely cheerful in the knowledge that he'd had a successful day and that he was going to spend the night with Tania – but he had an important task before he was due at her cottage about 1 a.m. after she had finished her dealing stint. His heart started to race with anticipation as he thought about the next few hours. This really was an adrenalin rush.

Much later, at his own cottage, Leo looked at his watch. It was a little after ten thirty. Going upstairs, he changed into a T-shirt, sweater and tracksuit, and put a pair of slacks, clean shirt and blazer on a hanger. He then took a medium-sized dark backpack from the wardrobe. As he picked it up, the effort it took indicated that its contents were fairly heavy. Going downstairs he opened the front door, having deliberately left some of the lights on in his cottage, locked up, then quickly looked up and down the lane. He walked over to his Mini and put the pack and his clothes on the back seat. He drove on to the lane with his lights off. It was not until he reached a T-junction half a mile down where the road normally became rather busier that he flicked his lights on and drove quickly but carefully to the hilly wooded area adjoining the Haslett farm. Turning his lights off, he reached for his backpack, left the car and disappeared purposefully into the woods.

At County View Eva, Vicky and Jay were sitting down after supper enjoying a second bottle of wine. Eva had taken Max to see a Harry Potter film that afternoon and had also indulged him in pizza. Consequently she, like the two who had eaten at Chepstow, was not particularly hungry.

As soon as Max had gone to bed, they'd started talking about the possibility of Vicky joining them. Right from the outset she showed her enthusiasm and reassured them that she didn't see this as a short-term stepping stone to starting on her own again.

'Frankly, I can't see where I'd get the capital from, and I've always really enjoyed being part of a team rather than having to shoulder all the responsibilities myself. The opportunity to work with facilities like these, and with the high-quality horses you have, is more than I ever dreamed would be possible.'

'What about your own horses and current owners?' Eva asked.

'Well, I wouldn't want to let any of them down, but on the other hand I can't see many owners wanting to move horses from the north of England all the way down here. There are two horses I particularly like and two youngsters which are coming on well. The two I own are Toss the Coin and Beatlemania. Two young horses are not yet named and are both owned by Colin Vickery who owns Happy Horoscope. He lives just outside Birmingham and I'm pretty sure he would move all three of them with me. That is, of course, if you're interested.'

'Your recommendation's enough, Vicky,' Jay reassured her.

'What about your staff?' asked Eva.

'As you know, I've only a small yard but I do have a couple who are very good. Dillon Payne and Emma Chapman are partners although they're not married. He's a good rider and could have been a professional but he's always struggled with his weight. Emma is just a damn good groom and a competent rider.'

'Would you want them to come with you?' Jay queried.

'Well, I would recommend them but it depends on your own staffing arrangements.'

Jay pondered for a moment. 'We normally have each member of our staff looking after three horses, so with five new ones we would be stretching our own resources. Do you think they would want to come?'

'I'm sure they would, but I'm equally sure they would only come together. They seem to be inseparable. But why don't you have them down, see if you like them, and you can assess their abilities at the same time? I'm sure I can get by without them for a day, particularly if you made it a Sunday when I tend to give my horses an easy day.'

This was agreed.

They then discussed finances and other important administrative details, and by the end of the evening everything had been arranged although, of course, the three horses owned by Colin Vickery would only move with his agreement. If he refused clearly they would have to reassess whether it was possible for Dillon Payne and Emma Chapman to join County View.

Two Sundays later Jay walked out to find a well-looked-after but obviously second-hand Citroën Xsara in the stable staff's car park. Standing next to it were a young man and woman in riding clothes, each holding a hat and a stick. He walked quickly over to them.

'You must be Dillon and Emma,' he said, and shook hands with them.

Dillon was about five foot eight, thickset, with a shock of curly dark brown hair with blond highlights. He looked fit, and from his physique Adam could well imagine he would have had great problems keeping to a practical riding weight. Emma was petite, with chestnut hair and a rather pretty face. Both of them were neatly turned out.

'Come on,' he said, 'I'll introduce you to Danny, my head man. He'll show you around. He'll get you to groom a couple of horses, which you can ride.'

Dillon nodded but said nothing. Emma enthused: 'We're really looking forward to it. I do hope we'll be able to work here. Miss Benson has been so good to us, and it looks an amazing place. I know you've got some wonderful horses.'

'Well, let's see how it goes,' replied Jay, and he turned and walked over to the yard. He quickly found Danny, who was expecting the two young people, and Jay left them in his capable hands, asking Danny to give him a call when they were pulling out for the gallops.

'Of course, guv. Now come on, you two, and I'll introduce you to the horses.'

Half an hour later Jay got a call on the intercom from the yard and Danny said they were about to pull out. Jay walked into the kitchen and suggested to Eva that she might like to come and watch.

Twelve of the horses were going up the gallops that morning. Danny was leading them. He'd put Dillon just behind him and then Emma, so that Jay could have a good look at how they rode. For a second opinion, David Sparrow was immediately behind the two of them.

A few moments later the string came sweeping past Jay and Eva. There was no doubt that Dillon had style and looked relaxed and confident. Emma was fine, but from her frequent glances over towards the Land Rover it was obvious she was nervous and desperately anxious to impress. As soon as the canter was over, Danny led the two of them over to the schooling hurdles. Both their mounts were experienced. Although Dillon's could take a good grip, Emma's was a very quiet mare and she was being given every chance to show her ability.

Danny and the Sparrow put themselves on the far side of the two horses so that Jay would have an uninterrupted view of Vicky's two young staff. The schooling went perfectly well. It was clear that Dillon was a cut above the average work rider, while Emma was totally competent and was clearly getting a little more confident as nothing untoward had happened, either on the gallops or over the hurdles.

Jay had already arranged for Danny to have a cup of coffee with the two of them, then bring them over to Jay who'd have a chat with them; he and Danny would compare notes later on. Two hours later the youngsters were on their way back to Cheshire, with a promise from Jay that he'd give them his decision the next morning. He, Eva and Danny sat round the kitchen table.

'What d'you think?' he asked, looking at both his wife and the head man.

'Well, they looked all right to me,' said Eva. 'They were both polite, well turned out, and I couldn't see that either of them did anything wrong. I didn't have much of a conversation with them, as you know.'

Jay turned and looked questioningly at Danny.

'Well, we haven't got many better than them in terms of riding in the yard. She seems a perky little thing, but he's not the most outgoing bloke I've ever met. I will say this – he rides bloody well.'

'D'you think you could work with them?'

'I don't see why not. With these new horses coming from Vicky's we're certainly going to need two more staff, and she says they're OK. One interesting thing he asked me was if there was any shooting around here. It seems it's a bit of a passion of his. I told him the farmers were always happy for people to go and shoot their rabbits or pigeons, and that we'd got one

79

or two pheasant shoots around here but that they were pretty pricey. He asked if I knew the game-keeper, and told me he'd done a bit of freelance gamekeeping up north as a result of which he was allowed to have a few days' shooting. He was also happy to do some beating. I said that if he came down here I'd be happy to make the introductions and then it would be up to him.'

'That's interesting,' said Jay. 'He can certainly always have a go at keeping the rabbit population on our gallops under control. Right, I'll have a word with Vicky, but as far as I can see we are all happy for them to join us.'

Eva and Danny nodded their agreement.

Chapter Six

Robin Haslett, a champion amateur jockey, was popular with his peers because he worked hard and was successful without being arrogant. As Jed had suggested to Jay, he could almost certainly have made a very good living out of being a professional jockey if he had wanted to. He was fit, strong and polite, with a ready sense of humour that had made him many friends in National Hunt racing. The chances of anyone superseding him in the near future were fairly remote but he still behaved modestly and took nothing for granted.

He was making his way, with his sister Penny, to Wincanton where he was riding in a two-and-a-half mile amateur steeplechase. Leo Forsyth was also riding in the race on a horse trained by David Frost, one of the horses that Jay had refused to have moved to him when Adam had suggested it. For once his father wasn't able to watch Leo as he had an extremely important business meeting in London. He had assured his son he'd have the race recorded and would watch it later on and call him in the evening.

When he arrived in the weighing room, Robin was greeted cheerfully by both amateurs and professionals alike and he headed towards a space next to Leo who greeted him warmly.

'That horse you're riding today looks quite useful,' Robin volunteered. 'I've got a feeling that you and I might find ourselves fighting out the finish between us.'

'I hope so,' replied Leo with a grin, 'but if we do you'll probably beat me.'

'Of course I will,' joked Robin. 'I've arranged for you to have an extra seven pounds slipped into your weight cloth after you've weighed out.'

Leo chuckled appreciatively.

Both of them changed, walked out and helped with the saddling of their horses.

David Frost, the young trainer who was responsible for Inside Track, had a quick word with Leo. 'Robin's horse is useful but your fellow has the ability to beat him. Don't take him on too quickly. I think you've got a little more pace than Moon Shadow, so I suggest you stay just behind him approaching the last and stay there with about fifty yards to go. If you give him a crack I think he'll get past Haslett's horse so quickly that it won't give the champ a chance to respond before the winning line comes.'

Leo nodded his understanding, walked back into the weighing room and waited to be called out to the parade ring.

The announcement was made and he followed his rivals into the large ring behind the grandstand where Penny was standing with David. Inside Track was almost black and his coat was gleaming in the sunshine. He was a big horse, and his ability to accelerate quickly was unusual in a horse of his stature.

The mounting bell rang and David legged Leo up. Most of the riders knew each other well, though a couple from the north kept themselves to themselves and cantered down to the start side by side.

Although amateurs, they and their horses were all experienced and the starter had no difficulty in getting them under orders. Within minutes they were on their way and jumping with the fluency expected of handicappers. Many of these horses had contested rather better races than today's before age had started to catch up with them and they'd moved down a grade to be owned and ridden by amateurs. Leo's horse was not one of these. He had been a successful point-to-pointer in Ireland before being spotted by David who had bought him from the owner/rider who was a friend of his. He had already trained a horse which he had bought for Leo and had placed it cleverly to win twice. He speculated that this would be an ideal second string to Leo's bow. Adam had accepted his advice and Leo was riding him for the first time in public. It was clear that Robin must have looked up the horse's form in Ireland to have made the comment he had before racing started.

Leo took his trainer's advice and sat a couple of lengths behind Robin during the early stages of the race. Going down the back straight for the last time they approached the open ditch in fourth and fifth positions respectively. The leader, who was clearly getting tired, made a hash of it and deposited his jockey on the floor. This left them lying third and fourth. There was no change completing the rest of the fences down the back straight, and turning for home they had three fences in front of them, including one on the bend. Again there was no change in position, but Robin's horse was now eating into the lead of the horses in front of him, and Leo stayed behind him as instructed. Entering the finishing straight, Robin had now moved into second place, with Leo still carefully tracking him, now a length and a half behind. Approaching the last the positions were unchanged, but Robin was now upside the leader. Landing, he quickly established the ascendancy, and Leo also passed the long-time leader and now closed the gap between him and Moon Shadow to barely a length. Robin's horse continued his strong gallop but Inside Track had no difficulty in matching the pace. With about a hundred yards to go, Leo urged his horse to greater effort. Inside Track responded by shooting past the champion's mount. Leo was now barely a length in the lead and the winning post was approaching rapidly. He was already savouring his win, but Robin Haslett was not champion jockey for nothing. A quick slap behind the saddle and energetic riding out with hands and heels brought the desired response from Moon Shadow. Inch by inch he crept up on Leo who was no longer urging his mount. With a mere ten yards to go Robin got his horse's head in front. Although a photograph was called for, both jockeys knew that Robin had won. Leo grinned magnanimously and leant over to shake hands.

'Tough luck, Leo,' said Robin. 'I thought you'd got me there.'

'So did I,' replied Leo with a rueful grin.

Going into the winners' enclosure, Leo looked cheerfully at his trainer. He was surprised when David gave him a hard look and said, 'I told you fifty yards not over a hundred. If you'd waited that bit longer he'd never have got back to you.'

Leo said nothing, but grabbing his saddle he walked angrily into the weighing room to weigh in. He was still highly resentful of the criticism when

Robin sympathized with him but kept his true feelings well hidden.

That evening Adam phoned his son to say that he'd had a look at the recording. 'Tough luck,' he said. 'I thought you were going to win.'

'So did I,' said Leo, 'but I guess the other horse was just that bit better.' He refrained from mentioning David's comment that he'd gone too fast too quickly.

'What news on the new horses?' asked his father.

'Well,' said Leo, 'I've already found three. Also, Vicky Benson, Jay's new assistant, is coming with three from her yard, and it seems that one of hers, Beatlemania, would suit me well. She's not prepared to sell him but she is prepared to lease him to me, and has indicated that she might be open to offers at the end of the season. That probably suits both of us as we'll not only know a bit more about his form but also how well I get on with him.'

'That sounds sensible,' said his father. 'Tell me about the other three horses.'

'I went with Jay to see all of them. Young Sport is an eight-year-old chestnut which has won two point-to-points in Ireland, three novice chases here, and been placed twice in two-and-a-half- and three-mile handicap chases. He's already at County View and won two weeks ago.

'Quiet Menace is a dark bay nine year old who went straight from bumpers as a five year old into novice chases. He won three but then his owner ran out of money and kept him at home for over a year but did hunt him. His previous trainer bought him and advertised him in the *Racing Post*. Jay had seen the horse run when he was younger and we went down to check him out. He ran two weeks ago and was placed. Jay sat on him and schooled him and we did the deal on the spot. He's here and Jay entered him for Sandown on Saturday immediately we left as he was racing fit. The third one, Grey Eagle, is also nine. He's a big grey who started as a novice hurdler, won two novice chases and was placed three times, and then moved up to three miles in handicap chases. He was also placed in a handicap hurdle, also over three miles. I liked him a lot and Jay feels that we might well be able to use him as a dual-purpose horse in both amateur hurdles and chases.

'They're being vetted in the next two or three days and will be with us by the weekend assuming they all pass.'

'That sounds great. So we're looking for just one more,' said his father. 'Now what do you feel about Saturday?'

His son paused. 'I think the horse will run very well. I rode him out earlier this week and schooled him. Jay's only reservation is that the ground at Sandown might be too soft for him. On the other hand the forecast is fine for the next three days so I'm very hopeful that the current soft going should be no worse than good to soft by the weekend.'

'Well, I hope you do run. I always enjoyed Sandown and it will be god to see you win at a top-class course.'

'Well, let's keep our fingers crossed, Dad. Don't bet too heavily on me.'

His father laughed. 'If only you knew,' he said enigmatically, but added nothing further.

'All right, I'll let you get to bed. I'm sure you've an early start tomorrow. Hope to see you on Saturday,' and he hung up.

Chapter Seven

The ancient turf, which dated back to the Middle Ages, was still in perfect condition. Small white pegs marked out a gallop which was the private property of Hubert Haslett, the owner of a huge farm which was commercially run but was not his main source of income. He had come from a long line of Birmingham industrialists who had made their fortunes producing components for cars and aircraft, and had diversified into machine tools and vehicle-tracking systems.

He had always been interested in horse racing, particularly National Hunt, and was genuinely amazed when his son Robin and daughter Penny had become stars at the local pony club and developed into riders of national acclaim in their sphere.

The two of them were trotting towards the bottom of the private gallop and chatting amiably. Some brothers and sisters do not get on well, particularly if they find themselves competitors in the same sport. These two were a striking exception. They adored each other and derived almost as much pleasure from the each other's success as they did from their own. They worked together, talked together, advised each other, and they constantly sought to fine-tune what each of them was doing. This particular morning they were trotting towards the bottom of a steep bank followed by their two Jack Russells. Like the riders, the dogs were siblings. Henry was slightly larger than his sister, Mouse. They were inseparable, and unlike some Jack Russells they were neither yappy nor bad-tempered. Both of them were full of character and even more energy. Every morning they would follow Penny and Robin out on to the gallops, and although they had no chance of staying with the horses once they went into a gallop, they followed them as if their lives depended upon it.

When Hubert realized that he had such talented children, he started to invest in decent horses for them. Initially they excelled at Pony Club and then local events, but it soon became obvious that they were going to concentrate on point-to-points. Robin became point-to-point champion, and two years later Penny was runner-up in the ladies' section. At that stage they sat down and had a serious conversation with their father. With a certain amount of reluctance, not from the financial point of view but from a safety one, he agreed to buy them good thoroughbred horses that could run in amateur races, and hunter chases while still riding in points.

He had long known Jack Symes, a previous National Hunt champion trainer, and had given him the task of finding six suitable horses which could be ridden by either or both of his offspring. This particular morning Robin was riding The Shepherd, and Penny, Lady Be Good. Both had already won several races, and Robin was already seven clear of his nearest rival in the current amateur jockeys championship. Penny was two behind her main lady rival, Naomi Norton. As always, they chatted cheerfully to each other until they got to the start of the gallop.

Their normal routine was to canter approximately half a mile up the least steep incline of the hill, before walking back with their happy and now heavily panting dogs to the bottom of the main gallop.

Every week the little white pegs were moved so that the ground didn't become too damaged. Weather permitting it was chain harrowed and perhaps rolled and left for a week or two to recover. With their small string and the enormous amount of land owned by their father, it was not difficult to ensure that in normal conditions they always had good fresh ground.

With a cheerful grin, Robin called, 'Come on, Penny, they're ready for some serious work. I'll beat you to the top.' The top was approximately a mile and a half from the start of the gallop, but the steepness of the slope made the workload much more like two miles. Within seconds they were side by side at racing speed. Robin, some six inches taller than his sister, didn't have quite her style but was a wonderful judge of pace, and there was no amateur, and not many professionals, as strong in the finish. Penny was neater, sat down into her horse more, and if anything looked slightly more like a flat jockey than a National Hunt one. The fact remained that both of them were highly competent. Halfway up the gallop there was a fairly sharp left turn which took them to the top of the hill where they always pulled up and walked down the other side, before walking and trotting back to the yard. As they turned the corner Robin was just half a length in the lead and glanced quickly over at Penny to see how she was doing. She gave him a knowing smile as if to say, 'I'm just waiting to take you when I feel like it.' Moments later there was chaos. Both horses were on the ground and their jockeys had been hurled from their saddles.

Robin was unconscious but Penny was just winded. She looked at the two horses, who were still on the ground, with complete disbelief and horror. Robin's horse had blood pouring from its front legs, and it was clear that one of them was broken. Fortunately hers, though cut, seemed at this stage to be more winded than seriously injured. Moments later Henry and Mouse arrived and stood silently looking at the terrible scene.

On their father's insistence they never went out without mobile phones, and Penny immediately dialled home and explained what had happened. Hubert made a frantic call to the local 999 service and then to Casey Jones, their vet. Even at that time in the morning he knew that she would be up because there were always horses needing treatment in her yard. She promised to be there in moments as she was only a short distance from the farm. She knew the gallops well so had no difficulty knowing exactly where to go.

When Hubert got there he was appalled. Somebody had strung a piece of wire across the gallop between two of the pegs, and it was clear that this was what had caused the mayhem. Although by no means an equine expert, he realized that Robin's horse was fatally injured, and was not too happy about the appearance of Penny's. It was not just a broken bone that could terminate a horse's racing career, if not its life – so could a badly injured tendon.

Penny was sitting next to Robin holding his hand and looking distraught. Her horse had got up and was standing next to Robin's stricken horse who, having tried a couple of times to rise, had given up the unequal struggle and was lying in a state of shock. In no time an air ambulance arrived and

Penny and Robin were loaded into it. Penny protested strongly but was overruled by both the paramedics and her father, who stayed and waited for Casey to arrive. It was not a long wait.

Within minutes Casey was there. She looked at the two horses and her face told him everything. She went to her medical equipment, produced a syringe, walked across to Robin's horse, found a vein in his neck, injected him and within seconds the horse was dead. This was not the first fatal accident which the Hasletts had experienced with their horses, and they had all agreed that shooting was the last resort.

Turning to the mare, she again produced a syringe. Hubert was horrified.

'Don't worry, I'm not going to put her down. I'm going to sedate her so I can take a better look, and we've got to get her to the clinic to scan her and see how bad the damage is.' She duly went ahead.

Not long after, the police appeared. By that time Casey's horsebox had arrived, the mare had been gently coaxed into the box and was on her way to the clinic. The dead horse would be removed by Hubert's farmhands and buried near where he had met his fate.

The local police were not used to anything like this, and indeed neither was Hubert Haslett. He showed them where the incident had occurred and said he was returning to his house.

As soon as he reached home he phoned the hospital to find that Robin was suffering from severe concussion and bruising, and a sprained wrist. None of these injuries, however, was particularly serious in the realms of National Hunt racing. Penny was unhurt and on her way home.

Once she arrived and learnt her mare was at the equine clinic she wanted to go. Hubert arranged for his chauffeur to take her there while he went to the hospital. At the clinic, Casey told Penny that the scan had been encouraging. It looked as if there was no tendon damage, just severe bruising and a very nasty cut on the front of both legs.

By the time she returned home the local press had been on, and not very much later a number of journalists from the national racing pages. Both Robin and Penny were well enough known for the incident to be significant, if not front-page, news.

Hubert soon returned with the news that Robin was now conscious, very sore and full of painkillers. It would be some weeks before he would be fit to race.

He was somewhat surprised when Jack Symes phoned to say he had heard the news from a friend at the *Racing Post* and was there anything he could do? Hubert explained the situation in more detail and added that he could not think who would have done such a thing.

After a few more minutes of conversation, Jack suggested that Hubert should contact Jay Jessop.

'You probably know that Jay has had some pretty odd and dangerous experiences with his horses and staff over the last few years, and he has very good connections with both private investigators and the police. I suggest you phone him and ask his advice. I'll be amazed if he doesn't come back with something which might at least help to put your mind at rest. This is an horrendous incident, Hubert, and the sort of thing we've got to stamp out in racing.'

As chance would have it, Jay was in his office when the phone rang and he immediately recognized Hubert's voice. They knew each other quite well as they had often met at various race meetings, and Jay had a high regard for both the Haslett children. Hubert described the events of the morning and told Jay that Jack Symes had suggested he ring him. Jay was horrified at the news and expressed his sympathy for everybody concerned, in particular the loss of the good horse and the injury to Robin.

As soon as the conversation ended, Jay phoned Harvey Jackson, a senior policeman whom Jay had come to know and trust over the last few years. A number of attempts had been made to injure Jay or his horses by unscrupulous men who stood to gain by incapacitating Jay in his riding days, or damaging County View as it grew to be the most successful National Hunt training establishment in the UK. These had included murder and kidnapping, as well as attempts to damage Jay's reputation. Harvey had become interested in racing and was now on very friendly terms with Jay.

The policeman listened intently to Jay's summary of the morning's events and gave his customary measured response.

'I'll give the local Chief of Police a friendly call and I'll be careful not to tread on his toes. These guys can be very sensitive about outsiders interfering on their patch.' He paused, and continued. 'You might consider getting Benny involved in this. I'll speak to Hubert Haslett and I'll also have a word with Giles.'

Giles Sinclair was the head of security at the BHB.

'It would be much appreciated,' Jay replied.

Within minutes he was explaining the situation to Benny. 'Well, thank God none of your horses or you were involved,' the East Ender commented with feeling. 'You'd better let this Haslett know that I'd like to have a chat with him and, if possible his children. I'd also like to have a look around. If there's a local pub I'll go in and chat there. They're often a source of useful information.'

'Bless you, Benny. I'll call Hubert and let him know.'

Not long after, Benny called Jay back. 'I've agreed to help Haslett but there's another thought nagging at my mind. Could Leo be involved?'

Jay was taken aback. 'Why would you think that?'

'Well, he and his dad seem hell-bent on winning so it just seemed a possibility. If you don't mind, we'll keep an eye on that young chap as well.'

There was a pause. 'OK. I guess we've nothing to lose, but let's hope your hunch is way out.'

'Agreed, guv. Be in touch,' and the East Ender hung up.

Feeling that there was nothing else he could do, Jay quickly told Eva what had happened before going out to the yard to watch second lot and a schooling session which would involve Danny, David Sparrow, Leo Forsyth and young Ali. Walking over to Leo, who was now mounted, he told him the news, realizing that he was bound to know Robin and Penny rather well.

'Oh, my God,' Leo exclaimed. 'Is Robin still in hospital?'

'I think so,' replied Jay.

'As soon as this is over, I'll phone Mr Haslett and go and see Robin if he's up to visitors. He's a hell of a nice bloke and I've always got on really well with him.'

'I'm sure that would be appreciated,' said Jay. 'Now, come on, let's get on with the work.'

A few minutes later he was sitting in his Land Rover with Jed next to him watching the horses have a swinging canter up the all-weather gallop to warm themselves up before going over to the schooling fences.

At the end of the morning Leo came in to find Jay going through the next set of entries in his little office.

'Would it be all right if I don't come in tomorrow?' he asked. 'I've spoken to Mr Haslett and it's possible that I might be able to see Robin tomorrow morning. I've got to call the hospital first, and if he's up to seeing me I would like to pop over. If he can't I'll turn up as usual, but it will probably be a bit later because I won't be able to phone the hospital until eight o'clock.'

'Of course,' responded Jay. 'I'll assume you're not coming in unless I hear from you. Please do give Robin our best wishes if you see him.'

'I certainly will. It's really bad luck, isn't it?'

'Well, it is in one sense,' replied Jay, 'but normally one person's bad luck can often be another's good. It seems to have worked out like that for you.'

'What do you mean?' Leo almost snapped at Jay.

'Well, if Robin can't ride for a while it'll give you a chance to at least close on his lead, won't it?'

'I hadn't thought of that,' said Leo. 'I only thought about Robin getting better.'

'Quite right,' said Jay. 'I'm sure you did.'

Leo smiled at him and left the room.

Jay mused. Leo was oddly defensive there, he thought. It would be bloody unnatural if he hadn't already realized the opportunity this might well give him.

With that he turned back to his entries and thought no more about it.

Chapter Eight

Two men dressed in immaculate dinner jackets strolled slowly and casually around Le Club casino in Las Vegas. Although they looked relaxed, they were actually extremely alert and watching the various gaming tables and those playing at them intently. They were clearly comfortable in each other's company, and those around them knew that they were inseparable friends.

Icarus Mauros was a second-generation Greek immigrant. As a boy, his father had been smuggled out of Greece, where he lived near the Albanian border. At that time the Albanians regularly raided villages and small towns and abducted boys and young men, compelling them to join their troops in attacking the forces of the Greek government. Icarus's grandmother decided to send her son to her family in America where he would be safe from such a fate. The young man found himself in Ohio where he worked hard, saved a little money and married a young woman also of Greek origin. It was not long before Icarus was born. He soon showed himself to be of a very different character to his laidback parents. At school he worked hard but was already shining shoes in his spare time. He followed this by delivering groceries for supermarkets. He learned

ncing and earned money as an instructor
r Murray Dance Studios. He was fluent
well as the Greek spoken by his family
their friends and relations. This gave him
a great advantage as many of the Greek-speaking
community were unable to do serious business in
anything other than their native language. He started
selling insurance and then made investments in small
properties. He was soon a very comfortably off
young man. He decided to take a break and visit Las
Vegas.

Playing blackjack one evening, he found himself
sitting next to a handsome man of about his own age.
After a while they both got up and walked across to
the bar and started chatting. He learned his companion was also the son of an immigrant. Manfred
Rozenberg's parents had fled Germany to avoid the
Nazis and had set up a dry-cleaning and small
tailoring business in the Bronx. Like Icarus, Manfred
had other ideas. He studied accountancy at night and
soon had a worthwhile job with one of the smaller
New York Jewish firms. His slightly earnest but
charming manner attracted clients, and before long
he was encouraged to set up his own business. This
prospered, and after a couple of years of hard work
he decided, like Icarus, to have a few days' break in
Vegas.

The more Manfred and Icarus talked together the
more they felt at ease with each other, and they
agreed to meet again in Vegas in six months' time.
That was eight years ago – in the subsequent period
they had built up a very substantial insurance and
property business, and become the closest of friends.
They had also taken the huge gamble of buying a
piece of land on the edge of Las Vegas and

constructing a small but luxurious casino. named it Le Club.

Through their diligent research they had learned that in order to succeed they needed to employ a senior manager with considerable experience in running a casino and with a wholly blemish-free background. After a long and careful search they met Joey Costello who, although coming from an Italian background, had no known connections with the Mafia. This was an essential prerequisite as the Gaming Control Board delved meticulously into the personnel of any organization wanting to run a casino. Hand in hand with the police authorities, they had effectively run the Mob out of Las Vegas.

As they walked round their casino, the contrast in their appearance was striking. Manfred was tall, rather slight and, in spite of Jewish ancestry, blond with blue eyes. Icarus was shorter, thickset and with a distinctly olive complexion. Both of them emanated a quiet confidence. They made their way to an area of the casino set aside for sports betting. Multiple screens showed football, golf, basketball, baseball and horse racing. The various time zones of the USA meant that a range of these sports was available on their screens, along with comprehensive betting odds.

Pausing to look at racing from Saratoga, Icarus turned to Manfred. 'I'd like to talk to you about horse racing,' he said. 'Let's go and have supper.'

They both lived on the top floor of the casino in separate suites. Neither was married but neither led an exactly celibate life. Their wealth and influence made them more than attractive to a wide range of women. They had also cultivated charming manners.

Apart from their suites, they had a large private dining room with its own bar and a comfortable sitting area where their high rollers were often entertained. At times this included politicians, entertainers and even some of the important members of the Mob – but only as clients. Although at pains to stay on the right side of the law, they had important and sometimes lucrative associations with a number of people who were far less fastidious in their attitude towards operating legally.

Icarus poured out two large single malt whiskies then picked up the phone and ordered grilled jumbo shrimps with a salad and a bottle of Californian Chardonnay. They were not great wine drinkers and very often stuck to whisky all day and into the early hours of the morning, but they felt like a change that evening. Both could take their liquor, but they were not consistently heavy drinkers and were seldom, if ever, the worse for wear. It could be far too costly in their line of business.

Once the meal had been served, Icarus started talking.

'As you know, a number of casinos are hooking up with the Hong Kong Jockey Club to have betting on their races over here. It looks as if the idea will receive government approval and will go ahead. The other day I was chatting to that Englishman, Adam Forsyth, who sometimes comes and plays here. In fact he is a pretty frequent visitor these days. He and I get on very well together. He's a pretty sharp poker player, and although he will sit down at high-limit tables, he keeps his own gambling under strict control. He's not a nervous player, but he never lets things get out of hand. He's also a bit of a ladies' man – he doesn't hesitate to pay top bucks.

'It seems he's chairman of a group of racecourses in Britain – he showed me a tape of his racecourses and some of the races. Over there jump racing has a big following, whereas in this country few of us know anything other than the Maryland Cup.

'As I watched his tapes I became more and more fascinated. A significant number of horses fall in their jump races, which are split into two categories. Quite small obstacles are called hurdles. The bigger ones look plain suicidal to me and are called steeplechases. It occurred to me that this sort of racing could be a very profitable addition to our sports betting if we could find some way of showing it in our own and other casinos. As you know, it's far from the most profitable sports betting activity, but if we were able to have races with greater uncertainty it could be very much to our advantage. Also it would give us something different. Horse race gambling is huge in the UK so why shouldn't we cash in on it here?

'Forsyth also mentioned that the government has announced it will license a super casino in Britain. The plan is that in the next two or three years this will be tested and then followed up by a number of other big operations as long as no one fouls up.

'If the casino industry is really going to open up over there, it would be worthwhile having a look at it. We both agree that there's not a lot more we can do to develop business in Le Club, and the cost of opening another Vegas casino would be huge. It is possible that it would be cheaper to have an operation in the UK. What's more, it wouldn't be a bad idea to spread the risk to another market.'

Manfred was looking intrigued. He knew that this was no idle dream and that Icarus would already have something hatching in his fertile brain.

His friend continued. 'I thought it would be worth our while visiting England and having a look at what goes on there. Forsyth has already said that he'd be very happy to show us around and I have the feeling that, although he is quite reticent in talking about himself, he's probably a big player in England. He just seems to be a man who keeps his cards close to his chest and knows where he's going. He's a charmer, but I doubt if he's a guy it would be safe to cross.'

Manfred thought for a moment. 'Well, it wouldn't do us any harm to have a few days off,' he agreed. 'Joey Costello is more than capable of running the casino while we're away.'

Again, Icarus picked up the phone, dialled a number and waited a few moments. 'Hi, Joey,' he said. 'Manfred and I are in the hospitality suite. Come up and join us when you can.' He listened to the reply and put down the phone. 'He'll be with us in five or six minutes,' he said.

Sure enough, a few minutes later there was a knock on the door and in walked an extremely handsome man dressed just as immaculately as the two casino owners. He was in his late thirties but looked younger. Waving to the bar, Manfred said, 'Help yourself.'

Joey walked over, poured himself a club soda over a glass half full of ice, and sat down on the settee between his two employers. He looked from one to the other questioningly. It was Icarus who kicked off.

Over the next few minutes, taking it in turns, they outlined their plan to Joey. He thought for a moment.

'Do you have any contacts in England apart from this Adam Forsyth?' he enquired. They both shook their heads. 'Leave it with me,' he said. 'I think I might be able to help you there.'

101

Manfred recalled that Honey, Joey's sister, had worked in London for a few years and had only returned to Vegas a few months earlier. Although nothing specific had been said, he and Icarus had always felt her return had been rather hurried and out of necessity rather than due to homesickness.

With that they turned their attention to the casino itself and to some of the big players who were there or who were expected in the next few days. As was their custom, they briefly reviewed their security and anti-cheating procedures which were critical for the profitability of such a business. The complicated and increasingly clever ways in which professional gamblers tried to cheat meant that casino operators had to be extremely vigilant and use more and more sophisticated surveillance and other techniques to ensure they were not taken for a ride. This area of activity was Joey's prime responsibility. Anyone he caught breaking the rules was removed from the casino very quickly, and was made to understand that he would not be welcomed back again. Wishing them a good trip, Joey then rose and left them.

Icarus and Manfred each had a whisky, and decided to call in on the surveillance room. This housed the closed-circuit television which gave a panoramic view of their casino and also allowed them to home in on any table they wished. Tonight there was nothing that warranted their attention, although they observed that a well-known senator and a couple of lesser film stars were playing. Returning to their suite, Icarus drew gently on the illegal Havana cigar he was smoking.

'I think I'll give Anna a call,' Manfred announced. 'I'll see you in the morning.'

Icarus chuckled. 'Don't wear yourself out,' he said, and smiled as Manfred let himself out of the suite.

Anna was his partner's flavour of the month. The daughter of a San Francisco businessman, she had come to Vegas for a weekend three months ago, had met Manfred, and had barely let him out of her sight since. She was evidently something of a bedroom athlete and had met a partner with equal stamina.

Icarus finished his cigar, went downstairs and walked once more round the casino. Seeing nothing of note or interest, he made his way back up to his suite and went to bed. He watched what he thought was a rather uninspired middleweight fight, and turned the TV off before it had finished. He doused the lights and was soon fast asleep.

Three days later they flew to London, where they were met by a chauffeur. They had been put in touch with a firm of lawyers recommended by one of Joey's London contacts. The man they were going to meet was Sol Jacobson, a civil rather than a criminal lawyer who was a well-known and successful specialist in property deals and tax avoidance. A number of his activities had been looked at by both the police and the Serious Fraud Squad but nothing had ever been proved which could lead to a prosecution.

Through one of his clients he had met Honey and her current boyfriend, who had proved useful to him on a number of occasions. Unlike the casino owners, he knew why she had left London rather rapidly.

The car took them to a small but exclusive hotel. The Belgravia Boutique deliberately kept a low profile as many of its clients did not want their whereabouts known. They included a number of South American and Middle Eastern diplomats, as well as a fair sprinkling of members or associates of the underworld.

The two casino partners had separate bedrooms with a communal sitting room between them. They looked around what would be their accommodation for at least the next few days and were satisfied it was well up to their demanding standards. They had been equally impressed by the head porter, who had a cheery manner and a Cockney accent. The manager was a suave and rather intense Italian who gave the impression of being distinctly tough beneath his charming exterior. He reminded them of Joey.

Having unpacked and settled in, Icarus phoned Sol who immediately invited them both to dinner that night. Icarus thanked him but declined the offer. 'We're a bit bushed,' he said. 'I think we'll probably have a light supper in our room tonight.'

'Perhaps we could meet tomorrow? How would it be if I came round mid-morning? We can talk confidentially in your room.'

'That sounds great,' said Icarus. 'Would eleven suit you?'

'Fine. See you then.'

Icarus informed Manfred of the plan. They went to their separate bathrooms, showered, and reappeared wearing the thick white terry towelling robes provided by the hotel. The both laughed at their twin-like attire.

Manfred opened his briefcase and took out some papers. 'When are we going to contact Adam Forsyth?' he asked.

'Not until we've talked to Sol Jacobson – hopefully he'll have found out a lot more background for us. I like Forsyth but he is almost too good to be true. I'd be interested to see what you make of him as you've not spent as much time with him as I have.'

On the plane they had discussed the possibility of buying into or even obtaining control of Adam's racecourses, although it was only a wild idea rather than a serious plan. That night, as they talked about it again, their enthusiasm grew. Here was a way of getting a foothold in an entirely new market, and they had never been afraid of taking a calculated risk. After further discussion they decided to put it on their agenda with Sol Jacobson the next morning, although making it sound a matter of interest rather than a pressing desire.

As they watched the world news, they ate a simple supper of smoked salmon and a side salad. They demolished nearly half a bottle of single malt whisky, before turning in to get a good night's sleep prior to their meeting the next day.

Sol arrived punctually the next morning. He was a short, well-built man in his early fifties, clean-shaven and with short grey hair. He wore large horn-rimmed glasses, behind which shone a pair of extremely shrewd grey eyes. He was dressed in a dark blue double-breasted suit with a pale blue shirt, a plain dark blue tie and highly polished Gucci slip-ons. They were later to learn this was his standard dress during working hours. At weekends he allowed himself the luxury of exchanging his double-breasted blue suit for a single-breasted medium grey worsted one, with a white shirt and a black and white polka-dot tie. Those who knew Sol sometimes wondered if the gleaming Gucci shoes were actually glued to his feet. They also wondered what he did with the very substantial income he clearly earned.

Although they had talked a couple of times on the phone, this was the first occasion they'd met, and while they exchanged pleasantries it was clear that the two sides were weighing each other up.

Although Sol had worked for a number of distinctly dubious characters, he always insisted he would never became involved in anything dishonest or illegal himself. He never missed an opportunity to state his passionate belief that everyone was innocent until proved guilty and that, as long as he worked within the strict letter of the law, it was up to him to exploit every possible loophole or nuance on behalf of his clients, however unsavoury they might be. One of the main reasons that so many of his clients were either active criminals, or sailed very close to the wind, was that experience had shown him these were the people who could pay his high fees and normally would without a murmur of complaint. Even the police and those lawyers whom he frequently found himself up against respected him, although he was not particularly liked.

Without wasting time, they ordered coffee and soon got down to business. Icarus and Manfred took it in turns to explain that they were looking to expand into Europe, and Britain in particular, in more ways than one. The fact that the government had indicated it would give the go-ahead for a major casino was of real interest, especially with the possibility of a number of other super casinos to follow. It was this, they stressed, that had excited their initial interest. They also explained the Hong Kong betting development which made them think that British racing, and in particular National Hunt racing, could provide a useful additional medium for their clients to gamble on. After meeting Adam Forsyth at Le Club, it had occurred to them that owning a few racecourses might give them further opportunities to enhance their foothold in the British gambling market.

'So how do you think I can help you?' was Sol's first question.

'We'd like to have a really detailed report into the likelihood of further casinos being licensed in the UK, and how we could best pursue the opportunity of gaining such a licence.'

Sol made a quick note. Looking up, he waited for them to continue.

'This man, Adam Forsyth,' explained Manfred, 'has visited our casino on a number of occasions and has been very affable to Icarus. He gambles extravagantly but is always in control. When he was with us recently we learnt that he is the chairman of a group of small but evidently quite successful racecourses. We understand that, although he's chairman and a major shareholder, he doesn't have a controlling interest. We would like a full background on all the shareholders and any information which might direct us to those most likely to sell, if we decide this would be an interesting investment for us.'

Icarus quickly added, 'We would want a very thorough financial analysis of the holding company, and if possible the contribution which each course makes to the consolidated profit and loss. As Manfred said, all the background on the directors, including any dirt you can dig up.'

Again Sol made some brief notes on his yellow legal pad.

'Lastly,' continued Manfred, 'we'd like to learn as much as we can about the way in which betting takes place, both at the racecourses and on the internet. We'd like to go to two or three race meetings here,

and if you had any contacts with a significant bookmaker who we could meet, that would also be very
helpful.'

Sol made further notes, then looked up. The two
American business partners added nothing more.

The lawyer quickly glanced at his notes and then
addressed them both in his precise way. 'The information about the casinos will be no problem, but it
will take a little time. I can tell you that there appears
to be some concern that such licences should not be
acquired by the Mafia or any of the other major
criminal organizations in the USA, the Far East or
Russia in particular. It's not even certain a super
casino will be licensed.'

Icarus and Manfred looked at him impassively.
'How long will this take you, Sol?'

'Probably four or five days,' was the reply.

'That seems reasonable,' Icarus agreed.

'As far as Adam Forsyth and Tolchester Holdings
are concerned, that may take a little longer. I know of
Adam Forsyth. He's a highly successful entrepreneur
in a number of different businesses. He's also a
significant figure in British racing. I don't know him
personally but I'm sure it shouldn't take too long to
discover most of what you want to know about him.
Until I've found out who the other directors are, I
won't be able to give you an idea of how long this
may take altogether.'

'We may be able to help there,' suggested Icarus.
'It's our plan to meet him for lunch or dinner and
hopefully get an invitation to one of his racecourses.
As Manfred said, I was on very friendly terms with
him in Vegas.'

Sol nodded. 'That, of course, would be helpful,' he
agreed. He paused, making a few more notes before

he continued. 'The bookmaker situation is no problem. There is a very significant bookmaking operation run by two brothers, Garry and Tony Kent. My company has worked for them on a number of occasions, and I know both of them personally. I'm sure I could arrange for you to meet them at one of the major racecourses near London. They are entertaining company but sail rather close to the wind, though they have never been arrested or prosecuted for anything more serious than speeding or a parking fine. They are, however, known to be quite closely connected with significant criminals from the East End of London,' he warned.

'As long as they can give us the low-down on the gambling market in this country, we're not too worried about their background or business ethics,' Icarus replied. 'It sounds as if it might be quite amusing to meet them.'

For the first time Sol let a glimmer of a smile play round his mouth. 'You'll certainly find them amusing,' he said, 'but don't be taken in by their rather jovial and good-humoured façade. They're a pair of extremely sharp cookies.'

The Americans smiled and Manfred, with a chuckle, replied, 'We can't wait to meet them.'

Sol put the top back on his fountain pen and asked, 'Is that all for the moment?'

The two Americans looked at each other and nodded. 'Yes, thank you,' Manfred replied.

'Right, I'll be getting on with it,' said Sol. He stood up abruptly, shook their hands and walked across to the door.

Icarus beat him to it, opened the door and with a broad smile said, 'We look forward to doing business with you, Sol.'

'Thank you,' replied the lawyer. 'Me likewise,' and turning on his heel he walked down the corridor to the nearby lift. Without looking back, he pressed the button, waited for the lift to arrive, got in and disappeared.

Icarus walked back into the room and gave Manfred a meaningful look. 'Not exactly a charmer,' was his colleague's assessment, 'but I have a feeling he's a guy who delivers.'

'I agree,' said Icarus. 'Now let's have a drink, and find ourselves somewhere to eat.'

'I guess that head porter might be our man when it comes to knowing the best watering holes in this city,' replied his friend. 'He probably knows a lot more than that too,' he added with a wink.

'Well, let's find out,' suggested Manfred. They put on their jackets, checked they had their wallets, and made their way down to the front hall where they were greeted cheerfully by Andy Best, the head porter. After they explained their requirements, they were asked what sort of food they liked. 'Something very English,' was the reply.

'Does beef appeal?' he enquired.

'You bet.'

'Right, I'll send you to Simpson's-in-the-Strand. There'll be a table waiting for you by the time you get there, and you'll have a choice of the best lamb or beef that Britain can provide. It's rather old-fashioned but the service is excellent and the wine cellar is first-rate.'

'We're not too much into wine,' explained Manfred, 'but I assume they have a reasonable selection of whiskies.'

'A racing cert, gentlemen, and some you'll probably never have heard of.'

'I doubt that,' suggested Icarus. 'We pride ourselves on knowing all the single malts as well as the blended products of your Scottish Highlands.'

'In that case you'll be in good hands,' replied Andy, who had by this time hailed a taxi. Opening the door, he ushered them in and instructed the driver where to take the two hotel guests. He returned to the lobby, phoned Simpson's and made the reservation.

Andy was a colourful character with a wide circle of contacts throughout the whole London hotel industry. Many were head porters or head waiters, with a sprinkling of security men. He was also Benny's brother-in-law. The two of them were close friends and avid football fans, although supporting different London teams. Since Benny's connection with County View, Andy had also taken a much keener interest in horse racing, particularly the jumping game.

Twenty minutes later Icarus and Manfred were sitting in the club-like atmosphere of the ground-floor restaurant at Simpson's. Theo, the waiter, who had been briefed by Andy Best, made sure they were comfortable, and soon there was a bottle of Glenmorangie on the table, along with a bottle of still mineral water.

They decided on the rib of beef, then over coffee Icarus phoned Adam, explained they were in London for a short while and asked whether it would be possible to meet for dinner. Adam proved to be free that evening so, having no other plans, they readily agreed. They were invited to meet him at the Mirabelle at eight o'clock and were assured that any black cab would know the way. Not being a man to waste time, Adam said he looked forward to seeing them and ended the call.

Returning to the hotel, they assured Andy Best that they'd thoroughly enjoyed their meal and asked him how long it would take to get to the Mirabelle.

'Only ten or fifteen minutes from here, depending on the traffic. You're certainly hitting the best restaurants in London,' he informed them with a broad grin.

They went into their room, phoned Joey at Le Club, and were told that nothing out of the ordinary had happened and all was well. He enquired how things were going in London and Manfred explained that they'd had an interesting meeting with Sol that morning and were meeting Adam Forsyth for dinner that night. Joey seemed particularly pleased that the meeting with Sol had gone well.

'Don't worry about anything here,' he assured them. 'I'll call you if anything out of the ordinary occurs. Have fun!'

Both the casino owners had complete trust in their right-hand man and gave the matter no more thought. They did, however, agree that they would probably have to handle Adam Forsyth with tact that night if they were going to get information out of him without appearing too inquisitive.

With nothing else to do before dinner, they settled down to read the wide range of newspapers which had been put in their suite. They then switched to satellite television where they watched the business bulletin and the CNN News until it was time to get ready for their meeting with Adam.

Chapter Nine

Promptly at eight they entered the Mirabelle restaurant in Curzon Street and were immediately impressed by its rather laidback style. They'd already been told a little of its history by Andy, and realized that it was one of the most famous restaurants in London with a top reputation since the end of the Second World War.

Adam was sitting in the bar and rose with a welcoming smile and an outstretched hand as they walked towards him. He suggested they went straight to the table, and soon they had their customary malt whiskies in front of them while Adam had a dry sherry.

After polite questions about their flight and how comfortable their hotel was, they ordered their food. Icarus opted for avocado vinaigrette and Manfred for Parma ham. Adam chose the terrine and strongly recommended the Dover sole. Having had substantial quantities of meat at lunchtime, the Americans happily settled for this too.

When Adam enquired about the purpose behind their visit, it was Manfred who led off.

'We both needed a break. We've only visited London once before and felt it was high time we put that right. You also aroused our interest in your jump racing, and we thought we'd come and have a close look at it for ourselves. We're hoping that invitation to one of your racecourses is still open, and the head porter in our hotel has also suggested we ought to visit a place called Sandown Park which he assures us is one of the top jumping tracks and is also not very far from central London.'

Adam nodded. 'Of course you must come to a Tolchester track. How about the day after tomorrow? We've got what looks like an interesting card at Essex Park, and it's only an hour and a quarter's drive from London. I'll pick you up and we can go together. It will give you a chance to meet Norman Parry, one of our directors. His family owned the course until it became part of Tolchester. If my memory serves me right, there's a big meeting the following weekend at Sandown. Will you still be here then?'

Icarus replied. 'Absolutely. We planned on at least a couple of weeks.'

The conversation paused for a moment while the first courses were served. Then Manfred rather casually enquired of Adam, 'We'd love to hear about your company and the racecourses which are part of your group.'

Adam was seldom happier than when talking about his businesses, in particular Tolchester Holdings. He filled them in on the racecourses and how they had come together. He was proud but not over-cocky about his role in persuading the various owners to join forces.

This time Icarus asked a question. 'Tell us about these owners. I'm always intrigued about business-men who get together in a sort of partnership. So often it can lead to friction which had not been taken into account at the outset.'

114

Adam agreed. 'That's true, but in fact we all get on rather well together. It was clear that combining our forces would give us greater strength in a number of ways, and in particular in ensuring our racecourses had good strong fixtures.' He briefly explained how the fixtures were distributed by the BHB. He also explained the importance of gaining sponsorship to ensure that prize money attracted good-class horses.

'Tell us a bit about these directors,' Manfred pursued. 'I'm always interested in business personalities.'

Adam obliged by listing the directors and explaining that the four of them had owned racecourses. He left it at that without being indiscreet in any way, but did answer briefly but accurately Manfred's supplementary question about their backgrounds. 'All were beneficiaries of inherited wealth with their main interests in agriculture, some property, and a significant portfolio of equities which were left to them by their parents. All are from established families, and none of them could remotely be described as nouveau riche. Jon Gormley is more involved in business than the other three and sits on a few boards. Like me he has a few City contacts.'

'Who owns what?' enquired Icarus.

Adam listed their names and the racecourses they had owned. 'Why do you ask?'

'Oh, just in case we meet any of them at the races,' was the smooth response.

Adam nodded and moved on. 'Well, as I said, you will meet Norman at Essex.'

He was bit more specific about Jay and Percy, explaining that they had been invited to join the board because of their high-profile reputations in racing, and also the fact that both of them were very successful businessmen in their own right.

'They sound an interesting pair,' commented Icarus.

'You'll certainly meet Jay at our racecourse,' replied Adam. 'He always supports our meetings and he's bound to have at least one, if not more, runners. He's a charming man but extremely efficient and outstandingly successful in whatever he turns his hand to. He's known Percy Cartwright since their university days. Cartwright has built up a worldwide insurance business and is a major owner at County View, Jay's training yard, as well as being a director of that company. It was at university that I met them originally, although I didn't know them as well as I do now.'

'They sound busy people,' commented Manfred.

'There's an old saying this side of the Atlantic and it may be with you too: if you want a job done choose a busy man.'

Both the Americans laughed.

The atmosphere was so friendly and relaxed that Icarus felt he could explore Adam's reaction to their idea of having National Hunt racing in Le Club, and possibly syndicating it to other casinos for their sports betting operations. Giving his partner a quick wink, he launched into a somewhat edited version of their idea.

'We would really have liked to provide a telephone betting service and make the English races available via satellite. Unfortunately, because of the recent changes in telephone gambling laws, in particular relating to poker, this would be illegal. However, the government seems set to allow a deal between the Hong Kong Jockey Club and some Vegas casinos. This means we are still interested in the possibility of showing UK jump races in our casino. It would give us an edge over flat racing. How would we go about getting permission?'

'Well,' explained Adam, 'there are two racing television channels which between them cover all the races at all the racecourses. In addition to this, the BBC and Independent Television cover a number of races. Although the UK rights are tied up, I can't see any reason why racecourses wouldn't sell you their rights for exclusive showing in US casinos. I'm quite sure we at Tolchester would be interested in such a deal.'

Manfred and Icarus both feigned surprise. 'Do you think that would really be a possibility?'

'I'd have to talk to my other directors,' replied Adam, 'but I can't see why they should object, particularly as it would provide an additional source of income. The only problem I foresee is that there is a significant time difference.'

'Yes, we thought about that,' replied Manfred, 'but we actually see it as a positive rather than a negative. Your daytime races would be shown in our casinos about eight o'clock in the morning until midday, and your evening races from say eleven until two in the afternoon. Although this isn't a peak time for our players, there are various important matches on the East Coast and we often have a fair number of sports gamblers in the casino. What's more, we thought that such a new idea could build up interest and be used as a hook to get people into the casino at a time when they might not normally come. Once they're in, we know that they'll nearly always play something, even if not getting heavily into the sports betting itself.'

'Well, in that case I think it might be a possibility. I'll phone the other directors in the next two to three days and get their initial reaction. But I usually get my way,' he added with some confidence. 'What's more, if it turned out to be a success with our racecourses, I can't see why you wouldn't be able to do similar deals with other courses.'

The two Americans looked at each other as if it was a new idea to them. 'That might be really interesting,' said Icarus, and Manfred nodded enthusiastically.

At that stage Adam looked at his watch. 'I don't want to be rude,' he said, 'but I've got a breakfast meeting tomorrow so I think I'd better be on my way. I'll be in touch with you tomorrow to arrange Essex Park and about Sandown on Saturday – that, of course, is assuming you're still interested.'

'Absolutely. We most certainly are.'

'Well, you might well meet my son at Sandown. I think one of Jay's runners is likely to be in an amateur chase where Leo is due to ride. It's a bit of an outside chance, but we're rather hoping he might be amateur champion this season.'

Both the Americans looked impressed. 'Well, that would be something, I imagine,' exclaimed Icarus.

'It would certainly be a huge delight for his old father,' smiled Adam. He put his napkin on the table. 'Right, gentlemen, I'll settle the bill on the way out. If you want to stay on and have a few more drinks, please be my guest.'

'That's very kind,' replied Manfred, 'but we're still feeling some effects from the long flight so I think we'll take a leaf from your book and have an early night too.'

They made their way out and Adam gestured to the head waiter. 'You'll send the bill on to my office as usual.'

'Of course, Mr Forsyth,' was the immediate reply. 'I hope you and your guests have enjoyed the evening.'

'We certainly did,' Manfred reassured him, 'and I'm sure you'll see us here again before we go back to America.'

'It will be a delight,' replied the head waiter. 'Might I be rude enough to enquire where you're staying?'

Adam told him.

'Ah well,' replied the head waiter, 'Andy, your head porter, knows me well so just ask him to give me a call and I'll make sure you're well looked after.'

'Thank you very much,' Manfred smiled warmly. With that the three of them left the restaurant. Adam's car was waiting for him, and he insisted on dropping them off at their hotel before Jamie took him on to the Barbican flat which he used on those occasions when he had either a very late night or an early start. He much preferred staying in his house in Berkshire, but he'd long ago decided that he didn't like trains and that the traffic jams during the rush hour on the M4 were neither an efficient nor a relaxing way to spend a significant part of his day.

Relaxing at their hotel, the two Americans were well satisfied with their progress.

'What shall we do tomorrow?' Manfred asked his partner. 'We can't sit here all day.'

'Let's ask Andy. He's bound to have ideas. What about a casino tomorrow evening, and a visit to one of the betting shops Adam mentioned?'

Manfred agreed. 'See you in the morning,' he yawned, and made his way to his bedroom.

Icarus glanced at the *Evening Standard* provided by room service, and then followed his partner's lead and settled for an early night. It made a change from Vegas, he mused to himself.

Adam let himself into his Barbican flat. It was far from spartan and as he closed the door he turned to see the silhouette of a tall dark-haired figure in the

119

doorway to the sitting room. She walked slowly towards him and led him to the bedroom. Gently she took off his jacket and tie, undid the buttons of his shirt and kissed him on the lips. 'Get into bed and I'll bring you a nightcap.'

She returned with a silver tray on which were two frosted glasses and a bottle of Dom Perignon. She poured each of them a glass and looked lovingly into his eyes. Cilla had been Adam's lover for over five years and had kept to her side of the bargain – she was always available when he wanted her, cooked for him when he was tired of eating out, and was the soul of discretion. The few times they were seen together in public caused little comment as her position as a top business columnist made her an obvious target for Adam's need for good PR. In return, her wardrobe was sensational, her jewellery exquisite, and the rent on her own flat paid for. No money ever changed hands.

She slipped off her robe and slid into bed next to him. Thirty minutes later a tired but contented Adam drifted into sleep. His thoughts were not of his mistress breathing gently beside him but of a very different South African blonde who had given him lunch a few days earlier.

Chapter Ten

Jay was just about to leave his office to watch first lot when the phone rang.

'Have you seen page five of the *Post*?' It was Frank Malone.

'No.'

'Well, read it and call me back.'

Jay had seldom heard Frank speak so tersely and certainly not to him. Reaching across to the pile of un-looked-at newspapers which were normally reserved until after first lot had been completed, Jay found the *Racing Post* and turned to page five. The headline riveted him: BRUTAL ATTACK ON AMATEUR JOCKEY.

Jay quickly read the copy beneath.

Jeremy Lloyd Paterson, the well-known amateur jockey now lying in second position in this year's championship, was brutally attacked as he left a nightclub in the Chelsea area last night. Lloyd-Paterson is well known for his high-profile night life which includes frequent visits to exclusive nightclubs where he is known to rub shoulders with a number of members of the Royal Family.

It reported that Lloyd-Paterson's father, who had been a well-known point-to-point rider in his youth, had bought a dozen horses for his son to ride which were split between three significant trainers. He clearly hoped that his son would follow in his footsteps, and indeed Jeremy had a great deal of natural ability. The previous season he had come third in the amateur championship, and this year he was now lying second, two wins ahead of Leo. This was mainly as a result of his father's horses performing consistently well. Apart from a few rides on other people's horses – all trained by his father's three trainers – he gained few outside opportunities. It was not that his ability was in question, but he was far from reliable in terms of turning up and was often not at his physical best when he did.

On leaving the club the night before, he had been attacked for no apparent reason as he was about to get into his Lotus. There was a rather waspish comment that it was surprising he felt safe to drive at three o'clock in the morning after spending several hours at the club in question. The report also remarked on the coincidence that Robin Haslett had been the subject of an attack of a very different nature. Although nothing specific was said, there was a clear inference that perhaps the two incidents were not unrelated. No mention was made of the fact that Leo's performances had taken him up to Lloyd-Paterson in the last week and that both were beginning to close on the out-of-action Robin Haslett.

Jay put down the paper with an ominous feeling. After a few moments' reflection he phoned Frank.

'What d'you think now?' the bookmaker demanded. 'Were my thoughts that fanciful?'

'I admit it looks suspicious, but I still find it hard to believe that either Leo or Adam are involved in this. It's beginning to look too bloody obvious.'

'It might look bloody obvious,' was the response, 'but thinking it and proving it are two vastly different issues.'

Jay reluctantly agreed with Frank's point. 'Well, I'll make sure Benny's aware of this, but God knows, he seems to have enough on his plate at the moment. Thanks for letting me know.'

'All part of the service,' Frank assured him in a rather more light-hearted tone than had been in evidence up until that moment.

Jay phoned Benny, who seemed to take the news more or less in his stride. 'Well, we know something's going on. Young Leo's behaving a bit strangely, and with the events surrounding the amateur championship it seems, to say the least, bloody odd, we also know his father's been backing him pretty heavily.

'As far as last night's concerned, toffs' nightclubs are a bit outside my league, but because this double-barrelled name seems to be pretty upper-crust the chances are it's come to Harvey Jackson's attention. I'll give him a call and see if he's got any handle on it. The other thing I'll do is give Marvin a buzz. He's more likely to move in – or know people who move in – those circles than me and my mob.'

Jay couldn't help smiling at some of Benny's phraseology but thanked him and rang off, saying he'd obviously be pleased to hear any news or hard facts which Benny could uncover.

After a little more thought he walked into the kitchen and told Eva the news. She put down *The Times*, which she read avidly every day, and paused before she spoke.

'You seem to have assumed that Leo and Adam are up to something. Do I know all the facts?'

Jay explained that Leo was being very reserved, almost secretive, and had changed from being fairly casual about the championship to being almost obsessive.

'Well, I'm not that surprised. Adam seems to be putting more and more pressure on him – far more than we thought when we first talked to him about this. He may be frightened of his father or just anxious to please him. It doesn't mean he's prepared to resort to violence to gain his ends. Who have you really talked to about this apart from Frank, Benny and now me?'

'No one.'

'Well, why don't you discuss it with Percy or Howard? Percy has a cool brain and Howard seems to have an instinct about people's honesty. Also, he knows a lot of people involved in racing and betting – remember he comes from the East End and was a bookmaker in his youth. You've nothing to lose.'

Jay saw the wisdom of her words and promptly returned to his office and phoned the two County View directors. Both listened carefully but declined to comment in any detail. The fact that Benny was involved seemed to reassure them, and each promised to call Jay if anything useful occurred to them.

Jay was relieved that his two friends now knew of his concerns, but he still had an uneasy feeling about the whole situation.

Chapter Eleven

Essex Park was one of the Tolchester Group of racecourses. It reminded Jay very much of Warwick. A bend away from the grandstands swept left-handed up a fairly steep hill before a fairly sharp decline at the beginning of the back straight. Here the fences and hurdles were more or less on the flat, as was the turn at the far end of the course bringing the horses back to the finishing straight. This was slightly uphill. Unlike Warwick, there were no buildings in the middle of the course, so there was an uninterrupted view of the whole course.

Jay had No Pushover owned by Pete Fulton running in the first race, which was a maiden hurdle. This meant that none of the runners had won a race at the time of starting. No Pushover was ridden by Ali who was getting more and more competent and confident. Although only finishing fourth, he would almost certainly have been much nearer the winner, if not actually challenging for first place, had the horse immediately ahead not run across him as they approached the penultimate hurdle. He quickly checked his mount, but this resulted in the horse having to check its own impetus going into the hurdle and ballooning it rather than taking it low and quickly. The resultant three lengths' loss of position proved critical in the run-up to the winning post.

Peter Fulton was philosophical about the outcome of the race. 'At least he wasn't hurt, and we know he's got ability even if we didn't pick up any prize money.'

'Absolutely,' agreed Jay. 'He'll almost certainly come on for the experience of that race.'

Peter declined Jay's offer of a drink in the bar as he had a meeting in London later that evening and was in a hurry to get away. Jay promised to phone him the next day and tell him how his horse had come out of the race, and said he was quite convinced he'd be able to give him another run in ten to fifteen days' time.

Jay and Howard had a cup of coffee together and waited for the fourth race in which Howard's horse, Brave Quester, was running. This was a novice chase and Quester was highly fancied as a result of his previous win at Plumpton. It was not just this victory which had made him a firm favourite with the book-makers, but the fact that he had run up a sequence of three consecutive wins over hurdles the previous season. David Sparrow was due to ride Howard's horse as he had in all his previous runs.

Time passed in friendly and general chat about racing. Howard said he had had a quiet word with Kipper Fish, one of his East End friends from way back. Kipper was heavily involved in the betting scene and would keep his ears open. Soon it was time to collect the saddle and get their runner ready for his race. The saddling and the preliminaries in the parade ring went without incident. All the runners were by now experienced with racecourse routine, even if for some it was their first run over fences.

Jay's main rivals were Kelly's Hero, who had come second in a good novice chase at Sandown, and Dream On, who'd won a rather moderate contest at Huntingdon. Jay was quietly confident that, barring accidents, Howard's horse would win. His jumping was immaculate, and he was blessed with the ability to quicken at the end of even a two-and-a-half-mile race.

The first circuit passed without incident, and the sixteen runners streamed past the winning post for the first time, closely bunched with the exception of two horses which were beginning to struggle at the tail of the field. Brave Quester was placed approximately seventh as they started the climb up the hill away from the stands. He was just behind Dream On and both were still moving easily in the same position as they approached the first of the fences after the downhill run. At this moment the horse immediately beside the County View runner slipped, fell and brought down the horse immediately behind them. This in no way interfered with Brave Quester and, watching the race carefully through his binoculars, Jay was not at all certain the Sparrow had even noticed the incident.

The two horses clambered to their feet, and one jockey was up immediately trying to grab his mount's reins without success. The other jockey lay motionless, and was soon attended by the paramedics. It transpired he was only winded. He was helped up and both riders were soon on their way back to the weighing room in the ambulance.

The two loose horses, instead of following the other runners, ran to the first fence down the back straight. Faced with the obstacle and with no jockey, one of them turned round and started galloping back towards the grandstand. The other horse followed his riderless companion.

The race was rapidly developing into a three-horse battle. Kelly's Hero, the second favourite, and In a Hurry, which had not won over fences before but had good hurdle form, were a couple of lengths ahead of Brave Quester. These three had broken away from the rest of the field which was now trailing by ten lengths. David Sparrow had his horse nicely tucked in on the rails behind the leaders. Turning for home, to David and Jay's slight surprise, In a Hurry lived up to his name, accelerated past the leader, and was going with consummate ease as he jumped the first fence in the home straight. David reacted quickly, slapped his mount's neck and quickly matched the other horse's acceleration. They both swept past Kelly's Hero who, although not struggling, was just continuing at the same steady pace. Jumping the penultimate, the two horses were upside. At that moment the two jockeys realized that there was potentially a major problem. The two loose horses were still galloping together, had rounded the bend and were making their way down the home straight in the wrong direction, presumably looking for where they had entered the track from the parade ring. They were rapidly approaching the two leaders but at that stage were well away from them. However, they were suddenly faced with the last hurdle in the finishing straight, swerved away from it and found themselves going straight at the two leading horses.

Unfortunately, they ran across them, and both jockeys were forced to take evasive action. By the time they had a chance to straighten their mounts it was too late and both of them had gone past the outside of the final fence. There was nothing they could do apart from slow their horses down, hack up to the finishing post, and turn round waiting for the race to finish before they disconsolately made their way to the exit from the racecourse. Meanwhile Kelly's Hero had continued at his steady but uninspiring gallop and had achieved an unexpected, undeserved and bloodless victory.

Jay and Howard looked at each other with an air of resignation. 'Damn and blast it,' was Howard's vocal reaction. His internal language was much stronger than that, but with ladies present he restrained the more violent phrases which were poised to spring from his lips.

'What do you think?' he asked Jay.

'Well, let's find out what the Sparrow's got to say – but it looks to me as if we would have won it.'

Moments later Jay's suggestion was confirmed by the Sparrow. He was his normal down-to-earth self and, looking at Howard, was adamant. 'He really would have won, sir. The other horse was going well but not nearly as well as I was, and I hadn't asked him for any extra effort apart from when we went past the winner.'

'Ah, well,' sighed Howard. 'He's come out of it unscathed, and he won't get an extra penalty which he would have done if he'd won.'

'I agree with you. Let's try and look on the bright side.'

Jay and Howard said a few more encouraging words to David Sparrow and made their way towards the owners' and trainers' bar. Earlier on Jay had spotted Adam and Norman Parry, along with two smartly but casually dressed men of very different appearances. He assumed they were business contacts of Adam's, and was certain he'd not seen them before. He noted that Norman Parry was talking earnestly to Adam's two guests. Going across to the bar, he ordered an orange juice for Howard who was driving himself home, and bought himself a Scotch to which he added a dash of water, feeling he needed to steady his nerves after the drama of a few moments earlier. Adam walked across, politely interrupted their conversation and apologized to Howard.

'Perhaps just before you leave you could spare me a moment. There are a couple of friends I'd like to introduce you to,' Adam told Jay.

'Of course. As soon as Howard and I have finished.'

'We won't be very long, as I've got a long drive ahead of me,' Howard explained.

Jay continued. 'Well, I'm in no particular hurry. David Sparrow has a spare ride in the next race, and I won't be leaving until he's finished and talked to the other owner and trainer. He's driving me home, so I can indulge in something rather stronger than I normally do at this time of day.'

Adam looked at him and grinned. 'I should imagine the last few minutes have been a bit nerve-racking for both of you.'

'You can say that again,' Jay said with feeling.

Having said all they really could about the unfortunate conclusion to Quester's race, Jay promised to call Howard the next day and to come up with a couple of alternative engagements for the horse. 'He certainly appears none the worse for today's exploits,' he reassured his still rather deflated friend, 'and we know he's on top form after today's excellent run until the incident.'

Draining the last of his orange juice, Howard shook Jay by the hand and, giving a nod and a wave in

Adam's direction, he left the bar. Jay picked up his glass and walked across to where the other three men were engaged in earnest conversation, Norman Parry having left the bar a few minutes earlier.

Jay noticed that the two strangers were drinking spirits, and from the smell he guessed bourbon of some sort. He was right, for the Americans had earlier discovered there was no malt whisky in the bar. Adam was sipping his customary glass of champagne.

'These are friends of mine from America,' explained Adam, introducing Icarus and Manfred. 'They're over here on a short holiday, and expressed an interest in seeing some National Hunt racing and learning as much as possible. That's why I brought them here today, and they're off to Sandown on Saturday.'

Jay smiled at them both. 'I'm glad to hear it,' he said. 'It's one of the great British sports.'

'It certainly appears to be exciting,' volunteered Manfred. 'You must be pretty sore at the outcome of the last race.'

'That's true,' admitted Jay, 'but that's National Hunt racing. Our misfortune as Lady Luck hardly smiled on us in the first race either. The owner of Kelly's Hero must think this is his lucky day.'

'I guess a fair number of bookmakers think the same,' suggested Adam. 'Your horse was a pretty hot favourite, and the bookies must be counting their winnings.'

'Well, it's incidents like that, horses who get it wrong or who fall, that make National Hunt exciting. It's more difficult for the punter to forecast the outcome compared with a great number of flat races where form tends to be a reliable guide. Having said that, there are plenty of hot favourites on the flat that fail to make it past the winning post first.'

The two Americans nodded. 'As you know, there's very little jump racing in America,' Icarus said, 'but Manfred and I have backed a fair number of losing favourites in our time.' Manfred smiled in resigned agreement.

As Adam had said nothing about their casino or the business they were in, they left it for Jay to ask or for Adam to volunteer the information. But neither broached the subject, and Jay continued, 'I might well have two or three runners at Sandown on Saturday. The going's a bit wet there at the moment for two of my potential runners, but the weather forecast is good. If it does dry out enough, I'll probably have a runner in the novice hurdle and the handicap chase, and Adam's son is due to ride in the amateur contest.'

'We're not particularly familiar with either of those races,' Icarus explained. 'What are they?'

Jay went on to explain that novice races were for horses that had not won a race the previous season, and handicaps were for reasonably experienced horses who would be carrying varying weights according to their past racecourse performances.

'That's much the same system as we have in our American flat races as far as handicaps are concerned,' Manfred commented.

'I think that system is more or less universal wherever horse racing takes place,' Jay agreed.

'Adam tells us that you are the champion jumps trainer and have been for a number of years now.'

Jay modestly nodded, without embroidery.

'How many horses do you have in your yard?' asked Manfred.

'Approximately a hundred and fifty,' Jay replied, 'thirty of them very young horses who we are bringing on.'

'How on earth do you keep track of them all?' Icarus asked.

'With difficulty,' Jay smiled. 'To be serious, a lot of the horses I've had for two or more years and they rapidly became familiar and even friends. Also we have an excellent and loyal staff, and very quickly I get to associate horses with the grooms who look after them. I can assure you if I get a name wrong I get some pretty old-fashioned looks from their minders who become very protective of their charges.'

'I can imagine that. It must be very exciting for them when their horses do well, and disappointing if they don't.'

'That's absolutely true. If they get hurt or, worse still, killed, most of the staff grieve as if it's a member of their family. By the way,' he said, 'if you do come on Saturday, do get Adam to let me know. I can leave some badges for you, and if you'd like to contact me before my first runner, you can accompany me while I'm saddling and then come with me to the paddock. Both the owners are very easygoing characters and I'm sure they wouldn't mind being joined by friends of Adam. Needless to say,' he said, turning to Adam, 'that includes you.'

'I'll probably take you up on that,' said Adam, 'but of course I don't need a badge to get in. Tolchester Holdings has reciprocal deals with nearly every racecourse in Britain as far as directors are concerned. The badges for Icarus and Manfred I'm sure would be very welcome.'

'I look forward to seeing you on Saturday,' replied Jay. 'I must be off now.'

He shook hands with the two Americans and then Adam, and said, 'Give me a buzz when you've got a moment. I'd like to talk to you about Leo.'

133

Adam looked concerned.

'No, it's nothing to worry about,' Jay reassured him. 'Just an update on how things are going.'

With that he made his way to the weighing room where a slightly resigned David was waiting for him.

'How did it go?' asked Jay.

'The bloody horse ballooned every fence!' replied the young jockey. 'He needs a lot more schooling before he runs over full fences again, and certainly before I ride him.'

'Well, I think we can both put this afternoon down as a bit of a disaster. Did Ali go back with our horses?'

'Yes, guv.'

'OK, over to you.' Jay tossed the car keys to the Sparrow and led the way to his parked car.

Chapter Twelve

Saturday morning came and the two Americans had their normal early breakfast before reading the papers. Andy Best had arranged for each of them to have a copy of the *Racing Post* and they were both studying the paper generally and the Sandown races in particular. Some of it they didn't fully understand but they felt it was important to absorb as much background as they could before they went.

At about half past nine the phone rang. It was Sol Jacobson saying that he would be going to Sandown and would introduce them to the Kent brothers. Manfred, who had answered the phone, asked Sol to hang on for a moment and, putting his hand over the mouthpiece, said quickly to his friend that it looked as if there could be a possible conflict.

'Not at all,' said Icarus. 'Let me have a word with him.'

'Hi, Sol,' he said. 'We're going to Sandown with Adam Forsyth. He's going to watch his son race. We're also meeting Jay Jessop who we saw earlier this week. It seems likely that Percy Cartwright, another of the directors, will be there. We met Norman Parry at Essex Park the other day.'

'That's no problem,' said Sol. 'The Kent brothers are going to be very busy, and if I introduce you to them you can perhaps make arrangements to meet them some other time. They might even be free to have dinner with you tonight.'

'That sounds great,' said Icarus. 'Have you got any more information for us?'

'It's coming along well,' the lawyer replied, 'but give me till say Monday or Tuesday. I'll call you then and hopefully arrange for us to meet. Anyway, I'll see you this afternoon. It looks as if it's going to be a good day weather-wise. I hope you enjoy yourselves.'

With that, in his usual somewhat abrupt way, he hung up.

Icarus explained the situation to Manfred, and they agreed that if the meeting with the Kent brothers went well, they'd see if they could have dinner with them that night.

At half past eleven Andy rang to inform them that a Mr Forsyth was downstairs waiting for them. They put on their jackets, grabbed raincoats, and within minutes were following Adam out to his waiting car. He ushered them into the back, while he sat in the front next to his chauffeur, Jamie. They were soon on their way west. At that time of the morning traffic was light, and thirty-five minutes later they were pulling into the owners' and trainers' car park at Sandown Park on the outskirts of Esher. Jamie quickly opened the rear door, while Adam let himself out of the front and stood waiting for his two American guests. They made their way over to the owners' and trainers' entrance where, as promised, Jay had left badges for the two Americans. They were given race cards, and followed Adam into the racecourse.

They were impressed. The parade ring was large and immaculate, and Adam pointed to the sizeable, attractive brick building with the winner's enclosure in front of it. This housed the jockeys' changing room, the weighing room and also the administrative offices of the racecourse. He then led them into the grandstand, showing them the various restaurants and betting facilities, before going through the stand on to the grass bank between the grandstand itself and the racecourse.

They were surprised by the size of the racecourse. Adam pointed to the famous rhododendron walk which led from the course to the parade ring, and explained the various features of the jumping course. He told them how the six fences down the back straight were famous in jumping, and that it was generally thought that if a horse got the first one right he normally would clear all six. A mistake at any of the earlier ones often resulted in a loss of momentum or errors later on.

He also explained that the last three fences were known as the railway fences. They could see the railway line behind the racecourse, so understood the origin of the name. These jumps came quickly one after the other and demanded concentration as well as natural ability. Pointing out the bend round to the finishing straight, he explained that after the famous Pond fence there was a steep incline where the outcome of many races had changed dramatically. On the first circuit the steeplechase fences included an open ditch. On the final circuit the open ditch was omitted and a plain fence situated alongside it was substituted.

'Come on,' he said cheerfully, 'let's go and have some food.' He'd booked a table in the restaurant, and they were soon seated with a great view of the course itself. Champagne appeared without any apparent request. Manfred and Icarus followed

Adam's choice of prawn cocktail and grilled gammon, and all of them settled for cheese and biscuits rather than a dessert.

They watched the first race from their table, but as soon as it was over Adam shepherded them downstairs as the first of Jay's runners, Green Agenda, was taking part in the two-mile handicap hurdle. He was owned by Percy, who had seen Jay and said he would meet him in the parade ring. Adam led them over to the saddling enclosure where Jay and Danny were calmly saddling the horse. Jay gave them a quick wave, before completing his chores. He then patted the horse on its neck, said something to Danny and walked across to greet Adam and the two Americans.

'What are his chances?' asked Adam.

'I'm not often this confident, but I'm pretty sure he'll be in the first three,' Jay replied. 'He's won his last two races, but although this is a tougher contest the uphill finish will suit him and I'm seriously thinking of moving him up to two and a half miles anyway. What's more, he's won his last two races on the bridle. If you're thinking of backing him, I don't imagine he'll be particularly generous odds,' he continued. 'Come on, let's get into the parade ring.'

They strode to the parade ring and Jay stood chatting to them. They were soon joined by Percy and Jay introduced the Americans to him, explaining that he was the owner. Adam added that Percy was one of the directors of Tolchester Holdings.

The Americans were aware of this and made a mental note to talk to him about the racecourses if the opportunity arose. The jockeys came in and David Sparrow was briefly introduced to the two visitors. He had already met Adam, and of course knew Percy well. He politely touched his cap to all of them, and before any further conversation could take place the mounting bell rang. He and Jay hurried across to Green Agenda who was now standing facing the centre of the ring held by Billy Franks, one of Jay's long-standing stable staff. Sparrow was legged up and the two friends went back to join the rest of the party.

Looking at the two Americans, Jay said, 'If you follow me I'll show you where we'll be watching the races. You can then go and have a look at the book-makers if you want to.'

They nodded and the five of them set off together. Seeing the rails bookmakers, Jay explained that these were the pitches owned by those bookmakers who had credit clients and who took large bets as well. The more normal run-of-the-mill bookmakers, who were still capable of taking large bets, were in three rows behind them in front of the other end of the grandstand. As the Americans walked towards the bookmakers, Sol appeared out of nowhere to greet them.

'If you're going to have a bet, come with me,' he said. 'Even if you're not I'll introduce you to the Kent brothers.'

With the race approaching, all the bookmakers were doing a lively trade. Sol quickly introduced Manfred and Icarus to Garry, who was standing there with an assistant. Tony was walking up and down the rows of other bookmakers looking at anything un-usual in the odds they were offering. Garry, who was expecting the introductions, was polite but clearly under some pressure.

'Perhaps we could meet for a drink after the third race,' he said. 'Would you like a bet?'

Icarus noted that Jay's horse was 2 to 1 favourite. Seemly Haste was second favourite at 4 to 1, the rest were 6 to 1 or more, with the exception of The Last Bid which was 5 to 1. Neither of them would normally have bet in a situation where they knew nothing about the horses or their form, but as a matter of politeness both of them had £50 to win. Adam, who had a bet with another bookmaker, almost bumped into them as they started on their way back. He smiled politely at Sol, who nodded and disappeared. As they walked back towards the grandstand, Adam looked enquiringly at his two guests.

'How did you meet Sol Jacobson?' he asked.

Manfred quickly answered. 'An old friend of ours in Las Vegas asked us to look him up, and he very kindly entertained us the day after we arrived before we saw you.'

Icarus smiled to himself. Coffee in their hotel was hardly Sol entertaining them, he mused.

'During the course of the conversation we explained to Mr Jacobson that we were interested in learning a bit about racing and gambling over here and he said he would introduce us to the Kent brothers who he seems to know reasonably well.'

'Yes, I can imagine he would,' was Adam's enigmatic comment. 'They are extremely successful bookmakers, but I believe they have a rather interesting background. Still, as far as I know they've never done anything illegal, or if they have they've never been caught,' he added with a chuckle.

The Americans smiled at him. By this time they were back in front of Jay and Percy, and climbed the few steps to position themselves alongside the owner and trainer. Jay normally watched races by himself but felt it would be impolite on this occasion, which is why he had suggested they all meet to watch the race together.

The two-mile race started at the beginning of the finishing straight, and within moments the horses were streaming past the grandstand, having already jumped two hurdles. Climbing away round the bend, the nine-horse field was still closely bunched, and jumping the hurdle on the bend the experienced handicappers all cleared it smoothly, although it could be tricky as it was slightly downhill. Entering the back straight, they met the first of the hurdles. By now the field was becoming more strung out. Green Agenda was lying in second position, only a length behind The Last Bid. The two leaders stayed in this order rounding the final bend, but suddenly Seemly Haste emerged from the pursuing pack and made rapid progress before settling in behind the County View horse. Turning for home, the leader was given a quick slap behind the saddle by his jockey and increased the pace. The other two quickly responded and there was no change in the order. Approaching the last obstacle, David Sparrow brought Percy's horse from behind The Last Bid. He closed down to within half a length of the leader as they jumped the last, but now Seemly Haste made an effort and was soon between the two leaders but still half a length down. With a sudden change of pace, he accelerated smoothly away from the hurdle and was soon a length ahead of the other two. David Sparrow responded rapidly and rode as hard as he could. Green Agenda made rapid progress to join Seemly Haste, leaving The Last Bid to head the pursuing pack and struggle for third place. The two leaders fought neck and neck and flashed past the winning post locked together.

The party looked enquiringly at Jay as the announcement came over the loudspeaker that there was a photo finish.

'I've no idea,' Jay answered their unspoken question. 'It was a bloody close call. Let's go and see what the Sparrow thinks.'

Walking quickly towards the end of the rhododendron walk, they waited for the Sparrow to be led in by Billy. All the horses were steaming. Jay looked enquiringly at his jockey.

'What do you think?'

'I've no idea, guv. It was really tight. Either of us could have won. It could even have been a dead heat.'

They walked towards the winners' enclosure, and almost immediately the Sparrow's premonition proved right.

'A dead heat,' was announced over the loudspeaker.

'What happens to the betting?' Manfred enquired.

'What price did you get?' asked Jay.

'2 to 1,' Manfred replied

'You'll get half the odds, so you'll get paid out even money. As the other horse started at 6 to 1, his followers will get 3 to 1.'

'Are you disappointed?' asked Adam.

'A little,' confessed Jay, 'but, to face facts, we were giving plenty of weight away.'

'I'm more than satisfied,' announced Percy. 'I think we may have underestimated the other horse. After all, he was placed in the County Hurdle at Cheltenham last year, and it looks as if he's just coming back to that form. Come on, let's have a drink.' With that he led them purposefully towards the owners' and trainers' bar.

'I'll just go in and see David as he weighs in,' said Jay. 'I want a quick word with him about the going and how he'll ride Front Line in the next race. By the way, if you want to be involved in the saddling or anything, we haven't got very much time.'

The next race was a novice chase and in this the County View runner was owned by Frank Malone. Jay had seen Frank earlier on but it was clear that the big bookmaker didn't want to gatecrash the party in the first race. By the time Jay had reached the saddling enclosure, having agreed with the Sparrow that he would ride a serious waiting game over the two and a half miles, Frank and Lance were already watching the horses walk round the pre-parade ring.

Adam and the two Americans had decided to have a quick drink and had agreed to join Jay in the parade ring.

They all met while Front Line was being led round the ring and the introductions were duly made. This time Jay was rather more cautious about the likely outcome of the race. Frank and Lance were extremely welcoming to the casino owners and had already met Adam on a number of occasions. Asked their purpose in visiting Britain, Manfred decided to be cautious in his reply.

'We're over here for a break but became interested in National Hunt racing as a result of Adam's involvement, and thought we'd like to learn a bit more about it. Needless to say, we were also intrigued to hear that you might be having some Las Vegas-style casinos in Britain.'

Frank nodded but quietly had a shrewd suspicion there was a little more to it than this. He said nothing, but enthused about his horse and announced he was far more confident of Front Line being in the winners' enclosure than Jay had indicated.

Within moments the Sparrow was once more in the ring. He was his usual polite self to the County View party, and was soon on his way accompanied by Jay to mount Front Line. This time the two Americans had decided not to have a bet but had yet to collect their rather modest winnings.

There were fourteen runners in this novice chase which started halfway down the back straight. It was a very competitive race. Three of the horses were running for the first time over fences, which was something of a surprise. Sandown was not an easy course for a horse to have its first experience over the bigger obstacles. On the other hand, all of them had won over hurdles. Of the remaining eleven, one had been placed fourth. Three, including Frank's horse, had had two chase wins, and the rest had all been second or third on more than one occasion. The quality of the field reflected the prize money of just under £20,000 to the winner.

The field was closely bunched over the first three fences, with the pace surprisingly being made by one of the horses which had only previously run over hurdles. This was probably, Jay surmised, to ensure that it had a clear view of the obstacles on its first time over the bigger jumps. Even so, the pace was still distinctly brisk but not suicidal.

There were no untoward incidents by the time they'd passed the winning post for the first time and made their way up the hill round the bend which eventually took them down the back straight. The downhill fence did catch out one of the first-time chasers, who fell, interfering with two of the horses behind him but only causing them to lose a length or two rather than bringing them down. Front Line, which was in the middle of the pack, had avoided any interference, and David maintained his position in touch without overexerting his mount. By the time they'd all cleared the water jump in the back straight, and were approaching the famous railway fences, the field was beginning to spread out. The hurdler was still in the lead but appeared to be tiring slightly and jumping his fences rather more deliberately than he had in the earlier stages. Two of the more experienced horses moved past him between the last two railway fences and were quickly followed by two more. The Sparrow quietly moved up into fifth position. Rounding the bend towards the Pond Fence, the tempo increased, two of the first four began to struggle and the hurdler dropped away quickly. David maintained contact with the two leaders but still stayed approximately a length and a half behind them. All three cleared the Pond Fence with fluency and made their way up towards the final obstacles.

As the two leaders fought it out for supremacy, David stayed in touch and was now a mere length behind the two of them. As instructed, he bided his time but closed to half a length behind the two leaders as they all cleared the last. With half a furlong to the line he asked for an extra effort. Front Line responded immediately and smoothly swept past the two leaders, and to the delight and very vocal support of the Malones, and the slightly more restrained enthusiasm of the rest of the County View party, won by a comfortable two lengths.

Frank and Lance rushed off with Jay to greet and congratulate David Sparrow, leaving Adam and his two guests to wander over by themselves and watch the mandatory photograph-taking of the horse and its connections.

Icarus turned to Adam. 'When's your son riding?'

'The race after next,' replied Adam.

'Do you mind if we wander around?' Icarus

continued. 'If it's all right with you, we'll catch up with you when the horse is being saddled.'

'That's fine,' said Adam, and seeing a racing friend of his he walked over for a chat.

Icarus and Manfred made their way to the Eclipse Bar underneath the grandstand overlooking the paddock. The Kent brothers were there waiting for them, each with a pint of lager in front of him. Tony paid them their modest winnings. Garry asked the Americans, 'What's your poison?' and Tony hurried away before returning with two Glenfiddich and a bottle of mineral water. They slightly diluted their drinks and toasted the two bookmakers. At this moment Sol arrived on the scene and declined the offer of a drink. It was Garry who spoke.

'Sol here has told us of your interest in learning a bit about the UK gambling business and bookmaking in particular. We'd be more than happy to pass on what we can.' Looking at Sol, he asked, 'Would you all like to join us for dinner tonight?'

Sol responded quickly. 'I'm afraid I can't. I've got a long-standing family engagement, but I'm sure that Icarus and Manfred would be delighted. Unless you've got anything else on tonight?' he quickly added, looking at the two Americans.

'I'm afraid we have,' said Manfred. 'Would Wednesday be OK? And we'd like you to be our guests.'

'Fine,' replied Garry, 'but we insist. Would eight thirty be too early?'

'It would suit us fine,' replied Icarus. 'Where shall we meet?'

'You're staying in the Belgravia Boutique, I believe?' Tony enquired.

'That's right,' replied Icarus.

146

'There's a restaurant called Motcomb's in Mobcomb Street which is only a short way from where you're staying. I'm sure your hall porter could point it out. Probably not even worth while getting a taxi.'

'That sounds great,' enthused Icarus. 'Well, I'm sure you need to get back to your pitch and we'd better go and give moral support to Adam Forsyth whose son is riding in the race after this.'

'Right,' said Tony. 'We look forward to seeing you next week.'

With that the two Kent brothers downed the rest of their lager as if programmed together and hurried back to the front of the grandstand.

Icarus looked at Manfred. 'Why did you say Wednesday? I thought we'd agreed tonight.'

'Let's not look too interested, and we're seeing Sol on Monday or Tuesday morning. We don't know what he might add.'

Icarus saw the wisdom of this. 'What's your take on them?'

'Well, they're certainly larger than life.'

'Well, I did tell you,' Sol reminded them. 'Don't give away anything that you really want to keep to yourselves. They're not the most discreet people in London, unless it's their own business,' he added hastily.

'Point taken,' Icarus assured him. 'Manfred and I will have a good council of war before we meet. Right,' he said, 'we'd better go and cheer for Adam's son,' and with that they gave Sol a big smile and turned to go.

'What are you up to?' Manfred asked. 'Do you want to join us?'

'No,' said Sol. 'There are one or two people here I need to talk to. Give me a call on Monday – I'll see how my people are progressing on your information and I'm sure we'll have enough to chat about.'

With that he turned and trotted off in his sparkling Gucci shoes.

'Sol seems a little less than enthusiastic about the brothers,' remarked Manfred, 'particularly as he introduced them to us and they have been clients of his.'

'Perhaps he's just anxious not to seem to be pushing them in our direction,' replied his partner, 'but all three seem a little tricky to me.'

'You're probably right,' agreed Manfred.

The two Americans walked out to the front of the grandstand just in time to see the race before Leo's finishing. Judging from the crowd's reaction it had been a thrilling one, and they guessed that a well-backed horse had probably won especially in view of the queues of punters lining up to collect their winnings.

They wandered slowly over to the now familiar saddling boxes and saw Quiet Menace, a large chestnut horse, being led around the pre-parade ring in the distinctive blue blanket with the County View initials on it. Moments later Jay appeared with a rather earnest-looking young man in riding clothes with a warm quilted jacket on top. This was obviously Leo Forsyth. They noted with interest that Adam was not with them. Jay walked across to them and briefly introduced Leo.

'What are your chances?' asked Icarus.

'Pretty good, but I've got a nasty feeling that I'll be beaten by Bronze Arrow, the favourite. He should have been ridden by Robin Haslett, the champion jockey, who's been injured. Warren Perry is riding him now. I'll probably be second favourite.'

The two Americans nodded understandingly. 'Come on, Leo,' Jay said. 'We've got work to do.'

The two of them walked across to one of the saddling boxes where Quiet Menace was led in by Emma, the new girl who had come with Vicky to join Jay's yard. The horse behaved as well as you'd expect from one who'd won as many point-to-points and chases as this fellow had, and the saddling exercise was completed smoothly with no trouble.

Danny looked questioningly at Jay, who quickly put a wet sponge into the horse's mouth and gave him a pat on the neck.

Turning to Leo, Jay said, 'You'd better go back and get rid of that jacket. It's not that cold today, is it?'

'No,' said Leo, 'and I'm riding in woollen colours, not the silks which I have to on occasions. I'll be plenty warm enough.'

'Right, I'll see you in a few moments.'

Leading the two Americans to the parade ring, Jay explained that this was a hunter chase and that all the runners in it had been qualified by being hunted. All the riders would be amateurs, some would be restricted to riding in point-to-points and this sort of race. Both Leo and Warren Perry had a licence which permitted them to ride in any amateur race. In fact, Warren was so experienced that he was able to ride in any race, although still holding an amateur licence. Leo was only a few rides away from achieving the same status, although he had nothing like the same experience as Warren. Apart from anything else, he was eight years younger.

Walking at a leisurely pace, they were soon standing in the middle of the parade ring where Adam Forsyth was already waiting. He smiled at them and they explained they'd already been over to see Leo's horse saddled and had met his son.

'Well, I hope he wins this afternoon,' said Adam. 'I've spent enough money on buying him horses, and I very much hope he'll win the amateur championship.'

Jay said nothing, but once again thought that Adam was inconsistent in his attitude towards his son's riding. One minute he was expecting the best, and the next minute, if put under pressure by Jay, he would claim he'd be happy for the young man to do well this year and hopefully challenge for the title the following season. At the back of his mind this worried Jay more than he was prepared to acknowledge to anyone apart from Eva.

A few moments later Leo joined them in the rather striking Forsyth colours of a red body, blue sleeves and a white diamond. The cap was red, white and blue hoops.

'I believe in being patriotic,' Adam explained to the Americans. 'That's why the colours are red, white and blue.'

'A few stars instead of the diamond and people might think you're American,' joked Manfred. Adam and Leo joined in the laughter.

The bell rang, Jay looked at Leo and said, 'All right, young man. Let's get on with the job. I've told you what to do, now just go and enjoy yourself.' With that he legged Leo up and walked back to Adam and the two Americans.

'What's the plan?' asked Adam.

'Well, it's a three-mile race, as you know, so I've told Leo to keep out of trouble for the first circuit and a half. Some of these amateurs are not particularly competent. I doubt if all the horses will get round. As

150

soon as they reach the beginning of the back straight the second time, I've told him to make sure he's first or second and as he turns for home approaching the Pond fence I want him to take the lead. His horse really stays and I'm hoping he'll prove too strong for Warren's horse. The big advantage that Warren has is that his horse can quicken at the end, but I hope that our horse will have more stamina and can sap the other's finishing speed by the time they've jumped the last fence.'

They left the parade ring and walked round to the stands where they stood in approximately the same place from which Jay always watched the races. They got a cheery wave from Frank and Lance Malone who had one or two of their friends standing with them and were clearly still enjoying their success in the earlier race.

The horses were all experienced so there were no incidents going to the start, the girths were checked and they were on their way at the first time of asking. As Jay had anticipated, some of the less experienced jockeys got over-excited by the big occasion and large crowd and set off too quickly. Leo stuck to Jay's instructions and was lying third in the main group of nine runners, letting the three tearaways go twenty or so lengths ahead by the time they'd got to the top of the bend, knowing full well they wouldn't last out. There were no fallers by the time they had reached the winning post for the penultimate time, but the field was now strung out and a number of the horses, including the first three, were beginning to struggle. They were soon engulfed by the main pack, and all three of them were pulled up by the time they'd got to the beginning of the back straight. Two more of the main group were also struggling which left seven in contention, with Leo now in third place and Bronze Arrow two horses and five lengths behind him.

Jay was pleased to see that Leo continued at the same pace in the same position jumping the first three fences down the back straight, but moved up to be joint second as they jumped the first of the railway fences. He stayed in this position jumping the next two, and it was clear to Jay that Quiet Menace was still moving easily. Warren Perry had covered every move made by Leo, and there was only one horse between them as they turned for home. Leo had now urged his horse past the leader and was in the lead making his way towards the Pond Fence. He gave his horse a quick kick and they cleared the fence three lengths ahead of Bronze Arrow who had now moved into second place. Leo then looked over his shoulder, which Jay didn't approve of but which was a common fault amongst amateur jockeys.

I'll have a word with him about that, he thought.

Approaching the penultimate fence, Leo gave his horse a slap on the neck and urged him to a greater effort. The horse responded, as Jay had hoped he would, and he gained another length on Warren's horse. He was now the best part of four lengths in the lead approaching the last fence, which again the partnership cleared smoothly. Leo now hit his horse twice behind the saddle, but the horse was going flat out and there was no additional speed to be found. He was, however, showing no sign of flagging and was now five lengths ahead of the favourite.

Jay was keeping his fingers crossed and Adam was saying, 'Hit him harder, Leo, ride him harder.'

Jay said nothing, but was slightly concerned to see Leo hitting his horse several times as if he could hear his father's urgings.

It was now that Warren Perry made his move. Giving his horse one slap behind the saddle, he sat down and urged him on with hands and heels. Slowly but surely he ate into Leo's lead, and with fifty yards to go his horse's head was alongside Leo's knees. Leo hit his horse four more times in quick succession, and in so doing rather unbalanced himself and the horse. Warren just kept on in the same way, and with twenty yards to go moved past Leo to win by a neck.

Adam was clearly furious. 'The young devil threw the bloody race,' he exclaimed angrily to Jay. The two Americans dropped back and said nothing.

Jay went to Leo's defence, although he was secretly displeased with the way in which he had used his whip. 'I thought he rode the horse very competently, Adam. Remember, he's up against a highly experienced and extremely talented rider. Let's not get too disappointed.'

Adam snorted. 'I'll give him a piece of my mind when we get to the winners' enclosure.'

Jay said nothing but gave Adam a hard look. He wasn't sure that it was taken on board.

In the winners' enclosure, it was clear from Leo's expression that he was crestfallen to have lost the race he'd thought he'd won. His father gave him no sympathy.

'You should have won that bloody race,' he ranted. 'You threw it away.'

Leo gave his father an enigmatic look and turned to Jay. 'What do you think, Mr Jessop?' he asked.

'I think you were beaten on the day by a more experienced and extremely good jockey. All you need, Leo, is more experience. Do you think you overused the whip?'

'He didn't use it very effectively,' commented Adam, and turning on his heel he walked away, clearly still in a bad temper.

Jay gave Leo a pat on the shoulder. 'We'll look at the race together on Monday. I think you deserve a day off tomorrow.'

'Thank you, Mr Jessop,' Leo said gratefully.

'By the way, Leo, I wouldn't be surprised if you're in front of the stewards for excessive use of the whip. You've got to give a horse a chance to respond to the whip and you didn't. What's more, by the time you were halfway up the run-in you should have known that the horse wasn't responding to the stick at all. You'd have been better off to just stay balanced and ride him out with hands and heels and perhaps the odd slap on the shoulder.'

Leo did not look pleased at this criticism and walked into the weighing room.

'Got a bit of a problem there?' asked Icarus.

Jay smiled. 'Youthful enthusiasm and inexperience. He'll probably get over it faster than Adam. That man really does want his son to win.'

'Is that for the son's sake or for his?' asked Manfred, giving Jay a penetrating look.

Jay shrugged and smiled. 'Who knows,' he replied. 'Come on, let's join Adam, buy him a drink and see if we can get him in a better mood.'

They found Adam in the owners' and trainers' bar with an open bottle of champagne in front of him. Against their normal custom, the two Americans joined him in a 'spot of fizz', as Adam called it, and so did Jay. The result of the race was not discussed again.

Adam looked at the two casino owners. 'Are you ready to leave now?' he asked, draining his glass.

'We'll just beat the traffic leaving the racecourse as there's another race to come.'

The two of them agreed and finished their drinks. Icarus turned to Jay. 'We've had a great day,' he announced. 'Thank you for looking after us.'

'It's been a pleasure,' said Jay. 'I hope I'll see you at other races before you leave.'

'You sure will,' replied Manfred, 'and thanks again.'

Both of them shook Jay's hand, and Adam gave Jay a far more friendly nod. I'll be in touch,' he said, and the three of them walked off.

Jay quietly poured himself what was left in the bottle of champagne when Frank and Lance joined him. 'Well, Mr Forsyth didn't look too happy about his son's result,' Frank commented.

'You're right,' said Jay, 'but I guess he'll get over it.'

'By the way,' said Frank, 'I noticed those two Americans chatting to the Kent brothers with a rather sharp-looking, smartly dressed man I vaguely recognized, but I can't put my finger on him.'

Jay raised an eyebrow. 'Well, they do own a casino and they are interested in gambling, so who knows? OK, Frank, I'm finished for the day. Well done with your horse. I'm thrilled for you.'

'So am I,' said Frank.

'It was great,' echoed Lance.

Jay smiled, shook both their hands, and made his way to the stable block. Danny was supervising Leo's horse being washed down, and assured Jay that all three horses seemed none the worse for their exertions. Leo had been to see his horse.

'I'll see you back at the yard later tonight,' he promised Jay.

'OK, and thanks for everything this afternoon. I'll give you a well-earned drink when you get back.'

'A touch of Jamesons would go down well,' the Irishman responded.

'It'll be there,' promised Jay, and he set off for the car park where David Sparrow was already sitting in the car waiting to drive his boss home.

As Jay had expected, Leo had been reprimanded by the stewards but he avoided suspension as it was his first offence. A somewhat subdued young man had showered and changed, and walked across to the silver Mini Cooper which he adored. His father would have cheerfully bought him something much flashier, but Leo was conscious of the fact that many of his peers were slightly suspicious of his extremely wealthy background. He did, however, add just about every extra that he could want. This included a CD player, a hands-off mobile telephone system, a black roof and a racehorse silhouette on the side doors.

His mood was somewhat mixed. He was disappointed at the outcome of the race and resentful of the criticism which he'd received. The fact was he knew in his heart of hearts that Warren was a better jockey than he was.

On the other hand he had got a date that night. He was meeting Tania, who he'd now been seeing for seven months. He kept this relationship very discreet. Tania was extremely bright but had dropped out of university. She dabbled with drugs but seemed to stop short of being an addict. She apparently paid for her somewhat extravagant lifestyle by dealing blackjack in one of the more exclusive casinos, supplementing her income by posing for pornographic magazines.

Although his father would have had a heart attack if he'd known of his association with Tania, she was bright, made him laugh, and had taught him things in bed which he'd never dreamed of, let alone experienced.

The phone rang and he saw it was his father. He ignored it and waited until the call had finished. He then switched on the voicemail and heard Adam in a somewhat placatory manner saying that he'd had tough luck in being beaten, and apologizing for his earlier criticism.

Leo frowned and switched the message off.

Back at their hotel, the two Americans reviewed the day. They were impressed with what they'd seen and had actually enjoyed the afternoon, but as always they were constantly looking for an angle that would benefit them. It was Manfred who came up with an interesting idea.

'We both feel there's mileage in the possibility of transmitting English racing to our casinos, and we know there's a bit of a problem with the time difference. We'd be showing their races between eight and eleven in the morning and their evening races from approximately eleven o'clock to two o'clock. We always have a reasonable number of sports punters in at that time, and this would not only give them an additional interest and opportunity but might give us a lever to entice more people into our casinos just to see what this racing is all about. Even if we don't make a lot of money on it, it could generate extra income on the more traditional gambling. We could promote it in the *Las Vegas Adviser* which hits two hundred thousand real punters.'

Icarnus nodded his agreement.

'What's more,' continued Manfred, 'Adam was talking about the fact that all these racecourses have annual members. These tend to be the really serious followers of racing and also, by and large, those with a few more bucks. Perhaps we could use these lists to set up special promotions and charter flights to Vegas. This would be particularly attractive if we owned racecourses or had a decent stake in them.'

The smile on Icarus's face made it quite clear he agreed, before he replied.

'I've been thinking of another angle. Adam was talking about a number of his courses having a fair amount of unused land and the possibility of building hotels on them. Getting a slice of one of the super casinos is going to be tough, and according to Sol they may not even happen. Why don't we build our own casino? Adam was saying how the racetracks were located in good catchment areas, so perhaps we could build a Le Club-type casino on one of the racecourses and develop a decent business, not only with the racegoers but also with the upper end of the casino market in this country.'

'I think that's a hell of an idea.' said Manfred, 'but let's not discuss it with Adam or anyone else, although it won't do any harm to let Sol know we're thinking along those lines.'

Chapter Thirteen

That night Manfred and Icarus went to the Empire Casino in Leicester Square. They found it very different to anything in Vegas. It was classy and well run, but small. Although very busy, it did not seem to have the really big betting customers which Le Club and most of the Vegas casinos had.

Sunday morning found them at a gym that Andy obviously knew well. He then arranged for a massage in their room and discreetly asked if they would like some female company for the evening. They both declined and spent the rest of the evening watching TV, including news from the States.

First thing Monday morning they phoned Jacobson and were told he had enough information for them to meet that morning. He arranged for his car to pick them up in an hour's time. They finished their breakfast and were ready to leave when Andy phoned to say a car was waiting for them. They were dropped outside an elegant Edwardian house in a row of similar buildings, most of which were now converted to offices.

Sol Jacobson walked across to the door and had already opened it when his secretary brought Manfred and Icarus out of the lift and along the corridor to his office. He shook both of them warmly by the hand.

'Would you like anything to drink?' he enquired.

Both shook their heads.

'Thank you, Muriel,' he said. 'Please make sure we're not disturbed.'

'Yes, Mr Jacobson,' she replied, and closed the door.

Sol motioned his two guests across the room to a round table which had a folder and his inevitable yellow pad placed on it. He motioned them to sit down, which they did far enough apart to see each other's faces. They adjusted their chairs so that they were looking at him.

'Well,' he said, 'I've got all the information which is available on the casino situation, but I must tell you that it looks as if it will be a couple of years before any decision is made with regard to future licences. There was a huge hassle after Manchester had been named as the site for the first of these super casinos, both Blackpool and London leading a strong protest, with a great deal of support not only from the localities concerned but also from a substantial number of Members of Parliament. The next round of licences, if and when they are granted, will be done under very close scrutiny, and I think the idea of any significant foreign investment is likely to be strongly opposed. What's more the new Prime Minister looks pretty anti the whole idea. Either way, I imagine this is a situation which is not likely to be of immediate interest to you.

'As far as Tolchester Holdings is concerned, we've made a great deal of progress. Shareholdings are as follows: Adam Forsyth has 20 per cent, Jon Gormley has 10 per cent, as do Jonson, Parry and Raymond. The public have 30 per cent, of which 10 per cent is owned by Lenton, Jenes and Stroud, known by its initials, LJS, a small private bank, 12 per cent by a venture capital company called New Opportunities, of which Forsyth is chairman and owns a controlling interest, and the other 8 per cent by a few private investors. Cartwright and Jessop each have 5 per cent.

'As I said, it is interesting that Adam Forsyth is a substantial shareholder in the venture capital company. This would give him control of at least 32 per cent of the equity and we suspect the bank would vote his way too. He has sent some very lucrative deals their way. He would only need one director or Jessop and Cartwright to vote his way to have control.

'As far as we can ascertain, all the racecourses are profitable. Tolchester racecourse itself is the most profitable and has had the most money ploughed into it, principally by Forsyth himself before the group was put together. Two of the others, Essex and Avon, are more profitable than the other two, and both have had their facilities improved and a significant amount of capital investment. The other two are less profitable, but it appears from the last annual report that there are plans to enhance both of these. Planning permission has been obtained for significant buildings to be put on Essex and we understand that this might include a small hotel. I believe you have met Parry?'

They nodded.

'Gormley is interesting. Although he inherited money he is clearly far richer now. It's not from his wife. He's a bit of a mystery and seems less interested in racing than the other directors.'

'Raymond and Jonson are the other directors. They have private incomes as well as the fees and dividends they receive from Tolchester Holdings, and appear to live quite modestly within their means, but two of them have their secrets. Parry, it seems, gambles heavily, and we understand that he is in debt to a number of bookmakers, including the Kent brothers who you've already met. Raymond is also interesting. Our detective work has uncovered the fact that he keeps a mistress in Holland Park who is some thirty years his junior. She lives very high off the hog and must represent very heavy maintenance. This would seem to be borne out by the fact that he has put up half of his equity as a guarantee to a well-known operator who specializes in lending substantial sums of money at high interest rates to people who can offer him cast-iron sureties against their loans.'

The two Americans looked at each other with interest.

'It seems that Gormley has a number of business interests in the City but is much more low profile than Forsyth and certainly not in the same league. Jonson appears to be the quietest of all and spends most of his time in country pursuits rather than at the races.

'Adam Forsyth also has an interesting side. Apart from owning the largest individual shareholding in Tolchester Holdings and apparently controlling New Opportunities, he seems to have an unusual method of operation when it comes to acquiring companies. Some of them he has just bought outright, put in his own management, built up their profitability and their balance sheet, and sold them on at substantial profits. He has a small group of extremely able and dedicated executives whom he uses as his company doctors. They have all been with him for at least ten years and are clearly well rewarded, hence their loyalty.

'He also has another more questionable way of operating. He buys into a company which is experiencing financial difficulties. He pays slightly over the odds for his equity, but also makes a loan to the company to enable it to invest in more up-to-date machinery, the purchase of smaller but complementary companies if appropriate, or any other sensible form of asset to develop the business. This inevitably results in the company increasing its indebtedness. At this stage Forsyth demands an additional chunk of the company's equity to ensure that he has a controlling interest. If the other shareholders are not prepared to agree to this, he demands the return of his initial loan which leaves them the option of either going into administration or agreeing to his demands. Twice companies have tried to call his bluff and each time he has withdrawn the loan and been prepared to suffer the loss on the initial purchase of his equity. He has subsequently picked up the companies for a song. The fact that he has done this at least twice has discouraged other companies from taking him on.'

'He certainly seems to know how to play hard ball,' commented Manfred.

Icarus smiled knowingly. 'I told you, Manfred, I didn't think he'd be a man to cross,' he reminded his partner.

'As far as Cartwright and Jessop are concerned, I think they would be very difficult to intimidate. Both of them are far too well off to be concerned at any potential loss they might suffer in their investments in Tolchester Holdings. I suspect they would also be the wrong people, if I may quote you, Manfred, to play hard ball with. They both appear to be squeaky clean.

'Anyway, all the facts and figures that I've been able to gather, and also notes on each of the directors, are in this folder. As I mentioned, at least two of them appear to have interesting hobbies. You might like to take it with you and consider it at your leisure. Please call me if you've got any queries or if there is anything else you feel I can furnish you with.'

'There is one other thing, Sol,' Manfred volunteered. 'We were wondering whether it would be possible to build a small but top-class casino on one of the racecourses in the Tolchester Group, something like Le Club but on a smaller scale.'

Sol thought for a moment. 'I guess it's a possibility but planning permission is always a big problem, and you've not only to convince the racecourse directors but also the local authorities, and then you'd have to get a casino licence. I think it might be a hard call but not impossible. Let me give it some thought and I'll come back to you.'

He passed the folder to Manfred who was sitting slightly closer to him than Icarus.

'Changing the subject,' said Sol, 'have you found the Kent brothers of any interest?'

'I'm sure they'll be most useful,' said Icarus. 'We seemed to get on with them rather well at Sandown. We haven't met them since, but we're having dinner with them on Wednesday. Would you like to join us?'

Sol declined, saying that he was meeting another client in Derby that night. Neither of the Americans was at all insistent. The invitation had been out of politeness, as they really preferred to have their meeting alone.

'As a matter of interest, where are you taking them?'

'Well, we enjoyed the Mirabelle so much,' Manfred replied, 'we thought we'd go there, and our hall

164

porter can ensure that we will have a table where we can have a discreet conversation, but they have insisted on a place called Motcomb's.'

'Oh, it's got that far, has it?' commented Sol, with some interest.

'It's nothing tangible,' insisted Icarus. 'It's just that overheard conversations can prove embarrassing, particularly if they're misinterpreted. Although we're in the gambling industry, we always try to err on the side of caution.'

'Very wise, very wise,' agreed Sol. 'My advice is to insist on the Mirabelle if you want to be discreet. Is there anything else I can do for you gentlemen this morning?' He had the knack of indicating when he felt a meeting had served its purpose, at the same time doing it in such a way that it would seldom cause offence.

'Nothing at all,' insisted Manfred. 'You've been most helpful, Sol, and we'll certainly be in touch when we've had a chance to digest the contents of this folder.'

With that Icarus and he stood up, quickly followed by Sol, who almost sprinted across his office to open the door for them.

'I've taken the liberty of having my car wait for you downstairs. Henry will take you wherever you want,' he informed them. 'Have a good day, and I look forward to seeing you soon.'

As soon as they left Sol unlocked one of his desk drawers and took out a notebook. He wrote quickly and then reached for a small tape recorder. Precise instructions were dictated before the tape was placed in an envelope which he addressed himself.

He rang Muriel. 'Send Henry up to me when he gets back, please.'

Forty minutes later the small package was personally delivered into the hands of someone Sol used for his most confidential activities and when discretion was of the utmost importance.

Icarus and Manfred descended in silence, to be met by Muriel who smiled and led them across the foyer to the pavement where the car was waiting for them. They both thanked her, got into the car and asked Henry to take them back to their hotel. During the journey they made no reference to their discussion at all. They occasionally asked the driver about some striking building or other point of interest which they passed.

Back in their rooms, they sat down and looked at each other. 'We really ought to have got another copy of this document,' Manfred announced.

'We don't want to get it copied here,' Icarus said. 'You read it first while I phone the States, then I'll read it and we can discuss it after we've had some lunch and both of us have had a chance to think through what we might do next.'

Icarus phoned downstairs and asked for Andy. 'We'd like a good American-style steak if we can get it in this town,' he informed the head porter.

'The Rib Room at the Carlton Tower is the place for you,' came the reply. 'What time would you like me to make a reservation?'

'Let's say, about one thirty,' said Icarus. This would give them a good hour to read the documents, and knowing how quickly they absorbed this sort of information he was quite sure that would be adequate.

He then phoned Le Club and was put through to Joey, who was still patrolling the gaming rooms. He was not at all surprised, even though by now it was approaching three o'clock in the morning in Vegas. The club's clientele were not small out-of-town gamblers who wanted early nights or to spend their time watching shows or getting smashed in the many and varied bars which were open twenty-four hours a day.

Icarus explained to Joey that they might be staying on for a while longer, and was assured that all was well on the home front.

'Sol has been enormously helpful, but we might want somebody who can do a little discreet detective work for us. It also might entail a little leaning on one or two people,' he told his trusted employee.

'Leave it with me. I'll get back to you within twenty-four hours,' he was promised.

Manfred finished his reading, passed the folder across to Icarus and walked over to their bar. Reaching for a bottle of Glenmorangie, he looked enquiringly at Icarus, who nodded. Two generous measures were poured into the beautifully cut crystal glasses with which the hotel had stocked their bar. Adding a dash of water to each, he passed one to Icarus while he picked up the other. Burying himself in the *Financial Times* and the *Wall Street Journal*, he let his partner plough through the documents that Sol had given them. Twenty minutes later Icarus had finished reading and replaced the papers in his document case.

'Let's go and have some lunch,' he said. 'I think I'll bring this with us. We wouldn't want it getting lost or falling into the wrong hands, would we?' He grinned.

Manfred smiled back in agreement.

Going downstairs, they were met by Andy in the lobby who walked out of the hotel with them and gave them directions for the five- or six-minute walk to the Carlton Tower. On reaching the hotel, they soon found the Rib Room and were greeted like long-lost friends by the head waiter who took them to a table by the window overlooking the square in front of the hotel, and looked meaningfully at the bottle of Glen Grant which had been placed on the table.

'If you would prefer a different whisky, that can of course be arranged, gentlemen, but Andy thought you might like to try this as a change from Glenmorangie which I believe you have favoured in your hotel room.'

The two Americans laughed. 'That Andy is something, isn't he?'

The head waiter joined in their amusement. 'Now, what would you like to eat? I believe you had steaks in mind.'

'That's right,' agreed Icarus.

'We have fine T-bones here. I can also strongly recommend the sirloin.'

Both the Americans settled for his recommendation, confirmed that they liked their steaks rare, they both liked green side salads and they would forgo anything to start. They sat back and grinned at each other. 'That seems to have been a useful morning's work,' Manfred announced. Icarus agreed.

'Well, let's just enjoy our food and the whisky and talk business when we get back to the hotel,' he suggested. Manfred nodded agreement, and they talked about the fight which they'd watched on television the night before and the US stock market until their steaks were served. Silently but appreciatively they demolished their food, but declined coffee, deciding they would have that back in their room where they could also enjoy a Havana cigar each. They settled their bill, walked briskly back to the Belgravia Boutique, ordered the coffee and made their way to their room, Icarus still firmly clasping the document case under his arm. They let themselves in, picking up a message from the Kent brothers which had been slipped under their door. This confirmed that they looked forward to meeting at the Mirabelle not Motcomb's. Removing their jackets, they waited for their coffee which arrived in minutes.

Icarus kicked off. 'Well, it looks as if there are two who might be vulnerable to our approaches, and even if we get their 20 per cent and manage to get the other two 10 per centers on our side, Adam Forsyth would still probably have the ability to block us, particularly with the support of Cartwright and Jessop.'

Manfred nodded his agreement. 'We're clearly going to have to get him on our side, but we've got to think of an angle which is going to make it attractive for him. Once we've shown our hand we're going to be a bit vulnerable, aren't we?'

'That's true,' agreed Icarus. 'Do we try and get a substantial shareholding and then approach Adam, or do we do it the other way round?'

Manfred thought hard for a moment. 'Tough one. I see Forsyth reacting in one of two ways. If we show him we're committed and have already obtained at least 20 per cent of the equity, this might convince him of our enthusiasm enough for him to throw his hand in with us. Initially he would still have control, but I'm sure we'd have ways of changing that situation before too long.'

Icarus smiled grimly. 'I think we can take that as read.'

'The other possibility is that he's really offended and feels we've gone behind his back, and with the support of Cartwright and Jessop, along with, we have to assume, that of the venture capital company, he'd have the whip hand.'

Icarus pondered. 'I think this calls for a charm offensive, though I still think we'd be better off doing it from a position of strength.'

'You're probably right, but I also believe we're going to need some help from whoever Joey finds for us'

'Seems likely,' his colleague replied. 'Now let's think about our conversation with the Kents on Wednesday.'

On Wednesday night the Americans were settled in the Mirabelle a good twenty minutes before the Kent brothers were due. They'd already decided to tell the Cockneys a fair amount about their plans without being too indiscreet. As Manfred had said, 'We'll have to give them a bit of bait if we're going to catch them.'

The brothers entered in their normal ebullient way and, after vigorous handshakes, sat down facing the two casino owners. All four of them polished off a dozen oysters, and for once the two Americans were drinking dry white wine while the bookmakers were sticking to their customary lager. The conversation skipped from jump racing, to the decline in the value of the dollar, the fact that the bloody do-gooders were stopping reasonable people smoking in public, and the Kent brothers' firm belief that global warming was all a lot of tosh. By the time this free-ranging conversation had come to a pause, the main courses were cleared and brandies and coffee put in front of them. The two Kents and Icarus settled back with their Havana cigars, enjoying the last few weeks of this being possible in a restaurant, and they all sipped their brandies.

The contented silence was broken. 'Well, what can we do for you?' asked Garry in his normal direct manner. 'I can't imagine you two gentlemen have flown all the way from Las Vegas just to have an afternoon's racing and then meet us here to talk generalities about what went on at Sandown last Saturday.'

The two Americans glanced at each other and Icarus, with one of his most charming smiles, said, 'Of course we did. What other purpose could we possibly have?'

Both Londoners joined in the mirth and laughed at Icarus's transparent flannel.

'Seeing as you have been direct, we won't beat about the bush,' Icarus continued. 'You know that we own a very successful and exclusive casino in Vegas.' The bookmakers both nodded. 'Well, a lot of people don't realize that quite apart from the normal table gambling games, sports betting is an important part of a lot of casinos. It's very significant with us and we'd like to make it bigger.

'We met Adam Forsyth when he visited our club, and he got us interested in your jump racing. There is nothing really like it in the States.' The brothers nodded understandingly. Icarus pressed on.

'It looks certain that a number of casinos will have betting on Hong Kong racing. We thought it was worth seeing if there was some way in which we could screen racing from the UK into our casino, possibly franchise it out to other casinos as well, and

171

improve not only our turnover but also our profitability. It seems to us that it's much harder for
favourites to win in National Hunt racing that it is in
flat racing.'

'As it happens, that's not the case,' Garry interrupted. 'The proportions are about 30 per cent flat
and 36 per cent jumps, but that still leaves a lot of
beaten favourites.'

It was Manfred who continued. 'That's one of the
two main reasons why we came over. We'd also
heard about these super casinos. Although they look
unlikely now, we thought it might be interesting to
see whether there is an opportunity for our type of
club over here. If we did such a thing it would be very
much like Le Club – upmarket and appealing to the
serious gambler rather than the casual visitor who
goes to a casino sometimes at weekends or on
holiday. We had a look at that new casino near
Leicester Square but it's still not in the same league
as anything in Vegas.'

This time it was Tony who spoke. 'Well, we know
plenty about horse racing as you realize, and the
bookmaking side of that, but damn all about
casinos as neither Garry nor I find them very
interesting. If that doesn't offend you,' he added
hastily.

'Good God, no,' replied Icarus. 'As far as we're
concerned it's strictly a business. You'll seldom see us
gambling unless it's to be sociable with one of the
really high rollers who needs to be well looked after.'

'OK,' said Garry. 'Let's leave the casinos to one
side. I'm sure that Sol will be able to help you there
if you decide you want information. He seems to
have contacts in just about every business in the
country.'

'That's what we thought,' agreed Icarus. 'He does seem to be very well connected and to be a man of integrity.'

'That's for sure. It's one of the reasons why so many villains use him,' explained Tony. 'They like a man who will keep his mouth shut. He also has a very good record when it comes to representing people the police would like to have behind bars, or the tax authorities would dearly like to see paying large sums of money.'

'We'd already heard that,' said Manfred, 'which is one of the main reasons we are using him over here.'

'Well, how can we hep you as far as the horse racing's concerned?' asked Tony.

Manfred took a gamble. 'We'd be interested in getting the television rights in the States for some of the racecourses in this country. We realize it might be difficult with some of the very big racecourses which are owned by the Jockey Club or which stage really big races like the Grand National, but from our point of view medium or smaller sized courses would be fine. We wondered whether you knew any of these which might be struggling, or have directors who might be susceptible to a good offer for their US TV rights – particularly if they've got financial problems.'

The two brothers looked at each other. 'And what would be in it for us if we did give you this sort of information?' Garry's question was almost aggressive.

Icarus ignored the tone and, looking the Londoner straight in the eye, replied, 'We don't expect anyone to do anything for nothing, Garry. You agree to give us that sort of information and, depending on how good it is, we'll make you an offer. This could be a one-off payment up front which would be doubled if the information turned out to be worthwhile, or you might be more interested in a percentage of what we make. Obviously that would take longer and you wouldn't know exactly what your reward would be.'

After a few moments' silence, Garry responded. 'We might be able to do some sort of business. Tony and I will need to think about what information we could give you, and also if it would be worthwhile for us.'

With that he drained his brandy. 'Who's for another?' he asked. Both the Americans decided that being sociable was probably a good idea and, slightly against their better judgement, they agreed. An hour later the Kents were distinctly the worse for wear, having drunk most of a bottle of brandy. Icarus and Manfred had been extremely circumspect in the amount they had consumed, although ensuring that there was always some in their glasses to give the appearance of enjoying themselves as much as the Cockneys.

At ten to one Icarus looked at his watch and explained that the two of them had to telephone their casino in the States as they had something important to discuss with their manager before the busy part of the evening got under way in Vegas. The Kents seemed perfectly happy with this and bade them warm farewells.

On the way out Manfred stopped and paid the bill. 'Good thinking,' Icarus said approvingly. 'It's the sort of gesture that will probably stand us in good stead eventually.'

They walked out into Curzon Street where the doorman already had a cab waiting for them. As was their usual practice, they said nothing important on their way back to the hotel, or indeed until they were settled in their towelling robes, Icarus drawing contentedly on another cigar, while Manfred sipped a large cup of decaffeinated coffee.

'Well?' he asked his partner.

'We've certainly given them something to think about. It will be interesting to see what they come up with. I've got a feeling they probably know quite a lot about the less public aspects of a lot of important people's lives.'

'Well, let's hope that includes some of the directors of Tolchester, as well as any other courses which might be of interest to us.'

'All courses would be of interest to us. It's just how much they would cost us,' was Icarus's response.

Manfred nodded in agreement, drained his cup and got up. 'I'm bushed,' he said. 'I'm off to bed.'

'I'll be doing the same as soon as I've finished this cigar. See you in the morning. I think our dinner guests tonight may have fairly thick heads tomorrow.'

'Well, if they don't they deserve to,' smiled Manfred, and turned to walk back to his room.

Back at the Mirabelle Garry and Tony were far from as drunk as the Americans thought. They were considering the conversation.

'This could be pretty useful for us,' commented Tony. 'If we had a real contact with a few racecourses we could control who had books there and who had the best pitches. It would also give us another opportunity for inside information.'

'The thought hadn't escaped me,' his older brother grinned. 'Let's play these two gents along but keep our options open. This might well fit in with my meeting with Oscar in Paris. Boxer and his mates have been busy – I've got a list of nine informants on our payroll and Oscar is meeting me in Paris to tie it all up.'

'I'll drink to that,' chuckled Tony, and poured the last of the brandy into their glasses.

Chapter Fourteen

The following morning Icarus opened up his laptop and switched it on. There was one significant new email from Joey.

Expect a telephone call from Kerry Nixon. He will help you. Regards, Joey.

He beckoned Manfred, who read the brief message and nodded. Icarus responded to a couple of other messages then closed the computer down.

"Well, I suppose we'd better have serious thoughts before we see this guy,' suggested Manfred. 'What do you think we should do?'

'My view is for him to contact the two that look as if they've got a weakness and approach them to see if they're interested in selling. We're not too sure quite how well off they are, although they're likely to have some sort of financial problem from what Sol said. At least we can find out if they would be amenable to us taking some sort of action, and we needn't do anything if we feel we ought to contact Adam first of all and try and get him on side. They won't know we are behind the contact anyway. We need to be very careful with Norman Parry. He didn't seem stupid but I'm not sure he likes Adam.'

His partner nodded.

At that moment there was a knock on the door and

their breakfast trolley was wheeled in. After they had finished, both of them showered and were dressed for the day when the telephone rang.

'Could I speak to Icarus or Manfred?' a voice with a very slight accent which Manfred did not recognize enquired.

'Who's calling?' was Manfred's response.

'My name is Kerry. Joey asked me to call.'

Manfred's tone was distinctly warmer as he continued. 'Ah yes, Kerry. We were expecting you. How are you fixed today?'

'I checked where your hotel is,' he replied. 'I could be there in half an hour or any other time which suits you today. I am working this evening, however.'

'Hang on a moment,' Manfred said. He put his hand over the receiver and enquired whether half an hour seemed suitable to Icarus. His partner indicated he was in agreement.

'Right. If you know where we are, we'll see you soon.'

'Half an hour later there was knock on the door. Icarus opened it and in walked a man at least six foot two tall. He had the physique of a prizefighter but not the face. Bright blue eyes shone out from an intelligent-looking young face, topped with a thatch of unruly blond hair. He held out his hand and shook both the Americans' in a surprisingly gentle movement. The apparent gentleness did not fool either of them. It was quite clear this was a man with a seriously powerful body, and although his movements were somewhat deliberate, they had the relaxed grace of a snake which was capable of striking like lightning. This was a man to be respected.

Although they did not know it, Nixon was the son of a Ukrainain diplomat who had been based in

England. Christened Jonus Buktas, he already spoke good English by the time he travelled to England aged twelve. He managed to get a place at St Paul's School where he proved to be an extremely adept scholar, and gained entrance to London University to study engineering. By the age of eighteen he had almost completely lost his native accent.

He was already showing a considerable hostility to his homeland and the way it was run. His father, using every diplomatic channel he could, managed to get him British status.

During his last two years at university he began to frequent a number of shady bars and clubs in and around the Soho area. His charm and obvious physical power attracted attention not only from women but from men who saw him as a possible useful accomplice in their criminal activities. Drugs and illegal immigration became two of his specialities. He also gained a reputation for being an efficient and totally trustworthy enforcer. In the last few months he'd moved away from drugs, which he considered were becoming far too risky, but was still involved in illegal immigration. Most of his money was now earned as a very highly valued bodyguard and enforcer. His two aides were called Boris and Valdas. They were also Ukrainian.

Nixon had chosen his Christian name because he had a school friend from that part of Ireland, and his surname because of a secret admiration for the disgraced American president.

'And of what service may I be to you?' he asked, looking from one American to the other.

'Well, there could be quite a number,' replied Icarus, 'but firstly, there are two men we'd like you to contact. We'll give you their names and addresses in

179

a moment. They both own shares in some racecourses in Britain and we want to know if they might be interested in selling. For your information, one is a heavy gambler and appears to owe a lot of money to more than one bookmaker. We believe most of it is to one company. We're not too sure about the financial status of the other one, but he does appear to have an extremely high maintenance mistress.'

At this point Manfred butted in. 'I assume that you don't mind being rather forceful if it seems necessary?' he enquired tactfully.

'Of course not,' came the curt reply.

'Mind you, at this stage we would prefer you to be as gentle and polite as possible. We don't want to alarm these two and have them go running to their board colleagues, although, frankly, we think that with the skeletons they have in their cupboards that's unlikely. It's essential they have no clue of our possible interest.'

Their visitor grinned.

'Do you mind if I ask where you come from?' Icarus enquired. 'By the way, I'm of Greek origin, and Manfred is of German.'

'I was born in the Ukraine.'

Manfred walked over to the desk, wrote down their names and mobile telephone numbers. He then handed Nixon a number of sheets of paper from the file which Sol had provided. 'You might like to read these background notes. Please commit them to memory as we don't want to leave them here.'

Nixon, walked over to the settee and sat down. It seemed he was a very fast reader as he quickly shuffled through the papers. It was equally clear that he had taken in the contents as he asked a couple of highly relevant questions. He then wrote down the two names and their addresses. Handing the papers back to Manfred, he looked from one to the other.

'And how much do I get paid?' he asked.

'What's your normal rate?' asked Icarus.

'I normally charge £1,000 a day if no violence is involved. If it looks as though that is going to be necessary, I shall assess the additional risk involved and talk to you about it. I would hasten to say that I've been involved in this sort of work in England for seven years now and I have never been arrested. I hope that may make you feel that you can trust me. If I need help I charge the same rate for any friends I use but will clear that with you first.' The Americans nodded. 'I'll start straight away then, as will my fee:' With a fleeting smile Nixon rose, crossed to the doors, paused, nodded to each of them in term and left.

'Joey's found us a cool customer there,' Manfred remarked.

'You can say that again,' agreed his partner. 'Let's wait for the action.'

Early the next morning, Kerry Nixon phoned Monty Raymond and Norman Parry. He very convincingly informed both of them that he was working on behalf of a large firm of bookmakers who were interested in possibly acquiring a shareholding in a number of racecourses, and that Tolchester Holdings was among those in which they were interested. He also indicated that his clients would be extremely generous in the terms they would offer for any shareholdings. With little difficulty he persuaded them that discretion was of the utmost importance and that they could rely on any conversation with him being kept completely confidential. He trusted that the same would be true of them. Individually they both assured him of their discretion, and seemed more than a little interested. He wondered how hard they would negotiate.

The first meeting was with Monty Raymond. Nixon had arranged to meet him at the Scratchwood service station on the M1, pointing out that it was about as anonymous a place as he could possibly hope for. At four o'clock, he was sitting as agreed with a copy of the *Racing Post* in front of him and reading the *Financial Times*. Monty entered the café promptly and crossed the floor to Kerry's table. He was dressed in clearly expensive jeans, a white polo neck sweater and a suede jacket. He seemed very confident as he sat down. Declining Kerry's offer of a drink, he suggested they get straight down to business. Kerry explained that his clients were interested in acquiring shares in racecourses and possibly eventual control as part of their overall expansion plans. They felt that any development should be linked to their core business of gambling, but should also have good assets. He had been well briefed by the two Americans on what would seem a plausible approach.

Monty nodded his understanding and then, looking firmly at Kerry, enquired, 'And what price would they be thinking of paying?'

Kerry had been instructed to appear to bargain and to open at 50 per cent above the current AIM price. If Monty baulked at twice the current price, he could then resort to a degree of intimidation.

Kerry named the figure, and the man sitting opposite him smiled. 'You know as well as I do, Mr Nixon, there is no way I'm going to sell you my shares for that price. If you read the company's background you'll see that we forecast a significant increase in profits this year, and if we live up to our expectations the share price will get very close to the figure you've just offered. If I sell to you, you're also getting a foothold in potentially a very valuable piece of real estate.'

Kerry smiled pleasantly and nodded. 'Yes, I can see your point of view. What sort of figure do you have in mind?'

He was not sure whether it was over-confidence or desperation which led the man sitting opposite to say, 'Three times yesterday's closing price. At least that way you'll know that I haven't taken any steps to inflate the base figure before we conclude any negotiations.'

Kerry laughed sarcastically. 'I admire your sense of humour, Mr Raymond, but let's be realistic, there's no way anyone is going to offer you that for 10 per cent of a company, particularly one that will need heavy investment in improvements over the next two or three years.'

'In that case I'm not interested,' replied the Tolchester director.

This time when Kerry spoke there was hardness in his tone. 'Well then, I don't suppose you'll mind your wife and the newspapers knowing about your little love nest in Holland Park and the beautiful Tessa you look after so well.'

Monty's jaw dropped. 'You wouldn't,' he stammered. 'You wouldn't.'

'Oh yes, we would,' replied Kerry. 'Our last offer is twice the price at yesterday's close. Think about it, Mr Raymond. I'll be in touch, but don't think about it too hard.' With that he folded the *Financial Times*, picked up the *Racing Post* and walked rapidly out into the car park before getting into his BMW coupé and driving back to London.

Monty sat there, staggered, then hurried out to his car and drove home. In the local village he walked into the pub and ordered a large brandy. He quickly followed this with another, before driving the mile and a half to his home at a speed which he hoped would ensure that any passing police car would not stop him. As he had anticipated, the roads were virtually deserted, and he drew up in front of his house with a sigh of relief. His relief was even greater when his housekeeper greeted him with the information that Mrs Raymond had gone to London and would probably stay the night as she was going to the theatre at short notice with their daughter Veronica.

Walking across to his bar, he poured himself yet another brandy, lit a cigarette and inhaled deeply while he thought of the implications of his meeting that afternoon. His first instinct had been to call Adam but the more he thought about it the more he felt that would not be wise. Adam could prove as dangerous as the man he'd just met and would be completely unscrupulous in the use of this information to gain control of his shares for himself.

He was highly tempted to go and seek solace with Tessa for the night but dared not get into a car with the amount of alcohol he'd already consumed, and anyway felt that in his current state he might be indiscreet and indulge in pillow talk which would certainly not help his present situation.

In London, Kerry returned to his flat close to the Oxo Tower, made himself a cup of coffee, then sat down and phoned Icarus. 'Contact one has been made,' he told the American. 'I'm seeing number

two at ten o'clock tomorrow. I'll report back afterwards.'

The next morning, shortly before ten o'clock, Kerry
Nixon was sitting in another service station, this time
the one near Reading on the M4. Norman Parry
walked in. He was very different in appearance from
his fellow Tolchester director – taller, much thinner,
with sparse grey hair and a clipped grey military-
style moustache. He was neatly dressed in grey
flannel trousers, blue shirt, a dark blue double-
breasted blazer, and what was obviously a military
tie of some type. He spotted Nixon with the *Racing
Post* and the *Financial Times*, crossed over and sat
down, almost barking his surname at him. Nixon
leant across the table and shook hands with the older
man who did so almost reluctantly.

'Well, I thought I'd come and talk to you and see
what all this is about, but I have to tell you I can't
think of any way in which I would possibly consider
selling my shares in Tolchester. Apart from anything
else, the racecourse has been in the family's hands for
three generations.'

Nixon decided on a rather more direct approach
than yesterday. 'Well, I thought that 140p a share
compared with yesterday's closing price of 70p might
appeal to you,' he suggested.

The older man gave him a hard look. 'I can't
imagine why you'd think that,' he replied. His rather
arrogant manner was beginning to irritate Nixon,
who leant back in his chair and fixed the man opposite him with a cold stare.

'Well, it may not be of interest to you,' he replied,
'but I think it might be of interest to the bookmaker

185

to whom you owe a large sum of money. I'm told they are getting very impatient with your empty promises and no money forthcoming.' Lowering his voice, he said, 'I suggest you think about it carefully. Accidents can happen to people like you, or members of their family,' he added menacingly. He took a small notebook from his pocket, wrote down his mobile number, tore it out and put in front of the now almost speechless Parry. 'Think about it,' he said, 'but not for too long. I would seriously suggest you keep this conversation between ourselves. I hope I've made myself understood.' With that he got up and strode out into the car park, and again drove back to his flat in London.

He was slightly surprised that he'd still heard nothing from Monty Raymond, but decided it was sensible to bring his American paymasters up to date. He dialled one of the numbers he'd been given and Manfred answered.

'I'm ready to report,' said Nixon.

Manfred glanced at his watch and saw it was a quarter to one. 'We're just going out for a quick lunch,' he replied. 'Why don't you meet us here at quarter to three. Is that convenient?'

'Of course,' came the reply. 'I'll see you then.'

Icarus and Manfred had lunch at Motcomb's and returned to the hotel for coffee. Promptly at two forty-five Kerry arrived. He gratefully accepted a cup of black coffee but declined Icarus's offer of a cigar, then gave a detailed account of his meetings with both the directors.

'What do you think they'll do?' was Manfred's question.

Kerry replied almost immediately. 'I'm pretty sure that Raymond will go along with us. He may try to

186

get a little more money, mainly as a face-saver, but I think he's really shaken up at the prospect of his Holland Park activities being exposed. Parry is more difficult to call. He's arrogant, very full of his own importance, but I rather think he might be a bluffer. He's probably the most likely to speak to Forsyth, but on the other hand he's so arrogant he probably wouldn't want it to become general knowledge that he's been bloody stupid when it comes to running up a gambling debt.'

'Well, you've met them both,' said Icarus. 'What would you suggest?'

'I think we should let them sweat it out for a day. If we've heard nothing then I'll call both of them and be a little more threatening. Are you happy with that course of action?'

The Americans looked at each other and nodded. It was Icarus who spoke. 'We'll leave the decision to you. In some ways the less we know the better. I'm sure you understand. If you want to talk to us in confidence you can use one of our mobile phones so you don't have to go through the switchboard.'

'Is there anything else I can do for you?'

'It would be interesting to know which bookmaker he owes money to.'

'That's easy,' replied their guest. 'I already know it's the Kent brothers.'

The two Americans kept poker faces. 'We've met them,' Icarus informed their new employee. 'Do you know them well?'

'Only by reputation,' was the reply. 'They've built up a very big business from nothing, they're hell-bent on expanding it, and they let very little stand in their way.'

'That's interesting,' commented Manfred. 'Well, if you could let us have any other information on them it would be interesting. There's a possibility that we might do some business with them but it's at a very early stage of discussion at the moment.'

Kerry smiled at them. 'If you're going to sup with them, I suggest you use a long spoon, but if you've met them I'm sure you've already come to that conclusion.'

The Americans said nothing, but they both smiled.

'Well, if that's all I'll be on my way,' Kerry said. 'I'll let you know the minute I hear from either of them, but if I haven't heard by tomorrow evening I'll give you a call and we can discuss the next step.'

'Thank you,' said Manfred, and again crossed the room to open the door for the powerful young man, who nodded to both of them and walked out.

'Well, I guess there's nothing we can do apart from wait and see. It's interesting that he knew the Kent brothers are involved with Parry.'

'It sure is,' agreed Manfred. 'He seems to know a hell of a lot!'

Downstairs, Andy politely opened the door for the Americans' visitor and watched as he walked down the steps, crossed the road and got into his BMW which was on a nearby parking meter. He seemed very deep in thought and then made a telephone call. It was several minutes before he started the engine and drove off. Waiting until the car was on the move, but not before he had noted the registration number, Andy phoned Benny.

Andy had always got on well with his brother-in-law, Benny, and they often met for an evening drink when

Andy was not on late duty at the hotel. It was therefore no surprise when Andy phoned Benny and suggested a drink, but it was unusual for him to go anywhere other than the Thames Bargeman which was their normal venue, and certainly not during the day.

'I want to talk to you urgently. It's best if we aren't overheard,' the head porter explained.

Benny thought for a moment. 'Let's make it downstairs in the Oriel in Sloane Square,' he suggested. 'We can get one of those tables in the bar – nobody will overhear us there – and it's a short walk for you.'

This was readily agreed. Two hours later they were sitting with glasses of lager in front of them.

'I'm intrigued,' announced Benny. 'What's on your mind?'

'Well,' replied Andy, 'there's a couple of Americans staying with us. Evidently they own a casino called Le Club in Las Vegas and they're clearly well heeled. What is surprising is some of the company they've been keeping. So far in their first few days with us they've had Sol Jacobson in their room, they've met Adam Forsyth, the owner of the Tolchester racecourse group, and I hear from my friend at the Mirabelle they've entertained the Kent brothers. That in itself was bloody interesting, but today Kerry Nixon arrived for a second time.'

'Blimey,' exclaimed Benny. 'They're certainly mixing with some pretty interesting characters.'

'That's one way of putting it,' smiled Andy, 'but knowing your connections with some of the higher echelons of racing it just occurred to me that it was unusual for them to be meeting all of these characters unless they're planning something here.'

'I agree,' said Benny, 'and it is of interest to me. It seems that the Kent brothers are in some way connected with my friend Jay Jessop, and we've been asked to keep our eyes and ears open to find out if there's anything that he should know about. It's also of interest that Forsyth's son is now riding at Jay's yard. His father is dead keen on him becoming the amateur champion jockey. What's more, Frank Malone has told us there have been some major bets on the chances of his son becoming champion, and some strange incidents have occurred which have certainly enhanced young Forsyth's chances of achieving his or his father's objective.'

He went on to explain the three situations which had led to Jay's and Frank Malone's suspicions. 'What is interesting is the fact that these two Americans now seem to be in touch with Nixon who we all know is a very serious hard man and bloody dangerous too. So far I can think of no way in which he is likely to have been involved in these incidents unless he was responsible for either the wire being put across the gallops or young Lloyd Paterson being beaten up.'

'Either of those would certainly be his style of action,' agreed Andy, 'but does the timing fit in with these incidents? After all, to the best of my knowledge he only met the Americans the day before yesterday, and why would these two Americans be interested in the amateur National Hunt title?'

'That's a very good point,' agreed Benny, 'but something odd is going on there anyway. I'm becoming more and more convinced Harvey Jackson's view is true – coincidences do happen but seldom with the frequency which these seem to have occurred.'

'The other thing,' continued Andy, 'is how would these Americans be benefiting from this? I wouldn't have thought the money would be of any interest to them anyway.'

Benny sipped at his lager, before replying. 'I think you're right. Somebody is clearly interested in the outcome, and the betting is very significant for this title race. Frank says he's never known anything like it. He's known big wagers in the past on the Trainers' Championship and even the champion jockey's title, but never on an amateur.'

'Well, I guess if we can work out who's going to benefit from it, we've got some clue as to who's behind these incidents.'

'You're right,' agreed Benny. 'If we can find out who stands to win, we're halfway there. I'll keep my ears open, and get one or two of my friends to do the same. I'd be grateful if you could let me know what these two Americans are up to, and if they have any other unusual or interesting visitors.'

'Done,' agreed Andy. 'Now, how's the family?' They proceeded to discuss the health and activities of children and grandchildren, and then the rather disappointing form of their two favourite teams, West Ham United as far as Benny was concerned, and Charlton, in Andy's case.

'Well, I'd better get back to work.'

'Thanks, Andy. I owe you.'

'No, you don't, and I'll keep my eyes and ears open.' With a cheery wave, he was on his way.

This is getting interesting, thought Benny. As soon as Andy left he called his brother Angel and suggested they meet for a drink.

'Do you want me to bring along Harry and Robbie?' asked Angel. The four brothers were very

191

close. Robbie was a Cagney lookalike and wasn't as smart as the others. Harry had his own pub in Hackney and only helped Benny if things were really difficult. Benny suggested that it would be fine meeting alone. Both the brothers spoke as little about business as possible in their homes so they agreed to meet at one of their favourite places. The Reef Bar at Paddington was nearly always busy but they had a knack of getting a table where they could talk quietly, and the chances of them being seen or overheard by anyone they knew were remote.

At seven that evening they were sitting opposite each other, bottles of beer in front of them.

'I think we probably need to keep an eye on this Nixon,' Benny started, 'and it's not going to be easy. From what I've heard he's a very competent character and I'm sure he watches his back like a hawk.'

Angel nodded. 'We're getting a bit thin on the ground, aren't we? We're keeping an eye on both the Forsyths, the Kents, the Americans, and now we're looking at following Nixon. We're going to need some more help. Do you think Marvin might be able to give us a bit of extra manpower?'

Benny thought for a moment. 'I'm bloody sure he could, but we'd have to do that through Percy Cartwright. I don't think either Jay or indeed Marvin would be happy with us approaching him directly.'

'I'm sure you're right,' his brother agreed. 'I'll call Jay tonight and I'll see if Harry can lend a hand – particularly during the day when his pub is pretty quiet.'

They finished their beers and agreed to go and have dinner at an Indian restaurant on Hyde Park Square which they'd used a few times in the past. Both being hungry, they polished off their food quickly, and by a quarter to nine Benny was on his way home. Pulling up outside his house, he phoned Jay from the car and explained their situation.

'I'm sure Percy would be happy for Marvin to help you,' Jay assured him. 'I'll give him a call and either he or I will come back to you.'

Benny went into his house where Sonia, his wife, was sitting watching one of her favourite wildlife programmes. She asked how his day had gone, but after years of experience she didn't expect him to go into any great detail. He took off his shoes, put his feet up on a stool and sat contentedly next to her on the settee. He'd gone into the kitchen to make them both a cup of tea when his phone rang. It was neither Jay nor Percy but Marvin Lewis. Benny had worked with Marvin before when Percy's company had been faced with an attempted insurance scam. Marvin was head of security at Cartwright's organization and, like Benny, had a wide range of contacts. On the whole his tended to be at a rather higher level, mainly in the financial world, but he still had a number of skilled and experienced 'foot soldiers' as he liked to call them. Some of these were reliable private detectives, some of them retired policemen or members of Marvin's own security activities.

'I'll be delighted to help you,' he assured Benny. 'Shall we meet at our normal venue?'

'No problem,' said Benny. They agreed ten thirty next morning in the American Bar at the Savoy. Like most of the places where Benny or Marvin met in public, they knew they'd be able to get a table where their conversation would not be easily overheard. This would be particularly true at that time in the morning.

The next day at ten thirty the two men were sitting with cups of coffee in the American Bar. They presented a startling difference in their appearances. Benny was wiry, fit-looking from his regular attendance at the gym, with short greying hair, dressed in clean jeans, trainers, a polo neck sweater and a black leather jacket. Marvin was tall, elegant, immaculately dressed in a charcoal grey suit, with his trademark sparkling white shirt, contrasting vividly with his handsome black looks. Originally from the East End, he had been outstanding at school and was a Cambridge-educated linguist. They had grown not only to respect other but also to form a real friendship.

Benny quickly outlined what was going on: Leo Forsyth and the amateur championship; the three incidents, which looked to be escalating in their ferocity with the beating up of Lloyd-Paterson; the appearance of the two Americans and their links with Adam Forsyth and with the Kent brothers. Now out of the blue Kerry Nixon had turned up too. Benny's group were now so thinly spread that additional manpower was vital if they were to cover all the people involved.

Marvin rapidly grasped the facts and took a couple of sips of his coffee before responding. 'Well, I can certainly find you half a dozen reliable people to help tail this Kerry Nixon. I've heard his name as a hard man but that's as far as my knowledge goes. In view of the fact that he seems to be in some sort of liaison with the Americans, would you like me to take over part of their surveillance as well?'

'Can a duck swim?' was Benny's response. 'I'd bloody love it.'

'Right,' said Marvin. 'I'll get to work on that straightaway. Would you let your brother-in-law know I'm going to be involved?'

'I'll give Andy a call so that he can keep you informed of any developments as well as me. There may be occasions when time is of the essence to keep our tabs on these casino owners. I'll do it now.' Reaching for a mobile phone from his inside pocket Benny pressed a button and within seconds was talking to Andy in his hotel lobby. He quickly explained the situation and handed the phone over to Marvin. Their conversation was brief.

'I'll get my team together, I'll let you know their names, and then perhaps you and I can meet for a drink?'

'That would be great,' said Andy. 'Benny and I sometimes use Number One The Aldwych. How would that suit you?'

'Perfectly' replied Marvin. Is tonight at seven o'clock possible?'

'Absolutely. See you then.'

Marvin passed the phone back to Benny who made some comment about Charlton Athletic, chuckled at Andy's response and said he'd be there that evening as well, if possible. Marvin finished his coffee, looked at the bill and put a £10 note on the table. 'Come on,' he said to Benny. 'Let's get going. We've both got plenty to do. I'll see you at Number One tonight.' He waved to the waiter, pointing to the money on the table, and they both left the Savoy going off in opposite directions, Marvin on his way to Canary Wharf, Benny walking into Covent Garden where he was meeting Angel and Robbie to discuss how they were going to deploy their forces over the next few days.

Chapter Fifteen

Garry Kent boarded the Eurostar to Paris and settled himself in his first-class seat, unaware that he'd been followed by Angel who positioned himself in the nearest economy section hoping that this would prevent him being recognized by the bookmaker. He was wearing a reversible raincoat, light tan on the outside and dark blue on the reverse; in his pocket he had a classic French beret and a pair of heavy horn-rimmed glasses with clear lenses. It was his plan to change his appearance as soon as they left the station in Paris.

They had become aware of Garry's impending trip across the Channel as a result of an overheard conversation between him and Tony in their local near the Elephant and Castle. Angel had discreetly hidden behind the *Sun*, which he was apparently reading avidly from cover to cover.

Arriving in Paris, Angel kept a wary distance behind his quarry and was surprised to see that Garry simply walked out of the station, crossed the road and entered one of the several large cafés opposite the exit. They had assumed that he would take a taxi or have a car waiting for him, and Benny had arranged for one of his Parisian contacts to have a taxi waiting for Angel. Ringing the mobile number he had been given, Angel explained to the waiting taxi driver what had happened. He was quickly reassured that there was no problem and the man would stay on hand in case he was required later. He gave Angel a description of his white Citroën and the registration number, and repeated it slowly so he could write it down.

Before Angel entered the café he changed his appearance as planned, went in and saw Garry sitting at an empty table. He chose one a little way apart but in good view and took out a miniature camera he had with him. Garry ordered an omelette with a cafetière of coffee. Not knowing how long he would have to stay there, Angel ordered croissants and a mug of hot chocolate.

He did not have long to wait before a well-dressed man of medium height with a suntan entered the restaurant, looked around, and seeing Garry walked straight across to him. Surreptitiously Angel took photographs of him while he was still standing and shaking hands with Garry. Fortunately he sat almost facing Angel, who was able to get further shots of him full face as he turned to place his order. The two of them talked earnestly before Garry opened a small briefcase he was carrying and passed across two or three sheets of paper and also a sealed envelope.

If Angel had been able to overhear the conversation, he would have learned that this was a list of names and telephone numbers of contacts at a number of racing yards and details of the Swiss bank account into which their money would be paid, along with each informant's individual bank account number. The envelope contained a very generous initial upfront payment of the retainer which the Kents were paying Oscar.

After little more than forty-five minutes, the two of them got up and walked out. Angel left the required money on the table, pointed it out to the waiter, and followed them. Just outside the café the two men shook hands and went in opposite directions, Garry straight across to the station. Following him at a discreet distance, Angel saw him sit down in the bar and order himself a large brandy. He took out his mobile phone and made a brief call, before ordering another brandy and a black coffee while he read a number of papers which he had removed from his briefcase.

Twenty-five minutes later the next train to London was announced. Garry got up and made his way to the platform. Angel went into the toilets, removed his raincoat and beret and his glasses, and made his way towards the train, carrying the raincoat over his arm. Getting into the carriage, he phoned Benny to tell him he was on his way back and briefly described the meeting. He then phoned the waiting driver and explained he would not be needing him after all. He ordered a beer, took out a thriller which he'd slipped in the raincoat pocket before he left, and settled down for the return journey. He didn't attempt to follow Garry on this occasion, but made his way quickly back to the little office that Benny and his brothers used as their headquarters.

Less than an hour later the film had been developed and they had five prints of each of the photographs which Angel had taken. The face meant nothing to Benny, any of his brothers or his immediate contacts. By the end of the day they'd drawn a complete blank and decided to phone Harvey Jackson. Harvey asked them to leave the photographs at Scotland Yard for his attention, which

Benny promptly arranged. He phoned Jay to report on the day's activities and, after a quick beer with his brother, he was on his way home to spend a quiet evening with Sonia.

It was just before midday the next day that he received a call from Harvey Jackson.

'We know who he met. His name is Oscar Fry. He's a banker who was investigated for embezzling. He repaid the money he owed but was dismissed. The bank did not press charges as they didn't want any adverse publicity which might well have resulted from such a prosecution. It was known that Oscar left the country shortly afterwards and he's now living in Spain just outside Malaga. This possibly explains his association with the Kent brothers.'

Harvey had already relayed this information to Jay, who in turn had informed Frank Malone and Percy. He in turn completed the chain by calling Marvin.

'I'd love to know what was on those sheets of papers that were passed to Oscar,' was Frank's comment.

'So would Benny and Harvey,' replied Jay, 'but it's clear that the Kent brothers are up to something.'

'Surprise, surprise,' was Frank's sarcastic response.

The next day Jay headed towards the owners' and trainers' bar at Fontwell. He saw Frank standing outside. As soon as the bookmaker spotted him he walked quickly over and, taking Jay by the arm, said, 'I want a quiet word with you.' He walked over to one of the benches by the parade ring, which at that time was deserted as it was well before the first race.

'Jay, you'll probably think I'm jumping to mad conclusions but there are some strange things going on around young Leo. First of all, it appears his father has two more substantial bets on him winning the

199

amateur championship. They are not with the Kents. One you could put down to paternal pride, but two becomes a bit suspicious as far as I'm concerned. This is particularly so as there have been a number of other significant bets placed by a well-known gambler and I'm sure that he is doing so for somebody else and not on his own behalf. Interestingly, it seems the Kents are not taking any more bets on Leo.'

Jay looked hard at his owner friend and raised a questioning eyebrow.

'Added to this is the extraordinary event at Robin's gallops, the sudden illness of young Harry Fowler giving Leo an almost dead cert winner, and now Lloyd-Paterson has been beaten up. I tell you, Jay, I'm getting bloody suspicious. I think something's going on and somebody ought to have a good hard look at young Leo. It might not be a bad idea to check out on his father as well, but I suspect if he has done anything he'll have covered his tracks and won't be personally involved.'

Jay frowned. Although he didn't say anything, he'd started to feel uncomfortable about the events of the last few weeks, and also the fact that Leo was steadily climbing up the amateur jockey championship and was now in second place, although still a significant number of wins behind Robin. On the other hand, with Robin still sidelined, and Leo now assured of some plum rides as a result of Lloyd-Paterson's incapacity, it was by no means impossible that Leo should overtake Robin. If this happened he could imagine Adam Forsyth buying horses like a man possessed to ensure that Leo had enough ammunition to maintain his lead. Jay's silence spoke mountains to Frank. He hadn't built his vast betting operation just because he was good at figures and had a great personality. Behind his hearty appearance was a shrewd man with a great deal of experience of all aspects of human nature. He rapidly realized that he'd hit something which rang a bell with his trainer friend.

'If you want my advice you'll get Benny on to this,' he said. 'He's effective and discreet and totally loyal to you and County View.'

'I was thinking the same,' Jay replied. 'In fact, he's already looking at the Robin incident on behalf of his father, and this would really only add another dimension to any enquiries he makes. He's started to check on some of young Leo's activities and is trying to keep an eye on Adam, but it's a tall order. I'd sooner you kept this between ourselves,' he added. 'I don't want Eva or anyone else to be worried. It may all be pure conjecture on our part. We certainly don't want to cast doubts on young Leo's honesty if it all turns out to be without any foundation.'

Frank nodded his agreement. 'Fine,' he said. 'I'll feel more comfortable if we at least try and found out what's going on. I've got one or two of my lads keeping their ears very close to the ground, and we'll know what's happening on the betting front on a daily basis.'

Changing the subject he said, 'By the way, your two American friends are seeing a lot of Sol Jacobson, I hear.'

'Well, do you?' responded Jay. 'I've heard the same from a very good source who is passing on their movements to Benny. I can't see how they are connected with the Leo situation, even though they are very much in touch with Adam.'

'Coincidence again?' queried Frank. 'Come on, we've time for a quick drink before you get busy.'

Chapter Sixteen

Percy was sitting in the back of his car being driven home by his driver, Francis. He was tired and slightly bored, having had one of those days which had been filled with administrative detail and what he considered to be the trivia of running a major business.

His mobile phone rang and Marvin's distinctive voice spoke urgently. 'I need to see you. I've got some information which is highly relevant to one of your enterprises.'

Percy looked at his watch. 'What are you doing this evening?'

'Nothing that can't be changed,' the security man informed him.

'Come round and have dinner with me, and why don't you stay the night?'

'That would be great. What time would you like me there?'

'Let's say half past eight,' Percy replied. 'I'll phone Mrs Armitage and tell her there'll be two of us for dinner. See you then.' He cleared the line and immediately phoned his housekeeper and explained the situation. 'If you make it a cold supper you can leave it out for us and we'll look after ourselves.'

Rather reluctantly Mrs Armitage agreed. 'Is there any wine that you'd like me to open?' she enquired with her normal efficiency.

Percy thought for a moment. 'Pop a bottle of champagne in the fridge, and perhaps you'd be kind enough to open a bottle of the Chilean Merlot.'

'Right, sir,' she said. 'I'll probably still be here when you arrive to check that everything is satisfactory.'

'Thank you, Mrs Armitage. I'll be about another twenty-five minutes.'

Percy sat back and wondered what on earth Marvin could have heard that was so important. He was one of the coolest heads in Percy's organization and never overreacted to anything.

A short while later his car was making its way up the gravel drive and he jumped out. 'Shall I bring your briefcases in?' Francis asked him. 'I'll put the car away. I assume you're not going to use it again tonight, sir?'

'Certainly not,' said Percy. 'I'll see you at seven thirty in the morning.'

'Right, sir. Have a pleasant evening.'

Percy had barely reached the top of the steps when Mrs Armitage opened the door and welcomed him with her normal polite smile. 'I think everything is ready. Perhaps you'd check.' Leading the way into the kitchen, Percy saw that a saucepan of soup was already on the Aga for him to heat when Marvin arrived. Going into the breakfast room, he saw a large piece of cold roast beef with a mixture of salads, and on the side his normal cheese board with five different cheeses and a barrel of biscuits. Alongside this was the already opened bottle of red wine.

'Is that all?' his housekeeper enquired.

'Yes, Mrs Armitage, it really is. Thank you very much, and off you go.'

With another of her warm smiles, she made her way out, and a few moments later he heard the back door close.

He went upstairs, took off his jacket, slipped on an old golfing cardigan, came down, listened to his answerphone and made a note of the messages, none of which were urgent. He'd barely opened the bottle of champagne when the doorbell rang. Moments later he was leading Marvin through to his study, which had two comfortable chairs. He poured each of them a glass of champagne and looked at his head of security, who was also by now a very trusted friend.

'Well, what's the urgency?'

Marvin took a sip of his champagne and launched into a brief but very precise explanation of what had caused him so much concern. Percy looked genuinely amazed.

'Good God,' he said. 'I'd never have believed it.'

'Neither would I,' replied Marvin, 'but I double-checked before I mentioned it to you and there's absolutely no doubt that it's true.'

'Is it likely to become public knowledge, and even more importantly is it likely to lead to a prosecution?'

'At the moment it looks unlikely. It has been so cunningly covered up that unless the Tudors are prepared to go to the police no one else is likely to know. Remember, theirs is a privately owned company.'

Percy nodded. 'So you think he'll get away scot-free?'

'That's the way it looks, but it makes one wonder what else he's been involved in. It might have significant implications as far as you're concerned.'

'I agree,' said Percy, 'but for the time being let's keep this strictly between ourselves. I want to give it some thought before I discuss it with any of my colleagues.'

Marvin made no comment. 'You'll keep me informed if you hear anything else,' Percy continued.

'Of course, and my two friends are still searching to see if anything else crops up.'

'I won't ask you who they are,' volunteered Percy, 'but you might thank them on my behalf. Come on, let's go and have some food.'

The subject was not raised again over dinner as the two men enjoyed the food and the wine, spent a little time talking about other company affairs, but most of it on the forthcoming test match series between England and the West Indies. Although born and raised in England, Marvin was an avid supporter of the West Indies, and Percy, as a member of the MCC, was equally committed to an English victory. Time flew, and by a quarter past eleven the two of them agreed to call it a night. Percy showed Marvin his room, bade his friend goodnight and made his way to his own. The shock of the news he'd received kept his brain racing for a good twenty minutes before he managed to drift into sleep for the six hours before his alarm rang in the morning

By the time he got downstairs, Marvin was sitting in the kitchen and was being chatted to by the, as always, cheerful Mrs Armitage. He already had a half empty glass of orange juice in front of him and a steaming mug of black coffee.

'Good morning, sir,' she greeted Percy brightly. 'Your usual?'

'Yes please, Mrs Armitage,' he said, and within minutes he also had orange juice, black coffee and a bowl of blackcurrant yogurt in front of him.

'I've already offered Mr Lewis some breakfast,' she told Percy, 'but he was insistent all he wanted was juice and coffee.'

'A conservative creature of habit,' Marvin explained with his usual dazzling smile. 'Have you given any more thought to what we discussed last night?' he asked Percy.

'I most certainly have,' responded his host, 'and I've decided to do nothing for the moment. On the other hand it means that I can watch the gentleman's moves if he looks like encroaching more aggressively on my activities. As I said last night, any new information will always be appreciated.'

With that, he picked up *The Times* which, along with a number of other national newspapers, had been neatly placed at the end of the table. Marvin settled for the *Financial Times* and quickly removed the Companies and Markets section, scanning the index at the foot of the page to see if any of the companies mentioned were of particular interest. Drawing a blank, he moved to the stock market pages and checked the prices of shares of companies in which they were interested from their clients' points of view. Dramatic fluctuations in prices were often a warning signal that all was not well, or alternatively that business was booming. Either could have significant bearing on a company's insurance activities.

Finishing his coffee, Percy folded the paper and looked enquiringly at Marvin. His colleague understood the unasked question.

'No, I'm not going to Canary Wharf this morning,' he said, 'I've got a meeting with one of my banking contacts – not about last night's conversation,' he added hastily, 'and then I'll probably catch up with Benny at lunchtime to hear his news.' With that he got up, thanked Mrs Armitage for his supper the night before and her kindness in the morning, and followed his boss out to the drive. Frank was sitting in the Rolls Royce, but leapt out of it the moment he saw Percy. Grinning at Marvin, he nodded in the direction of the gleaming black Porsche which he knew belonged to the head of security.

'Blimey, is that old rust heap still going?' he enquired.

'Just hanging on. Do you know, it still does nearly thirty miles an hour,' Marvin replied with a deadpan face.

Frank chuckled and opened the door for Percy. Marvin waited for the Rolls Royce to leave and, giving Percy a farewell wave, he jumped into his car. It started with a noise which clearly demonstrated the inaccuracy of the recent conversation about his pride and joy.

The man they had been talking about was on his way to the City. He would spend the morning talking discreetly to two men with serious money who had been his close but anonymous business partners for many years. They were men who, like him, were unscrupulous, and were quietly building up a network with major and sometimes controlling interests in small or medium-sized companies in a variety of industries. The one thing these companies had in common was not very dynamic management but the prospect of rapid growth with the right guidance, an injection of capital and more aggressive leadership. The holdings were all held in an offshore company with puppet boards. He was either the chairman or a board member of these individual companies, but none of the directors had an inkling of his true financial interests and less still of his long-term plans.

After nearly two hours of detailed discussion, it was agreed they would expedite their planned strike on the Tudor company.

Eva's mobile phone rang as she got back from taking Max to school.

'Is this a convenient time to speak?'

It was a moment before she recognized Adam Forsyth's voice. 'Absolutely. What can I do for you?'

'Eva, I was very taken with your interest in art and I've just received an invitation for myself and one guest for the opening of the new French Impressionists exhibition at the National Gallery.'

She noted something of an emphasis on the 'one guest'.

'It's next Thursday evening, so it may be rather too short notice for you.'

She thought quickly. She would love to go but what would Jay say? 'I'd love to but can I check Jay's arrangements first and call you back before lunch?'

'Of course, my dear, and use this number. It's my personal mobile. I do hope you can come. It would make my evening. Talk again soon.'

You old charmer, she thought. What are you up to?

She waited until Jay came in for his morning break after the horses had all been exercised and reported the conversation. He looked at her and grinned. 'Well, I can't blame him if he fancies you, but why don't you go? I know you'd love to have a look at those paintings. I seem to remember you saying some of them have never been in England before.'

'That's quite right,' she agreed. 'Why don't you come up and stay the night in the flat and we can have a late supper together?'

'No, you go by yourself. We've got dozens of runners in the next couple of weeks so I'm better off here. Anyway, it will be good to spend a little time alone with Max. You're a big girl now and can look after yourself.'

Eva laughed. 'Don't start taking me for granted,' she joked. 'I'm not past it yet.'

'I certainly know that, and you can prove it tonight.' And with the roguish grin Eva adored, Jay went back into the yard with a mug of coffee in his hand.

Chapter Seventeen

Nixon had still not heard from either of the two Tolchester directors. He phoned Monty Raymond's mobile number and it was answered immediately. The man at the other end slightly surprised Nixon by announcing, 'I've been waiting for your telephone call.'

'I thought you were going to call me.'

'I misunderstood,' was the apologetic response.

'Well, what's your decision?'

There was pause. 'All right, I'll do it, but I want another 20p a share.'

Nixon paused before he answered. 'I told you that was my client's top offer.'

'Well,' replied Monty, 'I'll settle for what I've just said. I'm quite happy to do the deal today or as quickly as it takes. That's my final offer.'

Nixon was surprised at the firmness in the man's voice. 'You've thought of the consequences?' he asked.

'Yes, I have, and they would be extremely unpleasant. I realize that only too well. If I'm going to sell out I will only do so for a very good price and that really is my final offer.'

'I'll talk to my client,' replied Nixon. 'Are you around all today?'

'If I can't talk my phone will be switched off,' Monty informed him, 'but otherwise the answer is yes.'

Nixon paused, put down his phone and stared at it for a while. He was tempted to phone the two Americans but decided that perhaps he'd phone Parry first. He dialled the number and a starchy voice answered.

'I'd expected you to ring me by now,' was Nixon's opening question.

Parry snapped, 'Well, I didn't, did I?'

'What's your reply?'

'Not remotely interested' barked the older man, and put the phone down.

Nixon was genuinely surprised. He thought he'd really shaken Parry and gave the matter some thought before phoning Icarus on his mobile number. Icarus put his hand over the mouthpiece and informed Manfred of the situation.

'Well, let's go for the extra 20p with Raymond,' Manfred suggested. 'It's not going to break us and at least we'd get it tied up.'

Icarus nodded his agreement and told Nixon to put the wheels in motion. Nixon was clearly pleased. They then discussed Norman Parry's reaction.

'I think it's worth our while giving him a real fright,' Nixon suggested.

'That's fine by us,' replied Icarus, 'but we don't want to know any details.'

'Don't worry,' Nixon chuckled down the phone, 'you won't and I hope you won't even read about it. I'll talk to you soon.'

He phoned Monty Raymond back and said his price had been agreed and the papers would be ready by lunchtime the next day. He should go to a bank in Fleet Street where the transaction would take place.

He would call Monty later to finalize the time and contact's name.

Nixon then phoned a number and announced, 'I want to see you and Valdas at our normal place at seven thirty.' The man at the other end of the phone grunted, which Nixon knew was an affirmative.

At seven thirty he walked into the bar at the Eurostar end of Waterloo railway station. Two swarthy men, one in his late thirties and the other a good ten years older, were sitting with beers in front of them, drinking from the bottles. They both looked as though they were used to physical work rather than sitting behind a desk. Nixon sat down opposite them. He spoke quietly in a language which few, if any, of the other customers in the bar would understand. He then passed them a piece of paper with instructions and a hand-drawn map. He nodded to them, put his hand on the shoulder of Boris, the older one, muttered something and left. Valdas put the piece of paper in his pocket. The two of them got up, walked out, and fifteen minutes later they were sitting in a black and rather battered Peugeot. Underneath the bonnet, the engine belied the car's appearance, being highly tuned and capable of doing well over a hundred miles an hour.

Boris drove carefully across London and stopped at a lock-up garage in Wandsworth. Three cans were stowed in the boot and a small device with a lot of wires went into his pocket. Two large and ancient holdalls were already in the boot. They then crossed Harmsworth Bridge and drove down the M4, leaving the motorway at the Maidenhead exit. They went past the town and into the countryside a few miles north of the town itself, then stopped and looked at the map.

It was now dark. They followed the directions carefully, before driving past a gateway with large stone pillars and wrought-iron gates which were closed and almost certainly electronically controlled. They passed the gates and drove half a mile along the road, noting that the perimeter was guarded by a high stone wall. They turned, retraced their route and found that nearly a mile of the stone wall continued in the opposite direction as well.

Getting out, they saw to their surprise that there was just a post and rail fence running from it along what was obviously the boundary of the large house which they could see in the moonlight. They returned to the car. A few hundred yards further down the road they found a small lane with a convenient wide verge. They got out, took their two large holdalls from the boot, locked the car and went back to the post and rail fence. Valdas clambered over it and swore, cursing the fact he had not already donned the gloves both had brought with them. The top rail had barbed wire nailed to it – a precaution to discourage cattle or horses from chewing it. His hand was bleeding quite badly. He warned his companion of the hazard, he passed him the two bags and crawled under the bottom rail.

Although they both had torches, the moonlight was good enough for them to be able to make their way towards the house and its outbuildings without using them. Fifty or so yards from the building they paused. They looked carefully for any signs of security cameras but could see none. They gambled that there were no invisible beams which would trigger off an alarm system.

Pulling up the hoods of their jackets and slipping on their gloves, they made their way towards the buildings. Their objective was to find a garage. They soon saw a building with two large metal doors which were clearly electronically controlled and would swing up to allow access into or out of the garage. They carefully skirted round it and found a window. It was securely closed. Valdas produced a large sink plunger from his bag, damped the rim with spit and pressed it carefully but firmly against the lower window pane. He held it there and passed his companion a glass cutter. Within moments the pane was lying on the grass beside them.

Valdas waited while his companion carefully shone his torch on the window. They saw a simple catch securing the bottom of the window. Valdas reached through and undid it, and the two of them very carefully raised the window. It was surprisingly quiet and obviously well cared for. Clambering through the now open window, Valdas waited while Boris passed him the bags.

Shining his torch round the garage, he saw an ancient but gleaming Bentley. Next to this was a Range Rover Freelander, and beyond that a Fiat Punto. He carefully opened the door of the Bentley and liberally splashed around it the contents of the can of petrol he'd taken from one of the bags. Next he laid a trail of petrol across the floor, emptying the rest of the can over the Freelander. Turning to the bag, he produced another can and repeated the process on the Punto. There was a small amount of petrol left which he poured over the back seats of the Bentley.

He then passed the bag out through the window and his companion passed him a small device. He switched it on and adjusted a dial. It was a small detonator set to go off in twenty minutes' time. Placing it on the front seat of the Bentley, he quickly clambered through the window.

The two men then rapidly left the scene of their activities and returned to where they'd entered. This time both of them scrambled under the bottom rail and made their way down the lane to their car, checking there was no one around.

Fishing the ignition keys out of his pocket, Boris backed the car on to the main road and waited for the next eight or nine minutes to pass. Suddenly there was a loud boom and moments later they saw a sheet of flame leap out of the side of the garage. They assumed this was through the window which they had used for their entry. Without waiting, they drove quickly but not recklessly away from the scene, through Maidenhead on to the motorway and back to their home in Wandsworth.

Boris phoned Nixon and reported the events. Their employer just said, 'Good,' and hung up.

At ten o'clock the next morning Nixon went to Victoria station, found an unoccupied payphone and rang Parry.

'That was just a warning,' he said, and put the phone down.

Meanwhile, at the house forensic experts were going over the smouldering ruins of the garage and the shells of the three cars. A senior policeman rang the front doorbell and was shown into the study where a clearly shaken Norman Parry was sitting. He was drinking black coffee, the aroma and the shaking hands suggesting to the policeman that it was laced with brandy.

'I'm very sorry, sir,' the policeman said sympathetically.

'Not half as bloody sorry as I am,' Parry snarled. 'I've had that Bentley for twenty years and looked after it like a baby.'

He seemed much more concerned about the Bentley than the building or indeed the incident.

'Well, it was clearly arson,' continued the policeman. 'Can you think of anyone who might want to do such a thing?'

'No,' snapped the older man, 'unless it's some bloody local vandals.'

'I don't think that's very likely,' replied the policeman. 'This looks like a well-planned exercise and we've found what looks like the remains of a fairly sophisticated detonating device. Are you sure you can't think of anybody?'

'I've already answered that question. If I bloody well knew I'd tell you,' he added vehemently.

The policeman sighed inwardly. He didn't believe the man sitting opposite him for one moment, but there wasn't much he could do. Reaching into his pocket he withdrew a wallet and placed his business card in front of Parry. 'Well, if you do think of anything please let me know. I'll report to you if forensics find anything useful, but I'm afraid it looks as if whoever carried out the crime knew exactly what they were doing. We'll search the perimeter and see if we can find anything there, but I'm not too hopeful.'

Leaving the building, he talked to the sergeant in charge of the half-dozen policemen who were there. He asked them to search the area carefully, and also to look round the perimeter. He then returned to headquarters in Maidenhead. An hour later the sergeant phoned.

'We've found where they gained entry, and it looks as if two people were involved from the not very clear footprints. It has been pretty dry weather as you know. We have however found some blood on the barbed wire and I'm getting the boys here to take samples. We'll send it back to you for DNA testing.'

'Well done,' replied his boss. 'I'll see you later.'

After scanning the papers, which included no mention of the fire, Nixon called Icarus and brought him up to date.

'What's your next move?' asked the American.

'I'm going to let him stew all today and I'll phone him this evening. 'I'll call him from a public phone box and put on my best Ukarainian accent.'

Icarus chuckled. 'Do you think that will frighten him more than what's already happened to him?'

'No,' replied Nixon. 'I just hope it will confuse him a little more.'

Icarus paused for a moment. 'I've got you,' he said. 'It makes sense. I look forward to hearing from you.' He put the phone down and brought Manfred up to date. In a fairly cheerful mood they walked to the Carlton Tower and enjoyed two more steaks.

The next day Benny phoned Jay. 'There was a big fire at one of the Tolchester directors' homes,' he announced. 'There are strong rumours going around that it wasn't an accident and there's something behind it.' He then proceeded to tell Jay as much as he knew.

'I think you might phone Harvey,' said Jay. 'I'm sure he'd be interested in what you've got to say.'

217

Benny was somewhat reluctant. Although he had a huge respect, indeed some liking for Harvey Jackson, he always felt slightly uncomfortable when talking to the senior policeman about news from his network. Nevertheless, he overcame his reluctance, picked up the phone and used the direct line which Jackson had provided if he needed to contact him. The policeman really didn't want his connection with Benny too well known, not from a sense of embarrassment but because Benny was the sort of contact who could be useful in many ways, particularly if his association with him was not public knowledge.

He listened to what Benny had to say with interest. 'That's very helpful,' he said. 'I'll make some enquiries through the local police force. If I learn anything significant I promise I'll come back to you. If you haven't heard from me within the next twenty-four hours it means we can see no particular connection or that we've no information as yet.'

'Thanks, guv'nor,' said Benny. 'It will be interesting to find out if there is anything suspicious behind it.'

At County View, Jay had been thinking for some time. He phoned Percy and brought him up to date. At the end of the briefing, Percy took Jay by surprise with his next remark. 'It seems to me there's a possibility that this could be a false insurance claim, or alternatively some sort of threat. We need to know if Norman has financial problems, and I'm sure the local police force will be looking into that if they think he is in any way connected with the fire. If it's some sort of threat, I wonder if somebody we know is behind it?'

Jay was genuinely puzzled. 'Who the hell do you think it could be?' he asked.

Percy spoke very slowly. 'Well, Adam Forsyth is pretty upset. At least two of the directors are refusing to go along with his way of thinking on the development of Tolchester Holdings and Parry is one of them. We know Adam has been quite unscrupulous in a number of his business dealings, and we are also beginning to wonder how far he is prepared to go to ensure his son wins the amateur title. It just seems to me that it's a possibility that bears serious thought and some investigation along those lines.'

For once Jay was almost at a loss for words. 'For God's sake, Percy, I know Adam's a tough man but do you really think he'd go so far as to damn nearly kill two young people just so that his son could win the championship?'

'Yes, I do,' said Percy emphatically.

'Well, I'm far from convinced,' retorted Jay. 'And can't believe he'd go to serious criminal lengths to persuade a director to vote his way.'

'We don't know it's the only director,' Percy countered. 'Remember, there are two others who showed only a lukewarm attitude, and one who was as hostile as hell.'

'What do you intend to do?' Jay asked.

'Well, I'm going to talk to Marvin and get him to give Benny as much support as possible, and then I'm going to put my suspicions to Harvey Jackson.'

'For Christ's sake, be careful,' said Jay. 'If you start making accusations like this and they get back to Adam, you're going to be facing a slander case. It's not only going to cost you a lot of money, it won't do your reputation any good.'

'I do realize that,' agreed Percy. 'I'll tread very carefully, and let's face facts. The three men I've mentioned are hardly likely to go shouting my suspicions from the rooftops.'

'I suppose not,' said Jay rather half-heartedly. 'Well, keep me informed.'

While Jay went thoughtfully into the yard to talk to Vicky and Danny about the next few days' racing, Percy wasted no time. Within a few moments Marvin was sitting opposite him and Percy was briefing him on recent events and his suspicions. Marvin in turn brought Percy up to date with his conversations with Benny.

'How do you think we should proceed?' asked Percy.

'I think that any input we can get from Harvey Jackson would be extremely valuable before Benny and I set any more wheels in motion,' the head of security suggested. 'Why don't you try and get him now?'

Percy nodded his agreement. Punching in Harvey Jackson's direct line, he was somewhat surprised and relieved when the policeman answered the phone immediately. Percy explained his thinking, and also Jay's reservations concerning his theory about various incidents and Adam Forsyth's possible involvement.

He was encouraged when Jackson was far less dismissive than Jay had been and explained that Benny had already spoken to him. Once more he trotted out his personal philosophy about apparent coincidences seldom really happening in twos and threes. He'd also learned enough about Adam Forsyth's background to know this was a man who was, to say the least, a very hard nut. Some would even describe him as downright unscrupulous, if not actually guilty of criminal behaviour.

'I totally agree with your decision to get Marvin and Benny to look into the background of this, and as soon as I've got any information from Maidenhead I'll contact Marvin direct. I'll also see what I can find out about our Mr Forsyth.'

Marvin had obviously gained the gist of the conversation and, getting up, told Percy that he would bring Benny up to date and the two of them would meet as soon as Jackson had come back.

Later the same evening, Kerry Nixon left his flat and took a black taxi to Charing Cross station. Phoning Parry's number, he found himself speaking to a woman. 'I'll get my husband,' she informed Kerry, who had put on his best Ukrainian accent. 'Who shall I say is calling?'

'It's Cross Channel Securities, madam,' he answered. 'Your husband has spoken to me about a possible share transfer.'

The wife obviously knew nothing about any such transaction, and from her tone of voice was less than interested. 'I'll get him,' she announced.

A few moments later Parry was on the phone. He was obviously slightly puzzled when he was greeted with, 'Hello, Mr Parry,' in a rather guttural voice. 'I'm phoning on behalf of a colleague who has spoken to you a couple of times. He believes that you will now be prepared to sell your shares in Tolchester Holdings at the price he offered when you last discussed it. The offer is still open and he is convinced you have had an opportunity to see *all* the advantages that such a transaction would have for you.'

'This is nothing short of blackmail,' Parry stuttered.

'I know nothing about that, sir. All I've been told is to inform you that the money will be waiting for you between ten and eleven tomorrow at the Chancery and Chapplestone Private Bank, 20 Fleet Street. There will be a share transfer certificate waiting, and the moment you have signed it and passed it to the manager he will give you the money in cash.'

There was a long silence at the other end of the phone. Eventually Kerry said, 'Are you still there?'

'Yes,' retorted Parry. 'I'm thinking about it.'

'Well, my colleague suggested you should think hard, very hard, before you turn it down.'

There was another pause. 'All right,' he said. 'I'll do it. I'll be there,' and he slammed the phone down.

Kerry then phoned Raymond. This time there was no argument and he explained the same mode of transaction, but this time setting the meeting at between two and three o'clock. He certainly didn't want the two Tolchester directors to be aware of each other's activities. Once it was all set up, he phoned Icarus. His mobile telephone was switched off so Kerry left a message to call him tomorrow morning, any time after six.

Chapter Eighteen

Icarus and Manfred were having another rather late dinner with the Kent brothers. It seemed that the two were launching something of a charm offensive and were saying they'd be delighted to continue assisting the Americans in their attempt to get television rights at certain racecourses.

'Have you thought of buying into any racecourses?' Tony asked.

Both Manfred and Icarus were surprised at the question. 'Hell, no,' was Manfred's immediate reply, accompanied by a gesture from Icarus which obviously showed he was in agreement. Clearly, the Americans were slightly disconcerted. 'Why would we want to do that?' asked Icarus.

'Well,' responded Tony, 'if you had control of the racecourses there would be no argument about you being allowed to broadcast their races in America.'

The casino owners allowed this proposition to hang in the air, apparently considering it. 'We'd have to think about that,' was Manfred's response. 'Racecourses are quite complicated businesses to run, particularly if you don't know anything about them, and I imagine with the amount of real estate they're sitting on they'd be pretty expensive. What's more, we known damn all about jump racing or even the rules over here.'

This time it was Garry who spoke. 'There are always good deals to be done and, as far as running them is concerned, we could make sure that you had good managers. We'd be very happy to act in a general overseeing capacity in view of the many thousands of miles you'd be away from the actual courses. If you decided to take that route we might even consider buying a shareholding in the courses with you.'

The two casino owners looked at each other. 'Clearly this is a bit of a surprise package for us,' replied Icarus. 'We'll have to think about it, but anyway we are most grateful to you for even considering a deal. We'll certainly be back in touch with you,' and he carefully steered the conversation away from the subject, enquiring how well the Kents knew Sol and what their relationship was with him.

The two brothers were rather vague in their response, and claimed that Sol had helped them with a couple of company purchases they had made.

Icarus and Manfred were far from convinced.

Deep in thought, the two Americans returned to their hotel room. For once Manfred poured the two large whiskies and set them down on the table in front of the settee. Both of them took a significant gulp before looking at each other.

'Where the hell did that come from?' asked Icarus. 'Do you think there's been some sort of leak?'

'Well, at first I thought there must have been, but who would know apart from Adam, Nixon and Joey? I'm sure that Nixon's two henchmen don't know who he's working for, and if Nixon is Joey's man, which we have every reason to believe, he's hardly going to shoot his mouth off. In fact, from our fairly brief contacts with them I would have said he was like a bloody clam.'

His partner nodded in agreement.

There were several seconds of silence before either of them spoke again.

'Well, Sol warned us that these two guys were well connected and far from stupid, so perhaps they've been having us watched. They may have seen Kerry Nixon visit us.'

'OK,' replied Manfred, 'but unless they've got ...' He leant across and whispered in Icarus's ear. He stopped in his tracks. 'Oh hell, that hadn't occurred to us.' They both looked shaken.

'I need some fresh air,' said Icarus.

'Me too,' said Manfred. Getting up they walked out of the room, took the lift, and apparently strolled down the street like two men taking a breath of fresh air before they turned in.

Outside, Manfred stopped and looked at his friend.

'If we are being bugged, who the hell do we get to check this out for us? Who of the people we know here are possible suspects?'

Icarus thought. 'Adam might want to know what we're up to. We've already expressed an interest in doing business with him, Nixon knows what we're up to, the Kent brothers seem to have guessed, even it's a wild one, and Sol knows about our various plans. We can't go to any of them without potentially tipping off the person who may well be having our room bugged.'

'Talk about a rock and a hard place,' commented his partner.

They strolled on in silence, apart from Icarus stopping to clip the end off a cigar, light it and puff nervously at it as they walked round the block. Suddenly he stopped. 'What about Andy?' he suggested. 'If he doesn't know somebody who'd do that sort of job for us, nobody will.'

Manfred thought before replying. 'I guess we've really got nothing to lose. I can't think of anyone else.'

'Agreed,' said Icarus. 'We'll talk to him in the morning.'

It was a surprised Andy who at half past seven the next morning got a call from the Americans' room asking if he could spare them a moment.

'We'll be down in a moment,' Manfred insisted.

'Let's take a stroll,' Manfred suggested as they met Andy, who felt distinctly uneasy about the sudden air of confidentiality which seemed to have developed between the two guests and himself, but followed them into the street.

'We think we may have a real problem, Andy,' announced Manfred. 'Something came up in one of our conversations which would indicate that there's a strong possibility our room has been bugged.'

Andy stopped dead in his tracks. 'Blimey, guv'nor,' he said. 'The management would have a bloody fit. Think of the implications with all the diplomats we have staying here.'

Icarus couldn't help smiling. 'Yes, I can see it would be, to say the least, a touch embarrassing for everyone concerned,' he agreed.

'How can I help?' asked Andy. 'Do I tell the management?'

'Christ, no.' replied Icarus. 'That's the last thing we want. To be frank, Andy, we thought you were the sort of guy who might know somebody who could come in and do a sweep. There would be real loot in it for both of you – particularly if it helped us find out who is behind it.'

Andy thought carefully. 'This is bloody tricky,' he mused, as much for his own benefit as that of the Americans. 'You have to give me a few hours. In the meantime I suggest, gentlemen, that you carry on talking as if you didn't think you had been bugged so we don't alert whoever is behind it to the fact that you're on to them.'

With that Andy turned and hurried back, promising he'd be in touch as soon as he had some news. Returning to the hotel, he was very thoughtful as he told his assistant that he was going out.

Phoning Benny, he told him that there was something important he needed to discuss with him and they agreed to meet at No One The Aldwych as soon as Andy came off duty at four thirty that afternoon. Benny was intrigued. It was unlike his brother-in-law to sound either excited or agitated, and he certainly gave the impression that something was bubbling away.

Promptly on time Andy walked in to find Benny already seated with two glasses of lager in front of him. Andy grinned, sat down and took a long gulp. He then put the glass down and, looking straight at Benny, told him the news, leaving out none of the details of his extraordinary conversation with the two Americans.

Benny whistled. 'Christ, I wish we'd done that before they moved in,' he said.

'What shall we do?' Andy demanded.

'Well, first of all we'll get somebody to do what we've been asked. Old Sparky Benson will do that without any trouble. But while we're at it, I think we ought to put another one in. Sparky is an absolute genius and I'm sure while he's looking around he can find a spot where they'd never think of looking. What's more, they'll probably think it's highly unlikely that lightning's going to strike twice in the same place.'

Andy grinned. 'You're a bloody genius, you know, Benny.'

'I do my best,' was the modest reply, accompanied by a deep chuckle.

Benny immediately pulled out his mobile phone, called Sparky and explained he needed a job done quickly, possibly that night. Sparky said it would be no problem and requested details. Benny handed the phone over to Andy, who briefed the bugging expert in a matter of moments.

'I'll meet you at the hotel,' he said, 'but I'll call you back to make sure they're going to be there, or if they're not that they're happy for us to go in.'

He finished the call with Sparky, took out his own phone and called Icarus on the mobile number he had been given. Icarus answered. Andy explained that he could get someone who was completely discreet round that evening within about an hour to an hour and a half. Icarus was more than happy.

'We were going out but we'll hang on if this is important,' he informed Andy.

'If you like, guv'nor. I'm very happy to come round and stay with him the whole time he's doing it. I don't know the geezer but he does come very highly recommended.'

Icarus sucked his teeth. 'Go ahead and fix him up. I'll talk to Manfred. Call me back in ten minutes and I'll say if we'll be here or not.'

Icarus explained the situation to Manfred, who immediately made a decision. 'Look, we've arranged to see the Kents tonight. It might seem a bit suspicious if we cancel at the last minute, particularly if both of us do, and anyway you never know what we might glean while talking to them. Let's keep our cards very close to our chests.'

Icarus nodded his agreement. They waited for ten minutes and, as promised, Andy phoned promptly. They assured him that they trusted him completely and looked forward to hearing whether or not they were being bugged or if it was just a weird coincidence.

Showering, putting on clean shirts and freshly pressed trousers and jackets, they were soon on their way to the Wolseley where the Kents had booked a table. Unbeknown to them, they were being followed by Jerry Downs, one of Benny's men, and also another guy who an expert would have known was a professional at tailing. He watched Jerry as carefully as he did the Americans. Approaching the Wolseley, Jerry Downs was still unaware that he was being followed. He waited for a few moments before entering the restaurant and looked to see where the Americans had gone. He saw they were standing on the balcony shaking hands with two men whom he recognized immediately as the Kent brothers. He wasn't particularly familiar with the Wolseley but he was observant enough to note that the tables up there were rather more widely spaced than the ones downstairs. Smiling apologetically to the head waiter, he explained he'd come into the wrong place and retreated quickly. Turning round the corner in Piccadilly, he went down past the side entrance of the Ritz and phoned Benny.

'Go and have a cup of coffee or something at the café opposite and give them forty-five minutes,' his East End chum instructed. 'Come out and keep in the shadows of the shops opposite. If any copper asks you what you're up to, say you're a reporter and hoping to get a quick interview with one of the celebs inside.'

Benny had already taken the precaution of giving a forged press pass to the man he'd employed as a tail.

Meanwhile, the other tail watched everything carefully. He had not bothered to go into the restaurant as he knew full well who the Americans were meeting. He waited for a few moments before walking down past the Ritz where he noticed the glow of a cigarette end as Jerry took the opportunity to have a quick drag before going into a café in which he knew there would be no smoking. The second tail walked slowly down, pulling a packet of cigarettes out of his pocket and put one between his lips. Casually he approached Jerry.

'I see you're smoking, mate' he said in as broad a London accent as he could summon. 'Could you give me a light?'

Jerry nodded and reached into his pocket for the lighter he always carried. In a flash a flick knife was in the other man's hand and it was driven straight in between the ribs just below the East Ender's heart. With a noise between a gasp and a gurgle, he shuddered and sank to his knees. The other man carefully wiped the blade on his victim's coat and walked nonchalantly away. He had checked there was no one else nearby.

Turning into St James's, he crossed the street, walked down to Piccadilly Circus and took a tube to Knightsbridge. There he got out, hailed a taxi and went home to his apartment.

Once inside Kerry Nixon removed his gloves and checked all over his raincoat to see if there were any marks. There were none. Putting the gloves and the raincoat into a small holdall, he looked carefully at his shoes. Again he could see nothing, but with his immaculate attention to detail he removed those and his trousers and placed them in the bag as well. He then changed into a pair of jeans, a heavy polo neck sweater and a dark blue windcheater.

Taking the lift to the basement garage, he ignored his BMW and got into an old Peugeot, drove through the City and down into the old dockland area. Parking and locking his car, he carried the holdall which he had removed from the boot, unzipped it and walked across to a nearby building site. Outside it were a few broken breezeblocks which had clearly been rejected as construction had got under way. He picked up two sizeable lumps of masonry, popped them into the holdall, zipped it up, walked down to the river and out on to a small pier. Making sure that he was in deep shadow on the edge of the Thames, he tossed it as far as he could, brushed his gloved hands together, walked back to his car and drove home.

Benny was sitting at home watching TV with Sonia, when the phone rang.

'It's Luke here. Dad's dead.'

Benny nearly dropped the phone. Luke was Jerry Downs' son and Benny's godson.

'What the hell happened?' he asked.

'He's been murdered,' said Luke. 'The police have just been round to tell Mum and me. She's distraught.'

'I'll be round in a few minutes,' he promised. 'Give her my love. I'll see you.'

Sonia, knew immediately from the look on his face that something serious had happened.

'What's wrong, Benny?'

'Jerry's been murdered. I'm off to see Mavis and Luke now.'

had happened and that they wanted information. Benny made a quick mental note of where Angel had been and named a number of places which he would cover himself. This would take both of them well into the early hours of the morning and they agreed that they'd meet at Benny's place at eight o'clock unless one of them dug up some dramatic information in the meantime.

Benny then phoned Harvey Jackson's number and was not surprised he was on voicemail. 'It's Benny here, Mr Jackson,' he announced to the tape. 'I know the guy who was murdered near the Ritz tonight and what he was doing. He was a close mate of mine and I'd like to talk to you. I'll be obtainable on the phone until about four o'clock this morning and then I'm going to grab some sleep, but I'll be on hand again from eight in the morning. I hope I haven't disturbed you. Goodnight, Mr Jackson,' and he hung up.

Driving slowly and thoughtfully, Benny made his way to the first of the drinking clubs. He was recognized by the doorman and went down into the bar. Morgan Blackstone, the owner, was sitting at a table with a group of his regular cronies. Seeing Benny, he stood up and came across, giving him a warm smile and a firm handshake. He immediately sensed that Benny was there on a serious mission. Benny nodded in the direction of the man's office. Morgan understood, turned and led him into the small glassed-off area where he did what little paperwork was needed to run the club, and closed the door.

Benny succinctly described how Jerry had been murdered, making it clear that they wanted information urgently and that it would be well rewarded. Morgan understood and said he'd pass the word round.

As Benny left, his phone rang. It was Harvey Jackson, the policeman he'd phoned as soon as he left the Downs' House.

'I've got a little information for you, Benny,' he said. 'Jerry was murdered in Arlington Place which runs down the side of the Ritz. He was apparently standing in one of the doorways not very far from the pub on the corner. Whoever did it must have been very quick because a fair number of people go in and out of that pub or use that entrance to the Ritz at that time of night. The main entrance on Piccadilly is closed. Jerry was smoking a cigarette when it happened so he was probably standing still. He was certainly facing his killer who knew how to handle a knife. The stab was just under the heart and death would have been almost instantaneous. That's all we know for now. There will be a post-mortem first thing in the morning. We'll keep Mrs Downs and Luke informed about what's happening. If I get further information you'll have it straightaway.'

'Thanks, Sid. Much appreciated.' Starting his car, Benny made his way to the next port of call. By half past three in the morning he'd covered eleven bars, clubs and snooker halls, and was completely bushed. Getting back to his house he let himself in quietly and, removing his shoes, crept upstairs into the spare room. Taking off his jacket and trousers, he pulled up a duvet, set the alarm on his wristwatch, and fell into a deep sleep before the watch brought him reluctantly back to consciousness.

At eight o'clock Angel and Benny were sitting in his kitchen eating a huge fry-up provided by the ever busy Sonia. Neither had any new information, but they both realized it was unlikely that even the East End grapevine would have worked that quickly.

They made a list of other places they would visit, and phone calls to make, and were both drinking their second mug of tea when Benny's phone rang. It was Harvey Jackson.

'You've got some information for me, Benny.' His manner was abrupt as always on the phone.

'Yes, Mr Jackson. Could you spare me a few minutes this morning?'

'Sure,' said the policeman. 'Let's not meet near the Yard. How about the Pegasus just off Berkeley Square?'

'Done,' said Benny. 'I know the pub well. It's one of Jay's favourite haunts. It's only just around the corner from his London pad.'

'I know,' replied Jackson. 'That's how I got to know it. Paddy Mullins, the publican, is on good terms with me. He'll give us a room upstairs. Just ask for me when you get there. If I'm not there he'll show you up until I arrive. Would eleven o'clock suit?'

'Sure.'

'By that time I'll have been able to find out anything that the boys at this end have put together,' promised the policeman.

'Thanks, Mr Jackson,' replied Benny. 'If I've got any more news by then you can be sure you'll get it.'

'I know, Benny,' replied Jackson. 'See you in a couple of hours.'

At five to eleven Benny walked into the Pegasus and asked for Mr Mullins.

'That's me,' said the burly man in shirtsleeves behind the bar. 'What can I do for you?'

'I'm meeting Mr Jackson,' he replied.

'Ah, he's here already. Come with me.'

He went upstairs, opened a door, and there seated in a surprisingly large room at what Benny suspected was a large card table was Harvey Jackson with a rather younger and earnest-looking man next to him. 'This is Detective Sergeant Barlow,' explained Jackson. He's one of my personal assistants and he's been digging into the events of last night. Sit down.' He motioned Benny to one of the several empty chairs round the table.

'Tell Benny what we know, Gordon,' Jackson instructed the young detective sergeant.

Very deliberately the policeman withdrew a notebook from his pocket, opened it and glanced at it. 'We know the murder took place at approximately nine thirty last night. We also know that Downs had walked into the Wolseley Restaurant and looked around, spoke briefly to the head waiter and walked out. He apparently walked round the corner into Arlington Place, which runs down past the side entrance to the Ritz, and stood in a doorway smoking a cigarette when his assailant approached and stabbed him once – very accurately under the heart. He would have died almost instantaneously. The assailant was obviously a fairly cool character because he wiped the blood from the blade on to his victim's jacket and left the scene. As far as we can tell, nobody saw the incident, but two of our men on the beat did notice a tall man walking quickly but not obviously in a hurry down past Fortnum & Mason towards Piccadilly Circus. They noticed him, not because he was doing anything suspicious, but simply because he was taller and appeared to be intent on going somewhere rather than the few other people walking along at that time of night who were meandering, chatting to each other or looking in shop windows.'

Referring to his notebook again, he continued. 'We also know that two Americans joined the Kent brothers, the bookmakers, at their table upstairs. We've not yet been able to trace who these two Americans are.'

'I can tell you that,' interrupted Benny. 'Their names are Icarus Mauros and Manfred Rozenberg They own a casino called Le Club in Las Vegas, and they are currently staying at the Boutique Hotel in Belgravia.'

Both the policemen looked slightly surprised. 'And how would you know that, Benny?' questioned Jackson.

'Because Jerry Downs was following these two men on my instructions.'

The two policemen now looked really surprised. 'And why would that be?'

'Well, Mr Jackson,' said Benny, 'you may know that there have been some strange betting activities taking place in conjunction with a young amateur jockey called Leo Forsyth. You probably know he's the son of a highly successful, very tough businessman called Adam Forsyth who controls the Tolchester Group of racecourses. I and my friends have been engaged to try and find out what's going on behind this betting, and also to get to the bottom of the wire incident at the Hasletts' farm and the subsequent beating up of Lloyd-Paterson.'

Jackson paused to let this information sink in. 'Well, we've also got something of an interest in Tolchester Holdings,' he said. 'One of the directors has suffered a major arson attack at his home and he refuses to admit that it could be deliberate, although we know it most certainly was.'

Benny surprised Jackson again. 'Well, Marvin Lewis, Percy Cartwright's guy, has been keeping an eye on these two Americans, and also on the directors

238

of Tolchester Holdings. It seems that two of the directors, Monty Raymond and Norman Parry, have been seeing a Ukrainian who uses the name Kerry Nixon in this country.'

Jackson whistled between his teeth. 'We know this man well. He has been connected with a number of violent incidents, and in some cases lethal ones, but so far none of them have been pinned on him. He's extremely clever and doesn't take unnecessary risks. He also only works with a very small group of foreigners who are capable of being just as violent as Nixon but don't have his brains.'

Jackson paused, and smiled before continuing. 'My, Benny, you and your chums are busy little bees, aren't you? Where the hell are you getting all the manpower from?'

Benny grinned. 'Well, the short answer to that is that Marvin Lewis, Percy Cartwright's head of security, is working with me on some of these fronts and he's covering quite a lot of the ground. As you know, Marvin and I have worked together before and the relationship is always very easy. We don't tread on each other's toes, and in fact we rather like working together. I've got a few other mates helping too.'

Jackson smiled again. 'Some would say you were rather odd bedfellows, but I remember that's very true from previous activities. Well, let's get back to the question in hand. Let me summarize my understanding. There is some odd betting going on which indicates that somebody expects Leo Forsyth to win the amateur championship, though at the time when the bets were first placed he was well behind the current champion. Since then an attempt has been made to at least injure the champion, if not actually kill him, and one of his best horses had to be put down. Next, one of Forsyth's amateur rivals was taken ill the day after having dinner with Forsyth junior. He was unable to ride, Forsyth got the ride and duly won. Thirdly, another key amateur with a lot of rides was beaten up so badly he had to give up his rides for some weeks, and again the beneficiary has been Leo Forsyth.'

'That's exactly the situation,' Benny said. 'On top of that, we have been checking on young Forsyth and he has been making rather mysterious nocturnal visits to some land near the Hasletts' farm, but we haven't yet found out exactly what he's doing. Incidentally, he's also having an affair with a croupier at one of the better-known London casinos. It's known that she is a drug user and she also enhances her income by posing for porn magazines.'

Jackson raised an eyebrow. 'We weren't aware of that. So, we have two American casino owners who have suddenly appeared, are having numerous meetings with both Adam Forsyth and two of the more dubious bookmakers, the Kent brothers, and are now in contact with Nixon. They have also had a number of meetings with Sol Jacobson, who we all know is more than happy to work for some of the more shady characters on the London scene.'

'A slight understatement,' grunted Benny.

'Next, one of the directors of Tolchester Holdings is subjected to an arson attack and refuses to cast any light on a possible motive.'

Benny interrupted. 'Here again I can add to our knowledge. Marvin has been checking on Tolchester Holdings and it seems that Norman Parry has an expensive gambling habit, and Monty Raymond an extremely expensive bird he keeps in Holland Park. Each of them has 10 per cent of the equity of

Tolchester Holdings. Over the last few days both of them have been tailed by Marvin's men and they have both been to a small private bank in Fleet Street. Marvin is of the opinion that both of them have sold part or all of their equity in Tolchester Holdings to finance their two expensive habits.'

'Now that is interesting,' said Jackson. 'What's the name of the bank?'

Benny told him and Jackson made a note. Passing it to Barlow, he said, 'I want you to find out all you can about the bank. Be heavy if necessary and find out what, if any, transaction took place between these two men on their separate visits to the bank.'

Benny decided not to mention Marvin had a very good friend in a senior position in the bank.

The young policeman took the paper, folded it and carefully put it into his notepad.

Jackson looked from Barlow to Benny. 'Anything else?' They both shook their heads. 'Right, let get on with it. Keep in touch, Benny.'

'Of course, Mr Jackson.'

They all rose and made their way downstairs. The policeman stopped to thank Paddy Mullins, while Benny made his way to his car. He swore when he saw the parking ticket, got in, phoned Marvin, and drove off to meet him in Covent Garden.

Nixon's mobile rang. He immediately recognized the number. There was no greeting, just, 'The bug isn't working. Find out why.' The line went dead.

Nixon swore to himself. It was one thing to get it in before the Americans arrived – a totally different proposition to search their room. For once he was at a loss.

Chapter Nineteen

At the end of the afternoon Leo entered Jay's office. Looking slightly uncomfortable, he announced. 'I've had a telephone call from Angus Lanton. He's asked if I can ride The Illuminator and Sultan in Waiting next week.' Still looking anxious, he waited for Jay's response.

'Well?'

'I thought I should ask you before I committed myself.'

'I bet you did,' Jay laughed. 'Of course you can. You're an amateur and you're not employed by us, even though you work extremely hard here.'

Encouraged, Leo continued. 'He's promised me at least another three rides on each of them in the next few weeks.'

'That's fantastic news, Leo,' replied Jay. 'That'll certainly give your attempt to win the amateur title a real boost.'

'Yes, I suppose it will,' the young man replied with rather forced diffidence. 'It's OK then?'

'Of course,' replied Jay. 'See you in the morning, Leo.'

The younger man grinned, turned round and closed the door after him.

Jay gazed thoughtfully at his pad and picked up the internal phone connected to the yard. 'Is Vicky around?' he asked Danny, who had picked up the receiver.

'Yes, do you want her?'

'No, just give her a message. Could she pop in and have a word with me when she's finished what she's doing. There's no hurry at all.'

'Right, guv'nor,' came the cheerful response.

Jay thought for a moment or two, then resumed the paperwork which was so much part of running such a large training establishment but was not one of his favourite aspects of the job. Forty minutes later there was a knock on the door and Vicky walked straight in. She'd very quickly made herself an integral part of County View and Jay had come to respect her judgement more and more. She was rapidly becoming the confidant and sounding board which Jed had been for so many years.

'Take a seat,' he said. 'Why don't you have a cigarette? I'm going to have a cigar.'

'Thanks, Jay.' She reached into a pocket of the light jacket that she wore around the yard when not riding and produced a pack of tobacco and a small machine which she used to expertly roll her own cigarettes. Jay finished completing the form he had been working on, leant over and lit her cigarette, then clipped a cigar and lit it.

'Leo's popped in and sprung a bit of surprise,' he said. 'I'd like your views.' He summarized the conversation which he'd had with Leo and waited for Vicky to respond. She pursed her lips and thought hard before venturing an opinion.

'Well, it's fantastic for him, but what's Angus up to? These are top-class horses and they're capable of winning much better prize money than they're going to pick up in run-of-the-mill amateur hurdles and

243

chases. Last season Sultan in Waiting was one of the top novice chasers, and The Illuminator won some very decent handicap hurdles. He was second in that big race at Kempton. I agree. It's very strange. Do you think Angus has been paid for this?'

'We know that he's a good trainer and we also know that the yard does gamble from time to time, as far as I know rather successfully. However, there does seem to be somebody seriously concerned about young Leo winning this title and I wouldn't put it past his father to do some sort of deal to ensure that he gets a number of almost cast-iron winning rides.'

'You know him far better than I do,' said Vicky, 'but if he picked up six wins between these two horses plus those he has with us, he would be very much in the driving seat with Robin still not fully fit.'

'That had occurred to me,' Jay agreed, 'and when I put the point to young Leo he seemed rather diffident, almost pretending he hadn't thought of that likelihood.'

'Well, there's nothing we can do about it. As far as we know they aren't breaking any rules or doing anything illegal. I guess all we can do is wish the lad the best of luck.'

'I know,' sighed Jay. 'There's something about this whole thing that makes me feel distinctly uneasy.'

Vicky got up, and with the broadest of her grins said, 'Jay, worrying about it isn't going to change anything. Let's just see what happens and hope Leo doesn't have an accident.'

'Of course, but I'll tell you something else: his riding style has changed quite significantly in the last two or three weeks.'

'He's certainly more polished,' his assistant agreed. 'Is that what you mean?'

'There is a more determined streak in his riding now than I noticed when he first came to us, and in spite of the warning he got from the stewards at Sandown he's still pretty whip-happy in my view.'

'Perhaps you ought to remind him of that,' Vicky suggested. 'It's not particularly good for our reputation if a young amateur who has most of his rides out of our yard has a reputation for hitting the hell out of his horses.'

'Perhaps I will,' agreed Jay, 'but I don't know if you've noticed, he's not someone who takes criticism too kindly.'

Vicky smiled. 'Did you and I at his age? I know I wasn't too amenable to people telling me how to ride my horses.'

Jay joined in her laughter. 'I guess you're right, but I'll still have a gentle word with him. Anything in the yard I ought to know about?'

'No. Everything seems fine. I think our runners over the next few days are in good form. I'll be disappointed if most of them aren't placed, and we ought to pick up a few wins between them. Have a nice evening. See you in the morning.'

Making a mock bow, Vicky turned on her heel and walked out of the room in a way which generated thoughts in Jay's mind which would not have gone down well with Eva if she'd been aware of them.

After finishing off the entries due for the following day, Jay made his way back to the house. He sat down in the kitchen and poured himself a glass of wine and offered Eva one, who refused. He related the events of the afternoon, which Eva took in her stride. 'I really don't see what you need to be worried about. If it's bugging you, why don't you give Benny a call?'

245

Almost because he could think of nothing better to do, Jay got out his mobile phone and punched in his East End friend's number. He explained what had happened that afternoon and asked Benny whether he'd be able to scout around Angus Lanton's yard and see if there was anything that would throw light on the offer for the spare rides.

Benny listened and then whistled. 'Blimey, guv'nor, I don't know where I'll get the men from. We seem to be following half the bleeders in the south of England at the moment.'

Jay couldn't help but laugh. 'All right, forget it.'

'No, no, no,' insisted the East Ender. 'Leave it to me. I expect I'll dig up something from under a stone somewhere.'

Jay laughted again. 'Thanks a bundle,' he said. 'I owe you.'

'You bloody do,' replied Benny. 'I'll keep you to that,' and with another chuckle he put down the phone.

He was having a drink with Angel at the time and told him of the new request which had come from Jay. If anything Angel was even more sceptical about their chances of finding the manpower to do this. A few minutes later they were joined by Andy Best, who clearly saw that they were giving some matter deep consideration.

'You two look as if you're hatching the bloody Gunpowder Plot,' was his opening remark.

Angel explained what their concern was.

'Well,' said Andy, 'I might be able to help you there. You never asked before, but I've got a few mates who have retired from portering and get bored. They'd be happy to earn a bit on the side. They're all from our sort of background and they don't have any airs and

246

graces just because they've been head porters at posh hotels. How much work do you think is involved in this?'

Benny thought for a while. 'They'd probably need to go down and spend a couple of days going round the local pubs and finding which ones the stable staff use. With a bit of luck five or six nights should do it. We've found when we've worked with stables before that they're seldom free at lunchtimes for long enough to get to a pub, but in the evenings a lot of them just let their hair down. Most of them are really interested in their horses. They're always more than happy to talk about them, and most of them boast that their horses are better than they really are. What we're after is anything we can learn about why these two horses have suddenly been made available for an amateur jockey who's making a really concerted effort to win the championship.'

'Understood,' said Andy. 'I'll talk to two or three. I'll come back to you and let you know when they can start. By the way, do you want them to know they're working for you?'

'Preferably not,' said Benny. 'They're going to be happy just working for you.'

'If they want their loot they'd better be,' Andy announced. 'They're all old mates of mine and they know when to keep their mouths shut.'

Garry and Tony were sitting in Garry's office the next morning. They were reviewing a number of sheets of paper in front of them and both had a distinct air of satisfaction about them. Tony summarized the situation.

'We've had eleven pieces of information from Oscar. Seven of them proved valuable but we have only acted on five, of which four were accurate. By adjusting our odds I believe we've made about an extra £200,000.'

'Yes, and we've had no press comment about anything unusual in the betting, although a couple of blokes at the races did jokingly ask me where my crystal ball was.'

'What do you think about Lenny Brown's contact at Jessop's yard,' Garry continued. Lenny Brown had phoned Boxer to say that one of his pals from the north of England had joined County View. He was always up for a bit of extra cash and he was bright enough to know if a horse was off colour or a really good thing. Boxer had buttonholed Dillon Payne at the races and had arranged to meet him in a pub opposite the station at Swindon. Dillon had shown great interest but Boxer had been very cautious about how much he told him.

'I think we should give it a go,' said Tony. 'It's a bloody big yard and they have runners in the really important races. That's where the big turnover is, and if we could have inside knowledge on one of those we could make some real money.'

Garry looked thoughtful. 'I want to keep this pretty tight. If we pick the wrong guy we'd be scuppered if it got out.'

'But we've met him, you know.'

Garry looked questioningly at his brother.

'When we were shooting in Cheshire with Adrian Sampson there was a young man there. He was neatly dressed but didn't look as if he had the dough to shoot at that level. I asked Adrian about him and he told me that he worked in a racing yard but helped him on the shoot part-time. He took his payment in a few days' free shooting.'

248

Garry looked interested but said nothing.

'I chatted to him a bit and got the impression he would always be open to extra work. So now he's at Jessop's. What I did learn from Adrian is that this guy doesn't drink, seems to have a steady girlfriend, and likes spending money.'

Garry was clearly giving the matter serious thought. 'OK, we'll give him a try, but tell Boxer to slow down now. We'll just see how things go with the seven guys we've got – eight including this new one.'

Tony got up. 'I'll go and see him straightaway. What are you doing today?'

'I thought I'd go to the Kempton evening meeting and spend most of the day here. What about you?'

'I think I'll have the afternoon at Warwick. It looks like the most competitive card of the day, and we've got that tip that Shadow Cabinet is going to spring a surprise. It's all right,' Tony added quickly, 'I haven't forgotten we're not going to do anything with this one.'

Garry nodded. 'We've already had one hot tip from that yard and I don't want to raise suspicions by going to the well too often too quickly.'

Tony grinned at his brother. 'And there was I thinking you were a gambler,' he laughed.

'Well, I'm bloody not,' replied Garry. 'It's the gamblers who keep us living like we do.'

Tony laughed again and went down to find Boxer.

Chapter Twenty

Eva arrived at the National Gallery to find Adam waiting in the foyer. She had put on a plain black velvet dress, and round her neck was a simple gold necklace with one huge diamond in the middle, a twenty-first birthday present from her father.

Adam hurried over, took her by the hands, kissed her on the cheek, and whispered, 'You look absolutely enchanting, Eva. Now let's go and look at pictures.'

An hour and a half later Eva was tired but exhilarated. The collection of paintings had been awesome, inspiring, and in some cases breathtaking.

Sensing that she was beginning to flag, Adam took her gently by the elbow and guided her out of the gallery. She looked enquiringly at him. He smiled enigmatically and pointed to his car.

Jamie saw them, and immediately jumped out to open the door. Adam ushered her in and walked smartly round to the other side to get in himself. He didn't need to tell his driver where they were going; within moments they had negotiated the rather complicated network of streets leading in and out of Trafalgar Square and were gliding up the Strand. They walked into the Savoy and straight through to the River Room restaurant. It was clear that Adam was not only known but expected. They were led immediately to a secluded table at the side of the restaurant.

'I'm so glad you enjoyed the paintings,' said Adam, and started to discuss one in particular which had clearly attracted Eva. She was waiting for menus to be presented when, to her amazement, the first course was served. A pot of Beluga caviar was placed in front of them along with the traditional accompaniments. A bottle of frozen vodka was produced, two tiny shot glasses were filled and the bottle put back on the table.

Eva was surprised and mildly amused. 'You took a gamble,' she said.

'I'm a risk taker, not a gambler,' he said, 'but instinct told me you'd not only be used to, but would enjoy, the very best.'

Picking up his minute glass, he looked at her and with a warm smile said, 'Here's to the rest of the evening.'

She smiled without actually answering, but sipped at her vodka. Eva had always adored caviar, and seeing that Adam was certainly not stinting himself, enjoyed what she knew would be a small fortune in little black eggs.

Intrigued as to what would happen next, she was only half surprised when each of them was presented with a roast grouse cooked pink, and again with classical accompaniments. The vodka was removed and a decanted bottle of exquisite claret put in its place. Even before she tasted it, she knew, as Adam swirled it round his glass before taking a sip, it would be the very best. She was not disappointed. Adam continued to engage her in conversation about the exhibition, always ensuring that he gave her time to answer his questions or express her own views.

After two glasses of wine, Eva's sense of humour got the better of her. Leaning towards him, she smiled and whispered, 'You know, Adam, I believe you're trying to seduce me.'

The response was instant. 'Of course I am, my dear, and I very much hope I succeed.'

Eva was stunned by his frankness. Before she could speak again, he covered the hand that was resting on the table with both of his and, in an extremely earnest voice with an expression to match, added, 'And I'm not joking, Eva.'

She withdrew her hand quickly. 'Adam, I'm married, I'm in love with Jay, and there's no way I would dream of being unfaithful with anyone. That would be even truer of a business partner and somebody I had thought until this evening was his friend.'

Adam was unfazed. 'I understand. As far as I'm concerned, with great reluctance, the matter is closed. There's no point in my saying that I won't always find you enormously attractive and indeed lust after you. However, you can be sure that, having made my play and failed, I will from now on behave like a true English gentleman – which I'm not,' he added with a chuckle, 'and I trust that we can always be good friends in the future.'

Eva thought for a moment. 'Adam, I've had a wonderful evening. In many ways I'm flattered by your proposition, and as far as I'm concerned the matter is closed as well. Now, let's enjoy the rest of the evening, and perhaps you'll understand if I say I'd like to go home in a taxi rather than in the back of your gorgeous car.'

This time Adam laughed out loud. 'You would be quite safe, I assure you, but I understand your point of view.'

They finished the grouse and they both drank filtered coffee. Adam finished with a brandy, while Eva declined any more alcohol. As soon as she had drunk her coffee, Adam rose and pulled out her chair. 'I'll be back in a few moments,' he informed the waiter, and led Eva out to the front.

'Rather than send you back in a taxi, please let Jamie take you. I could do with another drink to drown my sorrows,' he added with a mischievous smile. By the time he'd given her a peck on the cheek, his car had pulled up. He opened the door and helped her inside. 'See you at the races or County View fairly soon. Goodnight, and thank you for your charming company. Please give my best regards to Jay.' He closed the door, gave her a little bow, then turned and walked in his normal purposeful manner back into the Savoy.

Half an hour later Eva was lying in her bed in the little house in Hays Mews. She started to laugh. She had enjoyed the evening and couldn't help feeling that part of it was due to the flattery of having a really attractive and successful man paying her such ardent attention. At the same time she felt slightly sorry for him, an emotion she would never have thought he was ever likely to inspire. With a smile and a sigh, she turned over and went to sleep, wondering what sort of edited version of the evening she'd tell Jay the next day.

Chapter Twenty-One

Marvin walked into Percy's office and purposefully closed the door in a way that indicated to his boss that he was bringing important news.

'The Tudors are in your favourite pub in Barbados,' he announced. 'I understand they're staying there for the next four or five days if you still want to meet them discreetly and apparently by chance.'

Percy's favourite 'pub' in Barbados was the Coral Reef Club, an elegant and luxurious hotel set in amazing grounds which required a small army of full-time gardeners to maintain their customary immaculate condition. Although sophisticated and of international repute, it retained a friendly informality resulting from the fact that it was still a family-run business. Cynthia O'Hara and her late husband had owned the hotel since the 1950s, and she had continued to run it after his death. Although she was still very much a part of the management, the main responsibility now lay with her two sons, Patrick and Mark. Percy had stayed there at least once a year for the last decade. He loved the atmosphere and also the proximity to both the Kensington Oval Cricket Ground and a number of good golf clubs. The island, and that part in particular, was favoured by many of the leading owners and trainers in British racing, and if he sought agreeable company he seldom had any problem in finding it quickly

This was to be a brief and business-orientated trip. The Tudors to whom Marvin referred owned the company which they had discussed some days earlier when Marvin spent the night at Percy's home. They were cousins and their fathers had built it up after inheriting it from their fathers. After considerable thought and several discussions with Marvin, Percy had decided to talk directly to the two men running the company.

Percy rang for Moira, his PA, who came in with a notepad at the ready. 'I want you to book me a flight tomorrow to Barbados. I'll stay at the Coral Reef as usual, and make it an open ticket. I'll be back as soon as I've hopefully successfully conducted some business there.'

Moira knew better than to ask any questions. Fifteen minutes later she returned saying he was booked on the ten o'clock flight from Gatwick the next morning. 'Your usual suite is free and will be ready for you. The bill will be forwarded to me. There will be a car waiting for you at the airport to take you straight to the hotel. I've also booked a car to pick you up in the morning as I thought you might like to give Francis the chance for a few easy days.'

'You think of everything, Moira. What would I do without you?'

His PA of many years smiled and waited expectantly.

'That's all for the moment. I'd better start clearing up a number of items before I go. Tell Francis I'll be working late. Perhaps you'd phone the Turf Club and tell them I'll be dining about quarter to nine, and as far as I know I'll be alone. I'll talk to you when I've gone through this pile on my desk.' He looked at the stack of papers in front of him rather ruefully, and without saying anything else started to go through them methodically, glancing at some and studying others in more detail, dictating notes where applicable. Occasionally he just read something and made comments in his customary red ink. It was half past eight before he knew it, and there was a polite knock at the door. Francis came in and paused on the threshold.

'I don't want to hurry you, sir, but remember the Turf Club kitchen closes at nine.'

'Thanks,' responded Percy. 'If you'd be kind enough to put this briefcase in the car, I'll bring any other papers down with me in a few moments.'

'Right you are,' was the cheery response, and his chauffeur picked up the bulging briefcase, turned and made his way down to the basement where he unlocked the car, drove out of the garage and waited outside until Percy arrived. Twenty minutes later he was at the Turf Club and waited while Brian mixed him a Kir Royale which he took upstairs with him. Mr Payne greeted him in his normal cheerful and attentive way, and ushered him to a table where a couple of members he was on nodding acquaintance with were finishing their meal with a couple of the club's delicious sorbets. They greeted each other affably and, by the time Percy had decided on his dinner the two of them had finished theirs and were making their way downstairs to the bar where they would undoubtedly enjoy a brandy and curse the government for the rapidly approaching ban on cigar smoking, even in a private club.

Finishing his meal, he went out to find Francis waiting patiently, listening to some sports commentary which was turned off immediately he saw his boss approach the car. Jumping out, he opened the door and ushered Percy in, handing him a West End final edition of the *Evening Standard*.

Percy thanked him for his attention before looking at it. He then took out his mobile phone and punched the code which would take him straight through to Jay. At this stage he was still playing his cards very close to his chest. Apologizing for phoning late at night, although it was still not ten thirty, he explained to Jay that a sudden business matter had necessitated him going to Barbados for a few days, but he was quite sure it would be under a week.

'Hardly worth you going,' his friend commented. 'I assume you're staying at the Coral Reef.'

Percy confirmed that he was and then explained that if he possibly could he would add a bit of holiday on to the trip, though there might not be time for even one round of golf.

'Well, the cricket won't be that wonderful,' commented Jay. 'The test team are over here getting ready for their first match at Lord's.'

'I know,' grunted Percy. 'I've got a feeling I'm going to miss it. I hope to God we do well otherwise I'll never hear the end of it from Marvin.'

'I know,' laughed his friend. 'Well, have a good trip and see you when you get back. Things are all running smoothly here and I've got nothing particular to report to you.'

'What's the situation with young Leo?' Percy queried.

'He's now four in front of Robin and he's got some damned good rides lined up. Three of his own horses are looking very good for wins. He's picking up two or three of Lloyd-Patterson's better rides, and he's bound to get a win or two out of Angus's horses.'

'I see. What about young Haslett?'

'Well, he's back riding full-time now and he's ridden two more winners than Leo in the last five days. It's going to be tight, but between you and me, if I had to have a bet my money would be on Leo, though only just.'

'Well, that'll make Adam happy, though God knows how he'll react if Leo gets pipped by one or two.'

'I know.' Jay's tone was rueful. 'Anyway, have a good trip. Call me when you get back.'

'Thanks, Jay, I certainly will,' and he hung up.

At three o'clock the next afternoon Percy was sitting on the balcony outside his Coral Reef suite, having had a quick shower and changed into a pair of shorts and a cotton shirt. He checked his mobile phone for any messages, but the two that were there needed no immediate action. The hotel reception assured him there was nothing requiring his attention. He went back to his room, changed into a pair of swimming trunks, and with a towel over his shoulder strolled down to the sea. He swam briskly out to one of the rafts moored a little way from the beach and soaked in the sun for ten minutes. After that he dived into the sea and swam just as briskly back to the shore, parallel to the beach to give himself a little more exercise before turning to make his way in to the immaculately kept sand in front of the equally luscious lawns. Waving cheerfully to a couple of the waiters who recognized him, he went back to his room, showered off the salt water and changed back into the casual clothes he'd been wearing before his swim.

Reluctantly he carried his briefcase out onto his veranda and started to wade through the pile of documents which he had decided he really ought to look at before he got back to London. He went down to the dining room half an hour before dinner and slowly slipped a glass of dry white wine in the bar, hoping to see his quarry. There was no sign of either of them, so somewhat reluctantly he sauntered into the restaurant and was slightly surprised at just how hungry he felt. Apart from the normal menu, it was one of the famous buffet evenings at the Coral Reef and Percy opted for this. From experience he knew that the food would be magnificent, and also he would be able to string out his dinner for rather longer than if eating from the menu. Hopefully this would give him more time to orchestrate the meeting with the two Tudors he'd come specifically to see. Theirs was a business which had been in the family for three generations, and on retirement of the two fathers they'd taken joint chief executive roles. Luke Tudor ran the manufacturing operation and the UK market, while Philip, two years younger, looked after the very considerable export business. Both of them admitted that finance was not their great strength so had happily agreed for an outsider to join the board as finance director on the recommendation of one of their non-executive directors. Everything had seemed to go well for the first two years, but the third year under this regime had just finished and to their horror a substantial profit had deteriorated into what was now looking like an almost certain and significant loss.

They were frankly unable to work out how this had happened as sales had been up on the previous year, but their manufacturing costs had spiralled in a way that Luke could not explain. Alan Pardew, their finance director, said that there appeared to have been a huge wastage in raw materials and parts, and productivity also seemed to have taken a significant turn for the worse.

The two cousins had come to Barbados to talk things over away from the day-to-day grind, and try to decide what course of action to take. They had been made a fair but not generous offer for the company on behalf of an unknown potential purchaser, through a small but well-regarded merchant bank. They were sorely tempted to take it and enjoy the rest of their lives in some comfort without the hassle of running a business. On the other hand, both of them were reluctant to give up the family control, or indeed quit the business on a losing note. The night of Percy's arrival they'd actually decided to eat somewhere up the coast at a small but wonderful restaurant called the Fish Pot. They stayed chatting to the owner after their meal had ended, and it was well after Percy had eventually decided to call it a night that they returned to the Coral Reef and made their way to their adjoining bedrooms.

As soon as he was awake the next morning, Percy phoned through to Canary Wharf and spoke to Moira and then to two of his directors, agreeing or commenting on the various documents and proposals which he'd ploughed through the night before. He still had a few which required his attention but these were less urgent than the ones he'd tackled the previous day. Checking his mobile phone and laptop, he found a number of messages and emails but none of them crucial. Hurrying down to the still deserted pool, he swam twenty lengths before going back to his room, showering and shaving and going down to breakfast. He discovered from the head waiter that the two cousins sometimes ate together in the restaurant, but sometimes on their veranda. Today they were clearly on the veranda. Checking with reception that they were indeed still in the hotel, he decided to devote the morning to finishing his paperwork and enjoying the sun.

At lunchtime he dressed in the same casual clothes from the day before. He always travelled with a minimum of luggage, working on the principal that good hotels had fast laundry services. He had compromised to the extent of packing one tropical weight suit and was very much hoping that no occasion would arise which would require him to don it.

Making his way down to the seaside restaurant, this time he was delighted to see the Tudors sitting at one of the tables almost on the edge of the sea. He ordered Caesar salad, ate it as quickly as he could without appearing to be in a rush, and then made his way back to one of the tables near the bar which had four easy chairs and a coffee table in front of it. He ordered a cafetière of coffee and a bottle of Perrier water. He waited until the two Tudors got up and walked casually across to them. They also had an interest in racing, and the three were on slightly better than nodding terms.

'What a pleasant surprise to see you here,' he greeted them. 'Would you join me for a coffee?' Having nothing pressing on their agenda, they readily agreed. Soon all three of them were sitting and smoking Havana cigars which Percy had brought with him. He was far from a penny-pinching man, but paying hotel prices for cigars which he bought wholesale just went against the grain.

The conversation ranged across the weather, the hotel, the forthcoming cricket series, some of the issues facing racing, and the stock market. This allowed Percy to enquire how their company was doing. There was a pause before Luke, with some reluctance, said, 'We've not had the greatest of years.'

Percy decided not to beat around the bush. 'I know,' he said. They looked amazed. The figures had only just been audited and had not been signed off. They were certainly not in the public domain.

Percy continued before they had a chance to comment. 'It so happens that an extremely bright young accountant, who has been working on your figures for your auditors, has also been looking at those of one of your suppliers. One of the senior partners of his company is a close friend of my head of security. The young man was so concerned about the situation which he'd uncovered that he went to see his boss. Knowing my company's involvement with one of your directors, he went to Marvin who immediately contacted me.'

The Tudors were looking completely mystified. 'To put it in a nutshell, your company's books show considerable expenditure with this other company for components. They also show that they've been paid for. The mystery is that there is no paperwork at your suppliers indicating that these were ever shipped or indeed that your payments have ever gone into that company's bank. Further investigation would indicate that your company's money is now sitting in a private bank account in Jersey.'

'Good God,' exclaimed Luke. Philip looked too shocked to speak at all. 'Are you saying that we have been cheated out of a large sum of money by one of our directors?'

'That's how it appears,' agreed Percy.

'But surely Pardew would have spotted this?' Philip interjected.

Percy gave him a hard look. 'How long has he been with you?'

'Three years,' they replied simultaneously.

'And how did he join you?'

'He was recommended by –' Luke stopped in mid-sentence. 'Christ almighty,' he said, 'the penny's beginning to drop.'

The two of them were clearly stunned at Percy's revelation. Before either of them spoke again, Percy asked another question. 'Have you been made an offer for you company?'

'Yes,' was the reply.

'Who by?' asked Percy.

'We don't know. One of the City venture capitalists approached us on behalf of one of their clients.'

'Is it New Opportunities by any chance?' Percy continued his interrogation.

'Yes,' replied Luke with evident surprise that Percy was party to this information as well.

'Do you realize the same director is on the board of that company?'

'Good God, no.'

'Well, I'm going to give you one piece of immediate advice. Under no circumstances sell your company, not a single share. Marvin is looking into the situation further and he and Neville Simmonds, the partner I mentioned, will come and see you as soon as you get back to England. You're then going to have, I suspect, a simple choice. Confront your director, get the money back, get rid of him and your finance director, and go back to running what I am sure is a perfectly successful and well-managed business. If you need a new finance director, let me know. I'm sure I can help. The alternative is to go to the police and prosecute. That would probably be very satisfying in many

263

ways, but would do little for your reputations, take a long time, be very expensive, and there's always the off-chance, though I doubt it, you might lose. Anyway, you don't have to make up your minds now. Just don't sell any shares,' he stressed again. 'I don't know what your plans are, but I suggest you have a few more days' break here, think things through carefully, then get in touch with your lawyers, but make sure your finance director knows nothing. Just tell him you're considering the option of selling the company and it might be advantageous to indicate that you're leaning towards that route.'

The two brothers nodded. Clearly they were still in a state of shock and confusion. 'I'll leave you to think it over,' said Percy. 'If you'd like to join me for dinner, I would be very happy to discuss any further points that occur to you. If you both feel that you hate seeing your two board colleagues get away with it, I can assure you they won't. This will cause them an enormous amount of personal grief without their activities in your company ever becoming public knowledge.'

The brothers were obviously relieved. They got up and both shook Percy warmly by the hand. 'Why don't we meet on our veranda at half past seven?' Luke suggested. 'We can have a drink and chat over anything that occurs to us by then, and we insist on you being our guest for dinner.'

'All right, if you twist my arm. I'll see you at half past seven.' Percy flashed each of them what he hoped was a reassuring smile and went back to his room.

Shortly after half past seven that evening, Percy was sitting with the Tudors on their veranda. All were enjoying long gin and tonics. They explained that after deep discussion they were leaning towards the first of Percy's suggestions and would prefer to avoid litigation. They enquired, more in hope than expectation, as to how Percy saw their tormentors being punished.

'At this stage I think I'll keep it to myself,' he told them. 'I promise you'll know when the time comes. In fact I think some of it may be a fairly public humiliation.'

From the look in their eyes, it couldn't be too public or too great a humiliation. They finished their drinks and went in to what turned out to be a surprisingly convivial dinner in view of the situation facing the two cousins. Percy warmed to them as the evening progressed.

Chapter Twenty-Two

Jay's thoughts were interrupted by the ring of his cell phone. Picking it up he saw that it was Frank Malone. His friend and owner's cheery tones boomed down the line.

'There's an interesting development on the betting front, my friend,' he announced. 'The Kent brothers must have taken some fairly substantial bets on young Leo winning the amateur championship because they've been laying off a significant amount and even approached me. They were prepared to accept tempting odds from my point of view, but I declined.'

Jay was intrigued. 'That's a bit unlike their normal form, isn't it? I thought that was the sort of risk they normally took quite cheerfully.'

'It is, and all I can think is that either their book's become very exposed, or alternatively they're pretty confident that young Leo is going to win.'

Jay thought for a moment. 'Well, I don't know about their exposure, and you know much more about their normal behaviour than I do, Frank, but young Leo's got a pretty fair chance of pulling it off now, you know. He's five ahead of Robin with only a few weeks of the season left, and now he's got these two horses from Angus I'd say he's probably favourite to win. Robin's best horse went lame in its last race, and although he's largely recovered he's not accepting more than one or two rides on the same afternoon whereas a few months' ago he'd think nothing of getting up four times.'

'I know,' agreed Frank, 'but it's still odd. I've never known this sort of betting interest in the amateur championship before. My guess is that somebody is really confident Robin's going to come second this year and it's a confidence which makes me very uneasy. I'm just hoping that nobody's planning any sort of follow-up attack on that young man. I was wondering whether you might have a word with Hubert Haslett and suggest that he employs somebody to make sure his son is watched all the time between now and the end of the season?'

Jay thought for a moment. 'I wonder if Benny could take it on?' he said. 'I'll have a word with Hubert and tell him your thoughts. Do you mind if I mention your name?'

'Not at all. I'd do it myself but you know him far better than I do.'

'All right. I'll give him a call and let you know his reaction. Thanks for the tip-off, Frank.'

Jay pondered Frank's ideas for some time. He then looked up the Haslett number. The phone was answered by the housekeeper who promised to get Mr Haslett straightaway. Moments later he was greeting Jay.

'What can I do for you?' he asked.

Jay recounted his conversation with Frank and explained Frank's concern about Robin Haslett's safety. The father was obviously perplexed.

'Do you think your Benny would add this protection to the investigation work he's been doing? We

267

know that young Leo's been involved in some pretty mysterious evening activities but so far we haven't been able to find anything which would endanger Robin or his horses, or indeed any real clue as to what he's doing.'

'I know,' said Jay, 'but I still think it might be worth the precaution as there are only a few weeks left. You might also consider asking him to move in with you.'

'I did that when he first came out of hospital and he was adamant that he was going to continue living in that cottage I renovated for him a couple of years ago. He's a fiercely independent young man and he values his freedom and privacy a great deal. I wonder if you would pursue the Benny avenue and let me know what he says.'

Jay agreed and phoned Benny as soon as he'd finished the conversation with Hubert. There was a moment's silence at the other end.

'I just can't do it, Jay. I'm already spread too thinly. I honestly can't lay my hands on any more people who I'd trust to carry out this sort of work.'

'I understand. Have you any suggestions?'

Again, Benny was silent for a while, before replying. 'There's a very good security firm which Marvin uses from time to time when he needs to augment his resources. I can't recall the name but why don't you give him a call and see what he can come up with? I'm really sorry I can't do it, Jay.'

'Don't worry. I'll call Marvin and I'm sure anybody he uses would be more than suitable. Talk to you soon.'

He promptly rang Marvin's mobile phone, which was on voicemail. His direct line at the office was diverted to his secretary who said that Marvin was unavailable for the next few hours but she'd make sure that he phoned Jay before the end of the day.

It was while he and Eva were eating their dinner that Marvin eventually phoned. Jay quickly explained the situation and Marvin's reaction was positive.

'I'll phone Don Ashton, the boss,' he promised Jay, 'and call you back.'

Half an hour later Jay and Eva were sitting watching the ten o'clock news when Marvin phoned again. 'He's both happy and able to undertake the work. What do you want to do next?'

'Let me have his telephone number. I'll speak to Hubert and let the two of them work it out between them. Thanks for your help, Marvin. It's much appreciated.'

'See you soon, Jay, and I hope the protection's not necessary.'

'So do I,' said Jay. 'I'm really uncomfortable about the situation and particularly with young Leo working in my yard.'

'I bet you are,' Marvin responded. 'Let me know if there's anything else I can do.'

Jay called Hubert and explained that Benny couldn't take the work on but that Marvin had suggested a company which he used whenever he needed extra manpower. Hubert thanked him profusely and promised to call Don Ashton immediately.

'By the way, Jay,' he added, 'I'm not going to let Robin know about this if Mr Ashton thinks it can be done discreetly without lessening the effectiveness of the protection.'

Jay laughed. 'Yes, I can imagine Robin would resent the implication that he can't look after himself. I'm sure I would have been just the same at his age.'

'Wouldn't we all?' responded Hubert, and for the first time Jay noted a slightly amused tone in his voice. 'I'll get on with it right away, Jay. Thanks a lot, and please thank Marvin for me as well.'

Two days later, Jay had finished supervising first lot and had had his usual frugal breakfast before changing and getting ready to go to Plumpton. Before he'd had a chance to go upstairs the phone rang and Benny's familiar tones came down the line.

'Are you going to Plumpton this afternoon, guv?'

'Yes. Although I've only got one runner, I'm taking Jed with me as he always enjoys it down there. That and Fontwell were his two local courses and he's bound to meet up with a few old friends.'

'I'll see you there,' Benny said. 'I've got some interesting news for you.'

With that he rang off, leaving a somewhat intrigued Jay at the other end of the line.

Three hours later he and Jed were standing side by side watching Opening Bid run in the novice chase. Though not one of the yard's stars, he was a very competent horse and was nearly always placed. His owners were a little way down the stand with their son and two grandchildren, watching the proceedings with that nervous excitement which all but the most hardened of owners experience before their horse runs.

The two-and-a-half-mile race went smoothly, and Jay's runner finished a creditable third. He met the owners and explained that unfortunately the two youngsters weren't allowed in the winners' enclosure, but he'd make sure the horse stopped for them to be able to give him a pat on his way back to the stables.

270

Having ensured that the course photographer took pictures of them with their doughty performer, he declined the offer of a drink saying that he had to have a quick meeting before getting back to County View.

They took his rejection with good grace, as he promised to let them know how the horse was the next morning and discuss with them where and when he might run again.

Avoiding the owners' and trainers' bar, he walked across to the parade ring where he saw Benny waiting patiently for him.

'Is Jed joing us?' the Cockney asked .

'No, he's going to supervise the horse. He and Cathy are staying the night with Peter Hammond, who you may recall had a few horses with Jed in his training days. Cathy's going to drive him back tomorrow.'

'No problem,' said Benny, 'but I wouldn't have minded if he was here with us. I always value his opinion.'

'What's going on, Benny?'

'Well, you know we've been keeping an eye on young Leo, and last night he visited the lovely Tania again. Angel and Ronnie were watching him and Ronnie followed him home where he went straight in and almost immediately to bed. Angel followed his lady friend and was staggered when she made her way to Garry Kent's home, let herself in and apparently stayed the night.'

'Bloody hell,' said Jay. 'What do you make of that?'

'Not much, guv'nor,' came the reply, 'but we'll be burrowing away like moles tomorrow. I thought you ought to know immediately.'

'Damn right,' said Jay, who did not often swear. 'Do you think he and Leo are connected in some way in this gambling that's going on?'

271

'Search me, but it's bloody odd. I wouldn't have thought Garry was Tania's cup of tea unless she's doing some part-time whoring to add to her other slightly unusual ways of earning a living, but I'll guarantee by the end of tomorrow we'll have a bit more news to tell you.'

'Thanks, Benny. I look forward to it. At least, I hope I do,' he added as an afterthought.

Driving back to County View, Jay's mind was racing. Every aspect of this gambling activity around the amateur championship was becoming more and more complicated. At first it had looked like a straight-forward toss-up between Leo and his father as to who was behind it, if not both of them. Now some sort of connection between Leo's girlfriend and the dubious Garry Kent had added another dimension to an already complicated scene.

He decided there was nothing more he could do that night so, concentrating on getting home as fast as he legally could, he put the matter out of his mind.

Frank Malone was sitting in his office with Lance.

'Close the door,' he said. His son did as he was asked, returned and sat opposite his father. His father beckoned him to move closer. Leaning across his desk he said, in about as quiet a voice as he was able, 'Something very strange is going on, Lance. We know the Kent brothers seem to have a bloody crystal ball because of the ways they've changed odds to both cut the long-price winners and lengthen those on favour-ites. Well, somebody seems to be on to them. In the last few weeks we've been getting a lot of bets. Somebody new to us has been betting against losing favourites and still backing the longer price winners.

Somebody seems to know exactly what the Kents know. He's playing them at their own game – but with us, not the Kents. Whoever it is clearly doesn't want them to know what he's doing. At first I thought it was coincidence and the bets were only in twenties or fifties, but gradually they've grown from fifties to hundreds, and this week we had a bet for five hundred quid.'

Lance whistled. 'So you're sure the Kents are getting inside information and somebody else is now getting it too?'

'It's a racing cert. I know the Kents are pretty damn sharp but they can't possibly be that sharp so often. They're bloody well getting information.'

'Who from?' demanded Lance.

'That's what we're going to find out,' his father replied.

'How the hell do we do that?'

'We tackle the guy who's putting on the bets, and we put the frighteners on him.'

'We're going to have to find out who it is first,' his son pointed out. 'Presumably he's not betting in his own name?'

'No, he's got a credit account, but we've traced it. You and two of Benny's friends are going to visit this gentleman, so take some sun cream with you.'

Lance looked puzzled. 'Why should I do that?'

'Because you're going to Malaga,' his father said, 'and you're going to meet an old chum of ours, Oscar Fry.'

'Bloody hell. D'you think he's behind it?'

'I'm sure he is. You know our Oscar. He owed the Kents a lot of money and somehow he's got out of it with both his kneecaps. He used to bet with us but nothing like the sums he did with them. My guess is that somehow or other he knows the information they've been working on and he started to bet in a small way. But you know our Oscar, greedy as hell, so after a while when nothing happened he started to take chances. It's a bloody miracle that the Kents haven't cottoned on to it before I have, and we need to get to him before they do.'

He reached into his pocket and drew out a piece of paper. 'Here's his address. I've told Benny. He's sending Angel and Robbie with you tomorrow morning. You're all booked on the seven forty, and you're meeting at the airport, so have an early night. Peter will drive you there tomorrow.'

'What d'you want us to do when we get there?'

'Get a signed and recorded confession from him, and then tell him to get the hell out of Malaga if he knows what's good for him. We want the names of any people he's getting information from, and then as far as I'm concerned he's on his own.'

'I don't want to get involved in any rough stuff, Dad.'

'You won't need to. Angel and Robbie will put the frighteners on him. If that's not enough, all you've got to do is to threaten to tell the Kents and he'll squeal like a pig. Don't phone me when you're over there, just wait till you get back unless you're in some real trouble.'

'OK, Dad.' A very thoughtful Lance got up and left the office.

'It wasn't him that's been attacking Haslett or that double-barrelled toff who got beaten up.' Seeing that there would be no comment at this stage, he continued. 'The other evening Robbie decided to have one more go at finding out what young Forsyth was doing on these nocturnal trips of his. As usual, he parked down the road and followed on his motorcycle with his lights off. That young Leo must have been trained by bloody Red Indians or the SAS. He moves through the woods as fast as lightning and dead silent. That's why Angel has lost him the three times he's tried it. Anyway, Robbie had a bit more luck, so to speak. Following young Leo, he thought he'd lost him when he could hear nothing. He hurried on and only fell over him, didn't he? Our young man had built himself a sort of hide and was sitting in it with a camera. He wasn't best pleased when Robbie fell all over him and brought half his hide down with him. He wanted to know what the hell Robbie was doing following him in the middle of the night. Robbie said that he was a gamekeeper and had seen Leo moving suspiciously with a large pack on his back. Leo explained that his hobby was night-time wildlife photography, in particular badgers and owls, but on this particular occasion had been hoping to get some roe deer. Robbie had rather put paid to that. He went on to explain that his photography was done under a different name as he thought his father might think it was a bit sissy, but he'd had pictures published in magazines like *Country Life* and *The Field*, and some of the wildlife newsletters. Robbie thought that would be it when the youngster suddenly said, "Wait a minute. This is National Trust land. I've never known them to have gamekeepers out at night. They couldn't afford it."

'Robbie had to think quickly. He said that this was a short-term measure as there were some rare birds, which of course he wasn't at liberty to name, nesting in the area and they were worried that vandals would try and steal their eggs. Leo was less than convinced, but Robbie took his cue and beat a hasty retreat, promising that he'd say nothing to anyone about who was taking these photographs. Well, that's it in a nutshell, Jay.'

There was silence as the other two took this in. 'Well, it would certainly seem to rule Leo out of the Haslett incident, and we can only assume that whoever did that was responsible for the Lloyd-Patterson attack as well.'

'That puts us back to square one,' Eva remarked.

'Well, I'm not so sure, darling,' Benny said. 'We may have got a bit of interesting information coming our way, but I don't want to say what it is yet in case it turns out to be a red herring.' He drained his cup, stood up, and with a cheery grin, announced, 'I'll be off now. I've got a few other things to do as you know, Jay. Anyway, it looks as if you haven't got a bleeding cuckoo in your nest, doesn't it? I'm off to meet Marvin.'

With a smacking kiss on Eva's cheek, and a playful punch in Jay's ribs, he was on his way to the beaten-up BMW whose exterior appearance belied a finely tuned and powerful engine beneath the bonnet, an engine which was looked after lovingly by a retired Formula One mechanic who was one of the more obscure members of Benny's large clan.

Two hours later, Benny was having a cup of coffee with Marvin in one of the many little cafés in Covent Garden when his phone rang.

277

'Jackson here,' the policeman's distinctive tones came across the air. 'We've got a really hot lead on your friend's killer. Can we meet later this morning?'

'Like a shot.' Benny was enthusiastic. 'I'm with Marvin. Can he come?'

'Of course,' came the reply. 'See you upstairs at the Pegasus at half past twelve,' and Jackson hung up.

'I'll pop into the office for an hour, Benny, and see you later at the pub. Let's hope it's something really firm.'

Benny hoped so too, and the pair of them parted company.

At twelve fifteen Benny was already seated in the pub. A few minutes later Marvin arrived and they talked rather inconsequentially waiting for Jackson to arrive. Promptly at twelve thirty he walked in accompanied by DS Barlow. He nodded to the publican, pointed upstairs and received an affirmative smile. He beckoned the two unlikely allies to follow him. Entering the now familiar room, Jackson closed the door after them and motioned for them all to sit down.

'Barlow's come up with something very interesting,' he said. 'Tell them.'

The Sergeant, as always, produced his notebook, flipped it open and studied it briefly before speaking. 'I had a phone call from a sergeant at Savile Row police station who was on the beat with me when I first joined the force. He and I have remained close friends. We keep in touch and he knew I was working on the Arlington Place murder.

'The night of the murder they picked up a down-and-out who, under normal circumstances, they would have left alone. They know him to be harmless. However, on this occasion he was so drunk he

278

was staggering around near Piccadilly Circus and they were frightened he'd do himself some serious injury or cause an accident. They took him in for his own protection and he spent the night in the cells. The next morning he insisted he'd seen a murder, and to be honest they thought he was hallucinating or had read about it and was trying to get some attention.

'They then realized that there was no way he could have known about it from the news, so he was questioned rather more carefully. His story was that he was dossing in a doorway in Arlington Place and saw a man walk down and stand almost opposite. He lit a cigarette and was smoking quietly when another man approached him. The man stood in front of the smoker and took something from his pocket. His back was to our informant so he didn't know what it was. The next thing he saw was the smoker lying on the ground. The other man bent over him, appeared to stroke him or do something to his jacket, then stood up, looked all around and walked back up to Piccadilly. For a moment he paused under a street lamp and our informant got a good view of his face, although he was some way away. He described him as tall, fairly young with short blond hair and athletic looking. He was wearing a dark raincoat. He walked purposefully but without any haste up to Piccadilly and turned right down towards Piccadilly Circus. That's all he was able to tell us. The down-and-out went over to the prostrate man, saw he was dead and beat it.'

Jackson interrupted. 'It fits in with what the two men on the beat reported. At the moment we're working with the guy on a photofit picture and we're keeping him in custody so that he doesn't disappear.'

It was Marvin who spoke next. 'It sounds like a description of Nixon,' he commented.

'I know,' said Jackson. 'Of course, we've long had our suspicions of him.'

Benny had been listening intently. 'Why would Nixon be either following Jerry, or more likely following the Americans when it would seem that he was working for them?'

'Good question,' Jackson responded. 'Barlow and I have been trying to work that one out.'

'Surely they didn't feel they needed protection,' suggested Marvin, 'and, as Benny said, if Nixon was working for them why would he be following them?'

'Well, Jerry didn't know they were being followed,' Benny interrupted. 'He'd have told me when he reported the two of them had gone into the Wolseley and were meeting the Kent brothers.'

'Bloody odd.' Jackson took from his pocket a rather ancient-looking pipe, which was clearly already filled, and lit it – a sure sign that he was thinking hard. All four men sat in silence while Jackson puffed slowly.

'I've got a bit of news on the bank situation,' Marvin announced. 'It seems that Raymond and Parry were there to sell their shares in Tolchester Holdings. The odd thing is that the manager doesn't know who bought them, and so far no change of ownership has been registered with the Stock Exchange.'

Jackson nodded to Barlow. 'We've got the same information, but also a bit more,' he announced. Benny and Marvin both gave him rapt attention. 'It seems that shortly after the transaction had been completed another set of transfer certificates arrived made out to a different nominee along with the identical sum of money. The bank manager was perplexed and kept the money and the documents locked in a small safe in his office. Two hours later he received a phone call from the same man who'd originally spoken to him asking if the documents were ready for collection. He was staggered when he was informed that what appeared to be a different transaction had taken place. After a long pause he announced he would be sending the same courier who had delivered the documents and money to collect them within an hour.

'This time the bank manager was rather more attentive to the situation and handed over the documents himself. He insisted on a signed receipt. The courier spoke very little. The manager did detect what he considered to be a strong Eastern European accent. The man bore no resemblance at all to Nixon,' he added quickly.

'Bloody hell, what the fuck's going on?' Benny was clearly thinking aloud. 'Sorry for the French,' he nodded apologetically in Jackson's direction.

'Couldn't have put it better myself, Benny,' the policeman answered with a smile.

It was Benny who broke the short silence again. 'Nixon has two Ukrainians working for him. I know where they hang out. If I got that information to you, Mr Jackson, would you be able to bring them in for questioning?'

Jackson thought for a moment. 'Don't see why not. We can start on the "Are they illegal immigrants" tack and see what develops as the questioning goes on.' He turned to Barlow. 'Give Benny your mobile phone number and get on to it with my authority the minute he phones to say where they are.'

'Yes, sir.'

Jackson looked at the two men facing him. 'Anything else?' he asked. They shook their heads. 'Right, let's keep in touch. It'll be interesting to see what develops from these interviews. Meanwhile, I'll keep you informed of what happens with our eye-witness when he's gone through the identification procedures.' With that he got up, signalling that the meeting was at an end. Barlow jumped up beside him and quickly opened the door for Benny and Marvin. Both turned to the two policemen and, thanking them for their help and information, went downstairs, smiled to the publican and walked out into Hill Street. They walked side by side for a while in silence.

'I think I could do with a drink,' said Benny, 'and a stiff one at that.' Marvin nodded his agreement. They walked into the first pub they came to and Benny beat Marvin to the bar. 'What's your poison? I'm going to have a large rum and Coke.'

Marvin settled for a glass of what turned out to be very indifferent house white wine and they sat themselves down in a corner. It was Benny who spoke first. 'What the hell's the connection between all these things?' he mused. 'Damned if I can see it.'

Marvin took a somewhat disdainful sip of his wine before replying. 'Well, the three connecting links appear to be Tolchester Holdings, Adam Forsyth, and the Kent brothers. But why are two Vegas casino owners interested in any of that?'

'It's a bloody shame that we didn't have our bug in earlier,' observed Benny, 'but Sol Jacobson appears to be another link.'

'I'd thought of that,' agreed Marvin, 'but if we or Jackson tried to question him about any of them he would claim client confidentiality, so I don't think that's going to prove very fruitful.'

Benny shrugged his shoulders in a gesture of reluctant agreement.

Putting his half-finished drink down, Marvin stood up. 'I'm going back to the office. There are a few calls I want to make and I'll let Percy know what we've learned this morning.'

Benny nodded. 'I think I'm going to have another drink and give it a bit more thought,' he said. 'Be in touch, mate,' and he patted Marvin on the arm. Marvin flashed him his characteristic smile, squeezed Benny on the shoulder and left the pub. Benny drained his glass, walked over to the bar and ordered another. He returned to his seat, pondering the more and more complex set of circumstances facing them.

Back at Canary Wharf, Percy immediately agreed to see Marvin who brought him up to date with the developments of the morning. Percy got up, crossed his office floor and gazed out of his window down at the Thames. 'I wonder if any of this has a connection with what we discussed the other evening?'

'I just can't see it. As far as we can tell the Americans have only recently come here, I can't find any financial or other connection they have in the UK, and their meetings with both Forsyth and the Kents appear to have been racing connected. Of course, we've no idea what they've been discussing with our friend Mr Jacobson.'

'Fair point,' agreed Percy, 'and we're not likely to find out easily either.'

Marvin agreed, pointing out that Jackson had said much the same only a couple of hours earlier.

'Well, I guess we're just going to have to wait and see whether this eyewitness produces anything and, assuming Benny tracks down the somewhat mysterious Ukrainians, whether the police can extract anything from them.'

Marvin got up. 'Right, boss, I'll let you get on. You'll know as soon as I have any news.'

Percy smiled. 'I know I will, Marvin. Keep up the good work.'

Walking towards the door, Marvin stopped, turned round, and with his broadest grin announced, 'The West Indies are doing well against the MCC,' and leaving it at that opened the door and walked out.

'We'll see,' called Percy, just before his employee had the opportunityto close the door, and chuckled to himself as he turned his attention to the computer screen in front of him.

Idly logging on to the Tolchester share price, he noticed there had been no movement in the last few days, and further investigation indicated no comments or interest. As a director of the company he would have been surprised if there had been – very surprised.

Sitting with Jay over a cup of coffee after watching his horses on the County View gallops, Frank looked serious.

'How confident are you that Truly Tested will win this afternoon?'

'He worked very well yesterday,' replied Jay. 'He's well handicapped and the ground should suit him. If I were to put a figure on it, I guess I'd say I was 80 per cent confident, and as you know that's high for me.'

Frank thought. 'Well, it's interesting that the Kent brothers were offering a full point more than the rest of us last night, and I'm looking forward to seeing how the market shapes later today. I don't know how the Kents do it, but they seem to be guessing when the horses are going to run above their normal form and, perhaps even more surprising, when they're going to be disappointing. I know we can all of us get lucky by taking a chance from time to time, but they seem to be having a particularly hot streak. I'm certain they are getting inside information.'

Jay shrugged. 'Well, as you know I'm not deeply into gambling, Frank, so I wouldn't know, but I still think Truly Tested will run very well today.'

'I hope so, friend,' replied the big bookmaker, and draining his coffee he got up. 'See you at Ascot later.' Crossing the kitchen, he gave Eva a hug and enquired if she'd be there.

'No.' She explained that she was on the school run and would be picking up Max and a couple of his friends.

'Ah, the joys of parenthood,' Frank chuckled, and with a cheery wave to both of them made his way to his car.

At Ascot all the preliminaries had taken place, and Jay and Frank were standing chatting to Mark Harlow, Truely Tested's owner.

'I see we're favourite,' Mark commented, 'but the odds seem to have lengthened a bit. We were 3 to 1 in the papers this morning, but I see some of the bookmakers are offering 7 to 2, and the Kents 4 to 1.'

Jay shrugged. 'It's all a mystery to me how these prices move,' he said, 'but I still think your horse will take all the beating.'

The two-and-a-half-mile hurdle race was run at a sensible speed. There were ten runners and they were all decent horses competing for the £25,000 first prize.

David Sparrow had kept Truly Tested in the middle pack during the uneventful first circuit of the track, and heading for home up the long finishing straight he moved into fourth place. David urged him to make ground on the three horses in front but a kick and a slap on the shoulder produced no response.

David now got seriously energetic and resorted to a couple of cracks behind the saddle. There was still no response, and approaching the last hurdle Truly Tested had back-pedalled to be overtaken by three more horses. Jay was genuinely puzzled and turned to the clearly disappointed owner.

'I can't imagine what's gone wrong,' he said. 'He was fine yesterday morning, but that just wasn't the same horse.'

'I know,' replied Mark. 'Let's hope it's nothing serious.'

'I'll go and have a look at him in the stable,' said Jay.

As they walked across, they bumped into Frank. 'Very disappointing,' he said. 'What are you two doing?'

'I'm going to have a look at the horse and then I'm going for a drink afterwards,' replied Jay.

'I'll come with you, Mark,' Frank said. 'We'll see you in the owners' and trainers', Jay.'

Jay went off to find his horse. He was not particularly surprised to find he was being dope tested. This was normal procedure when the favourite or a heavily backed horse ran disappointingly.

'What do you think?' Jay asked Johnny Wall, the racecourse vet.

'Well, I know he's just had a race but he doesn't look 100 per cent to me,' replied the vet. 'Still, the blood test will soon tell us what we need to know, and you'll have that within the next few days. At least

I can say that nothing's seriously wrong with the horse, and there's certainly nothing wrong with his legs.'

'I suppose we must be grateful for small mercies,' said Jay ruefully. 'Thanks, Johnny,' and he made his way to the owners' and trainers' bar. He assured Mark there was nothing fundamentally wrong with the horse and he'd let him know the result of the blood test. He'd also have Chris, his vet, come and give him a thorough once-over the next day.

A still rather dejected Mark finished his drink, shook hands with both of them and left. As soon as he was out of earshot, Frank leant forward and said quietly but vehemently, 'Bloody suspicious, Jay. There was a hell of a lot of money against your horse winning. It was backed bloody heavily on the exchanges to lose. Do you think somebody got at him?'

'God knows,' said Jay. 'I can't explain the bad run.'

'Well, needless to say the Kents have made a minor killing on your horse's bad run,' Frank continued. 'I'll keep my ears open but the blood test should be fascinating.'

'I agree, but I can't think what can have gone wrong. Perhaps we're just beginning to get a virus in the yard and he's the first to go down with it.'

'Could be,' agreed Frank, 'but I doubt it.'

The following morning there was a knock on his open office door and Jay looked up from the list of entries he was making to see Ali standing in the entrance.

'Could I have a private word with you, Mr Jessop?' his conditional jockey enquired.

Oh, hell, thought Jay. He's going to resign and I really don't want to lose him.

'Come in, Ali.'

287

The young man took a step forward, turned, closed the door and walked across to the desk.

'Please sit down.' Obviously nervous, Ali perched himself on the chair. 'Well, what can I do for you?'

Ali reached into his pocket, brought out a small plastic bag and passed it across to Jay. In it were obviously used shavings from a horse box along with some small pellets. Jay looked enquiringly at the young man.

'Yesterday morning I saw Dillon come out of Truly Tested's box with a food bowl in his hand. I thought this was surprising as he doesn't normally look after Truly Tested but on the other hand Emma, his girlfriend, does. He then walked round to the back of the muck heap and appeared to bury whatever was in the bowl. Frankly, I thought nothing more of it until our horse ran so badly in his race yesterday. It all seemed very odd, so this morning I went to the muck heap and could see where it had been disturbed. I dug around a bit with my hands and retrieved this. I fetched a plastic bag for the sample, and thought I'd better bring it to you.'

Jay leant back in his chair and thought hard. 'Thank you, Ali,' he said. 'Please don't mention this to anyone else – and I do mean anyone.'

'Of course not, sir.'

'Thank you, again, Ali. Off you go, and behave as if nothing's happened. As soon as I know what's in the bag I'll let you know, and I'm obliged to you for being so conscientious and so discreet.'

Ali got up, obviously relieved, gave a rather nervous smile to Jay and scurried out of the office as quickly as he could.

Jay sat back and, after thinking for a moment, phoned Chris, his vet.

'I've got something which I need analysed quickly,' he said.

There was a pause at the other end of the phone. 'Jay, I'll do it as quickly as I can but I really can't get over to you. I've a big operation to undertake in just a few minutes. Is there any chance of you getting it over to me?'

'I'll bring it myself,' replied Jay.

'Wow, it must be important,' was his vet's response.

'I'll be with you in twenty minutes.' He carefully put the bag into his pocket and walked out to Eva.

'There's something I need to chat to Chris about. I'm nipping over to Cirencester. I'll be back within an hour. I'll take my mobile phone with me in case anyone needs me urgently.'

Eva looked at him questioningly. It was obvious that her husband had something serious on his mind and that he was in a hurry. 'Will you be back before lunch?' she asked.

'Absolutely,' he replied, and walking quickly out of the house, jumped into his car and drove off.

Arriving at Chris's clinic, he walked into reception where Carol, one of Chris's nurses, was acting as receptionist.

'Good morning, Jay,' she said. 'I was expecting you. Chris said you'd be on your way. Hang on just a moment and I'll fetch him.'

A few moments later Chris, dressed in his operating gown, came out. He beckoned Jay into his office and closed the door. 'What's this all about?'

'Yesterday Truly Tested ran at Sandown and performed appallingly. He was blood-tested, as one would expect. Young Ali came to see me earlier today and said he had observed Dillon leaving the horse's box yesterday in a rather suspicious manner. After

289

the horse had run so badly, he remembered the incident and decided to recover this sample, which he had observed Dillon burying in the muck heap, and brought it me. It needs to be analysed urgently.'

Chris took the bag and carefully emptied a little of the contents on to his desk. He looked up at Jay. 'I think I can tell you what this is even before I analyse it,' he announced. 'It's almost certainly Monensin – pellets used in pheasant rearing. It's an anti-parasite drug, but given to a horse it would almost certainly affect its heart. I'll get them to the lab now, and come back to you by the end of the day to let you know if my suspicions are well founded.'

'Thanks,' said Jay, 'and let's keep this between ourselves for the moment. If your suspicions are right I'll have to get on to Giles Sinclair at BHB Security immediately. I imagine they'll want to analyse it themselves.'

'Fine,' said Chris. 'If they do I'll make sure I keep some of the contents of this bag just in case anything goes wrong with the sample you send to the BHB.'

Still very worried, Jay thanked him, and hurried back to County View. Walking into the house, he beckoned Eva into their sitting room where he closed the door. He quickly explained the situation.

'Where the hell would he have got that from?' his wife asked.

'You know how keen he is on shooting, and presumably he could have laid his hands on them at one of the places he's been recently.'

Eva walked over to him and gave him a hug. 'Just relax,' she said. 'It's serious but at least if we get information to the authorities first they'll know that it was certainly not our doing. With your reputation I can't believe they would have thought that, anyway.'

She gave him a reassuring peck on the cheek and said, 'You go back to the office. I'll have lunch ready in about twenty minutes. How about an omelette?'

'Sounds fine to me,' her husband said.

That evening, just before Eva, Max and Jay were due to have dinner, Chris rang back.

'Hi, Jay, it was exactly what I thought it was.'

Jay thought for a moment. 'What effect would it have had on the horse?'

'Well, it would certainly affect the horse and he would probably lose stamina.'

'How long would it last?' was the next question.

'It would depend on the size of the dose, but it would need to be given in small quantities for a couple of days. A really big dose would have affected the horse's behaviour before he got to Sandown and might have proved fatal.'

'Thanks, Chris, for doing this so quickly.'

'If there's anything else I can do let me know, and if the horse doesn't seem OK tomorrow I'll come and have a look at him. If Giles Sinclair wants to talk to me, give him my number. I imagine they've got plenty of experts who'll know all about the effects of Monensin.'

'Thanks again,' said Jay. 'Love to that gorgeous wife of yours. Tell her I think she ought to come out of retirement.'

Chris's wife had been a very competent amateur jockey some years before but had very sensibly given up her dangerous hobby when she started to raise a family.

'No way,' was the laughing reply.

Jay phoned Giles Sinclair straightaway and gave him the information. He also explained Dillon's apparent involvement.

Giles thought for a moment. 'You're going to have

to get the police involved, but I suggest you phone Harvey first. He'll mark their card for them – they'll move more urgently and be less sceptical than if it comes from you. I know you're well known in the area, don't get me wrong – it's just that a senior policeman like Harvey can get things done a bit more quickly.'

'Understood,' was Jay's answer. 'I'll do it straight-away.'

Moments later he was talking to Harvey, who promised he'd phone the Gloucestershire Chief Constable immediately. He'd ask him in turn to phone Jay as soon as he and Harvey had finished their conversation.

It was less than twenty minutes later when Jay's phone rang. Jay and the Chief Constable had met on a number of occasions and were on cordial terms.

'I'm getting two men to come over to you now,' the policeman informed him. 'Is he at your yard at the moment?'

'Yes, and I'll make sure he stays,' Jay promised. 'It's getting near the end of the day but I can always find an excuse for keeping him.'

Sure enough, twenty minutes later a police car drove up and two uniformed officers got out. Jay led them over to the staff canteen where Danny had persuaded Dillon, Emma and a couple of the other stable staff to have a cup of tea with him while they talked about the next few days' racing.

Dillon was cautioned and, although obviously shaken, said nothing and remained calm as he was handcuffed and led away.

Emma, however, became hysterical. Danny and Jay had to prise her off Dillon, as she clutched him, sobbing, 'I told you not to do it, I told you not to do it.'

'Shut up, you stupid bitch,' he snarled, and the two policeman stopped to see what else would come out.

Danny put his arm around her shoulders. 'What's happened, Emma?' he said.

'It's his bloody shooting,' she said. 'He'll do anything to get money to go shooting. Some bloody bookmaker paid him to put that stuff in the horse's feed. I told him not to do it. He never listens to me.'

The two policemen looked at her. 'You'd better come along with us too,' said one of them. Looking at Jay, he added, 'Could someone bring her down? We don't want her in the same car as this fella.'

'I'll do it,' promised Danny. Leading Emma gently by the arm, he took her across to his car and drove out and up behind the waiting police car which moved off to the local police station.

Two hours later the Chief Constable phoned Jay. 'He's confessed everything. He claims it was some bookmaker called Garry Kent who paid him to do it, but frankly we've never heard of him.'

'I have,' said Jay, 'and if you speak to Giles Sinclair at the BHB he'll certainly be able to give you more information. I think you might find Harvey Jackson helpful too.'

'Thank you,' came the reply. 'We've driven young Emma back to her cottage, but I'm not sure she should be alone.'

'Thanks,' said Jay. 'I'll make sure one of the stable girls stays with her tonight.'

Finishing the call, he phoned Frank Malone to update him.

'I bloody knew the Kents were up to something,' he said. 'Well, this ought to cause them a few headaches. I imagine they'll be charged with a pretty serious offence. You and Mark have certainly got a

Chapter Twenty-Four

Boris and Valdas were taken completely by surprise by the ring at the front door and their rapid arrest by the four plainclothes policemen outside. Two of them had been standing to one side so as to arouse as little suspicion as possible. Once the door was opened the four of them pounced together. A little further down the corridor were four armed officers as a precaution in case any violence was offered. Within minutes the two handcuffed Ukrainians were on their way to Savile Row police station.

Nixon was blissfully unaware of this; he made a point of keeping at arm's length from his two cronies and met them in person only when absolutely necessary. For this reason he had located them in one of the seedier parts of Wandsworth, well away from his luxurious apartment on the south side of the river facing Canary Wharf.

They were kept separate, and DS Barlow and his colleague undertook the questioning. Valdas denied all knowledge of anyone called Nixon and protested that if he was given access to his flat he'd be able to show them his work permit. He gave permission for a policeman to go and search in his absence, explaining where his papers were. Similar permission was obtained from Boris, and less than an hour later the papers were in Savile Row.

It took only a few moments for an immigration expert to determine that both sets of papers were forgeries, although he had to confess they were very good ones. From the look on the Ukrainians' faces, it seemed likely that they were genuinely amazed and not a little angry that this had proved to be the case.

Although Boris maintained a stoic refusal to admit to knowing anything about Kerry Nixon, Valdas was made of less stern stuff. He eventually admitted that he had gone to the bank on both occasions on Nixon's instructions. It was the information that somebody had been murdered, apparently in connection with Nixon's activities, which led to this confession. Faced with his friend's admission, and clearly weighing up the odds, Boris decided that the consequences of being charged in connection with a murder were a greater hazard than the likely wrath of Kerry Nixon. He was banking on the fact that their paymaster would be safely behind bars by the time he knew of their betrayal.

Further questioning threw little additional light on this particular event, but it did make it clear that Nixon had been involved in a number of violent and unsolved incidents. They knew nothing about Nixon's other contacts but Valdas did eventually admit responsibility for the arson attack on Norman Parry's home, although vehemently insisting they did not know who the person was or why Nixon had instructed them to carry out the attack. After consultation with a senior officer, it was agreed that the two men would be charged with arson and kept in custody. They would also be isolated from each other. Jackson was then informed of the situation. The arson case against them was made virtually watertight when the DNA from the bloodied fence proved a match with Valdas.

As he'd promised, the policeman phoned Benny and Marvin and told them of the recent developments. He also added that the down-and-out informant had identified Nixon from a number of photographs put in front of him. The plan was now to arrest Nixon himself and put him in a live identity parade before questioning him about his activities with the bank and their now strong suspicions that he was the murderer of Jerry Downs.

'Now might be the time to have a serious chat with our American visitors. It will be interesting to see how they react to the fact that Kerry Nixon – who they've certainly been seeing a significant number of times, if not employing – is suspected of murder.'

'That ought to rattle their cage, Mr Jackson,' Benny said. 'I'd like to get my hands on this bastard, if it is him who did in poor Jerry.'

'A sentiment I deeply sympathize with, Benny, but I'm sure you realize that it's just not possible. We'll have to be satisfied with putting him behind bars for a long while.'

'Right, Mr Jackson,' agreed Benny, while quietly pondering the fact that life would be, to say the least, pretty uncomfortable for Nixon if any of Benny's East End friends were doing a stretch in the same nick.

Sitting in his car outside his home, Benny mulled over the events of the last two or three days and the information he'd received. He made up his mind. It was time to take the initiative. Within minutes he'd called both Marvin and Angel and had set up a meeting, saying to Marvin he'd hatched a plan which

297

could be a bit dodgy but he'd like Marvin to be included.

'D'you think we could use your office?' asked Benny. 'We need somewhere really discreet.'

'Of course,' said Marvin. 'How soon?'

'I've got to pick up Angel – half an hour approximately?'

'Fine,' said Marvin. 'See you.'

Forty minutes later the three of them were sitting in Marvin's office. He explained the plan that he'd been hatching in detail to both of them, and also that he'd need some outside help. They both readily agreed with his proposals, and after two more telephone calls everyone involved had been contacted and briefed. There was a real sense of nervous tension and anticipation as they parted and prepared for the next day.

Jay was about to go into a meeting of the National Trainers Federation when his phone rang.

'It's Vicky here. We've got a problem.'

God, thought Jay, that's all I need with everything else that's going on. 'Yes?'

'There's no sign of Leo. It's only forty minutes to the next race, and I can't get hold of him. I've tried his mobile every few minutes for the last half-hour.'

'Have you had any news at all?'

'No. I phoned Danny. He's heard nothing. We can't think what's happened. If there'd been an accident, surely the police would have phoned one of us, unless … ' She left the sentence hanging in mid-air.

'Unless it's fatal, you were about to say,' Jay completed the sentence.

'I suppose so,' was the somewhat reluctant reply.

'There's only one other amateur jockey here,' she continued, 'and that's Robin Haslett.'

Jay almost laughed. 'For God's sake, Vicky, you can't put Leo's main rival on a horse which has got a hell of a good chance of winning. Apart from anything else, Adam would go into bloody orbit.'

'I suppose he would,' she agreed, 'What shall I do?'

'Well, unless he arrives in the next few minutes we're going to have to withdraw the horse. Let me know as soon as you have any news. I'll get the receptionist here to phone and give you her number, and she can get me out of the meeting. Obviously I'll have to turn my mobile off while I'm in there.'

Going into the meeting, Jay was greeted warmly by the nine other members of the National Trainers Federation, all of whom he knew well and most of whom he was on good terms with. He explained that he might be interrupted and the reason why.

Jack Symes, the previous champion trainer, who now sat on the committee in an advisory role, commented, 'It's odds on he's gone to the other Bangor, Jay.'

Jay thought for a moment. 'Oh God,' he said, 'I bet you're right.'

Bangor-on-Dee, where the racecourse is situated, is close to Wrexham. There is also another Bangor, on the Menai Straits close to Anglesey. Leo would not have been the first jockey to make that mistake. In fact, Brough Scott, in one of his *Racing Post* articles, recounted how he'd been asked to ride a horse for a trainer for whom he'd never ridden previously. He went to the wrong Bangor, failed to get to the correct racecourse in time, and was never invited to partner one of that trainer's horses again.

There was a ripple of laughter round the room, and they all got down to business. Twenty minute later there was a knock at the door. The young lady from reception entered and whispered something to Jay. He nodded to his companions, left the room and took the call from Vicky.

Before she started to speak, Jay broke in.

'He went to the wrong Bangor.'

'How the hell did you know that?'

'He's not the first to have done it, and I guess he probably won't be the last. Anyway, is the horse all right?'

'Yes.'

'What about Leo?'

'Very dented pride, but that's all.'

Jay chuckled. 'God help him when he tries to explain that incident to his father.'

'I guess you're right', said Vicky. 'Will I see you tonight?'

'No. I think I'll probably be back from London after you've gone home. See you in the morning, and I'm sorry for the wasted day.'

'So am I. I think the young idiot would have had a very fair chance of winning.'

Chapter Twenty-Five

Garry was frightened. He was not sure how long he'd been in this small dark room, but the events of the last few hours seemed like a bad dream. That morning, as normal, Boxer had arrived to collect him, and drove carefully down the short lane from the end of his drive to the main road into London. Two cars were blocking the road and appeared to have had a head-on collision. Both drivers were standing in front of their vehicles arguing furiously.

Boxer stopped the car. 'I'll see what's going on and how quickly we can pass them, boss,' he said.

'Get one of the buggers to move as quickly as possible,' Garry snapped. 'We haven't got all bloody morning.'

Boxer did as he was told. Garry was watching from the back seat of his vehicle when to his amazement the side door opened and a man with a stocking pulled over his face pointed a gun straight at the middle of his chest.

'Get out,' the muffled voice commanded. Before Garry knew what had happened, another figure, also disguised with a stocking, leant over and grabbed him, hauling him out of the car. The gunman prodded him in the ribs, while the other man pushed him unceremoniously towards the two cars. Boxer was standing there, ashen-faced. One of the other two men held a gun to his ribs. These two were wearing dark glasses and Garry suspected that their coffee-coloured complexions were out of a bottle.

The back door of one of the cars was opened and he was shoved in. He was pushed to the floor. His assailants sat in the back and pinned him down with their feet, one on his neck and one in the small of his back. A thin leather strap was produced and within moments his hands were tied behind him. A blanket was then thrown over him and the feet were removed. Not a word was spoken, but he heard the driver's door open and the engine start. He then heard another engine start, and it was clear that the apparent head-on collision was nothing more than a charade. Garry's car moved off and, for what seemed an interminable time, he stayed, hot and sweaty with fear, under the blanket.

Meanwhile the fourth man had pushed Boxer back to the Bentley and made him open the boot. Boxer was pushed into it and the lid slammed down on top of him. The man returned to his car and followed the other one, containing Garry, towards London and then to a large industrial site which had a number of containers parked neatly side by side. Driving past the containers, the two cars hooted at a large gate which was set into a chain link fence with razor wire round the top. Apart from the gate man, two unprepossessing guards with Dobermanns on leashes stood there. The gate was opened and the two cars drove up to a warehouse. Three hoots on the horn, and the large sliding doors into the warehouse were pulled back. The cars went in, and the men replaced the stockings which had been removed from their faces for the drive to London. Garry was hauled out of the back with the blanket kept over his head so he had no idea where he was or what his surroundings were. Stumbling between the two men, after three or four minutes he was pushed down some stairs. He heard a door open, was thrust inside, and he heard bolts being shot across the outside of the door. The blanket was still over his head, and the strap had not been removed.

Wriggling and shaking like a wet dog, he eventually dislodged the blanket, only to be confronted by total darkness. Having tried to find some means of possible escape, he gave up and in a resigned manner sat down with his back against the wall. He had no idea who these men could possibly be or what had triggered this violent and frightening attack.

Meanwhile, the driver of the front car phoned Benny. 'The package is safe,' he announced.

'You know how to look after it,' was Benny's reply, and the line went dead.

After what seemed like hours since he'd been unceremoniously dumped in his windowless darkened room, Garry heard the bolts being pulled back on the door and it opened to reveal the silhouettes of two men. As he struggled to get up, one of them crossed the small space, brusquely pushed him to the ground and turned him over. With his knee in the small of Garry's back, he undid the strap, got up and gave him a far from friendly kick in the ribs. Not a word was spoken but Garry heard something being put on the floor. By the time he'd got up the door was closed again. Garry gingerly crawled across the floor to explore what had been left. It turned out to be two buckets – one with some water in it, the other empty but with a nearly full roll of toilet paper. Feeling thirsty Garry was tempted to drink from the bucket, but being far from certain of the origin of the water he restrained himself and settled instead for splashing his face and drying it with some of the toilet paper. Although he now felt slightly more comfortable physically, his anxiety had not been reduced a single jot.

Tony was sitting in the office wondering what the hell had happened to his brother. He'd phoned his mobile five times without any response. He was reluctant to phone the police to see if there had been any accidents, and his attempt to contact Boxer had proved equally fruitless.

As a last resort he phoned Tania who assured him that she'd heard nothing from her father and indeed had had no contact with him for the last three days. That had not been a particularly satisfactory meeting as her father had once more lectured her on her drug-taking habits and had only advanced what she considered to be a pittance instead of the substantial sum she had demanded.

Tony became more and more perplexed, and indeed worried. This just wasn't like his brother. He went down to the main office to enquire obliquely if Garry had been in touch with anyone there and pretended to busy himself assessing the bets which had so far been laid that day, and checking whether any of them needed his attention or if the odds on any particular horses needed adjusting. He was just leaving the general office and making his way up to his own when his mobile rang. It was an hysterical Boxer who was literally gabbling down the phone.

'For Christ's sake, shut up,' snapped Tony. 'Slow down and tell me what you're talking about.'

Still in an agitated voice, but this time at least intelligible, Boxer recounted what had happened to him and Garry that morning in as much detail as he could. A passer-by had heard his yells and let him out of the boot.

'Christ,' said Tony. 'Get back here as fast you can, and I mean bloody fast.'

He sat down behind his desk and lit a cigarette. After one puff, he crossed to the filing cabinet at the side of his office, opened the doors, took out a glass and a bottle of Scotch and poured a generous measure. Going back to his desk, he sat down, took a large gulp and three or four nervous drags on his cigarette. He phoned Boxer, who answered immediately.

'How much longer will you be?'

'Depending on the traffic, twenty minutes to half an hour,' was the shaky reply.

'Make it twenty minutes, and think about who we can talk to who might be able to give us a lead on who's behind this.'

'OK, guv.'

'Bloody think about it and think hard. I'll see you in twenty minutes,' repeated Tony, slamming down the phone.

In twenty-five minutes, a still visibly shaken Boxer knocked on his door and went straight in. Tony made him go over the events as far as he knew them again, forcing Boxer to speak as slowly as possible so he could concentrate on the rather sparse details at the other man's disposal. He got up, walked across the room, picked up another tumbler and poured Boxer a rather less generous measure than he had already consumed himself. He then replenished his own glass.

'Who might get a handle on this?' he demanded.

Boxer was ready with the answer. 'I'd like to talk to Micky Hobbs and Pinky Lamb,' he answered, naming two of his mates who'd done 'bird' at the same time as he had.

Tony neither liked nor trusted either of them and suspected they were not above being copper's narks, but in desperation he could think of no other course of action.

'Arrange to meet both of them as soon as possible. Don't say anything on the phone, and warn those toerags that if they let any of this out of the bag, particularly to the filth, they'll be in trouble which would make bloody Broadmoor seem like a Butlin's holiday camp.'

Boxer threw down the rest of his Scotch, gave Tony the ghost of a smile, and left the room promising he'd be back as soon as possible.

'Bloody right, you will,' was the only response, and Boxer hurried down the stairs.

Meanwhile, Garry was left sitting in the cellar room into which he'd been hurled. The warehouse above him was an Aladdin's cave filled with extraordinary items – obsolete transistor radios, pirate DVDs, pornographic magazines, cases of flick knives – anything that could make a quick buck if turned over in quantity, and almost certainly obtained from dubious sources. The only thing they had in common was that they always did their job.

They were all the property of Happy White, so called euphemistically on account of the continuous scowl which adorned his huge moon face above an equally massive and powerful body which was rapidly running to fat. Happy had had many brushes with law and order during the forty-seven years of his life to date but, by cunning ruthlessness and the odd thousand-quid bribe, had so far remained the right side of prison bars.

Although Benny had never been involved in any of his illegal activities, Happy owed the East Ender a great debt from the past. When little more than a small-time fence, Happy had been warned by Benny that one of his rivals had set him up for a thorough beating on his way from dog racing at Walthamstow. Happy had struck first, and not only did his rival and two of his henchmen need hospital treatment, but information about some stolen army rifles led to the detention of all three at Her Majesty's pleasure. It was this debt which Happy was repaying by allowing Benny the use of the small room in the cellar of his warehouse.

As the completely isolated Garry became more and more desperate, Boxer had been meeting what he hoped were his two informants. Neither had heard anything, but both swore they'd let him know if any unusual rumours about bookmakers came to their ears. They said they would do their rounds straight-away and come back to him one way or the other before ten o'clock that night. That time came and both reported they'd drawn a blank. A desperate Tony tuned in to every radio station to hear the news, and to the BBC, Sky and ITV news to see if there was any mention of an incident that might be covered on national or regional newscasts. There was nothing. Garry had just disappeared without trace.

Tony was so worried that he even considered phoning the police. This was absolutely his last resort and anyway, he reasoned, if they'd come across anything suspicious which seemed relevant to Garry they would certainly have contacted Tony before anyone else. Garry had been a widower for many years and had resorted to occasional high-class hookers rather than an ongoing relationship to satisfy the physical needs which he felt only occasionally.

At twenty-one, Tony had been madly in love with a sultry girl of Italian origin who in his eyes was every bit as beautiful as Sophia Loren. His plans to marry her were dashed when her parents forbade her to have anything more to do with him, and within months she was married to an ardent Roman Catholic whose father owned a very successful Italian restaurant in Soho.

Tony vowed he would never allow himself to be so vulnerable again, and his subsequent love life was consistent with this objective. He had had a series of girlfriends, all between the ages of eighteen and twenty-two, who were as blonde and slender as the love of his life had been dark and voluptuous. As soon as one of these 'trainee women', as he described them, became what he considered to be too emotionally involved or greedy, he moved on to the next.

At the moment he was between 'wifelets', as Garry referred to them jokingly, and was in no particular hurry to replace the last one. Reluctantly he went to bed after a few stiff drinks but slept only fitfully, hoping for a call from his brother, or at least someone with information.

At seven thirty the following morning there was a ring at the front door of Tony's Blackheath flat. Rushing to answer it, he found a small package had been put through the letterbox. He opened the door and, seeing no one, he ran to the window and was just in time to see a leather-clad motorcyclist disappearing down the road. He tore into the kitchen, feverishly grabbed a pair of scissors and cut off the outer wrapping to find a small cardboard box inside. Removing the lid, he reeled in horror. Wrapped in a small plastic bag was a human finger in some sort of liquid. Underneath it was a piece of paper. Reading the contents, he gasped.

You will shortly be instructed to meet somebody. You will be asked some questions. You will answer them fully and honestly. If you don't do exactly as you're told you'll start getting more of your brother's body in bigger instalments each time.

This and another finger had been provided by one of Benny's friends who owned an undertaker's business. He reasoned that the corpse being cremated the previous day would not really miss the digits.

At about the same time that Tony had received his gruesome package, an almost identical one had been pushed through the letterbox of Tania's small flat. Having had a very late night, she slept through the ringing doorbell and didn't move until well after ten o'clock. Getting up, she went into the kitchen to make a strong cup of coffee and noticed the package on the floor inside her front door. Picking it up, she took it into the kitchen and dropped it on the work surface while she switched on the kettle and put three heaped spoonfuls of instant coffee into the bottom of a mug. Waiting for the water to boil, she tried to tear off the wrapping with her hands. Finding it difficult, she fetched a sharp kitchen knife and, like her uncle, opened the box and discovered the identical contents. Reading the note, she screamed and had what would certainly have passed as hysterics. Shaking, and at a complete loss, she sat down. Hearing the kettle click off, with a far from steady hand she poured boiling water on the coffee and placed the mug by the open box with its offending contents. She slumped on to the one chair in the kitchen and thought frantically. Her first instinct was to call her father. His cell phone rang several times before switching to voicemail. She cut off the recorded message and immediately phoned her uncle. Gabbling out what had happened, she was met by a moment's silence.

'Grab a taxi and come over to my flat. Bring the package and letter with you. Don't speak to anybody and come straightaway.'

'I'll have to dress first,' she told him, 'but I'll be there as fast as I can.' She ended the call without waiting for a reply and rushed into the bedroom. Grabbing underwear, a pair of jeans and a sweater, she pulled them on, rushed into her little bathroom, washed quickly and hurried back to the kitchen. Snatching up her handbag, she shoved the offending package into it, unlocked the door, went outside and slammed it shut. Knowing she would have problems finding a cab, she walked down the road, jumped into her car and drove as quickly as she could into London and on to the office in the Elephant and Castle. Nobody questioned her as she went through the general office, although a number of the staff noticed that the normally glamorous and heavily made-up young lady looked far from well groomed that morning. Without a word, she walked up the few steps to her uncle's office, opened the door and rushed in. Tony was sitting behind his desk talking to Boxer. He gestured for the man to leave and got up and gave his niece a hug. The emotion welled up in her and she broke into uncontrollable sobs. Holding her tight for a moment, eventually he led her to the chair in front of his desk and sat on the edge of it watching her. He reached for a box of tissues and handed it to her. After a few moments she took a hold of herself, wiped her eyes and looked fearfully at her uncle.

'What's happening? Where's Dad?'

'I wish I knew the answer to both of those questions, sweetheart,' he said. 'I've had exactly the same package as you.'

'What are we going to do? Shouldn't we go to the police?'

'God, no,' was the response. 'If this is a gangland operation they'll kill him and we'll probably never even see the body.'

The girl moaned.

Her uncle continued. 'Let's wait for the telephone calls,' he said. 'Your father's bound to give them both our mobile numbers so I suggest you wait here with me. Have you had anything to eat?' She shook her head. Opening the door, he went downstairs. Boxer was sitting dejectedly behind the little desk which he used as his base when not out with either of the brothers or running some errand for them. 'Make us a pot of hot coffee and get a bacon sandwich from round the corner,' he instructed the ex-con, 'and be quick.' Turning, he went upstairs and rejoined his clearly terrified niece. Ten minutes later Boxer appeared with a somewhat ancient tray, two mugs, a large pot of coffee, a carton of milk and a large bacon sandwich. Tony poured each of them a coffee. Tania shook her head when he held the milk carton over one of the mugs. He passed the black liquid to her, followed by the sandwich. She looked at it with some distaste, but Tony was adamant. 'You've got to eat,' he insisted. Reluctantly she took a bite, followed by a gulp of coffee. They sat in silence while she continued to nibble the sandwich, and they both drank their coffee. Before they had finished, Tony's phone rang.

'You've got our package?' a muffled voice demanded. Tony confirmed he had and started to talk. 'Shut up,' snapped the voice at the other end. 'Get a piece of paper.'

Tony did as he was told.

'OK,' he growled. The muffled voice then gave him instructions.

'You'll never see your brother again if you don't do exactly as we say, or if you're followed. Understood?'

'Understood.'

'And when you come you might as well bring his daughter with you,' the voice continued.

Tony should have been surprised that they knew where she was, but it was clear from the efficiency with which the operation had been conducted that they would almost certainly have known where Tania was. In fact, as he thought later, they'd probably waited until she was there before they had made the telephone call.

Tony beckoned his niece downstairs where he spoke to Boxer. 'I'm taking the Volvo,' he announced, and put his hands out for the keys. The car in question was an elderly but very serviceable Volvo estate which Boxer used to get to and from his home and also for any of the chores which he did on behalf of the brothers. Tony felt that his Mercedes sports was a little too noticeable and he had no idea where they were going anyway. He opened the door for Tania, slid in behind the steering wheel and drove off in the direction of Epping Forest. Arriving there, he took the road he'd been told and was soon parked in a clearing reserved for people to leave their cars before enjoying a walk or a picnic in the forest. A few moments later an equally nondescript Ford Cortina drew up with two men inside it. The passenger front door opened and out got a man whom Tony recognized immediately.

Lou Bostock was one of three brothers who were well known in the East End. Fifteen years earlier they'd come down with their father on a freelance security job for one of the bigger London companies who required a few extra bodies for a specific assignment. The old man had enjoyed it so much that he'd set up there, initially freelancing for other companies but gradually building up his own set of clients and a reputation for performance. They'd worked on a number of occasions with Benny and, like many of the East Ender's acquaintances, were not averse to taking on assignments with no questions asked. Indeed, it had been touch and go on many occasions as to which side of the table they sat during their not infrequent attendances during visiting hours at both Wandsworth and the Scrubs. Lou stopped outside Tony's car and beckoned for him and Tania to get out.

'Lock it,' he said. 'You're probably going to be away for two or three hours.'

Without another word, he walked back to the car and gestured for the two of them to get in. His brother, Scott, was sitting next to him. Tony was worried and Tania was terrified. They drove off and nothing was said for over half an hour, then Lou reached beneath his feet and passed back two small hessian sacks. 'Put these over your heads when I tell you and leave them there until I say. If you know what's healthy you won't try and see where we're going.' Ten minutes later he gave the instruction. Neither of the passengers was inclined to argue and they quickly pulled the musty sacks over their heads. The car stopped, and they heard gates open and a grunted greeting. The car moved forward again and this time they heard metal doors being slid back. Unbeknown to them they were being taken to the same warehouse where Garry had now been for more than twenty-four hours. They were told to get out of the car but to keep the sacks over their heads. Each of the brothers took one of them by the arm and they were led to a room where they were seated on chairs. They were then told they could remove their hoods. They looked round and found themselves in a medium-sized room with a small window too high to look through and completely bare walls which had not seen a paintbrush for several years.

Scott sat opposite the girl. Lou instructed Tony to follow him. They went four or five yards down a small corridor when Lou opened another door. In the room was a trestle table with a wooden pallet propped up in the middle which was held in position by a rope over the top and tied to the table legs. There was one chair at the door end of the table and another in the middle rather like an umpire in a tennis match. Lou sat on it and gestured to the other chair. Almost as soon as Tony sat down, a voice addressed him from the other side of the pallet. It was rather a cultured voice and one which Tony could not place. The speaker was Marvin Lewis whom Benny had conscripted for the questioning on the basis that his own voice was probably too familiar and Marvin's cultured tones would add to Tony's confusion.

The questioning started immediately, and as Tony answered Marvin made notes on the other side of the table. Tony could see a recording machine in front of him and knew that at least his side of the conversation was being clearly recorded. After about forty minutes, the questions ceased, Marvin nodded to Lou who took Tony back to the room where his niece was sitting. Scott got up and, taking the girl surprisingly gently by the arm, led her out to the room where Tony had been questioned.

Tony was gestured to sit down, and Lou sat casually and clearly at ease in one of the other chairs.

'What the hell's going on?' demanded Tony.

'Shut up,' was the only reply.

Lou took out a packet of Silk Cut, offered one to Tony who gratefully accepted, lit one himself and leant over and lit Tony's. The silence was resumed.

Meanwhile in the other room a similar scenario was taking place. Marvin asked Tania all the same questions he'd asked her uncle, listening for any obvious inconsistencies. It was clear she was too frightened to lie or prevaricate. He then turned his questioning to the subject of her relationship with Leo and her interest in horse racing generally. It took a lot to surprise Marvin in his course of employment but her answers genuinely amazed him. After a while he paused, nodded to Scott, who again surprisingly gently led her back to the room where her uncle was sitting. He was on his third cigarette and she gratefully accepted a Silk Cut from her captor. She turned to speak to her uncle and was immediately silenced.

'If either of you speak we'll hood both of you,' Lou announced, and there was little doubt that he meant every word.

In Marvin's room, Sammy, the third brother, had brought Percy's investigator a bottle of sparking mineral water and a cup of black coffee. Marvin took a long pull at the water bottle and a sip of his coffee. He nodded to Sammy who left the room. A few minutes later he came back with a hooded Garry.

315

Angel was on the other side of him. The bookmaker was firmly pushed into the chair, Angel left the room, and Sammy leant over and pulled off the hood none too gently. Garry looked round at his surroundings and at the upright wooden pallet. Before he had a chance to say anything, Marvin started the questioning from the other side of the table as soon as he heard Sammy click on the recorder. He went through the same questions that he'd asked both Garry's relations and then moved on to talk about the mysterious changes in the odds on a number of horses. The accuracy of the information which clearly lay behind the questions astonished Garry. He would have been less mystified if he'd known that they were based on extensive research by Giles Sinclair's team in the BHB's security department. This had been supplemented by some pretty vigorous questioning of Oscar in Spain by Lance, Angel and Robbie, whose only regret had been that they couldn't stay longer to enjoy some of the sunshine of the Spanish coast.

At the end of his questioning, the hood was replaced and Garry was taken back to his room. This time there was a chair, a small plastic table and a little torch. Two ham sandwiches and a bottle of water were placed on it, together with a banana. Without a word Sammy left the room and with Angel's help slid the heavy bolts back in place. The two of them retraced their steps to the room where the questioning had taken place to find that the pallet had been taken down and leant against the wall, more chairs had been brought in, and Benny, Angel and the three Bostock brothers were waiting with Marvin. Marvin leant across the table and played the tapes. He was the only one who'd heard all three tapes so he waited for the information to sink in.

'Anyone want to hear it again?' he asked. Shakes of the head indicated they didn't. Marvin waited for someone to comment.

It was Benny who broke the silence. 'Stone the bloody crows. Who'd have guessed it? What do we do now?'

Marvin spoke. 'I suggest we hood all three of them again, take them back to Epping Forest, tie them up and just leave them there. I'll phone Harvey Jackson and tell him what we've learnt and I guess he'll make sure none of them leave the country even if he doesn't arrest them immediately. We'll meet him or one of his sidekicks as soon as possible and hand the tapes over, but we'll take copies first to make sure that we've got back-up in case anything goes wrong.'

'D'you think they'll go to the filth?' Lou asked.

'I doubt it very much,' was Marvin's reply, and Benny nodded in agreement.

'They're all bloody shaken up. They know they're in the wrong, and even if they do Mr Jackson will certainly make sure that any possible action against any of us will be nipped in the bud. You three are in the clear anyway. You've done nothing other than ferry Tony and Tania here and sit in during the questioning. The rest of us who've actually been a bit more physical have all kept our identities hidden, and even if any of the Kents suspected we were involved they haven't got a shred of evidence.'

'I guess you're right,' was Lou's response. 'Shall we do it now?'

'No time like the present,' said Marvin. 'Thanks for your help. You hang on a moment, Benny, and Angel, you just go as back-up in case the brothers here need any help but I very much doubt it.'

Marvin was right. The three Kents all put on their hoods without argument and squeezed into the back of the Bostocks' car with Scott in the front. Tania was sobbing in relief at joining her unhurt father. He was still too shaken to be in a comforting mood.

Angel and Sammy followed at a discreet distance, while Marvin and Benny reviewed the information they'd got and the action they were going to take. Marvin then phoned Harvey Jackson who fortunately answered his private line immediately. He briefly described the information they'd gathered and said that Benny would be on his way within half an hour once they'd taken a precautionary copy of the tapes. Jackson agreed to both courses of action and asked to speak to Benny.

'Does the Pegasus suit you?' he asked.

'Sure, Mr Jackson,' came the reply.

'Is half past one too soon?'

Benny looked at his watch. 'Let's say two o'clock to be on the safe side. The traffic can be bloody horrible at this time of day.'

The policeman agreed. Benny and Marvin left and found Happy who was sitting in his little glass-partitioned office looking at a pile of what appeared to be completely chaotic paperwork. Benny knew from past experience that this chaos belied the tight grip that the dealer had on his stock, his sales, what money he owed and what money he was owed. It was seldom that even the smallest detail escaped his attention.

'Thanks, Happy – I owe you.'

'No, you don't, Benny. We're all square now, but let me know if you need anything. It's bloody amazing what I get at times – and it's always cheap – specially for a mate.'

'I know, and I wouldn't ask any questions,' laughed Benny.

'And you wouldn't get any answers.' The fat man roared with laughter and, with his arm round Benny's shoulders, walked out to the beaten-up BMW.

As soon as the three Kents were dumped in Epping, Angel and the three Bostocks left and Benny phoned Jackson. He described exactly where they were, adding that they would probably be near a Volvo car with no distributor head waiting for help or walking from that spot to the nearest busy road.

As agreed, after 2 p.m. Benny walked into the Pegasus. Benny handed over tapes and the two of them went their separate ways.

It was nearly six o'clock that night when Harvey Jackson phoned Benny.

'Well, I think we've tied up all the loose ends,' he said. 'Would you and Marvin like to have a drink with me at the Pegasus?'

'I certainly would,' said Benny. 'I'll phone Marvin. What time would suit you, guv?'

'How about half past seven?' suggested the policeman.

Marvin answered his phone almost immediately and at seven fifteen the two of them walked into the now familiar bar downstairs at the Pegasus. Paddy Mullings saw them straight away, and with a broad smile indicated for them to go upstairs.

'You'll be moving in soon,' he quipped to Benny.

'Not a bad location. Could do worse,' was the quick retort.

They made their way up and knocked on the door.

'Enter,' boomed Harvey Jackson's voice, and they walked in. They were slightly surprised to see, not only a couple of bottles of wine and a selection of beers and glasses on the table, but also a veritable feast of cold food: pork pies, sliced ham, beef, salads, French bread, cheese, butter and pickles, were all laid in the middle of the table, with plates, knives and forks for three people already in place.

'I guess we could all do with a bit of sustenance as well as the booze,' Harvey said. 'Help yourselves to a drink and then we'll chat.'

Marvin, looking at the label on the wine bottle, settled for that and was joined by Harvey, while Benny took a bottle of lager.

'Right,' said Jackson, 'here's what we've learned. The Kents were indeed gaining inside information,' and he described the set-up. 'Anyway, you already know that, Benny, from your brother's conversations with Oscar.'

Benny managed not to look embarrassed.

'Nixon was actually working for Sol Jacobson. We now know it was Sol who had arranged for the Americans' room to be bugged. He was out to get control of the racecourses and was working with the Kents. His plan was to keep it as a very secret asset and use them as a money-laundering outlet. It seems he has his fingers in a large number of very dodgy but lucrative pies. The Americans were a useful smokescreen but were never going to be cut in. They were completely shattered when they found their attempt to get Raymond and Parry's shares had been thwarted, and we still don't know how that happened or who was behind it.'

Marvin smiled to himself but kept his own counsel.

'The betting on Leo was an entirely different matter. It seems that Tania had been going out with Robin Haslett – she evidently has a bit of a thing for amateur jockeys. When Haslett discovered what she did he dumped her, in her words 'like a bloody hot potato'. She was furious and told her old man. It was not by chance that she got to know Leo and saw him as a way of getting her revenge on Haslett. Garry was more than happy to support her in this, but he also saw it as an opportunity to make money. It was he who was responsible for the wire on one of the Haslett gallops and the beating up of Lloyd-Paterson. The Harry Fowler sickness was just pure coincidence. Also, Angus Langton owed him money so he arranged for those two horses to be available for Leo.

'The story about them getting big bets on Leo was all a smokescreen. The only decent-sized bet they had on Leo was from Adam Forsyth and that was far from huge. They were quietly backing Leo with other bookmakers and also on the exchanges. They stand to make a small fortune if Leo wins. Mind you, they're not going to be in a position to enjoy it as they've already been charged with their involvement in the two violent incidents and the attempted fraudulent activities in relation to their inside information. They will, of course, never be able to be involved in racing again. Tania's not actually done anything that she can be charged with, but with her father behind bars she's going to have to lead a rather more prudent life than she has until now, although a girl with her tastes, looks and morals might well decide to make a living in the oldest profession in the world.

'The Americans have done nothing illegal, although not for want of trying, so there's nothing we can do on that front.

'One last thing, and this has got to stay between the three of us tonight. I know you'd like to talk to your

321

Chapter Twenty-Six

Two days later, with Benny, Marvin and Harvey Jackson still sworn to secrecy, Jay, Vicky and Danny were sitting round the kitchen table at County View while Eva poured coffee for all four of them on the morning of Leo's big Cheltenham race. It was a hunter chase meeting so Leo's horse was Jay's only runner. It was always a competitive and popular meeting, but the focus of attention today was on the chances of Leo's horse, Quiet Menace, in the three-mile hunter chase. Robin Haslett was riding Poker Dice. He had now caught up with Leo in the amateur championship, and with only a couple of weeks to go there was a limited number of potential rides between them. Today's head-on between the two could well prove conclusive and the media was making the most of it.

There were mixed feelings among the four sitting round the table. Leo had ridden out first lot and had excused himself, saying he wanted to rest at home for a bit before getting to the racecourse early and walking the course in plenty of time for his race. It was an evening meeting so it would be mid-afternoon before the horse left.

It was clear they were all thinking about the coming confrontation between Robin Haslett and Leo, but it was Eva who broached the subject.

'Well, what do we think about this evening?'

'I've still got my doubts about Leo.' It was Danny who replied. 'I know Benny's proved that at least some of his nocturnal activities have been related to his photographic interests, but I still find it very odd that all these incidents have occurred to help his chances. Even if it's not Leo, somebody's been making huge efforts to ensure that he beats Robin.'

Vicky agreed. 'He's become increasingly secretive in the last few weeks. Although he's never been a really outgoing member of the yard, a number of the staff have commented that he seems more and more aloof.'

'Well, perhaps it's just the pressure that's getting to him,' suggested Jay. 'I know that I used to get a bit moody when big races were in the offing and a lot rode on them.'

'I think you're all adding two and two together and making twenty-two,' Eva snapped. 'Everybody's been putting the worst possible connotations on what he's doing, and even though Benny had found that at least some of our suspicions were wrong you are still not giving him even the benefit of the doubt. I hope that he wins this evening and goes on to win the championship. We all know he's worked damned hard on it, and there's absolutely no proof that he's had anything to do with these incidents. Equally, there's no proof that it's Adam. You're all putting the worst possible interpretation on a number of isolated incidents, and I for one don't believe either of them are remotely involved.'

Jay tapped the table. 'Come on, let's not fall out over it. Let's see what happens today, and after all if he does win it will be another winner for County View.'

There were smiles of agreement and, having finished their coffee, they all went about their next tasks before they got ready to make their way to Cheltenham.

At four thirty Jay had finished checking Quiet Menace in the racecourse stable block and was walking back towards the grandstand when he ran into Edward Gillespie, the racecourse managing director. They were long-standing friends and stopped to exchange pleasantries.

'I see you've got an interesting runner this evening,' was Edward's enthusiastic opening, 'and you've certainly produced the possibility of a fascinating contest for us.'

'And what would that be?' Jay responded rather archly.

'Well, seeing that just about every racing column is talking about the confrontation between Robin Haslett and Leo Forsyth, I'm surprised you ask!' quipped his friend. 'What do you think the outcome will be?'

'Are you talking about this evening's race, or the amateur championship?' asked Jay.

'Either or both, Jay.'

'Well, to be honest, Edward, I think both of them are too close to call. I think our horse has a slight edge over Robin's today, but Robin is the better and more experienced jockey. That's not to detract from Leo, who's made enormous strides in the last few months. As far as the championship is concerned, if you really press me I'd make Leo the slight favourite. Although Robin will get outside rides, and there's a lot of emotional support for him, Leo's horses with us are all in really good form and he's also got the additional ammunition of the horses which Angus has booked him for. As I said before, it's going to be a very close-run thing.'

'Well, I'll be watching with interest, and good luck this evening.' Edward gave Jay a playful punch in the ribs, turned and walked back towards the weighing room where, as always, he had pressing business to attend to.

The third race was Leo's hunter chase, the most valuable race on the card. Jay went to the weighing room and found Leo, who for once looked rather nervous. He was holding his saddle, standing slightly apart from the rest of the jockeys who were waiting for their trainers to arrive and relieve them of their burdens.

'Would you like me to come with you?' Jay enquired.

'No, you relax. I've got Danny with me and we'll cope perfectly well.'

Jay felt a pang of sympathy for the young man. He remembered how nervous he'd been at a similar stage of his career, and putting his arm round Leo's shoulders said quietly, 'You just do your best. You've come a long way since you came to us.'

Leo smiled at him gratefully. 'Have you seen Dad?' he asked.

'No, but he phoned a few minutes ago to say he was in the car park, so don't worry, he'll be here to encourage you.'

'I hope he won't just encourage me,' the young jockey replied. 'It would be nice if he was able to congratulate me as well.'

Jay chuckled. 'Time will tell, Leo,' he said. 'Now you just go and relax until you're called out.'

Walking thoughtfully round the back of the weighing room to where the saddling boxes were, Jay mused about this rather enigmatic young man. He was associated with an extraordinary and rather dubious young woman, and yet he had a passion for photographing nocturnal animals. His relationship with his father was just as much a conundrum, and indeed Adam Forsyth had become more and more puzzling in Jay's mind. Arriving at the saddling box, he cast the thoughts out of his mind as Penny led Leo's mount into a box, turned him round, and waited for Danny on one side and Jay on the other to position and adjust the saddle and breast girth.

Danny quickly rinsed out the horse's mouth with a sponge. Giving the animal a pat on the neck, Jay smiled at Penny and said, 'All right, get him on his way.'

A few moments later he and Danny walked into the middle of the parade ring where Eva and Adam were talking in a very friendly manner. The two seemed to have got on particularly well ever since Adam had discovered Eva's interest in art, and Eva had been Adam's guest at the National Gallery.

'Well, what's going to happen?' demanded Adam as Jay walked up to them.

'Leo's going to go very close,' replied Jay. 'I think it's a two-horse race to be honest. Three and a half miles over these fences can often provide huge surprises. As I said to you only a couple of days ago, Leo's come on in leaps and bounds.'

'What about the championship?' pressed Adam.

Jay repeated what he'd said to Edward Gillespie earlier.

There were eleven runners in Leo's race, and the bookmaking odds reflected the horses' ability and also the expectations of the punters. Robin's horse was 7 to 4, and Leo's 2 to 1. The third horse in the betting was 6 to 1, and the rest of the runners varied from 10 to 1 to 25 to 1. In a nutshell, the overall expectation was that it would be a two-horse race and a close one at that.

The previous day Jay had discussed tactics very carefully with Leo. He'd shown Leo a number of races at Cheltenham and described the importance of understanding the way in which the course had both uphill and downhill sectors before the famous and challenging uphill finish. Leo had never ridden at Cheltenham, which is why he had quite rightly elected to walk the course that afternoon.

Jay quickly took Adam by the arm. 'I think Leo's got an excellent chance. He's justifiably nervous, so let's be very cool. He needs encouragement and no advice other than what I've given him over the last twenty-four hours.' He looked Adam straight in the eye. 'Do we understand each other, Adam?'

Adam almost glared back at Jay, but eventually nodded. 'I understand,' he said. 'I know at times I let my enthusiasm for the boy to succeed run away with me.'

'Well, now's not the right time to do that. Here he comes.'

A moment later Leo was standing in front of them. He was clearly putting a brave face on the fact that he was genuinely extremely nervous, not only about the outcome of the race but also, Jay suspected, about riding round what was generally recognized as one of the toughest, if not the most daunting, steeplechase courses in Britain. The tension was broken by Eva who leant over and planted a big smacking kiss on Leo's cheek. 'That's for luck,' she chuckled. 'You'll get one on the other cheek if you win.'

He smiled gratefully. 'Well, if I do win I'll share the winner's bottle of champagne with you and the rest can buy their own.'

They all joined in the laughter in a very good-natured way.

Moments later the mounting bell rang and Jay hurried the young jockey away before anything could be said which might make him even more nervous. As soon as he had legged him up, Jay put his hand on the young man's boot. 'You've worked bloody hard, Leo. There's no reason why you can't win today. Just go out and do your best. We don't expect any more of you or Quiet Menace.'

'Thanks, Jay,' was the grateful response, and with a touch of his cap he concentrated on his horse as it was led round the ring and then down the chute on to the racecourse proper.

The race started almost in front of the stands, and the first circuit passed without incident. A strong gallop was set by Warren Parry, the highly experienced amateur who had beaten Leo at Sandown some weeks earlier and was riding Nuthatch, the third favourite. Robin was lying four or five lengths behind in third place, and Leo was tracking him carefully, making sure that each time they approached a fence his horse had a clear view and was not obscured by any of the horses in front of him.

Climbing the hill out of the back straight for the final time, Warren increased the pace and Robin Haslett quietly urged his horse into second place. Leo, who was now in fourth position, for a moment became over-anxious and gave his horse a slap on the shoulder. Realizing that he was probably moving too quickly, he settled down and let the horse continue at his previous pace until they reached the brow of the hill which swept down towards the finishing straight.

Jumping the fence on the top of the hill, Leo found that he was now upside the third horse and felt that Quiet Menace was moving very easily indeed. Resisting the temptation to overtake the two horses in front of him, he let his horse almost freewheel down the sharp downhill section before turning to face the infamous uphill climb at Cheltenham.

Approaching the third last fence at the bottom of the hill, Leo had a growing sense of optimism and fought furiously not to let his enthusiasm run away with him. He steadily made ground on the second horse, and jumping the second last almost upsides, landed half a length in front of him. Now there was only Robin Haslett ahead of him.

The excitement was mounting in his expectation of winning this major race at the most important steeplechase course in Britain. He took a deep breath and remembered his error once before at Wincanton. Moving towards the last, he let Quiet Menace approach the fence and jump it in his own style. He was now only three-quarters of a length behind Robin. He looked up the hill and saw there was still a long run in to the winning post, and sat still. He felt his horse almost willing him to urge him up to and past the horse in front. He continued to sit as still as he possibly could. There were fifty yards to go to the post and, feeling that Robin's horse had little left in its tank as he saw his rival urging his mount on, Leo allowed himself a brief moment of enthusiasm and hit his horse twice behind the saddle. Immediately a vision of Jay scolding him for excessive use of the whip at Sandown came back to him He settled down to put both hands on the reins, and with the occasional slap on the shoulder urged Quiet Menace past Robin's now clearly tiring horse. With almost consummate ease he moved away to win by the judge's decision of a length and a half.

He could hardly believe he'd done it. He pulled up well past the winning post and, as he turned to go down the chute back into the paddock and the winners' enclosure, the first person to congratulate him was Robin Haslett.

'Well done, Leo,' said Robin. 'It was a great ride you gave him.'

'Thank you, Robin,' replied Leo, 'but I know who the true champion is.'

'Well, that remains to be seen,' replied Robin.

'I don't think so,' said Leo, and with that slightly enigmatic remark trotted past Robin to be led into the winners' enclosure accompanied by the clapping and cheering of an enthusiastic throng. Dismounting Quiet Menace in the number one spot, he was surrounded by the County View group congratulating him with wild enthusiasm.

Eva lived up to her promise, and not only kissed him on the other cheek but on both cheeks, and gave him a great hug. There were tears in her eyes as she said, 'Leo, we're so proud of you.'

His father gave him a hug, stepped back almost embarrassed, and said, 'Well done, son. That was a great ride.'

Danny and Jay stood back until the time came for Jay to point out that photographs were in order. These were duly taken, with just about everybody in the party one side or other of Quiet Menace's proud head. Jay grabbed Leo by the arm and ushered him in to the scales, where he weighed in before Jay hurried him out again for the presentation ceremony and even more photographs.

Eventually Leo had the opportunity to walk quietly into the changing room. He went over to Robin and looked him straight in the eye. 'I'm not riding again this season. You're the real champion, and I've become equal to you only because of a whole lot of situations which I believe could have stopped you from being the true champion you are.'

Robin gazed at him in amazement. 'For God's sake, Leo, we've got another couple of weeks to go.'

'You have, I haven't. I beat you today fair and square in a great race on the greatest steeplechase racecourse in Britain. That's all I need. You're a true champion – now go and enjoy it. Next season if I come back it may be a different story. Then, hopefully, it will be just you against me without any of these horrible events that have happened.'

Haslett looked him straight in the eye. 'You're a decent bloke, Leo,' he said. 'This is going to cause a few ripples. There's been a lot of money riding on you winning.'

'Dame the money,' retorted Leo. 'I just want to enjoy this sport and hope that we'll continue to be friends.'

There was a pause before Robin answered. 'The very best,' he said, 'the very, very best.'

Leo changed and received congratulations and a number of back slaps, before he went out to meet his father and the County View group. Adam was ecstatic and everybody else was greeting him enthusiastically. The morning's doubts were forgotten in a moment.

It was Adam who raised his glass and said, 'For the amateur champion.'

Leo looked at his father and turned to the rest of the small group. 'I've got an announcement to make,' he said. 'I'm not riding again this season.'

Everybody was thunderstruck.

'What the hell d'you mean?' gasped Adam. 'You've got every chance of winning the championship, and what about all the money I've spent on horses for you?'

Leo looked steadfastly back at his father. 'That's just one of the reasons why I'm not going to ride again,' he said. 'Ever since you bought the first five horses there have been remarks made in the weighing room about me not winning the championship but having it bought for me. There have been hasty rumours about me be being involved, first of all, in Robin's accident, and then the beating up of Lloyd-Paterson. Frankly I don't think I would win the championship fairly and squarely. Today I beat Robin and nobody can cast any doubt that I did it on merit. That's enough for me. If it's not enough for you, Dad, tough luck.'

This time Adam was absolutely speechless. Eva went to the young man's defence.

'I think it's a very brave decision, Leo, and I think we should let it be known that this is the reason. Nobody can think for one moment you've lost your nerve, particularly after a ride like today's, and hopefully next season you can win it without all these dreadful incidents.'

Jay supported her, giving Leo an encouraging grin. 'It's not the end of the world, you know, even if you don't win next year.'

At last Adam found his voice. 'Well, I think we need to think about this,' he said. 'You don't have to make up your mind today.'

'Oh yes, I do,' said Leo. 'I'm sorry, Dad, I have already made up my mind. I know you spent a lot of money on buying the horses and having them trained, and the money you spent getting the rides from Angus, and also all the money you've lost on your bet.'

'What the hell are you talking about?' demanded his father. 'Sure I've bought you horses, and sure I had a bit of a bet on you at the beginning of the season, but I can assure you it wasn't a particularly big one. I just don't gamble over things that I have little or no control over. As for the Angus horses, I don't know what the hell you're talking about.'

Now it was the turn for everybody to look amazed.

'Look,' interrupted Jay, 'we've just had a great result. I really think that Leo's made up his mind and has probably chosen wisely, but as far as the other issues are concerned let's forget them for the moment and enjoy the present success.'

The tense atmosphere relaxed, and suddenly Adam put his arm round his son's shoulders. 'I'm proud of you, my boy. I'm sorry I reacted like I did. If that's your decision, you've certainly got my support.'

Eva suddenly laughed. 'Come on, Leo, where's that bottle of champagne you promised we could share?'

'To hell with his bottle of champagne,' said Adam. 'I think Leo ought to keep that for a quiet celebration. What would you like to do, Leo?'

'I'd like you to buy us all some champagne, and I'd like to ask Robin to join us.'

'What a wonderful idea,' said Eva, and to everybody's surprise Adam agreed.

Chapter Twenty-Seven

Percy waited until nearly seven o'clock, at which time the office was quiet and he had no more meetings planned. Picking up his phone, he dialled a number which was in his address book but was not used so frequently it was on his mobile. After three or four rings the phone was answered.

'Cartwright here,' he announced. 'I need to see you.'

'Good evening, Percy,' a rather cultivated voice replied.

'It's about Tudor Components and Holdings and it's rather urgent.'

There was a pause. 'I'm afraid it's not convenient for several days. I've a very full schedule.'

'I really don't care how full your schedule is. We're going to meet and we're going to meet this evening.'

It was clear that the man at the other end was both put out and perplexed by the tone of a man he'd always been on friendly terms with.

'I'm afraid that's just not going to be possible.'

'In that case you leave me no option other than to go to the police, and in particular the Fraud Squad.'

There was an audible gasp at the other end of the phone. 'What the hell do you mean!'

'Just get over here and I'll tell you. You know where my office is. My chauffeur will be sitting in reception downstairs and he'll bring you up. Don't worry, the meeting will be quite discreet. I'll see you in half an hour.'

After another pause, the voice snapped, 'Right,' and the connection was cut.

Percy sat back in his chair, reached into one of his drawers and drew out a folder. He was very familiar with the contents. Reaching into another drawer, he opened a box of Partagas Shorts, knowing he would certainly have finished it by the time his reluctant visitor appeared.

Enjoying the flavour of his cigar, he quickly flipped through the file again to refresh his memory. He then walked across to his drinks cabinet, poured himself a large dry sherry and phoned Freddy to give him instructions about bringing the visitor straight up.

He smiled grimly to himself. This was going to be interesting.

Twenty-five minutes later Freddy phoned from downstairs to say that he and Mr Cartwright's guest would be up in a few moments. Percy put his glass back into the cabinet and closed it. He was not in a mood to offer hospitality. A few moments later there was a knock on the door and Freddy opened it.

His visitor walked in and made no attempt to shake Percy's hand. There was a hard look in his eyes and Percy knew this would be a bruising encounter.

'Do sit down.' He gestured to the settee, walked across to an easy chair facing him.

'What the hell's this about, Cartwright?'

Percy noticed his Christian name had now been dropped.

'As I mentioned to you on the phone, it's about Tudor Holdings which you have been systematically cheating.'

'What the hell!'

Percy held up his hand. He pointed to the folder which he'd placed before the man in front of him. 'In there is clear evidence of the fact that you, with the help of your accomplice, Alan Pardew, have raided the Tudor Company. You have transferred funds from one of your companies to your private account in Jersey, you have billed the Tudors for components they have never received, and you are planning to take them over on the cheap. It's no use you trying to deny it. It's all there in black and white and has been completely validated by one of the top firms of auditors in the country. It's unfortunate for you that your company and the Tudors use the same auditors, and indeed the same very bright young man audited both your books.'

The defiance of the man sitting opposite Percy crumbled rapidly.

'I deny it, of course,' he said rather feebly.

'Of course you do,' said Percy, 'but that's neither here nor there. I'm now going to tell you what you're going to do. You're going to repay the whole of that money to Tudor Components and Holdings, plus the interest which would have accrued if they had still had the money. You will see the sums in that file, which you can take with you. You will also resign from every board on which you sit, and you will sell me your shares in Tolchester Holdings for £1.'

The man sitting on the settee was poleaxed. 'You have to be joking!'

'Oh no, I'm not,' said Percy. 'Unless you do as I say, the contents of that folder will be placed in the hands

337

of the police, and a note about the contents will be sent to each of your fellow directors on the boards on which you sit. There will also be a leak to *The Times*, the *Financial Times* and the *Daily Telegraph*, outlining your criminal behaviour. You have forty-eight hours to complete all these actions, otherwise you'll be looking at a significant period behind bars.'

The man sitting opposite him said nothing.

'One more thing,' said Percy. He got up, walked across to his desk and picked up two more sheets of paper. Both had his signature at the bottom and there was space for one more. 'Sign them,' he said. The man looked at him as if about to protest, but said nothing. He glanced at the papers and somewhat unsteadily signed them both. Percy walked across to his desk, picked up an envelope and a cheque. He picked up one of the documents, folded it, put it into the envelope and solemnly handed his guest a cheque made out for £1. 'That's all,' he said and, walking across to the door, opened it to find Francis waiting. 'Please take my visitor downstairs.'

Waiting for the clearly shaken man to leave, Percy stood to one side. The man got up. 'Don't forget your folder,' Percy said.

'I don't need it. Damn and blast you, Cartwright,' and with that the now ruined Jon Gormley walked out and followed Francis down the corridor to the lift.

Percy walked back into his office and closed the door. Crossing to the drinks cabinet, he opened it and this time poured himself a rather large brandy. He went to his desk and, with a grim but satisfied smile, picked up his phone and called Luke Tudor.

'I think you and Philip can open a bottle of champagne. It's all done.'

'Thank God, and thank you so much, Percy.' The voice at the other end of the line was both relieved and excited.

'It's a pleasure,' replied Percy. 'Now, have a good evening.'

'We will, but there's just one more thing I want to say. Philip and I have been talking about what would happen if things panned out satisfactorily, as they now have. We'd certainly like you to help us find a new finance director, and we'd be honoured and flattered if you'd join our board to replace the gentleman who's just left your office.'

Percy laughed. 'It's a very generous thought. In many ways I'd love to, but can I give it a little consideration? I'm pretty damn busy as it is, and I wouldn't want to take anything on I couldn't do properly.'

'We realize that,' replied Luke, 'but please think about it. We'd love you to be part of our company.'

'I really will,' Percy promised. 'Now, the two of you go off and celebrate.'

'Thanks again,' said Luke.

'It's been a pleasure,' replied Percy, who was smiling broadly as he put the phone down.

Two days later Jay and Eva were walking round the stables just after the staff had left. They enjoyed the sight of lovely heads looking at them over the half doors and the sound of contented munching on hay. Max was staying the night at a friend's.

Jay's mobile rang.

'Damn and blast! Can't we ever get a few minutes' peace and quiet?'

He answered the call. It was Percy.

'I know it's late but do you fancy bringing Eva up to London for a celebration tonight?'

'What are we celebrating?'

'Well, I've pulled off a bit of a coup, and I'd like you two to share it with me.'

'You sound very mysterious,' Jay commented.

'Oh, not really. It's just something I think the two of you might be interested in. Can you make it?'

'I don't see why not. We were going to have a quiet evening, but a good dinner with you will probably persuade Eva a night in London's not the end of the world.'

'Great. Where would you like to go?'

Jay thought for a moment. 'How about Amaya? We haven't been there for a long time. You know how much Eva loves Indian food, and it doesn't come better than there.'

'Done deal,' said Percy. 'How does eight thirty suit you?'

'Sure,' replied Jay, 'but forgive us if we're ten minutes late. You never know what the traffic's going to be like on the M4, even though we're going in the right direction. You've got me really intrigued.'

'Good,' said Percy. 'See you in a couple of hours,' and put down the phone.

Just after half past eight Jay and Eva walked into the restaurant and saw Percy seated at a table. He waved them over and beckoned to the waiter, who immediately filled the two champagne glasses already put in place for them. Percy was looking particularly cheerful and somewhat mischievous.

'So what's all this about?' asked Jay.

Percy reached into his pocket, brought out his wallet and took out two business cards. He passed one to each of them. They looked at them with

340

amazement. Embossed in gold was the horseshoe logo of the Tolchester Group. In the middle it said *Percy Cartwright* and underneath *Chairman*. They both looked at him dumbstruck. Eventually it was Eva who spoke.

'What the hell's been going on?'

'It's a long story,' said Percy. 'When the Americans came over, they started to make efforts to secure the shareholdings in the Tolchester Group. Although they were ready to play hard ball, we now know who was really behind the threats of blackmail and violence, including the arson attack on Norman Parry's house. What the Americans didn't know was that Sol Jacobson and Jon Gormley had similar plans. What was more, Sol had been tipped off by some member of their staff in Las Vegas who had advised them to use a man called Kerry Nixon. Kerry Nixon was actually working for Sol Jacobson, and evidently has been for some time. Before friends Icarus and Manfred arrived here, Sol had had their rooms bugged. As you know, Benny became aware of that when he was asked to have the room swept, although he did not then know who was responsible. He subsequently had a different bug put in so he and his crew knew what was going on and kept Marvin and me informed.

'At this stage Adam Forsyth phoned me and said he thought that something strange was going on. Raymond and Parry were being very cagey whenever he tried to talk to them about Tolchester, and Jon Gormley had not given him the support which he had expected of the board when changes were being made. He then discovered that enquiries had been made of the venture capital company to see if there was a possibility of them selling any of their shares.

At this stage Marvin had all the directors watched carefully without them knowing. Through our bugs we knew what the plan was in terms of Raymond and Parry selling their shares to a nominee fronting for the two Americans. Quite simply, we beat them to it. At the same time Adam went to Rupert Jonson and told him what was going on. Rupert assured Adam that he would not sell his shares and would support Adam in whatever he wanted to. The situation was then that Adam had 20 per cent of the shares, I had 25 per cent and you had 5 per cent. With Adam's blessing I went to the venture capitalist and they agreed to sell me their holding. Jon Gormley will do the same if he knows what's good for him, and he won't be making any money out of them. This now means that with your backing – I hope I'm not assuming too much – I now have 35 per cent of the shares myself and, with your support, 40 per cent. With Gormley's, that will make 50 per cent. Adam has decided that he's fed up with the situation and asked if I would take over as chairman. He and Rupert will support the expansion plans which we've all had, and he will concentrate on his other business ventures.

'He also wants to spend more time with Leo and surprisingly enough he's become very supportive of Leo's photographic activities. In fact Leo has just been offered a job with a wildlife magazine which almost certainly means he'll have to give up any hopes of winning the amateur championship next year. Surprisingly enough, Adam seems to be quite relaxed about this, and indeed rather enthusiastic. I know he hasn't spoken to you yet, but his plan is to discuss the future of the horses which he bought for Leo. Essentially he would like to keep those in training which you feel can go on to make progress beyond

342

the amateur and hunter chase fields. He would like one or two really decent horses, but is perfectly prepared to have two or three with you who would perform well at the Tolchester tracks, if not at the highest level. I've discovered there's a very reasonable core to Adam's personality. In fact, he's quite a softy in some ways.'

'I told you so,' said Eva, and smiled in a self-satisfied way at the two of them.

'So that's it in a nutshell,' concluded Percy. 'The police are wrapping up the criminal side of these various activities, and hopefully we can sit back and concentrate on what we do best – you on racing, Jay, you on Max, Eva, and me on insurance – and of course on Tolchester Holdings.'

'I'll drink to that,' said Eva. All of them touched glasses and then gave their attention to choosing their food.

Epilogue

The somewhat unlikely quintet of Marvin, Benny, Percy, Jay and Harvey Jackson were having dinner in Percy's private dining room in Canary Wharf. All of them had arranged for transport after the dinner so the wine had been flowing liberally as they reviewed the past few months, and the last few weeks in particular.

Harvey took a puff of his cigar and a generous sip of his vintage port, and chuckled.

'Well, life has certainly been far from dreary since County View and its associates first crossed my path. Are there any more surprises in store for me and my colleagues as we attempt to enforce a measure of respect for the law among certain members of the racing community?'

Percy also drew on his cigar, before answering. 'Come on, Harvey, we all know that, whatever the business, there are always people who will try and exploit it by cutting corners, telling half truths, or even seriously going out of their way to cheat. Racing's no different. It's just that it has a more glamorous profile, it's something the media love to write about, it has a huge number of personalities, both good and bad, and it takes place every day. Its not very surprising that it throws up crooks, but it also throws up some really dedicated, decent, hard-working and animal-loving people.'

It was Marvin who took up the conversation. 'Until only a few years ago I knew virtually nothing about racing and only read about it at the time of the Derby, Grand National and perhaps Royal Ascot. There was the odd sensational headline about cheating but it really hadn't impinged upon me at all. Now I realize it is a multinational industry, and although the vast majority are involved in it for the love of the sport, a degree of excitement, and perhaps the thrill of a big gamble, there are just a few who see it as an opportunity to cheat, lie and even threaten or violate people in their desire to make a quick buck. But I've also learnt it's not as easy as you think. The racing authorities around the world have got wiser and far more responsible. Governments are more and more concerned about the fact that gambling must be controlled, and the likes of our erstwhile friends from Las Vegas probably looked at London as a possibility to expand their interests because gambling in America has been seriously cleaned up. The Mafia no longer have real control or influence in Las Vegas. The threat to England and our super casinos is far more likely to come from Russia or the Far East. What I've learnt is that it's a wonderful sport, most of the people in it are fascinating, dedicated and real fun.'

They all turned to Benny, waiting for his contribution. He took a far from gentlemanly sip of port and virtually downed the contents of his brimming glass.

'Well, fellas, I think you're talking a lot of bleeding nonsense. It's all about greed, it's all about excitement, it's all about people wanting to win on and off the track, and it's all about the fact that nobody thinks

345

they're going to get caught. And we know that's not true, is it?' he said, giving Harvey Jackson an amused grin.

'No,' replied the policeman. 'Not if we've got help from people like you, Benny.'

It was Percy who roared with laughter. 'Well,' he said, 'on that note I suppose we ought to end the evening's serious discussion.'

'Is this what you call serious discussion?' queried Marvin. 'So what's going to happen about the Kents, Jon Gormley, Sol and the Americans?'

'Gormley realizes he's made a terrible mistake. He's got stacks of money. He'll keep his head down and think that he's lucky not to be behind bars. The Tudors just don't want to attract bad publicity.

'The Americans have had their fingers burnt and burnt badly. They've been told that they are definitely not welcome back and I can't see them wanting to return anyway. It would be hard for us to make an arson charge stick.

'Nixon will spend at least twenty years inside and it won't be any better for him than the Kents.'

'Why did he kill Jerry Downs?' Marvin asked.

'He felt Benny was getting too close and thought this would scare him off. He was wrong, wasn't he?'

'And what about Sol? Where the hell is he?'

'Well, he's done a lot of big criminals a lot of favours and I guess he called one in. You can be sure he always had an escape plan and the minute he heard Nixon had been arrested he put it into practice. So for the moment he's lying low, I guess, and spending his money carefully. But that just isn't his style. He'll get bored and do something flamboyant or plain careless. If the police abroad don't get him, some group of criminals or a high-class tart will be his undoing. You mark the words of a wise old copper. There's a £250,000 reward on his head, and if you want the real irony – it's all part of the cash we've seized from his own friends. Someone will be too greedy to resist temptation. There's not nearly as much honour among thieves as the fairy stories tell.'

'How did you get on to him?' questioned Marvin.

'Well, we got his mobile phone records, and an interesting notebook and some tapes in his office. We suggested to Nixon that Sol had implicated him to avoid a murder charge. We didn't say we hadn't caught him. Nixon was furious and told us all we wanted and a lot more besides. If we catch Sol, he's done for.'

At last Jay spoke.

'I'd like to thank you all for your help and support, and above all for solving the many mysteries and putting the bastards behind bars. I've also learned a real lesson, and that's not to judge people too quickly. A lot of us were guilty of this and no one more so than myself. It was only Eva who refused to share our prejudices. I also owe a big apology to Adam and Leo, but I can't see how the hell I can do that without letting them know what we suspected.'

'Let sleeping dogs lie.' Benny was adamant. 'Just take the two of them out and say how much you've enjoyed working with them this season. You can talk about Adam's horses for next year and assure Leo he's always welcome at County View, even if he's only going to ride in a few races or not all.'

It was clear from the nodding heads around the table that the others totally agreed with this suggestion.

'Is there any booze? I'm as dry as a bloody bone with all this chat. I thought this was a celebration not a wake. Now, will somebody give me a drink, and have you heard the story about the short fat guy and the six-foot blonde with the…'

A gale of laughter drowned the rest of Benny's chestnut.

Joey Costello let himself into his apartment. It was only a little after one o'clock in the morning, which was an early night for Joey, but for some reason he felt particularly tired that day.

Unlocking the door, he found that the deadlock was not engaged and he only had to use his Yale key. This was not a complete surprise to him as quite often his sister, who worked long and irregular hours at Las Vegas airport, spent the night with him rather than going to her apartment on the outskirts of the city. They were very close, and Joey was always delighted if she waited up so they could have a chat and a drink before hitting the sack.

He noticed that the drawing-room light was on but when he went in there was no sign of her. Crossing to the cocktail bar, he poured himself a large bourbon. He seldom drank at Le Club, but enjoyed a quiet drink before turning in for the night. Sipping it slowly, and not even bothering to turn the television on, he gradually unwound. Finishing the drink, he got up, turned off the light and walked quietly down the corridor. He opened the spare bedroom door where Honey always kept a selection of her clothes and what he called her 'travelling beauty parlour'. There was no sign of her. He was slightly puzzled as he made his way to his own bedroom. Switching on the light, he was startled to see his sister lying on top of the bed with her back to him.

'Hi, sis,' he greeted her. There was no response.

Walking round to the other side of the bed, he was about to shake her gently when he stopped in his tracks. There was a small hole beneath her heart, and a pool of blood had formed and congealed on top of his duvet. With a roar of grief, he sank to his knees and was about to touch her when he saw a piece of paper underneath her hand. Reaching across, he picked it up with trembling hands. The message was in Honey's own handwriting.

'Sol says hi. He'll be seeing you.'

For once in his life, true terror gripped Joey's heart. He knew he too was a dead man.

Dangerous Outsider

A mysterious young Irish trainer backed by a financier who wishes to keep his identity hidden, moves to England and proceeds to take on his successful English counterpart Jay Jessop. And at the same time strange accidents start occurring at Jay's stables: a fire breaks out, an attempt is made to discredit Jay by involving him in a drug-related incident, horses are abducted and the stable's champion jockey is enticed away. Finally an attempt is made on Jay's Head Man's life.

As the violence escalates, one suspect emerges as the mastermind behind all these events. And the final revelation of his identity and the motives behind all the brutal events stun the police, bankers and international racing authorities alike.

Available in paperback £6.99.

A Touch of Vengeance, Odds on Death and *Dangerous Outsider* establish Graeme Roe as an exciting storyteller who has joined the ranks of today's best racing mystery writers.

www.constablerobinson.com

If you enjoyed *Too Close To Call*
why not order these titles.

No. of copies	Order	Title	RRP	Total
		A Touch of Vengeance	£6.99	
		Odds on Death	£6.99	
		Dangerous Outsider	£6.99	
		Grand Total		£

Please feel free to order any other titles that do not appear on this order form!

Name: _____

Adress: _____

_____

_____ Postcode: _____

Daytime Tel. No./Email: _____
(in case of query)

Three ways to pay:

1. *For express service telephone the TBS order line on 01206 255 800 and quote 'ROE'. Order lines are open Monday–Friday, 8.30am–5.30pm*

2. I enclose a cheque made payable to **TBS Ltd** for £ _____

3. Please charge my ❑ Visa ❑ Mastercard ❑ Amex ❑ Switch

   (Switch issue no. _____)

   Card number: _____

   Expiry date: _____ Signature: _____
   (your signature is essential when paying by credit card)

Please return forms (*no stamps required*) to FREEPOST RLUL-SJGC-SGKJ, Cash Sales/Direct Mail Dept, The Book Service, Colchester Road, Frating, Colchester CO7 7DW.

www.constablerobinson.com

Constable and Robinson Ltd (directly or via its agents) may mail, email or phone you about promotions or products.

❑ Tick box if you do not want these from us